First Sight

www.transworldbooks.co.uk

Also by Danielle Steel

* Published outside the UK under the title PASSION'S PROMISE

For more information on Danielle Steel and her books, see her website at
www.daniellesteel.com

DANIELLE STEEL

First Sight

BANTAM PRESS

LONDON • TORONTO • SYDNEY • AUCKLAND • JOHANNESBURG

TRANSWORLD PUBLISHERS
61–63 Uxbridge Road, London W5 5SA
A Random House Group Company
www.transworldbooks.co.uk

First published in the United States
in 2013 by Delacorte Press
an imprint of The Random House Publishing Group

First published in Great Britain
in 2013 by Bantam Press
an imprint of Transworld Publishers

Book design by Virginia Norey

A CIP catalogue record for this book
is available from the British Library.

ISBN 9780593063170

Addresses for Random House Group Ltd companies outside the UK
can be found at: www.randomhouse.co.uk
The Random House Group Ltd Reg. No. 954009

The Random House Group Limited supports the Forest Stewardship Council® (FSC®),
the leading international forest-certification organisation. Our books carrying the FSC
label are printed on FSC®-certified paper. FSC is the only forest-certification scheme
supported by the leading environmental organisations, including Greenpeace. Our
paper procurement policy can be found at www.randomhouse.co.uk/environment

Typeset in Charter
Printed and bound in Australia by
Griffin Press

2 4 6 8 10 9 7 5 3 1

www.randomhouse.com.au
www.randomhouse.co.nz

To my greatly beloved children,

Beatrix, Trevor, Todd, Samantha,

Victoria, Vanessa, Maxx, and Zara,

may all your loves "at first sight," and otherwise,

turn out to be the right ones, and last forever.

I wish you joy and happiness forevermore.

With all my heart and love,

Mommy/d.s.

forevermore

first blush,
 first light,
  first crush,
   first sight,
magic moments,
  lightning bolts,
    rainbow's end
   and somersaults,
summer rains
  and cricket's wings,
    thunder rolls
and hearts
      that sing,
i looked into
    your eyes
  and saw
the dreams
  i'd heard of,
   never known,
  your gentle touch,
  your eyes
    so vast,
  and knew that
  finally
    at last
  the wishes
    of all my days
    had all
     come
      true,

the day
     your heart
         touched
             mine,
and with a clap
of thunder,
     i knew
without a moment's
     doubt,
         that i had
             fallen
     instantly,
         totally,
             absolutely
                 infinitely
and forevermore
     in love
         with you.

First Sight

Chapter 1

The pilot's voice on the Alitalia flight to Paris from Milan woke Timmie from a brief nap. She was exhausted after a week in New York, then two more in Europe, first in London, then in Milan. It was a pilgrimage she made twice a year in February and October for the ready to wear fashion shows, the famous "prêt-à-porter." She was the founder, guiding light, principal designer, and CEO of the most important men's and women's ready to wear lines in the United States, with subsidiary companies in Europe, which was what brought her to the European ready to wear shows twice a year. She showed her U.S. lines with the other American designers in New York during the first week, and then showed her French subsidiary lines in Paris. And in between, she attended the London and Milan runway shows. And she went to Men's Fashion Week in Paris as well, for her men's lines.

Timmie O'Neill had run her business single-handedly for twenty-three years, since she was twenty-five years old, when it all began. At forty-eight, her empire was so vast, it encompassed children's wear, home furnishings, and decorating accessories, including wallpaper, sheets, towels, and linens. Ten years before, they had added cosmetics, men and women's skin care products, and half a dozen perfumes, which had stunned them all with their universal appeal and almost instant success in every country where they were sold. Timmie O'Neill was a name that was known worldwide, and associated with style, fashion at a range of price points, and astonishing success.

The world of Timmie O had been a legendary victory for more than two decades, and now its founder and CEO was heading for Paris to oversee the October ready to wear show of its European-based lines. The rest of the American designers wore themselves out during the frenzy of fashion week in New York, without adding the insanity of the European prêt-à-porter. Only Timmie did both, with her boundless energy and success. But even she was exhausted after Milan, and absolutely drained when she thought of doing the show in Paris. The clothes they had shown in New York had been received with even greater than usual kudos from the press.

For her entire career, it seemed, Timmie O'Neill had had a Midas touch, and could do no wrong in the eyes of the fashion world. Even during the occasional seasons when she had been less pleased with their lines herself, or the critics had been slightly less in love with them, they had done staggeringly well nonetheless. Everything Timmie did, she did well. She threw herself into all she undertook with perfectionism and inimitable style and grace. She was relentless in how hard she pushed herself, far more than anyone else, and what she expected of herself. She had an uncanny knack for predicting what the world would want to wear, live with, and smell like, long before they thought about it themselves. Along with their clothing lines, their perfumes were among the biggest sellers in the world. She had chosen the scents and designed the packaging herself. There was very little that Timmie O'Neill didn't do well, brilliantly, in fact, except maybe cook. And dress, she liked to say. As sensitive and forward thinking as her designs were, she insisted that most of the time she didn't care what she wore herself. She had little time to give it much thought, although the clothes she designed had made her famous, particularly her signature sportswear, which managed to be simultaneously casual, easy to wear, and chic. There was a simple, clean elegance to everything she designed, and without even trying, or thinking about it, she herself was the epitome of casual chic.

On the flight from Milan, she was wearing jeans, a T-shirt, both of her own label, a vintage mink jacket she had found years before in the backstreets of Milan, and black ballerina flats she had designed the year before. She carried a large black alligator Hermès bag that had been the precursor of the Birkin, and was even more striking because of its size, and had real style because it looked well worn, after years of use on trips such as this.

The pilot announced their descent toward Charles de Gaulle Airport in Roissy, just outside Paris, as Timmie stretched her legs out in front of her in one of the plane's eight first-class seats. She had slept for most of the brief flight and through the meal. She was wiped out after the pressure, work, and revels of Milan. She had visited the factories that produced knits, bed and table linens, and shoes for them. The European ready to wear shows particularly entailed endless parties and socializing as well. No one ever slept till the end. There was a priest sitting next to her on the plane, who had said nothing to her during the flight, and was probably one of the few people who wouldn't recognize her, and wasn't wearing something she'd designed. They had nodded to each other politely when she took her seat, and ten minutes later, after glancing at *The International Herald Tribune* to see what they said about the collection she'd seen in Milan, and London the week before that, she was sound asleep. As the landing gear came down, she glanced out the window with a smile, thinking of Paris, and then turned to her two assistants, who were seated across the aisle from her. The priest had been happy to take the window seat, and neither of Timmie's assistants had disturbed her while she slept. They'd all had a grueling three weeks, first at the shows in New York, then London and Milan. Paris was their last stop, much to their collective relief.

All four shows were important, and the ready to wear shows in Paris were always high-pressure, fast paced, and stressful from beginning to end. Milan was an important mecca of the fashion world, but victory in Paris was what mattered to her most. It always had. Paris was the city she loved best in the world, and the one that had spawned her dreams. Timmie still looked sleepy as she handed some notes to her assistants, David and Jade. David had been with her for six years, and Jade for twelve. They were passionately devoted to her for her kindness, fairness, and all they'd learned from her personally as well as professionally. Everything about Timmie was inspirational, from the genius of her work, to the thoughtful, compassionate way she treated people. David always said she was lit from within, like a beacon that shined through the darkness, pointing out the path for others. And the best of her was that she was entirely unaware of how remarkable she was. Humility was unheard of in the fashion world, but all who knew her agreed that she was amazingly uncomplicated and modest.

She had a completely innate, instinctive sense about how to run her business, who she was designing for, and what they wanted to wear next season. She was quick to sense adjustments that had to be made, and never hesitated to make changes in the lines when necessary. There had been many over the years. She was never afraid to try something new, no matter how high risk. She was fearless in all she did. She lived life in bold strokes and had been a wonderful employer and friend to David and Jade over the years. Timmie was trustworthy, incredibly hardworking to the point of being driven, brilliant, creative, funny, compassionate, somewhat obsessive, a perfectionist in all things, and above all kind. The standard she set for competence, efficiency, creativity, and integrity was high.

David Gold had come to her right after graduating from Parsons as an aspiring designer, and Timmie had rapidly determined that his designs were prosaic and tended to lean more toward past styles that had been reliable and solid, but he had little of the forward vision toward the future that she looked for in design assistants. But she had seen in him something far different and more useful. He had a knack for ingenious marketing ideas, was supremely organized and attentive to details, and had an ability to keep vast numbers of people on track at the same time. She had singled him out of the design team rapidly, and put him to work for her as an assistant. He still came to the shows with her twice a year, but his responsibilities had grown exponentially in his six years with her. At thirty-two, he was a vice president in charge of marketing, and she reviewed all their publicity and ad campaigns with him. Together they had honed their PR image till it gleamed. He was brilliant at what he did.

As always, he had made everything about the New York and European shows easier for her. Timmie had often said that his business card should read "magician" instead of VP in charge of marketing. The creativity he had lacked as a designer he had a hundredfold when it came to ideas about marketing, advertising, and handling people, in ways Timmie insisted she couldn't have done herself. She was always fair about acknowledging others' achievements and quick to lavish praise where it was due. She was extremely fond of him, and had nursed him back to health herself during a bout of hepatitis four years before. They had been close friends ever since, and he revered her as his mentor, and said she had taught him everything he'd ever learned about the fashion industry, while Timmie claimed he had long since outstripped her skills. Their team efforts were a huge success to the immeasurable benefit of "Timmie O," the company as well as the woman.

Jade Chin had been an editorial assistant at *Vogue,* and had come to Timmie's attention at a number of shoots at the magazine, which Timmie often attended herself, to make sure that the clothes were photographed and perceived in the right way. Jade had been just as meticulous as she, just as maniacal about details, and never flinched at an eighteen-hour day. Timmie had hired her after she had been at *Vogue* for five years, crawling her way up the seemingly endless ladder, which would have eventually landed her a title as editor of some section of the magazine, at pathetically meager pay, with a multitude of perks and little recognition. Instead, Timmie had offered her a salary that had seemed huge to her at the time, and a job as her personal assistant. Despite opportunities to move into the corporate structure of Timmie O over the years, Jade had chosen to remain Timmie's main personal assistant for the past dozen years. She loved her job, and everything it entailed. And she and David were a good team. She and Timmie worked together with exquisite synchronicity, and she had a sixth sense for what Timmie needed, almost before it entered her employer's mind. Timmie had long since said that having Jade as an assistant was every working woman's dream. Jade had almost become the wife Timmie would never have. She thought of every last detail, and even carried Timmie's favorite tea bags in her handbag on every trip. Cups of tea would appear discreetly just when Timmie needed them most, along with lunch, dinner, snacks, exactly the clothes she wanted to change into for an interview, and a detailed accounting of who to call, who had called her, who Jade had successfully fobbed off for her, and a constantly changing sheet of appointments. She kept Timmie moving in the right direction, and always on track, while handling all the minor details for her, and making her life run smoothly at all times.

The three of them made a remarkable team. Jade and David allowed Timmie to dodge all the irritating details of her daily life, and focus on her work. As she put it, they made her look good, and feel better than she would have otherwise. Jade had been to Paris with her some fifty times in twelve years, and David maybe half as many. Paris was Timmie's favorite city on the planet, and although her U.S. business was based in L.A., she went to Paris every chance she got and traveled all over Europe to keep track of her subsidiary companies there. She had been far braver than most U.S. designers about putting down roots and starting companies in Europe. It had served her well. The trip to Paris never seemed too long to her, and she would go at the slightest provocation, and merest excuse. As she always did after the ready to wear shows in Paris, since they were the last stop in what she referred to as Hell Month, she was planning to stay on for two days alone after the shows to relax. After that, she would join Jade and David in New York, to talk to production people, visit their factory in New Jersey, and meet with their ad agency to discuss a new campaign.

Timmie was one of the few holdouts who refused to move her base of U.S. operations to New York. She preferred living in Los Angeles, and the life she enjoyed there, dividing her time between her beach house in the Colony in Malibu, and her city house in Bel Air. She had no desire whatsoever to live in a penthouse in New York, freezing in winter, and commuting to the Hamptons in the summer. She liked her life just fine the way it was, and insisted it worked for her. It was hard to argue with success. She hopped on a plane whenever necessary, at the drop of a hat, to go to Paris or New York, or Asia in some cases. David had tried to talk her into buying her own jet, and she insisted that she didn't need one, she was perfectly happy flying on commercial airlines, as she just had to Paris from Milan, and from London before that.

Considering how successful she was, Timmie was surprisingly unspoiled. She never forgot her simple origins, the luck that had started her on her career, or the coffee shop where she'd worked as a waitress, when she worked on her first designs at night, and bought inexpensive and unusual fabrics with her tips. She had been making clothes for seven years, before her first big break at twenty-five, when a buyer from Barney's noticed some of the clothes Timmie had sold to her co-workers, which were kicky, fun, stylish, and exquisitely made. She bought half a dozen of Timmie's best designs and took them back to the old Barney's store on West 17th Street, long before they moved uptown, and they were an instant hit. Her next order was for twenty-five pieces, then fifty. When the buyer ordered a hundred pieces the following year, Timmie quit the coffee shop, rented a crumbling warehouse in the L.A. fashion district, and hired a dozen girls from an unwed mothers' home to help sew. She had paid them a decent wage, which had been a blessing for them as well as for her. After that, she was on her way. By thirty, she was a nationally known success, and in the eighteen years since, she had skyrocketed into the stratosphere. But she never forgot how and where it all began, or how lucky she had been to be singled out, and blessed with success. Although there had been some tough bumps in her life since, she still felt fortunate in many ways. Most of all in her work.

Timmie looked out the window with a tired smile, as they landed at Charles de Gaulle with a sharp bump, and taxied down the runway toward the terminal, where someone from VIP services would be waiting for her. As usual, she was planning to hit the ground running, but at least she didn't have jet lag to contend with, since they had been in Europe for two weeks. She had interviews with French journalists in Paris for the next two days, and she was planning to meet with textile reps to choose fabrics for the following year's winter line. Although it was October, the ready to wear goods they were showing now were for spring and summer. She was already working on the next fall and winter lines. Cruise and resort wear were already in production, and would be shipped within two months. She was always working a year ahead, and had most of the following year's designs either sketched or taking shape in her head.

"Who am I seeing this afternoon?" Timmie asked, looking vague, as she glanced out at a gloriously sunny October day, which was a relief after five days of consistent rain in Milan. It didn't look as though the winter doldrums had hit Paris yet, much to her delight, although she loved Paris even in the rain. She always said that somewhere in a past life she must have been French. It was the city of her soul, although she had been twenty-seven the first time she had come, two years after the beginnings of her success. Her first trip had been to buy fabrics for her designs, and it was only after she opened European subsidiaries many years later that she showed her own designs at the Paris prêt-à-porter shows, a rare treat and honor for her.

The first time she saw Paris had been love at first sight for her. She loved everything about it. The weather, the architecture, the people, the museums, the art, the restaurants, the parks, the streets, the churches, the light, the sky. She had been so overwhelmed the first time she rode in a taxi up the Champs-Élysées to the Arc de Triomphe, she had started to cry. It was night, and an enormous flag was fluttering slowly in a summer breeze, lit up in the dark night, and she had never gotten over that feeling of awestruck adoration for the magical city, even now. Her heart always pounded with excitement every time she arrived. She had never gotten blasé about it, or taken its breathtaking beauty for granted. She had always said she wanted to get an apartment there one day, but somehow never had. She stayed in the same suite at the Plaza Athénée every time she came instead, and they pampered her like a deliciously spoiled child. She loved it, and as a result, had never gotten her own place.

"You're meeting with the fashion writers from *The Washington Post* and *The New York Times,* and some journalist from *Le Figaro,* after lunch," Jade said briskly, and then smiled as she looked at her. Timmie had a look on her face that she only saw in Paris. No matter how tired she was, or how exhausting the previous cities had been, there was a kind of glow about Timmie in Paris. She had a special kind of romance with the city, and people always teased her about it. "You've got that look," Jade said with a smile, as Timmie nodded, unabashedly happy to be there, whatever her country's views on the subject at the moment, or however much others liked to bash the French. Timmie always stood up for them staunchly. She loved the French, and everything about Paris. Sometimes she just sat in her room late at night at the Plaza Athénée, after she got home from business dinners, and looked out the window at the dark gray pearly light of the night sky, or a sunrise on a winter morning . . . spring . . . summer . . . whatever time of year, it was Timmie's favorite city, more than any other in the world. There was nothing else like it and it never failed to make her heart race.

Timmie absentmindedly ran a hand through her thick, long hair, and pulled it back in an elastic. She didn't bother to look in a mirror, or go to the bathroom to do it, or even brush it. She didn't care. She rarely thought about her looks. She was beautiful but not vain. She was far more interested in the looks she designed for others. Her lack of narcissism about her own appearance was endearing and refreshing. When she was working and busy, she looked like a long, leggy child who had wandered onto the scene and was pretending to be a grown-up. Her style was commanding, and her talent obvious, but at the same time there was a kind of innocence about her, a lack of awareness about who she was and the power she wielded. Timmie's real strength was pure raw talent, and incredible drive. She produced more energy than an electrical power plant, and Jade could sense her winding up now.

Timmie had a lot to do in Paris. They had fittings with the models scheduled for seven the next morning. She was driving three hours outside of Paris after that, to look at textiles at the factory, and see if they were willing or able to do some special fabrics she wanted. There would be more interviews after that, to talk about the collections she was showing, for both men and women, and she had just introduced a new perfume in September, which had been a major hit with the youth market. Young women all over the world were clamoring for it. Everything Timmie touched turned to gold, and was blessed with the sweet smell of success. In her business life, things had always been like that. In her personal life, she had been far more challenged. But to look at her, all one saw was a beautiful woman with a mane of thick red curly hair and big green eyes, who was totally unaware of how striking she was.

They stood up, waiting to leave the plane, and David took her alligator bag from her, and groaned as he always did when he held it. "I see you brought your bowling ball with you again," he teased, and she chuckled. He looked like a young male model, and Jade was as meticulously dressed as Timmie wasn't. If one had to guess, anyone would have thought that Jade was the designer and Timmie the assistant, although Timmie was capable of looking smashing when she chose to. Most of the time, she wore her own designs, mingled with vintage pieces she had collected over the years, and some fabulous Indian and antique jewelry she bought mostly at Fred Leighton's in New York, or at an assortment of jewelers in Paris and London. She loved unusual pieces, thought nothing of mixing real with fake, and on her no one ever guessed the costume pieces. She never hesitated to wear a diamond necklace with a T-shirt, or a gigantic vintage Chanel ring, from Coco Chanel or Diana Vreeland's collections of costume jewelry, with a ballgown. Timmie O'Neill was beautiful, in a strikingly natural way, but more than anything she had style, in a casual, mix-and-match bag-lady sort of way, as she liked to say herself. She was no bag lady, but she liked to think so. In fact, she didn't like to think of herself at all. She just got up and dressed in the morning, and let things fall into place. It always worked well for her, although Jade frequently said that if she had tried to put herself together as Timmie did, they wouldn't have let her in the back door of their hotel. But on Timmie, it all worked.

She looked striking and casually stylish as they finally filed off the plane, and David located the VIP woman to help them. He was happy to put Timmie's immensely heavy alligator bag on a rolling cart. It was full of notes and sketch pads, a book in case she wanted to read, a bottle of her latest perfume, and a ton of what Timmie called "debris" that was always floating around her purse. Keys, lipsticks, lighters, an ashtray she had stolen at Harry's Bar, or that they had actually given her when she tried to steal it, a new gold pen someone had sent her, and a dozen silver pencils, all of which weighed a ton as she lugged it all around. David always said you could open an office and start a business with what Timmie carried in her purse. It gave her a feeling of security to carry everything she needed with her. She didn't want to rely on having to find some essential item while she was away on a trip. So she took it all with her, as though she might never go home again.

They followed the VIP woman to baggage claim, where Jade and David would wait for their bags. There was a mountain of them, as Timmie always packed too much, and they had the entire collection with them packed in special trunks. The airline had been warned, and the trunks and boxes containing the ready to wear collection came out first. David had arranged for a truck to get it all to the hotel. He had offered to ride the truck with it, so Timmie could go ahead, but she said she preferred to wait. She wanted to make sure nothing got lost. It would be a disaster if it did. She left Jade talking to David, as they waited for the bags. Timmie walked away, watching people, and lit a cigarette. She had quit for years, but started again eleven years ago, after her divorce.

She stood quietly near a wall, watching people drift by carrying their bags, on their way to customs. As an American, with an entire clothing collection in tow, they had to go through immigration and customs as well. They had documents exempting them from duty and tax, although it was unlikely anyone would open any of their bags or trunks. They had paid five thousand dollars in excess baggage, which was roughly what they always paid, moving the collection from New York to London to Milan to Paris, and then finally back to L.A.

As Timmie smoked her cigarette, she kept thinking how far she had come from her beginnings. Staying at the Plaza Athénée in Paris was second nature to her now, and felt like home, but she had come a long way to get here. She never lost sight of that, and was often grateful for her achievements and blessings, and her serendipitous beginning, all those years ago at the coffee shop. It had been a long, long road from there to Paris, as she stood in her vintage mink jacket, wearing a large diamond bracelet on her wrist, which a few passersby noticed as she smoked. She was so casual about it in spite of its size, that it was hard to guess if it was fake or real. She absentmindedly pulled the elastic out of her hair, and her long curly red hair cascaded past her shoulders. She looked like a young Rita Hayworth in all her glory. Timmie looked nowhere near her age, few people would have guessed that she was forty-eight. At most she looked forty, if that. And in her case, it wasn't due to any special caution or attention, it was just good genes and blind luck. She hated exercise, had no need to diet, and rarely used beauty products. She splashed cold water on her face, brushed her hair, and brushed her teeth, and that was it.

Her eyes drifted to a young mother, struggling to get her bags off the conveyor belt. The woman had an infant strapped to her, while a two-year-old girl holding a doll clung to her skirts, and a boy who looked about four argued with his mother, and finally burst into tears. Both mother and son looked exasperated and harassed. Timmie noticed that the little girl was beautifully dressed. The boy was wearing short pants and a navy jacket. The mother looked tired as she struggled with the bags, and the little boy continued to cry. He wasn't having a tantrum, he was just upset. And without thinking about it any further, Timmie reached into the pocket of her jacket where she had a stash of lollipops that she liked to suck on whenever she had to draw. It kept her from smoking, and was a habit she'd always had. She pulled out two of the lollipops, and approached the mother of the crying boy. They were obviously French. Despite Timmie's passion for all things French, she had never learned the language, except for a few cursory words. She usually got by with gestures and smiles, and the driver she always used in Paris usually helped her out. This time, she was on her own. She managed to catch the mother's eye, showed her the lollipops, without the children seeing them, and smiled a questioning, shy glance.

"Oui?" she asked. The woman understood her, and hesitated. She looked Timmie over carefully, and was about to say no, as the children turned around to observe her. With her free hand, Timmie gently stroked the boy's fine, carefully cut Dutch boy hair, which surprisingly was the same color as hers, or the color hers had been at his age. Timmie's had settled into a burnished copper over the years. His was more carrot-colored, and he had the same pronounced freckles she had had in her youth. The little girl was blond with big blue eyes, as was their mother. The baby had no hair at all, and was observing the scene peacefully with a pacifier in her mouth, which was keeping her quiet. The two-year-old was sucking her thumb, seemingly unaffected by her brother's tears.

The mother nodded then, having seen Timmie's unconscious gesture, as she gently stroked the boy's hair and he stopped crying, and stared up at the stranger. The two women exchanged a smile then, as the young mother thanked her in French, and said *"oui,"* as Timmie handed both children the lollipops, and then helped the young woman with one of the bags, to get it on the cart. Both children politely said *"merci"* to Timmie, and then the family went on their way, as Timmie watched.

She had noticed from the tags on their bags that they had come from a French city, and not from the flight from Milan. The little boy turned and waved at her with an impish grin, before they disappeared, and the mother glanced back with a grateful smile, as Timmie waved back. Her eyes followed them until they were gone, and then David and Jade joined her. They hadn't seen her exchange with the two French children, but it wouldn't have surprised them. Timmie had a soft spot for kids, and had none of her own. She was always talking to children in supermarkets and airports, or while standing in line in department stores. She had a way with them that defied language and nationality, and bridged the gap between her age and theirs. She was just one of those people who liked children, and they seemed to sense that about her. She had an easy way of talking to them, which was unusual for someone in her position, with a career, and no family of her own. She always said that she was alone in the world. She had often said to Jade that she might adopt one day, but she never had.

Jade had biological clock issues of her own. At thirty-eight, she was worried that she'd never have babies. She had spent ten years as the mistress of a married man, and had finally broken up with him the year before, but had met no one important to her since. Her clock was ticking. And Timmie's had stopped ticking years ago. She felt too old to have a baby now, but adopting a child still appealed to her, in a distant dreamy way. She knew it was unlikely to be a dream she would indulge, but she still liked thinking she might one day, although she hadn't mentioned it in a while. David thought she should. He worried that she would be lonely in the years ahead without children. Even Timmie couldn't work forever. Or could she? She always said she planned to work until she keeled over at a hundred.

Jade thought the idea of Timmie adopting a child was silly, and that Timmie was fine as she was. She was a sophisticated, successful woman, who headed up an enormous conglomerate. She couldn't even begin to imagine Timmie with a baby. She knew, as Timmie did most of the time, that it was just a dream, and she would never do it. But on quiet, lonely nights, once in a while, Timmie still thought of the dream with an aching heart. Her life was lonelier than she liked to admit, and the prospect of being solitary for the rest of her life depressed her. It wasn't how she had expected her life to turn out. But over the years, much had changed. She was philosophical about it, enjoyed her life, and tried not to think about how much lonelier her life would be in her old age. Without ever intending to, she had wound up with a career, and no man or kids.

Gilles, Timmie's Paris driver, was waiting for them just beyond immigration and customs. He was a familiar, welcome sight, and greeted them with a broad smile and a wave. As always, a cigarette was firmly embedded between his lips, as one eye squinted to avoid the ever-present curl of smoke. He had driven Timmie for ten years, and had married and had three children in the years since. His wife was a pastry sous-chef at the Crillon, and between them they made a decent living, while his mother-in-law took care of their kids.

"Bonjour, Madame Timmie! *Vous avez fait bon voyage?* You made a good trip?" He spoke heavily accented, fairly accurate English, and always enjoyed driving for her. She was reasonable, friendly, and never made outrageous requests of him. She apologized profusely when she kept him out late, which never bothered him anyway. He liked his work, and the people he met. It made him feel important driving clients like her, and impressed the other chauffeurs. She was generous with her tips, and she sent him a suit for Christmas every year. As a result, he was one of the best-dressed drivers at the Plaza Athénée or any other hotel. She had also given him gifts for his wife and kids. He enjoyed her passionate love of Paris and all things French. She was a pleasure to drive and chatted with him easily, as she and Jade slid into the car, and David got into the luggage truck with their bags. It was not a job for a vice president of marketing, but he wanted to keep track of their things, so nothing got lost or went astray along the way.

"How are Solange and the kids?" Timmie asked pleasantly.

"Very good. Very big," he said, with a broad smile, still squinting in the smoke, as Jade rolled down the window with a disapproving look. Timmie didn't mind, and lit another cigarette herself. She always smoked more in France, since everyone else did. "We get another

baby next year," he said, looking happy about it. Timmie knew it was
their fourth. He had asked her about investment advice more than
once. He and his wife made a good living, and they owned their own
house outside the city, where Solange's widowed mother lived with
them. Timmie liked knowing about the people who worked for her,
and she had always been fond of Gilles. "It's good with you?" he
asked, glancing at her in the rearview mirror, as he darted expertly
through the traffic leaving Roissy. She always looked beautiful and
sexy to him, despite her age. He didn't have the age prejudices about
women that men did in the States. Forty-eight seemed young to him,
particularly looking as good as she did.

"Everything is fine," she said, looking pleased. "We're doing the
ready to wear shows next week. I might get some time to shop this
weekend." She was hoping that they would finish all their work by
Friday, so she could have a day or two to herself, to wander through
antiques shops and check the boutiques in Paris. She liked staying on
top of local trends, wherever she went, and the competition. But in
Paris, she also liked to wander along the Seine, visit the stalls of the
bouquinistes who sold old books, and just breathe deeply of the atmosphere of Paris. She liked going to church there too. Gilles always took
her to out-of-the-way places she wouldn't otherwise have discovered,
and tiny quaint churches she had never heard of before. She was fun
for him to drive around. He loved showing off the city to someone
who appreciated it as much as she did.

She had already told Jade and David that, once their preliminary
work was done, they could go away for the weekend. They both
wanted to go back to London to see friends. They didn't share her passion for Paris, and David had even said something about Prague.
There would be no meetings or interviews over the weekend, and
hopefully by then, all the fittings would be complete. The seam-

stresses Timmie had sent over would be working on alterations and last-minute adjustments all weekend, but were well able to manage it on their own. She would handle all the last-minute details herself, and with Jade and David on Monday. The runway show was Tuesday, and on Tuesday night Jade and David would head for New York. She was flying to meet them on Friday, after two days off on her own after the show. And if she got time to herself over the weekend as well, it was an added bonus, and an ample reward after three weeks of hard work so far. She didn't look it, or even admit it readily, but she was tired.

She and Gilles chatted easily on the drive into Paris, while Jade quietly read her notes. She left several messages on their office phone in Los Angeles, for when the office opened, and several more in New York. It was just after noon in Paris, and still too early everywhere else. Timmie's first interview wasn't until two-thirty, so she'd have a little time to get organized, and gather her thoughts before they got started. There was traffic on the way in, and they drove onto the Avenue Montaigne just before one. Timmie beamed the moment she saw the Plaza Athénée. It was her home away from home. She loved staying there, the elegance, the people, the exquisite service, and she loved meeting friends for lunch at de Relais.

"You always look happy in Paris," Gilles commented, as he opened the door for her, and the doorman smiled as he recognized her, and touched his hat.

"Welcome back, Madame O'Neill," he said, as Jade organized the removal of their hand luggage, and David pulled up behind them with the truck full of their bags and the trunks with the collection.

One of the assistant managers came out to escort her to her suite, as Jade quietly doled out tips, and told Gilles what time to come back. Timmie usually ate late in Paris, and liked going to little bistros, where they made no fuss about her, and she could eat simple French food. As she wandered up the steps, through the revolving door, and into the subdued opulence and elegance of the lobby, there was no denying she was an important person, as members of the staff acknowledged her, and the assistant manager preceded her to her room. Here, their paying attention to her didn't bother her quite as much as it might have in other places. She hated having a fuss made over her, but at the Plaza Athénée it seemed affectionate and familiar, and she smiled broadly as she walked into the same suite she had occupied for the last fifteen years. It had a living room and a bedroom, with long beautiful French windows hung with elaborate satin curtains. The furniture was worthy of a small French château, with gilt and mirrors, chandeliers in every room, and a bathroom where she loved to soak in the tub for hours. Her favorite chocolates and fruit were sitting on a table, with a huge vase of flowers from the manager of the hotel. She always felt spoiled and pampered just being there, and even though she knew the days ahead would be frantic, she was thrilled to be there for more than a week. Ten days in Paris would restore her, no matter how hard she worked. Even Hell Month was a small price to pay, in Timmie's eyes, for the sheer, unadulterated joy of being in Paris for a week.

The assistant manager bowed, left her keys on the desk, and disappeared as she took off her mink jacket, tossed it on a large velvet chair, and checked her messages on the desk. There were already ten of them, and four faxes from her office. Jade went through the messages for her, and said that all the textile people had confirmed their appointments, and one of the interviews had been put off for the next day. The days ahead were going to be busy, which wasn't news to either of them, and as they chatted, a room service waiter appeared with a tray with a pot of tea. The moment she arrived, they knew just what to bring her. It was Earl Grey with her favorite cookies. Impossible to resist.

"You're looking happy," David commented as he stuck his head into the room, and Jade showed the bellboy where to put Timmie's bags in the bedroom. Everything at the Plaza Athénée moved with the precision of a Swiss clock. David smiled at the beatific look on her face. She looked like a kid in her T-shirt and blue jeans, with her mane of red hair all over the place. She sat down happily on a couch in the living room, munching a cookie, and put her ballerina-clad feet on the coffee table.

"It feels so good to be here," she said, looking relaxed for the first time in weeks. She was beaming.

"Tell me that on Tuesday," he teased her. He knew that by then, they'd all be tearing their hair out over the collection, endless headaches with the models, technical problems with lighting and sound, and shaky places on the runway, all the usual miseries that plagued them during the shows, but for now, she didn't care. She was just happy to be there. "You really ought to get a place in Paris, since you love it so much here."

"I know. But I'm too spoiled at the hotel. This would be hard to beat." She waved vaguely at the flowers, the tea, the cookies, the huge silver platter of chocolates, and the elegant furnishings in the suite. "I feel like Eloise at the Plaza Athénée."

"Okay, Eloise, you've got an hour to change, if you're going to," Jade said matter-of-factly. "You've got two interviews back-to-back, a break, and then a meeting. Do you want me to order lunch?" Timmie shook her head. The tea and cookies were perfect, and all she needed for now. She didn't eat much, and was as thin as their models. Years before she'd had offers to model, which she had never bothered to pursue. She was far more interested, even then, in making clothes for them to wear, than in being one of them. But she still had the look.

"I'm not going to change," Timmie said quietly, glanced at her watch, and took a sip of tea.

She had a call to make to Los Angeles, to her current off-and-on male companion, although it seemed silly to call him at that hour. It was four in the morning in Los Angeles, and she didn't want to wake him. Zack had made her promise she'd call him when she arrived, even though it seemed foolish to her. But he said he liked hearing from her and knowing she'd landed safely, which touched her. Most of the time, he wasn't that interested or that attentive. But he surprised her with kind gestures now and then.

She knew he was still angry at her for not taking him on the trip. Often, like a child, he expected her to spoil and entertain him, and he had pouted for weeks before she left. He didn't believe her when she told him she'd be working the entire time, and would have no time to play, in spite of the time she hoped to have to herself over the weekend. But it wasn't worth his coming all the way from Los Angeles, for two free days she might not have anyway, if there was a crisis, or the two days she was planning to take off the following week. There was no point having him around while she worked night and day. She hadn't had a single day, or even hour, off so far on the trip. She was wondering if calling him from Paris would make things worse, or pacify him a little. It was hard to tell. She thought about calling him later that afternoon, but then he might be annoyed that she hadn't done what she'd said she would. She could always call him now, give him a quick kiss, and let him go back to sleep. She knew he hadn't forgiven her yet for leaving him in L.A. for three weeks, while she traveled to New York, and three very appealing cities in Europe.

Before she left, he seemed to feel, despite their somewhat casual relationship, that taking him along to play while she worked was his due. She hadn't agreed. It had been a bone of contention between them for weeks before she left, and still was. It was the nature of the beast with men like him, who went out with women like her. It was a role reversal she had never liked or believed in, but had found herself participating in, in recent years. Men like Zack seemed to her the only alternate option she had to solitude. It had its drawbacks, which she was realistic about, and at times its perks. Most of the time, he acted like a spoiled child. He was young, irresponsible, and completely self-centered.

There had been a number of men like Zack in her life during the past eleven years, since her divorce. She had been married for five years, and the years after her marriage had seemed far longer, and emptier for sure. She had filled them mainly with work and long hours, and devoted herself to building her empire year by year, with impressive results. There was little time or opportunity in her life for a serious companion, and she was convinced that by now she was no longer eligible for one anyway. Timmie always said that women in her position didn't attract men of equal importance or magnitude, or of comparable substance and moral worth. Women in her shoes seemed to be magnets for men who wanted her to do for them. She firmly believed that men her age, who were as successful and powerful as she was, usually allied themselves with women half her age, who were grateful to be the girlfriends or mistresses of important men. They molded themselves into the decorative role powerful men offered them, flattered their men accordingly, and were pleased to be trophies to be shown off and put on display. Timmie said that men who were her equals and age didn't want women her age, or who were as successful as they. It certainly seemed to be true in her case.

In all eleven years since her divorce, not a single appropriate equally successful man, even close to her age, had ever approached her. So the choice she was left with, in the same vein as other women like her, was either noble, dignified solitude, or the occasional companion, like Zack, who was usually younger than she was, in her case only by a few years since men half her age would have made her feel even more ridiculous, and would have bored her to tears. The problem with them was not so much one of age, but that they were not in love with her, nor was she in love with them. She could have forgiven much, if there had been love on both sides of the exchange, which, in eleven years of assorted partners, had never been the case.

The men she went out with often seemed to be actors or occasionally models, writers, artists, involved in some artistic pursuit, more often than not, to a mild degree. They were never successful, nor worked as hard as she. They were handsome, narcissistic, spoiled, superficially nice to her, at first anyway, and impressed with who she was, and sometimes jealous of it. They enjoyed the perks she provided. She was the giver in each of these relationships, and they the takers, and eventually the emotional inequities of the situation did them in. It wasn't the financial difference that spoiled it for her. It was the unavoidable fact that they didn't love each other. She had never fallen in love with any of them. Nor they with her. And within six months or less, they parted company, usually on decent terms. They helped to pass the time, and fill lonely nights and weekends. They were an antidote to loneliness, and a life that became too solitary with no companion whatsoever. Although she was always torn as to whether it was better to hang out with someone less perfect for a time, or remain bravely alone, hoping for the right one to turn up one day. There were times when she wasn't that brave. And then someone like Zack would come along, and she'd compromise for a while again, although sometimes being with them made her even lonelier than she already was, and sometimes it was okay. In exchange for their company, she furthered their careers, took them to events with her, the rare times she went, and invited them to her house in Malibu on weekends.

She hadn't really been looking for a man in the past eleven years. She had accepted her single state after the divorce and made her peace with it. She really didn't want to be with a man unless she loved him. But at times the companionship of a man was fun or even comforting, and flattered her. At forty-eight, she wasn't ready to give up on relationships forever. And the right guy might never come along. She knew the limitations of men like Zack, but until now, anyway, there were just no other options. And for what it was worth, Zack was company, and she was fond of him. She had liked him better until he had been seriously unpleasant to her when she wouldn't take him to Europe. That had been just a little too blatant, and it had turned her off. She had been somewhat cool with him after that and he had been petulant with her before she left, and ever since she told him he wasn't coming. She wasn't even sure they'd still be seeing each other when she got back. She hadn't made her mind up yet how she felt about it. She suspected the end was near, for both of them. In different ways they were both getting less than they wanted or felt they deserved. And once resentment set in, as it had now with him, the relationship never lasted long.

She had called him several times anyway since she left, to keep the option open, annoyed at herself for putting up with him. But she hated to be alone again. It was fun being with him sometimes, although she had no illusions about their future. Without love to fuel their relationship, sooner or later it would end.

Zack was forty-one years old, a sometime actor, and model. He had done several national commercials, and did fairly well. They met when he auditioned for a national campaign of Timmie O ads, and they started dating after he was turned down. He was a good sport about it, although she knew he was hoping she'd get him work one day. He mentioned it from time to time, which was uncomfortable for her.

He was boyish and playful, and irresistibly handsome. They had fun in Malibu on weekends, although sex had never been great for them. She had learned over the years that narcissistic men were far less sexual than others. They were much more interested in themselves, which wasn't a trait of Timmie's. She was neither narcissistic, full of herself, or selfish. Those who knew her well, like Jade and David, agreed that she was a truly good person, which was rare. Neither of them would have said the same of Zack.

Zack had never been married and was a professional bachelor of sorts, with no particular interest in getting married or having kids. All he really wanted was to have fun. As long as the relationship met those criteria or served some purpose for him, he was happy to stick around. He loved getting publicity with her, and was always on the lookout for situations and opportunities that would enhance his career. He preferred perks and lucky breaks to work. Timmie was the worker bee of the pair. Zack was not.

The relationship was what it was, and she had few illusions about it. It was fun while it lasted, and sooner or later, for one reason or another, she knew it would end. Her relationships with men like Zack never lasted more than a few months. The periods of solitude between them lasted a lot longer. She was never sure which she preferred, settling for the wrong guy, or being alone. Neither were options she loved, and they were the only ones she'd had for years.

She was hoping to keep the relationship with Zack going until after the holidays, because facing Christmas alone would be harder still. Being with less-than-perfect men who didn't love her seemed less painful to Timmie than being alone for holidays and weekends. So she put up with the inevitable disappointments and irritations, as long as they weren't too extreme. He filled a role in her life of some-time companion, and superficial lover and friend. He was handsome, charming when he wanted to be, and they often had fun when they went out together. He wasn't a bad guy, didn't do any harm, and once or twice a week, he kept her warm at night, which seemed like a good thing. And when it was over, as it would be inevitably, then she'd take a break for a while again, savoring her solitude, and convince herself she was better off alone. It was a dance she had done repeatedly in the past eleven years, she knew it well. It was the dilemma of most single women her age. There wasn't a high demand for forty-eight-year-old divorcées. And success seemed to be a romantic handicap for a woman at any age. She figured it would take a miracle to meet a man who was undaunted by her success and her age, didn't try to take advantage of her, and loved her for who she was, genuinely. There had been no miracles in Timmie's life in a long time, and she was no longer waiting for one. She had long since resigned herself to dating men like Zack, and made no excuses for it. Who she dated was no one's business but her own. She hurt no one, never threw her weight around with them, and she was always gracious at the end, which wasn't always the case with them. But Timmie was a lady till the end.

She picked up the phone and dialed his number in L.A., as Jade left the room without comment. She had seen a number of men like Zack come and go over the years of working for Timmie. She hated them. Timmie deserved so much better, but Jade also understood better than most the disadvantages Timmie was operating under. She'd had her own problems finding the right man, and knew the compromises one made, in her case a married man, which she would never do again, after ten wasted years and a broken heart to show for it. She had begun to think that maybe Timmie was better off with men like Zack, who looked like boys and pretended to be men. At least Timmie had no illusions about them. She never fell in love with them, and wasn't broken-hearted when it ended. The damage was limited. She never lost her dreams, in fact with men like Zack, there were no dreams at all. Just a pretty face, a handsome body, an easygoing guy in most cases, and another six months she didn't have to spend alone. It worked, as long as you never wanted more, and remembered what it was. The only real mistake would have been thinking it could be more. But Timmie never did. She knew the game and the breed too well. She kept her heart well protected, and didn't expect a lot from them.

Zack answered on the second ring, and was obviously asleep when Timmie called.

"Hi Zack," she said easily. "We just got to Paris, and I said I'd call. Go back to sleep. I'll call you later." She was about to hang up when he spoke. He had a deep sexy rumble of a voice, especially when he was in bed or asleep. She loved his looks and his voice.

"No, don't...I'm awake...so how's Paris? It sucks without me, right?" He was teasing, but not entirely, and even half asleep, there was an edge to his voice. She could easily hear that he was still angry about the trip he'd missed. She had no intention of discussing that with him again, or explaining for the hundredth time that for her this was work.

"Absolutely. It totally sucks." She laughed, thinking he was at least consistent. He had become obsessive about her inviting him on this trip. Their battles had raged on for weeks before she left, while she tried in vain to reason with him, and convince him that she needed to work on this trip, and go alone. "Why don't you go back to sleep? I'm going to work in an hour."

"Yeah, yeah, I know. You keep saying that. You can't be working all the time." It had been a recurring theme during their calls throughout the trip. He had been doggedly persistent, probably thinking she'd relent and invite him to come over halfway through, but she hadn't.

"Believe it or not, I am. These road shows for the ready to wear collections are a bitch." She was being honest with him, although he hadn't believed her all along. It sounded like a lot of fun to him. Models, parties, press, a round of activity in sexy European cities. What more could a boy want? It would have suited Zack to a tee if she'd let him come. She didn't want to have to worry about him while she worked.

"You could have hired me to model at least," he chided her gently, and she smiled. She knew that was what he wanted, or at the very least a free ride. There was no mystery to what he wanted from her in this instance—it was all up-front.

"They hire all the models in Europe, Zack. You know that." But he also knew she could have forced them to hire him, and she had chosen not to, which rankled him. It was in her power to get him jobs, or even create them for him. Timmie was adamant that she didn't want the men she dated on these trips. She never mixed business with pleasure. He would have been out of place here, unless she was serious about him, which she wasn't, and he wasn't serious about her either. They were just having fun together for a while, which didn't warrant a trip to Europe, in her mind. In his, he felt she owed it to him, for reasons that were mystifying to her. As far as she was concerned, Zack

was asking for too much, and she hadn't given in. "Besides, my darling," she added sensibly, without emotion, "you're too old for these
shows. The models are all kids, some of them are in their teens."

"Euro scum," he said succinctly, and she laughed. In some cases, he
wasn't far off the mark. All she cared about was how well they wore
her clothes.

"I'll be home in two weeks, thank God. I feel like I've been gone a
year," Timmie said, changing the subject.

"It feels like it to me too," he said, sounding warmer. He had actually missed her more than he expected to during her trip. And despite
all their arguments about it before she left, he was fond of her. She
was a nice woman, and treated him well. He recognized that she was
very good to him. "Just get your ass home, so we can play and hang
out in Malibu." She knew he enjoyed her house in the Colony, and the
weekends they spent there. She enjoyed them too. It was part of the
fair exchange they both tacitly agreed to by going out with each other.
Her lifestyle, in exchange for his companionship. It worked for both
of them, and they had good times together.

"I'll be home soon," she reassured him. "What are you up to this
week?"

"I have a go-see for a modeling job today, and an audition for a
commercial tomorrow," he said, sounding hopeful. He got a fair
amount of work, for a man his age.

"I hope you get it," she encouraged him. It was one of the things he
liked best about her. She was always so up and positive. Whatever
happened, she had something cheerful to say about it. She was never
a downer.

"So do I. I need the money," he said with a yawn. She could easily
envision him lying there, in all his boyish beauty. There was no denying that he was gorgeous, even if self-centered. Looks like his were

hard to resist. It was part of what had appealed to her from the beginning. It was fun going out with someone that handsome. For a while at least. "Well, don't have too much fun in Paris. In fact," he said, with a grin at his end, "I hope you have a lousy time there and miss me. Why should you have fun, if I'm not?" It was hardly gracious of him, but the comment didn't surprise her.

"I suppose that's one way to look at it," she said practically, only mildly shocked at how blatant he was about his feelings. "I think you'll get your wish. Starting in about half an hour, I'm going to be working my ass off." Work was work, even in Paris.

"Nice ass. I like it," he said matter-of-factly, missing her.

"Thank you. Yours is nice too." And in better shape than hers, although she didn't say it. There was no need to point that out. Why remind him? He was only seven years younger than she, but spent hours every day toning his body.

"Well, get yours home soon before I forget what it looks like." He was in better spirits with her than he'd been in in days, and was obviously beginning to forgive her. He was clearly anxious to see her when she got back, and she was relieved. She had no desire to end the relationship with him yet. Not until after the holidays at least.

"I'll send you a snapshot," she teased. "I'll have Jade take it after my next meeting." He laughed at her answer. She had a quick wit, and she was smart, he liked all of that about her. In fact, sometimes he liked her a lot more than he intended. He was just pissed about the trip. But not pissed enough to end the relationship. He had opted to pout instead. He was hoping she'd take him on the next one.

"Bring me back something from Paris," he said bluntly, almost like a child to a parent.

"Like what?" she asked, surprised. She had been generous with him so far, and given him a lot of clothes from her most expensive men's line. She knew he needed them, and it didn't cost her anything to do it. And she'd bought him a nice watch on his birthday. He was grateful, and not in the least embarrassed by the gifts.

"The Eiffel Tower maybe. I don't know. Surprise me."

"I'll see what I can come up with." It was like talking to a child sometimes. In his mind, she should spoil him. There was no pretense of equality in the relationship, and never had been, emotionally, intellectually, or financially. Equality was not the nature of relationships like the one she had with Zack. Their difference in age and economic stability skewed everything. She felt like his Sugar Mommy much of the time, which felt awkward to her, if not to him. For her, equality in relationships was a thing of the past, and she firmly believed not likely to ever happen again. It was the price she paid for success and age. "I'm sorry I woke you up."

"I'm glad you did. Maybe I'll get up and go to the gym."

"Have a nice day. I'll call you soon. Maybe over the weekend," she promised. "It's going to be pretty nuts here for the next few days." Just as it had been in New York, London, and Milan. It never even occurred to him to ask her how she was, or if she was tired. He knew she could take care of herself, and assumed she was all right.

"See ya," he said, and hung up. She sat staring at the phone for a long minute, as Jade walked back into the room.

"How's the prince?" Jade asked, as she glanced at Timmie.

"Okay, I guess. Still annoyed that I didn't bring him, but better now. He seems to be getting over it, although he wished me a lousy time without him." Timmie found it funny.

Jade didn't. "That sounds about right," Jade said sourly, putting a stack of papers on the desk for Timmie to sign. A flood of new faxes had just come in, which required her immediate attention.

Timmie looked up at Jade strangely, feeling numb, not even disappointed by her conversation with Zack. For all his blatant lack of sensitivity, he was familiar to her by now, and a comfortable presence in her life at times. She accepted him for who and what he was. The man she was sleeping with and not the man she was passionately in love with. Sometimes, Timmie knew, you couldn't have it all. You had to compromise. And she had, rather than be alone. Although his wishing her a lousy time without him had been a bit beyond the pale. "Sometimes I don't know why I bother," Timmie sighed, as they chatted.

"You know why you bother, and so do I," Jade said honestly. She always called things as she saw them. Timmie loved that about her. "Because being alone is lousy, and lonely," Jade went on. "So you settle for what you can get. And that's what it looks like. It looks like Zack. But the alternative, of no one, isn't so great either. It's not a lot of fun. And doing what I did, dating a married man, is worse. At least you won't get your heart broken. All he'll do in the end is piss you off, not break your heart."

"Not always," Timmie said honestly. "Sometimes they take a piece of you with them. Like your self-respect and self-esteem for putting up with the bullshit. After a while, it gets to you."

"So does a married man who won't leave his wife. Hell, Timmie, what other choice do we have? All the good ones are married." It was a mantra Timmie had heard before. Hers was that all men, the good ones at least, were terrified of her success.

"They can't all be married," Timmie said staunchly.

"Really? When was the last time you met a decent, respectable guy worth having who wasn't?"

"I don't know," Timmie said with a sigh, picking a chocolate off the platter. "I don't pay that much attention. I don't think I want a real relationship anymore. Why do I need one at my age? But I'm not sure

I want the Zacks anymore either. I always wind up feeling like their mother, and as though they expect me to meet their every need. That's not my job."

"Try telling them that," Jade said tartly. "Maybe we should both go into the convent, " Jade said, smiling at her.

"Not unless I get to redesign the habits. They've gotten seriously ugly," Timmie said pensively as though she meant it, and they both laughed. "I don't know what the answer is. At your age, you'll find the right guy one of these days. You just have to keep looking. At my age, I don't think I care anymore. In fact, I know I don't. The last thing I want now is to get married . . . so that leaves the Zacks . . . or no one. Noble solitude. I guess I'm ready for another dose of that sometime soon. I think this is on its last legs. It's starting to depress me. I'm tired of playing Lady Bountiful to bratty, immature male models and actors, or being bitched at when I don't want to. Where the hell do these guys get their sense of entitlement? I wish I had as much self-confidence as they do. Narcissists are just too goddamned much work," Timmie said with a shrug. Although he had been relatively pleasant, the call to Zack had done nothing to cheer her, and after three weeks on the road, she was exhausted, which dampened her spirits. She wasn't sure if she was looking forward to seeing him when she got home, or not.

"Maybe you'll meet someone here in Paris," Jade said hopefully, and meant it.

"Are you kidding? Who are we talking about here? The nineteen-year-old male models from the Czech Republic, or the angry French journalists from the left-wing press, or the other designers, who are either women or gay or both? I'm not looking for anyone. And anyone I'd meet here would be geographically undesirable anyway. The last thing I need is a guy halfway around the world, in Paris. But thanks for the suggestion," Timmie said, popping another chocolate in her mouth. Her metabolism allowed her indulgences few women could get away with.

"I think I'm going to try computer dating when we go back. I know four people who've gotten married this year to men they met on the Internet," Jade said, looking as though she meant it.

"Just be careful. I think that sounds scary," Timmie said, as she got up and started brushing her hair. Her first interviewer was due to arrive within minutes. The Paris rat race was about to begin.

"How much worse could it get?" Jade asked rhetorically. "I've had married, you've had assholes. The worst that could happen is that I meet a nice ax murderer, get married, and have babies. At thirty-eight, I can't afford to be too picky."

"At thirty-eight, you can afford to be as picky as you want. Don't settle, Jade," Timmie said seriously.

But she also knew that even Jade was older than a lot of men wanted. Men of all ages seemed to want twenty-two-year-olds. Grown-up women, with brains, had been becoming obsolete for years. And Timmie knew that she herself was no longer even in the running, for a variety of reasons, age, income, success, celebrity to a certain degree since her name was a household word all over the world, which didn't help either. All it drew to her were guys like Zack, or worse. She was still pondering it when Jade came back in to tell her that her first interviewer was waiting downstairs in the lobby. There was a wonderful area where they served tea and fabulous pastries. She liked meeting members of the press there, or in the bar. Timmie sighed when she told her. She looked beautiful, but her assistant could see how tired she was.

"Shall I have him come up?" Jade asked.

"I guess so," Timmie said quietly. She wasn't in the mood. All she wanted was to go for a long, quiet walk through Paris. She had three days of hard work ahead of her, and then, over the weekend at least, she could do whatever she wanted. She thought of Zack's comment while she waited for the interviewer to come to her suite. *"I hope you have a lousy time without me in Paris."* She'd been with men like him for too long. His saying that to her didn't even shock her anymore. She was used to men now who were handsome, and fun to play with, but it never occurred to them to take care of her and comfort her, or even rub her shoulders when she was tired. She carried the full weight of her life and responsibilities on her own. It was a burden she felt acutely at times, and she did now.

She stood up with a smile when the interviewer walked in. He was a tall, thin, balding, angry-looking man who was about to challenge her about the meaning of fashion. And suddenly, she didn't care about that either, as she pretended to greet him warmly, and smiled as she shook his hand, invited him to sit down, offered him tea or coffee, and pointed invitingly to the platter of chocolates.

"This is quite a hotel you stay in," he said after accepting her offer of coffee, and devouring four chocolates. "Does it embarrass you to live like this, and spend this kind of money, all earned from exploiting people and their whims about fashion?" he asked in a single breath between chocolates, as Timmie smiled kindly at him, and wondered what the hell to answer. It was going to be a long afternoon, she realized, as she looked at him, and knew that Zack's wish was about to come true. She was having a lousy time without him. But then again, had he been there, she might have had a lousy time with him too, depending on his mood. Nothing in life was sure.

Chapter 2

Both of Timmie's interviews on Wednesday afternoon were predictably tiresome. She had been doing interviews just like them for twenty-three years. She rarely enjoyed the publicity aspects of her work. What she loved was the designing, and coming up with fresh ideas for new collections several times a year. It had been even more fun since she had added all the additional lines to her company. The possibilities were infinite.

Presenting the collections at the ready to wear shows in New York and Europe was an important aspect of her work. It was particularly exciting for her since she was the only American designer to show her work in both American and European venues, which made the ready to wear shows that much more challenging for her. She took the ready to wear shows seriously twice a year, and it was crucial to her that their runway shows went off impeccably. She was a perfectionist about every detail. It nearly gave her an ulcer fitting the models to the clothes, seeing that every possible element was the right one, every accessory the perfect choice, and then watching everything intently in rehearsal. Timmie was normally good-natured and even-tempered, but it drove her insane if anything went wrong, or the models didn't look right when they were on the runway, if their hair was wrong, if they moved wrong, or some piece of an outfit got misplaced.

By Friday afternoon all the models had been fitted in the outfits they were to wear. The rehearsal was set for Monday, and after her last textile meeting on Friday afternoon, Timmie realized she'd had a stomachache all week. She had hardly eaten, and the less she ate, the worse she felt. Jade asked her if she was all right, before she and David left on Friday evening to catch the Eurostar to London. They had decided to spend the weekend there, and David had agreed to give up his weekend in Prague to accompany Jade. They were going to three parties, and he was determined to visit the Tate.

"Are you feeling okay?" Jade inquired again just before she took off. She looked concerned. She thought Timmie looked unusually pale, and she had seemed nervous and anxious all week. It wasn't surprising before the ready to wear shows. Timmie was always stressed before the runway shows, but this time she seemed more jangled, and Jade thought she didn't look well. She looked exhausted, and somewhat unnerved.

"Actually, I feel like shit," Timmie said with a grin. "I think I'm just tired. I wish Paris were at the beginning of Hell Month, instead of the end. By the time we get here for the ready to wear shows, I'm always beat. I think I wore myself out in Milan." Although it had been a good show there too, and she'd been pleased. She hoped the one in Paris would be as good. She had selected the best models in Paris, and so far the clothes had looked great on all of them.

"Take it easy this weekend," Jade said, looking worried, as David came to pick her up in Timmie's room. Their rooms were just across the hall from hers. "You don't need to do anything. It's all done." She knew Timmie was thrilled with the fabrics she had ordered for the following year. She had gotten everything she'd wanted, and they were having several fabrics woven especially for them. The clothes she would design using them would be totally unique. "Are you going to any of the parties here?"

"I should probably make an appearance at a few of them." A lot of the design houses gave parties in Paris, but Timmie O was not going to this year, which was something of a relief, and it was also why Jade and David were able to get away to London. Otherwise, they would have been stuck, working in Paris over the weekend. They also knew they would have to make up for not entertaining this time, by giving some kind of bash when they came back for the next ready to wear shows in February. But at least this time they were off the hook. "Maybe I'm coming down with the flu," Timmie said with a thoughtful look. "I'll be fine after a good night's sleep." She had been thinking about ordering room service that night, instead of going to one of her favorite bistros. She wasn't in the mood, and a quiet night in her room was suddenly a lot more appealing. She was planning to order soup, and go straight to bed.

"Call if you need us for anything," Jade reminded her, and gave her a hug as they left. She knew that Timmie would be happy wandering around Paris all weekend, and visiting her favorite haunts, unless of course she got sick, which she and David both hoped she wouldn't.

"I'm not going to need anything. You two just have fun." They were young enough to actually enjoy running off to London for a round of parties, even after three killing weeks of work. She had made a dinner reservation for them at Harry's Bar, on her account, which was yet another treat for them. And she felt a thousand years old herself as she climbed into a hot bath, shortly after they left. The chance to soak lazily in the warm water in the deep tub felt good after weeks of hard work, especially the last few days in Paris.

She thought about Zack, as she lay in the bath. She hadn't called him since the morning they arrived. There didn't seem to be much point, and he knew where she was. He could have called her and hadn't. But he was on her mind, so she sent him a brief e-mail when she got out of the bath, just to keep communication open between them. She didn't want to close any doors before she got back. She called room service after that, ordered chicken soup, read a chapter in the book she'd brought with her and hadn't had time to read so far, and fell asleep by ten o'clock.

She woke up at two in the morning, feeling violently ill, and spent the rest of the night throwing up. She felt absolutely awful, and finally fell asleep again at six in the morning, as the sky over Paris was beginning to lighten. The last thing she wanted was to be sick in Paris, and miss the opportunity to enjoy the city she loved so much. It was really miserable luck, and she obviously had picked up a flu on her travels. It was noon when she next woke up, and finally felt better, although her stomach muscles ached from retching all night. But at least when she got out of bed, she no longer felt nauseous. It had been a rough night, but the worst seemed to be over.

She called Gilles and asked him to meet her outside at one. She ordered tea and toast from room service, thought about calling Zack again, but by then it was three in the morning for him. It was odd how the familiarity of him called to her at times. Good or bad, he was after all the current man in her life, even if part-time. By sheer reflex, she had almost called him the night before, when she was sick. But theirs was not the kind of relationship in which she would have felt comfortable whining to him. She had a strong suspicion he would have laughed at her, or made light of it. Sympathy hadn't appeared to be his strong suit so far, in the four months they'd been together. Whenever she said that she was exhausted from a hard week, he had ignored the comment and suggested they go out, and several times she had, to indulge him, oblivious to her own needs, meeting only his. She took a shower, dressed in a sweater and jeans, comfortable shoes, and left the hotel. As promised, her driver Gilles was waiting outside, and smiled the minute he saw her.

He took her to all the places she loved to go to, but by four o'clock she was feeling sick again. She hated to waste a minute in Paris, and had wanted to go to Didier Ludot at the Palais Royal, to dig through their vintage couture, but in the end, she decided to skip it and go back to the hotel. She didn't feel up to shopping anymore. And as soon as she got to the Plaza Athénée, she went straight back to bed. By seven o'clock that night, she was throwing up again, even more violently than she had the previous night. Whatever bug she had picked up, it was a nasty one, and by nine o'clock she felt like she was going to die. She made one last trip to the bathroom, and this time nearly fainted on her way back to bed. She hated to admit it, but she was starting to panic. And after lying in bed crying for another half-hour, she began to think about finding a doctor. She was sure that all she had was stomach flu, but she was feeling extremely ill. And then she remembered the name of a doctor a friend in New York had given her, in case she ever needed a physician in Paris. She had saved his office and cell phone numbers on a piece of paper in her address book. Feeling slightly embarrassed, she called and left a message on his cell phone, and lay on her bed afterward with her eyes closed, feeling frightened to be so ill. She hated getting sick when she was on trips and far from home. She thought about calling Zack again, and felt stupid even thinking about it. What was there to say, except that she was feeling awful and had the flu? She didn't want to call Jade and David and upset them, either, so she lay on her bed, waiting for the doctor to call her back, which he did promptly. She was impressed when he returned her call within minutes and promised to come to the hotel at eleven.

The concierge called as soon as he entered the hotel, and told her that the doctor was on his way upstairs. At least by then she hadn't thrown up in nearly two hours, and she hoped it meant she was on the mend. She felt silly to have bothered a doctor for something that was surely minor, even if disagreeable, and he probably couldn't do anything about it anyway. She was feeling sheepish as she opened the door to him when he knocked, and even more so when she saw a tall, good-looking man with sandy blond hair in his mid-fifties standing there in an impeccably elegant dark blue suit and white shirt. He looked more like a businessman than a doctor, as he introduced himself as Docteur Jean-Charles Vernier. And when she apologized for disturbing him on a Saturday night, he insisted that he had been at a dinner party nearby anyway and didn't mind at all. He said he was delighted to help her, although visiting patients in hotels was not usual for him. Timmie knew he was an internist and a reputed professsor at the Faculté de Médicine. He had left the dinner party promptly after Timmie's call on his cell phone, although he was somewhat overqualified for what he was doing as a favor for her friend in New York. Timmie was grateful that she had made note of his name and number and had a doctor to call, other than a total stranger referred by the hotel. He was a well-known and highly respected doctor in Paris.

He followed her into the room, and could see that she was moving slowly, and seemed somewhat unsteady, and even considering her fair redhead's skin, she seemed unusually pale to him. He saw her wince when she sat down as though her whole body ached, which it did. Every muscle in her body felt as though it were shrieking. She'd been vomiting for two days.

Without saying a great deal about it, he took her temperature and listened to her chest. She had no fever, and he assured her that her lungs were clear, and then he asked her to lie down. As he put his stethoscope away, she noticed that he wore a wedding band on his left hand, and she couldn't help observing that he was a very good-looking man, with deep blue eyes and still-blond hair, in spite of a little distinguished gray at the temples. She couldn't help thinking too that she looked a total mess, not that she cared. She felt too sick to worry about how she looked. He smiled at her pleasantly as she lay down, and he gently moved his hands around her abdomen, and then frowned. He asked her then to describe what had happened, touched several places on her stomach again, and asked her if it hurt. She seemed to be most sensitive around the area of her belly button, and once when he touched her she gave a sharp gasp of pain.

"I think it's just the flu," she reassured him, looking worried, and he smiled. He spoke excellent English, but his accent was decidedly French, and so were his looks, although he was taller than most French men.

"You are also a doctor?" he asked with a somewhat mischievous look. "As well as a famous designer? I should be very angry at you, you have cost me a great deal of money. My wife and both my daughters have bought many of your clothes." She smiled at his comment, and he pulled a side chair up to the bed, and sat down to talk to her. He could see that she was afraid.

"Is it something awful?" She had decided sometime that night that it was probably cancer, or at the very least a perforated ulcer, but there had been no sign of blood in anything she threw up. She hoped that was a good sign, but she didn't like the look in his eyes. Something told her she wasn't going to like what he had to say, and as it turned out, she was right.

"I don't think it's awful," he said carefully, as she nervously twisted a lock of her long red hair. She looked like a little girl suddenly, tucked into the big bed. "But I am a little bit concerned. I would like to take you to the hospital tonight, and do some tests."

"Why?" Her eyes opened wide, and he saw fear turn to panic. "What do you think it is?" She was sure again that it was cancer after all.

"I cannot be certain without some scans, but I think it is possibly an attack of appendicitis." He was almost sure it was, but didn't want to make an official diagnosis without a sonogram. "I would like to take you to the American Hospital in Neuilly. It is a very pleasant place," he said reassuringly as tears filled her eyes. He knew the American Hospital would be less frightening for her than the Pitié Salpetrière where he often worked. He had privileges to see patients at the American Hospital too, although he seldom used them.

"I can't. I have a show on Tuesday, and rehearsals on Monday. I've got to be there," she said, looking nearly frantic, as he frowned.

"I can assure you that if your appendix explodes, Madame O'Neill, you will not be at your show. I know your show is important, but it would be irresponsible not to do some tests now." It was easy to see that she was feeling very ill.

"Would I have to be operated on if it is my appendix?" she asked in a choked voice, and he hesitated before he answered. He looked like a very elegant dinner guest who had wandered into her room from a party somewhere downstairs. But however worldly he looked, he sounded very much like a doctor, and she didn't like what he'd just said.

"Possibly," he said in answer to her question. "We will know better after the scans. Have you ever had this before? Or even something similar in the past few days or weeks?" She shook her head. She had felt a little queasy one night in Milan, but she thought it was something she ate. She'd had white truffles on pasta for dinner, and it had been extremely rich. Jade and David hadn't felt well afterward, either, and they had all decided it was the heavy white truffle dinner. In Milan, she hadn't thrown up, as she had for the past two nights. In the morning, after the white truffle pasta, she'd been fine. She didn't mention the truffle episode to him, for fear it would make him even more deter-mined to do the scans on her now, if he thought she'd had the problem for a while.

"I think I'm feeling better. I haven't thrown up in several hours." She looked as stubborn as a child, which he didn't seem to find particularly charming. He didn't like difficult patients in the middle of the night, and he wasn't accustomed to dealing with foreign VIPs and headstrong Americans. Jean-Charles Vernier was used to his patients and students doing what he said. As an illustrious professor, his authority was usually unquestioned. He assessed somewhat correctly that she was obsessed with her work. "What if I just rest, and we see how I feel to-morrow?" She was bargaining with him, and he didn't like it. He looked at her with considerable annoyance. He could see that she had no in-tention of going to the hospital if she could help it. She knew that if she did, and they operated on her, the show on Tuesday would be a mess. She had no confidence that anyone would pull it off as competently as she would herself, even David and Jade. She had never missed a ready to wear show in her entire career. And in addition to that, if at all possible, she had no intention of having surgery in France. She would take care of it when she got back to the States, hopefully, once she got home, or even in New York. "Why don't we give it another day?" she suggested. Her eyes were wide and very green in the star-tlingly pale face.

"Because it could get rapidly worse. If it is indeed appendicitis, you don't want it to explode." The very word nearly made her shake. The prospect of an explosion of any kind anywhere in her body did not have a lot of appeal.

"No, I don't, but maybe it won't. Maybe it's something else, some mi-nor thing, like the flu. I've been traveling a lot for the past three weeks."

"I see that you are a very stubborn woman," he said, looking at her sternly from his considerable height. "Everything in life is not about work. You must also take care of your health. Are you traveling with anyone?" he inquired discreetly, but it was obvious that there was no one sharing the room with her. The other half of her bed was untouched.

"My two assistants, but they're in London for the weekend. I could stay in bed until Monday, and even if it's appendicitis, maybe it will calm down."

"That's possible, but it sounds as though it has been acute now for twenty-four or forty-eight hours. That is not a good sign. Madame O'Neill, I must advise you that I think you should go to the hospital." His voice was firm, and he looked as though he was about to get seriously annoyed with her if she didn't do what he said. She didn't like his attitude, and he liked hers even less. He thought she was foolish, stubborn, and spoiled, and used to doing whatever she wanted. Another American obsessed with money and work. He had dealt with a few patients like her before, though generally the workaholics he saw were men. He wasn't enjoying this at all. He was a respected internist with a busy practice. He didn't have the time or disposition to argue with a patient who didn't want his help, no matter how well known she was. In his own field and realm, he was nearly as important as she was.

"I want to wait," she said stubbornly. He could see that nothing was going to move her. She seemed totally inflexible to him, foolishly so.

"I understand that, but I do not agree with you." He took a pen out of his inside jacket pocket then, and a prescription pad from his doctor's bag. He scribbled something on a sheet from the pad, handed it to her, and she looked at it, hoping it would be a prescription for some magical medication that would fix everything. Instead, all she saw was his phone number on the paper he handed her. It was the same number she had called and not a prescription at all. "You have my phone number. I have advised you of what I think you should do. If you don't wish to follow my advice, and if you feel worse, please call me at any hour. But then, I will insist that you go to the hospital. Will you agree that if you do not feel better, or feel worse, you will do as I ask in that case?" His tone was chilly and very firm.

"All right. Then I will," she agreed. Anything to buy time. She couldn't allow herself to get sicker until Tuesday night. And hopefully, whatever it was would have disappeared by then. Maybe it really was only the flu, and he was wrong. She hoped he was.

"We have an agreement, then," he said formally, as he stood up and replaced the chair he'd sat on to its original place. "I will hold you to it, for your sake. Don't be afraid to call me. I take calls at any hour." Although he wanted to impress her with the seriousnesss of the situation, he didn't want to appear too intimidating or frighten her unduly. He didn't want her to be afraid to call him if she got worse.

"Can't you give me something in case I get sick again? Something to stop the vomiting?" She was still feeling nauseous as she lay in bed and talked to him, but she didn't want to admit it to him. She had no intention of going to the hospital that night. He was probably just an alarmist, or maybe he was covering himself, she told herself. Maybe he was afraid of a malpractice suit if he didn't at least suggest the hospital to her. Her thinking was very American, and she didn't share any of it with him.

"That would not be wise," he said stiffly, in response to her request. "I don't want to mask whatever you have. That could be dangerous for you."

"I had an ulcer several years ago, maybe it came back again."

"That is all the more reason for you to have a scan. In fact, I'd like to insist on that before you travel again. When are you leaving Paris?"

"Not until Friday. I could come in on Wednesday, after the show on Tuesday afternoon." She was hoping to be fine by then.

"I hope you will. Call me on Wednesday morning, and I'll make an appointment for the scan for you." He sounded businesslike and cool as Timmie decided his ego was bruised because she wouldn't do what he said.

"Thank you, doctor," she said softly. "I'm sorry to have brought you here for nothing." She looked genuinely apologetic, and for an instant he wondered if she was actually a nice woman. He couldn't tell, all he had been able to see so far was how headstrong she was, and accustomed to getting her own way. It didn't surprise him, given who she was. His assessment of her was that she was probably used to having control of everyone and everything in her world. The one thing she couldn't control was her health.

"It was not for nothing," he reassured her politely. "You must have been feeling very ill." He correctly guessed that she was not the kind of person to call a doctor unless she thought she was dying, or very near. Jean-Charles had agreed to see her, as a favor to his patient from New York who had referred her. And there had been a tone of desperation in Timmie's voice that struck him, even before he recognized her name.

"I was, but I'm feeling better now. I think you scared me," she admitted, and he smiled.

"I wish I were able to 'scare' you into getting a scan tonight. I truly think you should. Don't wait until you feel very ill again to call. It might be too late then, and if it is your appendix, as I suspect, it could explode."

"I'll try not to have any explosions between now and Wednesday morning," she said with a grin, and he laughed as he picked up his bag. He liked her, despite the fact that he thought she was stubborn, and tough to deal with, as a doctor.

"I hope your show goes well," he said formally, told her not to get out of bed until then, and to rest as much as possible over the weekend, and a moment later, he let himself out.

After he did, Timmie lay in bed, feeling terrified, but also as though she had escaped a dire fate. She had adamantly not wanted to go to the hospital that night. It all sounded much too scary to her. She hated hospitals, and even doctors sometimes. She rarely went, unless she felt deathly ill, and admittedly she had. She lay quietly after his visit, and a few minutes later, she called Zack. She was feeling lonely and scared and reached out to him. She didn't want to worry David and Jade by calling them in London. By then it was three in the afternoon for him, and she assumed he'd be at home. He often was at that hour, particularly on a Saturday afternoon. He would be home from the gym, and it was too early to go out for whatever evening plans he had. But when she called, both at home and on his cell phone, it went to voice mail, and all she could do was leave him a message, tell him she was sick, and hope he'd call her back. She needed to talk to someone, and since he was the man she was sleeping with, however temporary their relationship, he seemed like a viable option. She just wanted to hear a familiar voice that would comfort her for a minute, a hand to hold on to in the dark.

She lay quietly in her bed for another hour, worrying about what the doctor had said, and finally around one-thirty in the morning, without throwing up again, she fell asleep. Zack hadn't called her back, and she had no idea where he was.

She woke up at ten the next morning, and miraculously felt better. She called Gilles and told him she wouldn't be going out. She had hoped to go to Sacré Coeur, because she loved hearing the choir of nuns who sang there, but she thought it would be smarter to stay in bed and not stir things up. She slept on and off all day, drank chicken broth, and tea, and finally ordered a little rice late that afternoon. She was feeling better by the time Jade and David came back that night, having had a wonderful time. They thanked her for dinner at Harry's Bar, told her about the parties they'd gone to, and David raved about the Tate. She never said a word to them about how sick she'd been, calling the doctor, or what he'd said about her going to the hospital and having scans. She felt as though she'd had a narrow escape. She went to sleep early that night. And on Monday she felt like herself again, which in her opinion proved the doctor had been wrong, no matter how illustrious he was. It had obviously been just the flu, and she was greatly relieved as she put on jeans and a black sweater, her black ballerina shoes, and went downstairs to supervise the rehearsal in the rooms they had reserved for two days for their show.

As usual, the rehearsal was an utter mess. It always was. People went the wrong way, heading onto the runway from the wrong direction, looking dazed, models showed up late, the lighting was wrong, the music they had brought with them got lost and was finally found after everyone had left. It was the chaos she had come to expect over the years at rehearsal, and it made her doubly glad that she hadn't been talked into going to the hospital, and maybe having an appendectomy unnecessarily. She didn't trust medical care in France. She even went to dinner with Jade and David at the Voltaire that night, and stopped in at one of the parties afterward. It was hosted by Dior, and as always at their parties, it was a fabulous event. They had Lucite floors set over a swimming pool, topless models everywhere, and Timmie was utterly exhausted by three A.M. when they finally got back to the hotel and went to bed. But she was relieved to notice that even though she was tired, she didn't feel sick at all. She felt absolutely fine and pleased to note the doctor had been wrong.

The next day their show went off as smoothly as it had gone badly at rehearsal the day before. She was extremely glad that she had been on hand. Without her meticulous eye surveying everything, she was sure that some of the details that mattered to her would have gotten lost in the shuffle. She didn't trust anyone else to run the show. They all congratulated each other, and at eight o'clock that night Jade and David flew to New York. The last of the shows was over, and all they had to do before returning to Los Angeles was attend several days of meetings in New York. Timmie planned to be there on Friday, and spend the weekend in New York after visiting their factory in New Jersey. She had meetings set up for Monday and Tuesday, and Tuesday night they were all flying back to L.A. Timmie realized that Zack still hadn't returned her call. She suspected that he was punishing her for not taking him to Paris, and saying she was sick on his voice mail had just encouraged him to punish her that much more. The opportunity was probably too good for him to resist, and he had gotten his wish. If sick, she was having a rotten time in Paris without him, so he didn't bother to return her call. Her being sick and having a lousy time had probably given him a sense of having the upper hand. It sounded twisted, but Timmie knew he had a petty side to him that held a grudge.

She was so tired after the show and after having drinks with several journalists and editors from *Vogue* at the bar that she ordered room service. Jade and David had already left for New York. Timmie and the journalists were all exhausted after the grueling weeks of the ready to wear shows. Having done double duty in New York and Europe, Timmie felt as though she was ready to crawl as she went upstairs. She didn't even bother to eat the dinner she had ordered, and fell asleep on her bed in all her clothes.

She had no idea what time it was when she awoke. It was dark outside, and all she was aware of was a stabbing pain in her right side. She was in such agony she could barely catch her breath, and this time she had no doubt what it was. Dr. Vernier had been right after all. She lay in her bed and cried, and frantically dug through the papers on her bed table, wondering where his number was. She was beginning to seriously panic when she found it, and, writhing in pain, she dialed his cell phone number. She saw on the clock then that it was four in the morning. And all she knew for sure was that she was in big trouble. She could hardly speak when he answered the phone on the second ring. For a moment, he had no idea who it was. She was sobbing, in agony and terror, and then in an instant, he realized who it was just as she said her name. And just as she had, he could easily guess what had happened. Just listening to her, he was sure that her appendix had ruptured, or was about to. He hadn't heard from her in three days, and had hoped that all was well and he'd been wrong. It was obvious now that that was not the case.

"I'm sorry to call you so late, doctor...," she said, gasping with the pain and crying. "I'm...in terrible pain....I..."

"I know." She didn't need to explain as he came instantly awake and sounded calm. "I'll send an ambulance for you at once. Stay in bed. Don't move. You don't need to dress. I'll meet you at the hospital when you arrive." He sounded cool and precise, and reassuring in his professionalism, like someone she could count on.

He could tell that she was in extreme distress and considerable danger. The situation was urgent.

"I'm really scared," she said, crying harder, and sounding almost like a child. "I'm in so much pain...what are they going to do?" She knew without asking him, and he didn't answer her directly. He just sounded reassuring and assured her everything would be all right.

"Are your assistants with you?" He wondered if she was alone. It sounded fairly dire to him, and he was worried about her. She had been foolish not to deal with it three days before, but it was too late now to worry about that. He was anxious to get her to the hospital and into a surgeon's hands. They would do the scans now in the operating room, while preparing to operate on her.

"They left for New York," she gasped.

"You're alone?"

"Yes."

"I'll have someone from the hotel wait with you. I'm going to call for the ambulance now. Madame O'Neill, everything will be all right," he said in a strong quiet tone, which made only a small dent in her panic.

"No, it won't." She was crying like a child, and he had the feeling that something more was happening than just her appendix rupturing. She was obviously overcome with panic, but he didn't want to waste more time.

"I'll meet you at the hospital when you get there," he said calmly, and hung up. He had no other choice. He was sending her to the American Hospital for her comfort, rather than the Pitié Salpetrière where he normally worked. He had privileges at both.

A few minutes later, Timmie rang for a maid, who very sweetly sat holding her hand until the paramedics arrived, and put Timmie on a gurney in her nightgown, covered her with blankets, and sped down the deserted hotel halls. The arrival of the paramedics had caused a considerable stir in the lobby and the assistant manager on duty appeared as she left. She was in the ambulance speeding through the night a few minutes later, crying softly. The paramedics spoke no English, and could say nothing to reassure her. Her eyes were filled with terror as they took her out of the ambulance, and the first thing she saw was Dr. Vernier waiting for her. He took one look at her face, and quietly took her hand and held it in his, as they rushed her into the hospital, and up to the operating room, which they were already preparing for her.

"I called one of the best surgeons in Paris for you," he said quietly, as they wheeled her into the brightly lit operating room, and she looked at him with wild eyes.

"I'm too scared," she said, clutching his hand, too paralyzed with pain to move anything else. "Please don't leave me here alone," she said, sobbing. He nodded and smiled at her, as a nurse approached with papers for her to sign. He explained to her what they said, and asked if there was someone they should call to tell them she was there, or in case the situation worsened. Timmie thought about it for a moment and told them not to call anyone. The person she listed as next of kin was Jade Chin, who Timmie explained was her assistant, staying at the Four Seasons in New York. She gave him her cell phone number, but told him not to call her unless something went wrong. There was no point upsetting her now. There was nothing she could do from New York. It struck him as sad as he listened to her that this woman who had so much, and was so important and respected in the world, had only a secretary to call now that she was ill. It told him a great deal about her life, the choices she had made, and the price she had paid for them. He felt sorry for her, as they did the scans and he held her hand. His prediction of three days before had proven to be accurate. Her appendix had ruptured, and toxins were rushing through her system as a result.

"Please don't leave me," she said, clutching his hand, and he held her delicate hand firmly in his own.

"I won't leave you," he said softly, as he watched the anesthesiologist prepare to put her under. They were moving quickly, and the danger was considerable now. They needed to remove what was left of her appendix and do what they could to clean out the area. Her eyes met his as the anesthesiologist spoke to her in French, and Jean-Charles Vernier translated for her, and continued to hold her hand.

"Will you stay even after I'm asleep?" she asked, as tears poured from her eyes.

"If you would like me to." His presence was calm, powerful, and reassuring. Everything about him told her she could rely on him. And in that single moment, she trusted him completely.

"I would . . . want you to stay . . . and please call me Timmie." He had called her Madame O'Neill again while translating and telling her what would happen. She was glad suddenly that she had called him. His was a familiar face. At least she had seen Jean-Charles Vernier before, and he had been highly recommended by her friend in New York, as an excellent physician. She knew she was in good hands, but she was terrified anyway.

"I'm here, Timmie," he said, with her hand in his, and his blue eyes firmly locked into hers. "Everything will be fine now. You're safe. I won't let anything bad happen to you. And in a minute, you'll be asleep. I'll see you when you wake up," he said, smiling at her. The moment she was asleep, he was going to leave and put on surgical garb. He had every intention of staying with her for the surgery, just as he had promised. He always kept promises he made. His patients knew that he wouldn't let them down, and Timmie sensed that now too.

A moment later the anesthesiologist put the mask over her face. Her eyes looked into Jean-Charles's, as he continued talking to her, and a minute later, she was asleep. He left the operating room briefly then to put on a gown and mask, and scrub up, and as he did, he couldn't help thinking about the woman they were operating on, and all that she had given up in her life, to trade her enormous success for even one person whom she could call in an emergency, and who could be there with her, to hold her hand. Before she had drifted off to sleep, he had thought he had never seen such sad eyes in his life, or someone so scared to be alone. And as he stood next to her, holding her hand, he had the impression that he was looking at a terrified, abandoned child.

Just as he promised her, he stood beside her and watched the surgery. It went well, and the surgeon was pleased. As the surgical team left the room, Jean-Charles Vernier followed her to the recovery room. He didn't know her at all, and had found her difficult and unreasonable three days before, and now all he knew was that whoever she was, and whatever had come before in her life, he sensed to his very core that he could not leave her alone. Someone had to be there for her. And he was all she had. He had sensed the overwhelming solitude and loneliness in her soul.

She saw him standing next to her when she woke up in the recovery room. She was still woozy from the drugs they had given her, but she recognized him immediately and smiled at him.

"Thank you," she whispered, and then closed her eyes again.

"Sleep well, Timmie," he said softly. "I'll see you tomorrow," he whispered, as he carefully took his hand from hers.

She was already sound asleep again, as he left the room, said good night to the nurses, and went out to his car. Everyone at the surgery was impressed that he was her attending physician and hadn't left her side.

He didn't know why, but he felt a deep sadness for her. Something in her eyes that night had told him that much had happened to her in her life, and none of it good. The powerful woman others saw, who ran an empire so successfully, had nothing to do with the one he had seen that night. The woman he had seen had wounds in her soul that tore at his heart. He was still thinking about her as he drove home, and watched the sun come up over Paris.

In the hospital in Neuilly, Timmie was lost in the arms of a deep, peaceful sleep. Without even knowing it, Jean-Charles Vernier had kept all the old demons of her past from engulfing her that night. And all he knew was that without knowing why, he had seen them in her eyes.

Chapter 3

Timmie was lying in her bed the day after her surgery, looking out the window, when Jean-Charles Vernier walked into the room. He was wearing his white coat, with a stethoscope around his neck. He had patients to see at his other hospital, and had visited them first, before coming to see her at the American Hospital in Neuilly. When he arrived, he had checked her chart and spoken to the nurses earlier, and knew that all was going well. They had told him she was still asleep, but had been awake that morning, was fully alert, and had taken very little pain medicine and he was pleased. She was still on heavy doses of IV antibiotics, to combat the infection from toxins released into her system, but he thought they had remedied the situation quickly after her appendix ruptured. And although it had been painful and frightening for her, she had actually been very lucky. It could have been a lot worse. After observing her closely for the next several days, he was sure they would be able to send her back to the hotel. He was anxious to check on her himself, and was smiling when he walked into the room. Since he had seen all his other patients, he could spend whatever time he needed with her without rushing. He saw that she looked tired, but far better than he anticipated after her ordeal the night before.

"Well, Timmie, how are you feeling today?" he asked in his heavily accented English, with his blue eyes observing her intently. She smiled when she heard him use her first name. She had half-expected him to revert to Madame O'Neill again, now that the crisis was over. She liked hearing him say Timmie. He made it sound very French.

"I feel a lot better than I did last night," she said with a shy smile. She was sore, and the incision hurt, but even that was less acute than the searing pain she'd had the night before.

"You were very lucky things did not get very much worse," he said as he sat down on the chair next to her bed, and then turned to ask her politely for permission. "May I?" He was formal, and yet at the same time warm, and she still remembered his holding her hand when she was terrified before the anesthetic. He had never let go of her hand once. And she saw the same kindness now in his eyes.

"Of course," she said about his sitting down. "Thank you for being nice to me last night," she said shyly, her green eyes meeting his intense blue ones. They were both remembering his holding her hand. "I get very scared sometimes," she admitted hesitantly. "It's a lot of old stuff from my childhood that creeps up on me, and when I feel frightened, suddenly I'm five years old again. I felt that way when I got to the hospital, and I really appreciate that you were there, and stayed with me." Her voice drifted off as she looked at him, and then she glanced away, as he watched her quietly from the chair. She was embarrassed to admit to him how vulnerable she felt at times.

"What happened when you were five years old?" he asked cautiously. He wasn't asking entirely as her physician, but he had seen something so raw and terrified in her that he had instantly seen an old trauma that was overwhelming her. It was hard to imagine what it was, although frightening things happened to children sometimes, which then pursued them for a lifetime, even as adults.

"My parents died when I was five," she said quietly. She didn't speak again for several moments, while he continued to watch her. He wondered if she would tell him what had happened after that. Although that in itself would have been enough, particularly if they had died in some traumatic way that had affected her, or if she'd seen it happen. And then slowly, she went on. "They had a car accident on New Year's Eve. They went out and never came back. I still remember when the police came to the house and took me away. I don't know why, but they picked me up in an ambulance. Maybe it was the only vehicle they had on hand at the time, or maybe they thought it would frighten me to ride in a police car. I've had a terror of ambulances ever since. Even hearing the sirens makes me feel sick." And of course she had been brought to the hospital the night before in an ambulance, which he suddenly realized must have been hard for her. There had been no other choice, given how sick she was. He knew then that her state of panic the moment he saw her must have been heightened, or even caused by that.

"I'm sorry, I didn't know. I should have picked you up myself at the hotel, but I wanted to come here and get everything ready for you, and make sure the surgeon and the operating room were ready for you." He apologized to her as she smiled at him. And he didn't normally pick up patients at their homes.

"Don't be silly. How could you know? And I actually felt so awful, I don't think it bothered me as much as it might have otherwise. I was scared out of my wits about what was going to happen when I got here." He smiled at her reassuringly, and she had the same feeling of safety being near him as she'd had the night before the moment she saw him, and then when he held her hand. He exuded solace and comfort, warmth, and something almost tender and very strong. He seemed trustworthy and reliable, and a good person. Although she hardly knew him, she felt protected by him, and totally at peace. He was a very gentle man.

"Where did they take you in the ambulance when you were a little girl after your parents died?" he asked with interest, keeping a close watch on her expression, and as he did, he could see something far-away and painful cross her mind. She almost winced at the memories that had come to life again the night before.

"They took me to an orphanage. I lived there for eleven years. At first, they said I would be adopted very quickly, and they sent me to several homes to try out." Her eyes looked sad as she said it, and although he said nothing to her, his heart ached for her. He could almost feel the pain she had felt as a little girl, suddenly orphaned and alone, in an orphanage among strangers. To him, it seemed like a terrible fate for a child. "Some of them kept me for a while, weeks, I think. A month maybe, it seemed like a long time to me then. Some of them only kept me a few days. I guess things haven't changed much. People want babies, newborns preferably. They don't want scrawny five-year-olds with bony knees, freckles, and red hair."

"That sounds adorable to me," he said to her, and she smiled ruefully.

"I don't think I seemed so adorable to them. I cried a lot. I was scared, probably most of the time. Maybe all the time. I missed my parents, and the people they sent me to seemed weird to me. They probably weren't, or no more than anyone else. I wet my bed, I hid in closets, I hid under my bed once and refused to come out. They sent me back the next day and said I wasn't friendly. The nuns scolded me and told me I had to make more effort after that. They kept sending me out to audition for the next three years, until I was eight. And by then, I really was too old. And I wasn't very cute then. One of the families I went to said my braids were too much trouble, so they cut off all my hair. I came back nearly bald, they just took a razor to my head and gave me a crew cut. It was pretty scary stuff for a little kid. And there was always some reason why they didn't want me and sent me back. Sometimes they were polite and lied about it, and claimed they had decided they couldn't afford to adopt, or they were leaving town, or the dad lost his job. Stuff like that. Most of the time, they didn't say anything. They just shook their heads, packed me up, and sent me back. I could always tell the night before, or most of the time anyway. I knew that look. It always gave me a sinking feeling in my stomach. Sometimes they took me by surprise, but mostly not. They gave me five minutes to pack my things, and drove me back. Some of them gave me a present when they did, like a teddy bear or a doll or a toy, kind of a consolation prize for not making the cut. I got used to it eventually, I guess. Except I wonder now if you ever do. I think now, with the perspective of time and age, that every time they didn't want me and sent me back, it broke my heart again. After a while, every time I went out to try out, I was scared. I knew it would happen again. It always did. How could it not?

"After I was eight, they put me in foster care, which is usually for kids who can't be adopted for some reason. Most of the time because their parents won't relinquish them for adoption. Mine were dead, but since no one else wanted me, I wound up in foster care. The theory behind it is excellent, because it's supposed to keep you from being institutionalized, and there are some wonderful people who foster children. But a lot of bad ones too. Some people see it as an opportunity for child labor and slavery, they cash in on the money they get, starve you, work your fingers to the bone doing things their own kids don't want to do, and they treat you like dirt. But eventually, I turned the tables on them. I did the worst things I could think of, to see how fast I could be sent back. I liked it better in the orphanage. I was in thirty-six homes in eight years. It became a joke. In the end, they stopped sending me out and left me alone. I didn't bother anyone, I went to school, I did the chores I was as-signed to. I was reasonably polite to the nuns and I walked out the door without looking back when I was sixteen. I got a job as a waitress and worked in several restaurants. I loved to make clothes with left-over bits of fabric in my spare time. I made them for myself, friends, co-workers. Making clothes was like making magic for me. I could transform a scrap of fabric into something beautiful, and make a waitress feel like a queen. In the last coffee shop I worked, my career started and my luck turned. I got a fabulous opportunity, and it's been a good life ever since, even a great one, most of the time," she said with wise, sad eyes that had seen too much in one life. "But I've noticed all my life, that when I get frightened, or something goes terribly wrong, or if I'm sick or upset, it all comes back to me. Suddenly I'm five years old again, I'm in the or-phanage, my parents just died, and I'm being sent to strangers who don't want me, or maybe even scare me to death. I think that happened to me last night. I was both sick and scared, and by the time I got here in the ambulance, I was so overwhelmed by panic I could hardly breathe. I had asthma as a little kid. Sometimes I'd pretend to have at-tacks in foster homes, so they'd send me back. They always did. No one wants a funny-looking redheaded kid on their hands with asthma on top of it. In the beginning, the attacks were real. Later they weren't. By then I didn't want to try anymore. I didn't want to put myself on the line. I didn't care about them, and I didn't want them to care about me. They didn't. The best thing that ever happened to me was leaving the orphanage and going to work. Then I was finally in control of my own life, my own destiny. No one could scare me anymore, or send me away. It sounds crazy to say it now," she said as she looked at Jean-Charles openly.

He was amazed by her honesty as she talked about it, and her air of calm and acceptance about everything that had happened to her. Hers was a story that tore at the heart, and it was even more amazing to know what she had ultimately become. Her success story was even more remarkable than most people knew. She had crawled out of a life that would have killed some people, and had achieved more than anyone could have imagined. She had climbed Everest, and reached the summit, successfully, more than anyone ever knew. Only a handful of her closest friends and associates knew about her past. She had never said it as bluntly or as honestly as she had just said to Jean-Charles. But he was a doctor and she figured he could take it. She assumed he had probably heard worse. Her history had become routine to her but it had shocked him anyway, and touched him deeply. He had even deeper respect for her after hearing what she'd shared. "It probably sounds crazy to you," she said again, "but I don't ever want to go back there, in any way. Or feel as though I am. I don't want to try and charm someone into adopting me, or do a song and dance for them. I don't want to be a ten-year-old slave in foster care, or even a thirteen-year-old that no one has hugged in years. I never want to be in that position again. Ever. I did enough of it then to last a lifetime. I don't ever want to be abandoned or go back to the orphanage again. I'd rather be alone." Or with men she cared little about. Her eyes were so intense, it was easy for him to see that what she had said came straight from the heart, and deeply touched his. And saddest of all, to him, was that she had gotten her wish. From what he could see, she was alone.

"What can you or any of us do to avoid being abandoned, Timmie?" Jean-Charles asked philosophically. "People have a way of leaving us in life, even if we're not orphans or five years old. People we love die, husbands and wives run away, we get fired from jobs, even if it's not our fault. And people who love each other sometimes hurt each other, even if it's the last thing they want or mean to do. Life is painful, and there are no guarantees. If you love someone, they can leave you, or send you back to the orphanage in other ways. We've all been there to some degree. But you far more than most. I'm sorry you had to go through all that, particularly as a young child. What a terrible life it must have been for you," he said sympathetically, and she smiled again. It was a sad, quiet half-smile that told him he was right. It had been eleven years of nightmares for her then. And the memories of it that had haunted her ever since. The ride in the ambulance had brought it all back to her. She could still remember the night her parents died as though it were yesterday. She had felt five years old again in the ambulance the night before. And when she got to the hospital, she had felt so small and vulnerable while he held her hand.

By the next day, the adult in her had taken over again, and the five-year-old was nowhere to be seen. But Jean-Charles had seen the terrified child clearly the night before, even though Timmie, with all her courage, power, and strength, was very much in evidence today. But when Jean-Charles looked at her, he saw something else as well. He saw the shadow of the child who had held his hand in the operating room, and clung to him as though her life depended on it. And perhaps it did. He had no idea how she had survived the challenges of those frightening years in the orphanage. But somehow she had. Whatever toll those years had taken, she was sane, whole, functional, successful, brilliant, and creative now, and no one looking at her would ever have suspected where she had started or what her life had been like as a child. No one could even begin to guess at the pain of her early years. But Jean-Charles had seen and heard it, and the bond between them was forever changed. He had had a glimpse both into her soul and into her past. He knew now that she had been traumatized for at least eleven years of her life, and maybe more. It gave him tremendous insight into her, she had taken a constant emotional battering and still managed to come out on top in the end. She was successful, powerful, a bright shining example of success, although Timmie doubted herself at times, more than anyone realized. She knew where the scars and the holes were in her soul. And much of what she did was to protect those old wounds from opening again. She couldn't afford it anymore. Her wounds had been hit too hard in the past. She couldn't risk reinjuring them again.

The French doctor had sensed all of that the night before, in the way she clung to his hand. It frightened him for her. What he had seen in her then, and even now to some degree, was a tsunami of pain so vast that it would have drowned everything around it, if it was ever unleashed. And it nearly had been the night before. Coming to the hospital had been terrifying for her and had reminded her again of how alone she was. It was like the old demons of her past reawakening and condemning her to the orphanage again. Jean-Charles being there for her had changed the agony of that reality for her. For even a brief moment, he had made her feel she was no longer so alone. She was grateful for it now, as they exchanged a smile and the past became dim again. In the end, however hard it had been, they were only ghosts and could no longer hurt her now. For all these years, Timmie had never allowed the past to haunt her, daunt her, stop her, cripple her. She wouldn't let it. She was too strong to let it stop her. Now and then it sneaked up on her, as it nearly had before the surgery, and then she consciously put it behind her again, where it belonged. She still honored the child she had once been, and all that had happened to her, but she couldn't allow a frightened five-year-old to run her life. She never had and wasn't about to start now. She had to be stronger than that, there was no other choice. Jean-Charles could see it all in the look on her face, and admired her strength and courage.

"You are an absolute hero," he said admiringly. She thought he was teasing her, so she smiled, but he wasn't. "I think you're the bravest woman I ever met." He understood perfectly now why she had been so upset the previous night. "Did your parents have no relatives that you could go to?" he asked with sadness for her and deep compassion, and she shook her head.

"All I know about my parents is that they were Irish and they died. There's nothing else to find out. I thought of looking up some relatives once when I was in Ireland. There must be thirty pages of O'Neills in the phone book. That's all I know. So I'm alone, except for wonderful friends I enjoy a lot."

But they both knew that when things went wrong, in some way, as they had with her appendix, there was no one to turn to, and she was entirely alone, except for people who worked for her, but they had their own lives. He remembered her giving him Jade's name to put on the forms as next of kin. That said a lot. There was no one else in her life to rely on, which was harder for him to believe in the case of a woman as beautiful and successful as she was. It was hard to imagine how she had wound up alone, unless it was what she wanted. And perhaps it was. He almost couldn't blame her, after a beginning like that. It would have been nearly impossible to open up, love, attach, and trust. And more than likely, he realized sadly, she probably never had. Fate was cruel at times, it had been to her, but materially, it had been kind. And she had worked hard to earn what she had. They both knew that material success was not enough for a good life. But it was something at least, and she loved her work. In her opinion, she had a very good life.

She looked peaceful and calm as she lay in bed and talked to him. He was touched by the confidences she had shared. He suddenly felt as though, as a result of her surgery and the powerful effect it had had on her, he had crossed the line from doctor to friend in a matter of hours, and he was deeply honored. He thought she was a remarkable woman. Timmie felt the newly formed bond between them too, and was equally impressed by him, as both a doctor and a human being. He was a deeply caring, warm person. His kindness to her had made her open up as she hadn't in years. She seldom, if ever, shared the story of her past, and rarely had in her life.

"I'm sorry to bore you with that miserable old stuff. I don't usually talk about it, but I felt I owed you some explanation after panicking last night," she said, looking apologetic. It embarrassed her a little to have shared so much with him.

"You were fine," he reassured her, "and you owe me no explanation. Surgery in a foreign country, when you're all alone, is a frightening thing. Anyone would be scared. And you have more reason to be than most. You were traumatized as a child. It doesn't surprise me at all that you don't have children," he said gently. "You must have been afraid to inflict the pain you suffered on someone else." Many of the people he'd met who had had agonizing childhoods had decided not to have children themselves. Timmie seemed fairly typical in that. And then he saw the look in her eyes, and realized he had hit another wound. He wanted to cut out his tongue, as her gaze met his. The pain he saw in her silenced him.

"I had a son who died," she said softly. Her eyes never left his.

"I'm so sorry," he said in a choked voice. "How stupid of me to assume . . . I didn't think . . . you told me you didn't have children when I asked . . . I imagined that . . ." She had somehow seemed to him the classic career woman who wouldn't have wanted kids, particularly with her childhood history of abandonment and loss. It never occurred to him for a minute that she might have had a child. Worse yet, one that died.

"It's all right. I've made my peace with it. It was a long time ago. He was four, and he died of a brain tumor twelve years ago. They couldn't save him. It would probably be different if it happened today. Chemotherapy and oncology are much more sophisticated now than then. We did our best." She smiled sadly at Jean-Charles then, and he could see her eyes were brimming with tears. They always were when she talked about him. She rarely did. "His name was Mark." She said it as though she wanted him to be remembered. He was not just a boy who had died twelve years ago. He was a child named Mark, whom she had loved and carried forever in her heart.

It was after that that her business had become an empire, and had grown to be so vast. A year later, in fact, when her husband left. It had been yet another nightmarish time in her life, and it was also why she no longer wanted marriage, or a serious man in her life. All she wanted now was peace, her work, and occasional men like Zack to keep her company on weekends. She didn't want to care too much or hurt again. She didn't want to love any man enough to care when he left her, as Derek had, or feel the agony of losing Mark, who had been the light of her life for four short years. Life was so much simpler now. There were occasional bumps in the road, but nothing she couldn't handle and no one she cared too much about. There were no great joys, nor major losses either. She didn't want to wind up down a black hole again, or wishing she were dead, as she had when Mark died and Derek left. She just wanted to go on now as she was—looking forward, and rarely if ever back, thinking about the collections she designed, worrying about the ready to wear shows, and enjoying her employees and friends. She wanted nothing more or different than she had. Jean-Charles could see that in her eyes.

There were doors in her that were tightly closed. She had given him a glimpse behind those doors, but Timmie wanted them closed. It was the only way to avoid the pain of remembering and reopening old wounds. Her face had seemed luminous when she talked about her son, but when she mentioned her husband, her face grew serious again. It was all behind her now, hopefully for good. She had survived during the hardest years of her life, and gone on, except for Mark, whom she had taken with her, tucked into her heart. He would always be with her. But she no longer wanted a serious man in her life, or even a child. The risk of getting hurt was just too great.

"I'm so sorry about your son," Jean-Charles said with a genuine look of sorrow and compassion for her. "And your childhood. All of it. You've had some truly shocking luck." He was bowled over by everything she had said. And he was grateful suddenly to have met this remarkable woman, and have her as a patient. He admired her a great deal.

"I guess. But I've had some good luck as well. You do the best you can with the hand you get. Sometimes it's hard, and sometimes it comes out all right. You deal with it as it comes," she said, looking tired. She had told him so much, she decided to tell him the rest. She could see in his eyes that he was wondering why she had no husband if she'd had a child, and he was too polite to ask. He assumed she had been married when the child was born, although she was brave enough to have had one on her own. Nothing would have surprised him of her now.

She told him what had happened to her marriage, simply, without bitterness or accusation, only facts. "My husband left me six months after my son died. His death put a terrible strain on both of us. We'd been married for five years, which isn't very long. He was the men's designer I hired when I started the men's line, and he was very good. We were good friends before we married. He's a decent man. I thought it would kill us both when Mark died, and it was never the same between us after that. We were both too devastated and distraught to take care of each other. And then I discovered what everyone else knew all along. He was bisexual, and married me to have a child. I got pregnant almost immediately after we got married. And our marriage was kind of a spur-of-the-moment thing. I wasn't even sure I wanted kids, for all the reasons you just said. He talked me into it, and into marrying him, to have kids. It turned out it was the best thing I ever did. And then, after Mark died, Derek told me he wanted out. According to him, having children was the only reason he married me. Neither of us had the heart to have another child, and he had another life I never knew about. We thought Mark was unique, and I think losing him ended the marriage. Everytime we looked at each other afterward, all we saw was Mark.

"Derek started drinking a lot after Mark died, got involved with another man, and fell in love. I don't think he wanted to drag me through the pain of that, he wanted to make a clean break, and so did I. Under the circumstances, I think it was the right thing to do. He left the business, got out of the marriage, and they've been living in Italy together ever since. I think he's happy, and I wish him well," she said quietly, as Jean-Charles absorbed the impact of yet another trauma she'd survived. "I gave him a big chunk of the business when he left, because he really created the men's line and put us on the map as an international success. So he retired, I went back to working like a maniac. The business became my life. I lived through losing Mark somehow, and Derek. Nothing could hurt as much as losing Mark," she said sadly, with tears in her eyes. "I hear from Derek once in a while. I think it's painful for both of us. It's easier when we don't talk. There's nothing left to say anyway. He's living with a man who used to be one of our models. They're happy. I have my life. So that was that. It was the end of an era for me.

"It's not a very happy story to tell. I don't think the marriage would have lasted anyway. You can't make yourself be something you're not. Mark kept us together, and when he was gone, Derek went back to the life he'd led before, and I didn't know about. People had said things to me once in a while, but I never believed them. As it turned out, it was all true and they were right. Having Mark made it all worthwhile, even for a short time. I wouldn't trade those years for anything. They were the best years of my life. Life is strange sometimes," she said with a sigh, "it gives you challenges and gifts you don't expect. Mark was a gift. A gift of pure joy. I'll never regret a minute of his life, or even marrying Derek to have him. My life is just very different now." She was very matter-of-fact as she said it. She accepted everything about her past, with all its regrets and sorrows. And in spite of that, she had gone on to make a decent life for herself, and those around her. And if she indulged herself with men like Zack from time to time, she did no one any harm, and they kept the demons of her past from haunting her too acutely.

Jean-Charles realized that she was a truly remarkable woman, and he had underestimated her at first. There was so much more to her than met the eye. She had the strength of a hundred people, and the heart of a thousand. And as they looked at each other in her hospital room, Timmie realized for the first time that she was holding his hand again. It was not a story one could tell without support, or to anyone but a friend, and now he was, in her mind as well as his. He had come into her life for a brief moment, to make a sudden episode of discomfort easier for her, but now when she left, she would take a piece of him with her, as one always did when one shared a part of oneself with someone else. She had opened her most secret places to him and shown her heart to him, as battered and bruised as it was. She often said that her heart was like an ancient Chinese crackle jar, full of cracks, but old and strong. He sensed that about her now, after hearing all that had happened to her. He had never respected anyone as much as he did her now. She was the most extraordinary woman he had ever met, and he respected her for all her courage, and lack of bitterness about the past. She seemed to view all of it as a gift no matter how great the losses or scars. There was something very beautiful about her and very proud. Even her scars touched him deeply now. There was nothing ugly or bitter about her.

"It's a shame you never married again and had more children," he said sadly. He was deeply moved for her, and aware of her many losses. In fact, she had lost everyone she had ever loved or cared about. Parents, son, husband. And survived it, even if scarred. She had only been thirty-six when her son died, and a year older when she got divorced. She had still had time then to start a new life, and had obviously chosen not to, for all the reasons she had shared with him for the past two hours. Jean-Charles wondered if she felt loving anyone again was just too risky. And perhaps for her it was. The time had flown, and hung in space now as they continued to hold hands. He felt close to her, closer than he ever thought he would, and yet he had no designs on her. He had no romantic feelings toward her. All he felt was a powerful bond from one human being to another, which was precisely what she felt for him.

"I don't want more children or a husband," she said calmly. "I never did after Mark died, and Derek left. He wanted another relationship, I didn't. I just wanted to be alone to lick my wounds. And I did for a long time. The business kept me alive. The rest was just too hard."

"And now?" Jean-Charles asked with curiosity. She had told him so much that he wasn't afraid to ask her more about her life. "There's no one in your life?"

She shrugged, and shook her head with a smile, remembering that Zack had never called her back. She had left him a message that morning about her surgery, and he hadn't called her. She wasn't even sure she cared if he did or not. There was no point counting on Zack. He would never deliver. He was too busy getting even for imagined slights and looking out for himself. There was no real malice to him, but no substance either. He was there for a good time, and had never pretended otherwise. "No one important," she said in answer to Jean-Charles's question. "People come and go in my life. I've made compromises I can live with, for short periods of time. I haven't had a serious relationship since I was married. I don't want one anymore. The price is too high, and I'm too old for that now," she said with a shy smile, and the French doctor laughed.

"At forty-eight? You certainly are not. Women much older than you fall in love again and get married. Love has no age. My own mother was widowed at seventy-nine and married again at eighty-five. She has been married for two years now and adores her husband. She's just as happy as she was with my father." Timmie smiled at the idea of an eighty-five-year-old bride. There was something deliciously sweet about it.

"Maybe when I'm eighty-five," she said with a wry laugh, still holding his hand. "I think I'll wait till then. I'm probably still too young to try again. I think I might wait till I have Alzheimer's, and then I won't remember what to be scared about. Right now, my memory is still too good. It would scare me to death." And in her case, with good reason. She had lost too much in her life, and been injured by too many people too many times.

"You're missing something," Jean-Charles said gently. "A great deal, in fact. You're missing love in your life, Timmie, because you're frightened. I don't blame you. But existing without love, if I'm guessing correctly, is a hard, lonely life." And led to the kind of panic he had witnessed the night before, where she was totally dependent on a stranger.

"It is hard," she acknowledged, "but it's safe. I have nothing to lose now." To him, it seemed a sad statement, particularly for a woman as wonderful as she.

They both remembered the name she had given on her next-of-kin form. Her assistant's name, and not a man or a husband, or even a boyfriend. She had no relatives or siblings. Having to list her next of kin always underlined to her where her life was, but it was a reality she had long since accepted. She knew it wasn't going to change. And providence put the people she needed on her path, just as Jean-Charles had been there for her when her appendix ruptured. Now they were becoming friends. She was aware that he admired her a lot, and she also saw something sad in his eyes. She wasn't sure if it was sadness for her life or his own, and she didn't want to ask. Confidences like the ones she had shared had to be given as a gift. You couldn't pry them out of anyone. They had to be freely given, and she could see that he wasn't ready to do that about his own life, and maybe never would. She had chosen to share her history with him, but she could sense that, like her, there was a part of him that was closed off.

"How did you manage not to become bitter?" he asked quietly. "You have so much reason to be." Yet he could sense that there was no rancor in her at all, against anyone. She had let it all go years before. He somehow suspected that she had never been bitter, perhaps devastated or sad. But she held none of it against anyone, not her parents for dying, or her ex-husband for leaving, or the doctors who had been unable to save her child. She was unlike anyone he had ever known, and he wished he could be more like her. In his case, he carried resentment for a long time, and regrets about the past. They saddened him deeply from time to time. She was an inspiration to him, and he knew he would long remember all that they had shared that afternoon. It was growing dark when he finally let go of her hand. They had sat and talked for hours. The nurses had peeked in to see how she was, and discreetly left. She was in good hands, and they didn't want to interrupt. They could see it was a serious conversation. Both Timmie and her doctor had looked intent as they talked, and now he saw that she looked tired.

"I've exhausted you," he said apologetically, feeling guilty for staying so long. But she was a fascinating woman, and the insights he had gained into her would never be forgotten. He knew he would always remember her with profound respect and admiration whenever he heard her name. And he hoped to see her again sometime when she came back to Paris. It suddenly seemed like a great gift of providence that he had met her at all. If her friend in New York hadn't given her his name, she never would have, and would have had to call the hotel doctor, whom she knew nothing about.

"It was good to talk to you," she said with a quiet smile, laying her head back on her pillow for the first time in hours. "I never talk about those things anymore." She had gone to therapists for years after her son's death and the demise of her marriage, and eventually she and her therapist had decided the work was done. It was as good as it was going to get. The rest she just had to live with and accept. The past was what it was. "It meant a lot to me to tell you about it. Sometimes we think we know who people are, and how they got there, but we really don't. You never know what people have been through, or how far they've come," she said wisely, as he nodded agreement.

"You've come far, Timmie," he said soberly. Farther than anyone he'd known. They had formed a bond the night before when he had been there for her. It was something she would never forget either. He had been right there for her, as few people ever were. And she sensed from talking to him that he was a man one could trust. "When are you going to let me go home?" she asked as he stood up. She had nothing and no one to rush home for, but she didn't like being in the hospital either.

"I don't know yet. Not for a while. Perhaps in a week. I'll let you go back to the hotel before that, and see how you feel. Are you going straight back to Los Angeles from here?"

She shook her head. "I was supposed to go to New York. I have meetings there next week, and one this Friday night."

"I'm not sure you'll feel up to it. You may be fit to travel in a week, but if I were you, I would go home and rest, at least for another week. You did have surgery, after all." She nodded.

She had been thinking of telling Jade and David to have the meetings without her. They could always bring her up to speed when she got home. The most important thing had been the ready to wear show, and she had done that. The rest didn't seem to matter quite as much to her now, and he could see that in her eyes. She wasn't fighting him to leave, which he had expected of her. She had turned out to be so much different than he thought at first. He had expected her to be spoiled, difficult, demanding, and overbearing, as witnessed by her success. Instead, she was anything but. She was warm, kind, strong, intelligent, reasonable, compassionate, and gentle. She didn't seem to have a mean bone in her body. And he liked her a lot. "Do you need anything before I go? More pain medication?" he offered, and she shook her head.

"I rarely take anything. This isn't so bad. I've been through worse." After talking to her all afternoon, he knew she had. She hadn't taken medication when Mark died either. Hiding from reality and her feelings about it was not her style. She faced things head-on. She always had.

"Call me on my cell phone if you need anything," he reminded her, and she smiled. He patted her shoulder, and she smiled at him again before he left. And after he did, she lay in bed and thought about him for a long time. She hadn't spoken to anyone like that in years, and never as honestly as she had to him, maybe in her entire life. She felt completely comfortable with him, and trusted him as she hadn't anyone in years. The crisis of the night before had knocked down barriers between them that might never have otherwise disappeared, and now they were gone.

And as he left the hospital, Jean-Charles thought of her in precisely the same way. She was one of those rare women to whom one could say anything, confide everything, and whom he would have liked to share his secrets with as well. For now, she had shared hers, and he wondered if he would share his with her one day. She had bared her soul to him that afternoon, and her history, however painful. He could see that parts of it were still raw for her, and perhaps always would be. Other parts had healed over time, although there were deep scars on her heart, and even her soul. He felt as though he had met one of the rare beings of his lifetime. And she was feeling the same thing, amazed at all she had confided in him. It had seemed completely natural to do so.

She had no regrets about sharing any of it with him. It occurred to her after he left her room that once upon a time it would have been nice to have a man like him to share her life with. She'd never had that. She and Derek had shared their interest in her business, and a child, and little else. They had never had a lot in common, except work. She had realized later how little she knew him, and how much less he knew her. Someone like Jean-Charles Vernier seemed more like an equal partner, a worthy opponent probably, an ally, and someone one could count on. But as always with men like that, Timmie reminded herself, he was also married. As Jade said, the good ones always were. She thought of it, as she drifted off to sleep that night, in the American Hospital, and remembered that she still had not heard from Zack. It was disappointing, as always with him, but no surprise. Disappointment was a way of life with men like him. Timmie had grown used to it over the years. She had been through so much in her life that disappointment seemed like a small thing. She had survived so much worse. And at the other end of the spectrum were men like Jean-Charles. Extraordinary, admirable, worthy of respect and trust. And for one reason or another, unattainable and out of reach. Most of the time, like Jean-Charles, they belonged to someone else. But she had been grateful to talk to him all afternoon. She had sensed that he was a kindred spirit. That in itself was so rare that even talking to him was enough. She had no need for more.

Chapter 4

For the next two days Timmie continued to recover well. She looked and felt better every day, and Jean-Charles came by twice a day to check on her. Usually, before and after his own office hours. On Friday, he came to see her for the third time that day, on his way home from a dinner party that he claimed had been deadly boring. He stuck his head into her room, wearing a dark pin-striped suit, and was pleased to find her awake. He looked as handsome and elegant as the first time she saw him.

She was reading an English magazine a nurse had found for her, and although she didn't mention it to Jean-Charles, she had just spoken to Zack. He had been predictably unsympathetic about her surgery, and teased her about it instead, as though it were a prank she had played. Nurturing was not his strong suit, and he treated even problems like a joke. He said, in a laughing tone, that that it served her right for not taking him on the trip, which seemed like pushing it to her. It never even occurred to him that she was upset or had been scared. It was inconceivable to him that someone as strong as Timmie would be afraid of anything, even what he considered minor surgery. She sounded fine to him, and she didn't say otherwise. She played it down for him. And she felt better now anyway.

She had heard from Jade and David several times that day too. Their meetings in New York had gone well, and they were managing fine without her. Jade had offered to fly back to Paris, and both of them were worried about her, but she insisted she was fine. There was nothing they could do for her anyway. All she had to do was rest, stay on the antibiotics, and regain her strength. She had walked up and down the halls, although slowly and cautiously and slightly bent over, several times that day. Only Jean-Charles knew how shaken she had been. To the others, she presented her usual show of composure and strength. She didn't like appearing vulnerable to anyone. It made her feel too exposed.

When Jean-Charles poked his head through the door, Timmie looked up and smiled. He looked dashing, slightly mischievous, and almost boyish as he strode into the room. He noticed that her color was better than it had been that afternoon, and she told him about her walks in the hall.

"What are you doing here at this hour?" she asked, as she would have of a friend, rather than her doctor. But doctors didn't usually visit patients at eleven o'clock at night. They had developed a special bond and enjoyed each other's company. They exchanged a warm smile as he sat down near her bed.

"I was on my way home, and decided to check on you," he said comfortably. "You're a very important person, after all." He was teasing her, and she laughed. She didn't mind it from him now.

"I'm a very bored person," Timmie said, putting the magazine down, pleased to see him. "I must be getting better," she continued, smiling at him. "I'm beginning to feel like I'm in jail. When are you going to let me out?"

"Let's see how you feel tomorrow. I suppose I could send you back to the hotel with a nurse," he said, looking pensive. He was going to miss his afternoon conversations with her once she left. While she was in the hospital he could drop in on her anytime.

He had rarely enjoyed as much interaction with a patient, and he liked hearing her thoughts on a variety of subjects about which she was knowledgeable and well informed. They had discovered that they both had a passion for art, and shared a great fondness for Chagall. She had one at the house in Bel Air. And he had begun to confide some of the details of his own history with her. He had told her the day before that he had gone into medicine due to the death of his sister from a brain hemorrhage when he was sixteen and she was twenty-one. Her sudden death had been a turning point in his life.

"I don't need a nurse," Timmie complained as he sat down in the chair next to her bed and she silently admired his suit, and wondered whose it was. It was beautifully tailored, and had clean, masculine, elegant lines. It suddenly made her wonder if he'd be offended if she sent him one of hers. He was always impeccably dressed. She liked the way he looked when he was casually dressed too. He had shown up that morning wearing khaki pants, a striped pale blue shirt and blazer, and brown suede loafers. He looked well in his clothes, and his style of dress was more British than French. Everything looked great on him since he was tall and lean.

"You do need a nurse," he assured her. "I have a strong suspicion that if you don't have one, you'll start running around, or going out." He had already told her that he wanted her on bed rest for a full week, which was beginning to seem like cruel and unusual punishment to her. She was feeling well enough to get up and move around.

"I wasn't exactly running down the hall this evening after dinner," she assured him, and he returned her smile. She had washed her hair that morning, and her curly copper mane was cascading past the shoulders of her hospital gown. He noticed that the Plaza Athénée had sent her a huge bouquet of flowers. David and Jade had sent her another enormous bouquet that they had ordered by phone from New York. The room smelled like a garden. "What was the dinner party like?" she asked him, looking like a child who had been left home with a baby-sitter, and wanted to hear all about it.

"Intensely boring," he said with a grin. "It was very stuffy, the food was bad, and someone said the wine was awful. I couldn't wait to leave." She didn't want to ask him, but wondered why he hadn't gone home with his wife. She had gotten the impression once or twice that he wasn't happily married, but he had never commented openly about it. He preferred to talk about his children. He had two daughters, Julianne and Sophie, who were respectively seventeen and fifteen, and a son, Xavier, who was in his first year of medical school and wanted to become a surgeon, which obviously made his father very proud. He had mentioned them to her several times, with undeniable pride. The girls were almost the same age her son would have been, and he had wondered more than once if it upset her when he talked about them. But as she inquired about them, he allowed himself to mention them when the subject came up.

"I'm not very good about dinner parties either," Timmie admitted to him, comfortably tucked into her bed as they chatted. It was fun having a visit at that hour, especially now that she was feeling better. She didn't even feel the IV in her arm. "I'd rather spend time at my beach house, or in some little bistro with friends. Going to parties is usually too much work." She worked too hard at the office to have much time to devote to her social life, although she sometimes got cornered into going to major Hollywood events. Particularly since her company frequently provided clothes for movies and dressed a number of Hollywood stars.

"Where is your beach house?" he asked with interest, enjoying the conversation. She was much more fun to talk to than any of the people he had dined with that night.

"In Malibu," she said easily, as she told him about it, and the long walks she loved to take on the beach. She didn't mention that she spent time with Zack there. He didn't seem worth mentioning, and she had refrained from talking about him. He wasn't important enough in her life to discuss with Jean-Charles. He was one of the compromises she made.

"I have always wanted to see Malibu," Jean-Charles said, looking pensive. "The photographs of it are beautiful. Is your house in the Colony?" he inquired, showing his knowledge of the area, and she smiled as she nodded.

"Yes, it is," she said quietly. "You'll have to come out and see it sometime." After she said it, they both fell silent for a minute, while both of them wondered if they'd actually ever see each other again. There was really no reason to, unless she came back to Paris and fell ill again. Or maybe after the exchanges they had had since she'd been there, perhaps they would actually become friends.

"I haven't been to Los Angeles in many years. I went to a very interesting conference and lectured at the medical school at UCLA," Jean-Charles said as he stood up again. It was getting late, and she was his patient after all, and needed her sleep. He said as much to her and she nodded. She was tired, but she enjoyed talking to him. "I'll come and see you tomorrow," he promised, "and we'll decide together when you can go back to the hotel. Perhaps Sunday, if you promise to behave."

"When do you think I can go back to L.A.?" She had been gone for weeks.

"We will see. Maybe at the end of next week, or before, if you're doing well." Jade had offered to come back to fly home with her, and

Timmie had insisted it wasn't necessary, although even carrying her oversize travel bag right now would seem like heavy work. But she was determined to go back to L.A. alone, and let Jade fly back with David from New York. It made more sense. "Sleep well, Timmie," he said, as he stopped for a last moment at the door, and she smiled at him from the bed.

"Thank you for the visit, doctor," she teased him, as he smiled at her, and then left.

She fell asleep, thinking about him, and wondering what his wife was like, if she was as sophisticated and elegant as he was, and at the same time as candid and open. He was an interesting mix of alternately formal and warm. He had shown her photographs of his very handsome children, and it seemed a foregone conclusion to Timmie that his wife must have been beautiful as well, since he and his children were. Timmie couldn't imagine him with anyone who wasn't, although she had noticed that he said very little about her, other than that she had studied law when she was younger, but never practiced, and that they had been married for nearly thirty years. It seemed a long time to Timmie, and sounded impressive, but it was hard to determine from the little he shared about his marriage if he was happily married to her or not.

Given the length of their marriage, Timmie assumed he was, but he was noticeably reticent about it, and made neither positive nor negative comments about his wife. He seemed very neutral about it, whenever the subject came up. That in itself made Timmie wonder about the status of his marriage, if he was happy or not. There was a noticeable absence of anecdotes about his wife. He either spoke of his children, or himself, but almost never his spouse.

One of the many things Timmie admired about him was that despite their many and often philosophical conversations, with many points of view in common, she never had the feeling that he was flirting with her. He was always careful, interested, and respectful, and never crossed any lines. His lack of overt flirtatiousness with her made her suspect that he was still in love with his wife, even if he said little about her, which seemed admirable to her. He was an easy man to admire, for his skill, his dedication, his knowledge, his fine mind, his culture, his sense of humor, and his concern about his patients. She had never been as well cared for by any doctor, and she had already decided to buy him a gift before she left. But she couldn't do anything about it until he let her out of the hospital and she got back to the hotel.

And when he came back to see her in the morning, in casual week-end clothes, corduroy slacks, and a gray cashmere sweater, she broached the subject of her leaving the hospital again.

"All right, all right," he teased her. "I can see you're going to harass me until I send you back to the Plaza." She had been on the IV antibi-otics for long enough, and he said he was going to give her the rest of what she had to take in the form of pills. He was very cautious med-ically, she had discovered, and extremely responsible. "I'll send you back to the hotel tomorrow," he conceded, "as long as you promise you won't do anything and you'll continue to rest. I suppose it's more com-fortable for you there." It was, but she had no complaints about the ser-vice or her accommodations during her four-day stay at the hospital, and he had continued to stop in to see her several times a day. He was attentive, and he practiced medicine with care, and attention to every meticulous detail.

He told her before he left that he was leaving for the night with his children. His associate would be covering for him, and he reminded her that she had his cell phone number, and if any problem arose, she wasn't to hesitate to call him. It reminded her of when she had called him on Tuesday night in excruciating pain. It seemed aeons ago now, after days of talking and getting to know each other. He was no longer a stranger, he was a friend.

"I'll come by to see you at the Plaza Athénée tomorrow when I get back," he assured her, and she knew he would. He always did exactly as he said. He was a man you could rely on. Everything about him exuded reliability and strength. "I'll be in Périgord tonight, at my brother's house. My children and I love it there."

After he left, Timmie realized that he hadn't mentioned his wife, which seemed strange to her. Maybe she didn't like Périgord as much as they did, or didn't get along with his brother. Anything was possible after long years of marriage. People developed habits and concessions, or drew lines in the sand about friends or in-laws they disliked. Jean-Charles had offered no explanation as to why he hadn't mentioned her. And Timmie somehow didn't feel it appropriate to ask, although they had shared deeply personal views about many things, from politics to art to abortion and the raising of children, a subject about which she knew little, since her experience at mothering had been all too brief. When she thought about it, she realized she envied him the weekend with his kids. She thought they were lucky to have a father like him.

It was quiet that night without him, and Timmie watched CNN on the television in her room. There were no shocking news events. And the reports from Jade and David in New York were good. They had two more days of meetings scheduled after the weekend, and were planning to be back in L.A. on Tuesday night. Timmie was hoping to be back with them by the end of the next week, and she was dreading the backlog of work that would have piled up on her desk in her absence, particularly while she was sick. She hoped she would feel equal to it by the time she got back. She was still tired after her ruptured appendix, and when she dressed to leave the hospital on Sunday, she found that she was exhausted by the effort, and almost sorry she hadn't agreed with Jean-Charles's suggestion to take a nurse with her. She had insisted that she would get all the care she needed from the hotel staff. Gilles had come to pick her up and take her back to the hotel. He said he was enormously relieved to see her looking so well, and he had brought her a huge bouquet of red roses wrapped in cellophane. She felt like a movie star or an opera diva as she left the hospital, on still slightly shaky legs with the flowers in her arms. And once there, she was surprised how nice it was to get back to the Plaza Athénée. It felt like a homecoming to her, as she walked into the luxury of her familiar room, and one of the maids helped her settle in.

Timmie showered as Jean-Charles had told her she could, ordered lunch from room service, checked her messages, read some faxes Jade and David had sent her, none of them earth-shattering, just informative. And then Timmie happily got into her bed, between exquisitely pressed sheets. Being there again felt like the height of luxury to her. Although everything at the hospital had been efficient, comfortable, and pleasant, there was no place on earth as wonderful as the Plaza Athénée, in her opinion.

She was happily tucked into her bed there late that afternoon, eating her favorite chocolates and sipping tea, when the concierge called to announce that Docteur Vernier had come to see her, and five minutes later, he came up. He looked relaxed and happy to see her as he strode into the room and told her she looked better already.

"It must be the chocolates," she said as she offered him one, and he resisted, with more willpower than she felt capable of. "How was Périgord with your kids?" she asked, without adding that she had missed him, but she was surprised to find she had. She'd had no one interesting to talk to since the previous morning when he came to see her at the hospital before he left.

"Excellent," he commented. "And how do you feel being back here?

As well as you did in the hospital yesterday, or have you already exhausted yourself?" He looked almost stern as he questioned her, and she laughed at him, which made him smile again. Her laughter was always infectious, and he was satisfied to see she had regained her mischievous look. She looked very well to him, and he was pleased.

"I haven't done a thing. All I've done since I got back this morning was lie in bed and eat."

"That's just what you need." He had already told her several times he thought she was too thin, which didn't entirely surprise him, given the business she was in. All American fashion people looked anorexic to him, although Timmie's slimness wasn't quite that extreme. But he could see that she had lost some weight that week, which was to be expected after her surgery. He could see easily that she was delighted to be back at the hotel, in the comfortable bed and surroundings, with her own nightgown on. She had even put on a pair of diamond earrings, and done her nails that afternoon. She was back in the lap of luxury again, and felt more herself than she had at the hospital in Neuilly. Now, as soon as he gave her permission to do so, she was going to fly the coop entirely. He hated to admit it to himself, but he knew he would miss her when she left. She was excellent company, and wonderful to talk to. Her anxieties that had been aroused the night of the surgery had dissipated days before, and she was confident and smiling again. She was now a woman of power back in her element. There was no question that after twenty-three years of remarkable achievement, elegant opulence suited her to a tee. He teased her about it as she offered him a glass of champagne, and he laughed and shook his head.

"I rarely drink," he said easily, not in the least bothered about it. The bottle of Cristal she held out to him held no appeal at all. "And I'm on call tonight."

"You don't drink?" She seemed surprised. He was a man of good habits, a fine mind, warm heart, and was devoted to his wife and children. One couldn't ask for more. She couldn't help thinking again that his wife was a lucky woman. Men like Jean-Charles Vernier were rare, and didn't come on the market often. Not in her experience anyway. They almost always stayed married to their wives. She couldn't even imagine Jean-Charles single, or involved with one of the young women the men she knew hung out with. Most of them were starlets, models, or bimbos. The thought of it was laughable. He wouldn't have put up with a woman like that for ten minutes. His standards were obviously so much higher, and he was truly a nice man.

She offered him a cup of tea, which he also declined. He didn't expect her to entertain him. He wasn't a guest, he was her doctor, as he pointed out to her with a smile.

"I thought we were friends too," she said, looking disappointed, as he laughed.

"That's true. I think we are. I enjoy our conversations very much," he admitted to her, and then he surprised her by what he said next. "I'm going to miss you when you're gone."

He liked their philosophical discussions about the human race, their frailties and predilections, the politics of their respective countries, and he had been deeply touched by her confidences about her previous life. He had been greatly moved by the stories of her childhood at the orphanage and in and out of foster homes, which would have destroyed most people and had only made her stronger. And he was deeply saddened for her about her son. Given his love for his own children, he couldn't imagine anything worse than losing a child. Yet she had managed to survive that too, and the betrayal by her husband. She had been through so much, and was still whole. She had won his profound respect in the days since her surgery, and he agreed with her that they had become friends, however odd that seemed at first. It no longer did now, even to him. He wasn't in the habit of becoming friends with his patients. But there was something warm and unusual about her, which drew him to her, and made him want to share his thoughts with her. He was entirely comfortable sitting in the living room of her suite and chatting with her. She had gotten out of bed to sit with him, among the profusion of flowers that had been sent to her by acquaintances in the fashion world who had heard of her surgery. Word of it had spread like wildfire, with Jade and David in New York.

"So what are your plans?" he asked her, looking relaxed. He seemed happier than he had before the brief weekend he'd spent with his children in Périgord.

"You tell me, doctor. How soon can I fly home?"

"Are you in a great hurry?"

"No," she said honestly, "but I should get back. I have a business to run," she reminded him, but he was well aware of it, and of how busy she was, and was likely to be when she went back.

"How does Thursday sound to you? Can you live with that?" He didn't want to rush her departure, but he knew he couldn't keep her at the Plaza Athénée forever.

"It sounds about right." And it would give David and Jade a day to organize things for her after they got back. "Can I go out a little bit before that? At least for a short walk." She had something in mind, which he didn't suspect.

"I think you can. Don't walk too far or do too much. Don't carry anything heavy. Be sensible, and you'll be fine."

"That's good advice about life," she said, and he smiled. "I'm always sensible unfortunately. I'm too old to be otherwise." That was not entirely true, but for the most part it was.

"Age has nothing to do with it. And you're young enough to be foolish if you want. It might do you good from time to time." He could only imagine the pressure she was under, with her work, and the stress when things went wrong. Fashion was a tough business, and he suspected she had to work hard and fight well to stay on top, which was where she'd been for twenty-three years. Right at the very top, always trying to outdo herself. It was no easy task.

She noticed, or had the impression, that he was reluctant to leave that afternoon, as night began to fall. And then she decided to ask him a random question, which was perhaps too personal. But she decided that if he didn't want to answer it, he wouldn't. He was a big boy, well able to defend himself, and she was curious to know.

"Did your wife go to Périgord with you and your children?" she asked, out of the blue, and he looked startled and instantly uncomfortable.

"What made you ask that question?" He was intrigued by her intuitiveness. She seemed to know many things, and accurately guessed the rest. She trusted her own instincts more than most.

"I don't know," she answered honestly. "You didn't mention her. That seemed odd."

"No, she didn't go. My brother and she don't get along." To say the least. He said that in fact, they had been feuding for years, over a house Jean-Charles and he had inherited together, and eventually had to sell because neither of them could agree on who would use it and when. Jean-Charles's wife hadn't spoken to her brother-in-law since, and refused to join her husband on visits to him and his wife in Périgord.

"I thought it was something like that." Timmie nodded. Her guess had been correct. It was a family disagreement of some kind.

"We don't always go places together," Jean-Charles said, as a muscle tightened almost imperceptibly in his jaw. There was something he wasn't saying, and Timmie watched his eyes, trying to sense what it was. "We're both very independent people, with widely diverging in-terests. Whenever I take the children there, she always stays home."

"Did you go to the dinner party alone the other night in Neuilly?" She was being frankly nosy now, and was aware that she had no right to know. She wondered what he'd answer, when he recovered from his surprise at the question. He was once again impressed by how astute she was.

"I did, actually. She doesn't like those people either. We rarely go out together, or enjoy the same friends. What made you ask?"

"Just a feeling I had. It's none of my business. I'm sorry I asked," she said politely, totally intrigued by the arrangement they had.

In some ways it was very French. People in France seemed to stay married forever, and resolved their differences by leading separate lives, rather than getting divorced as frequently as people did in the States.

"You're not sorry at all," he teased her. "You wanted to know. Now you do."

"Isn't it hard having separate social lives and weekend plans?" She wondered if he had a mistress, or saw other women, but she would never have dared ask him. She didn't get the feeling that he did. He didn't look the type to run around. And he had been circumspect with her. He was clearly not a flirt, with his patients anyway.

"If a marriage is difficult, and two people are very different, having separate lives can keep the marriage alive. After nearly thirty years, one can't expect things to be the same as they once were," he explained calmly. It was obvious that he had made peace with how he lived, and it worked for him.

"I suppose not," Timmie said politely. "I never got that far, I wouldn't know."

"Five years is respectable too. I think it's a shame the way people don't work things out, and just give up," Jean-Charles said, and then went on, "I think people should stay together for their children's sakes. They owe it to them, no matter how unpleasant things get."

"I don't know about that," Timmie said honestly. "I've never been convinced that people who don't get along and stay together make their children all that happy. They always wind up blaming their kids for the sacrifices they made. I think that takes a toll in the end. And why spend the rest of one's life with someone one doesn't like, or can't stand, or doesn't get along with? I can't imagine kids get a lot out of that, except the opportunity to share their parents' stress, which doesn't seem fair to the kids."

"We don't always get what we want in life," Jean-Charles said cryptically, "or what we thought we would. But that's no excuse to run away. People owe each other more than that, and their children certainly."

"That sounds like a hard life to me. I believe in making a serious effort, but not being miserable for the rest of your life. Sometimes it's better to admit you've made a mistake, or things have changed. I think now I respect my ex-husband for doing that, although it was hard for me. If he hadn't, we would have lived a lie forever. I'd rather be alone than do that." Jean-Charles obviously disagreed with her. He was defending a way of life, and the choices he'd made, for better or worse. In recent years, mostly worse.

"Sometimes you have to resign yourself," he said, helping himself to a chocolate, while Timmie watched his eyes with interest. She sensed easily that there was much he wasn't telling her.

"I don't agree with you," Timmie said quietly. "Resignation is a miserable way to live." She would have hated staying married to Derek, once she knew he was involved with another man. In the end, painful as it had been, Derek had done the right thing leaving her. It had been cleaner in the end, although devastating at the time. And she respected him for it now.

"There is a certain nobility in sacrifice," he said philosophically as she thought about what he was saying.

"They don't give prizes for that," Timmie said staunchly. "You just get old and sad and tired before your time, while you watch your dreams die. And why do that? There should be more to life than that."

He didn't answer her, and looked as though he was thinking about it. She had raised a number of interesting questions for him that week, and always gave him much to think about in the course of their conversations. In spite of everything that had happened to her, she was a woman who still believed that love was possible, for others, if not for herself. She too had resigned herself, and no longer believed in dreams. But she liked the theory, especially for others. The reality for both of them was actually similar, although he was married and she wasn't. They had each made their peace with what they didn't have in their lives, as many people did, and led their lives as best they could, filling their time by working too hard. He had his children, and she filled her nights occasionally with men like Zack.

They chatted for a while, and finally he got up regretfully. He was comfortable at the Plaza, talking to her, and would have happily continued to sit there for hours. But he had other things to do. Before he left, he promised to come and check on her the following afternoon. She had three days left in Paris.

When she got up and dressed the next day, she felt shakier than she wanted to admit, even to her doctor. She was feeling better, but still not herself yet. In spite of that, she forced herself to go out. The errand she wanted to do was in a shop only a few yards from the hotel on the Avenue Montaigne, which provided some of the best shopping in Paris. She wanted to buy a gift to give Jean-Charles before she left. He had been exceptionally nice to her, and taken excellent care of her, and she wanted to give him something to thank him for it, although she knew he didn't expect it. It was a gesture of gratitude and friendship she wanted to make to him.

Timmie went down to the lobby just before noon, and walked slowly toward the watch store on the Avenue Montaigne, feeling annoyingly like an old woman. She felt as though she had aged a hundred years in the last week. Her body was still feeling the effects of her ruptured appendix, and the antibiotics she was still taking made her feel slightly sick. But once in the shop she was distracted by the selections they offered her, and she found exactly what she wanted for him. It was a beautiful, simple platinum watch with a black face that she hoped would please him. The salesman who had helped her had assured her that if he didn't like it, he could return it for another watch he preferred.

She was pleased with her purchase as she walked slowly back to the hotel, through the lobby, and was relieved to get back to her suite. Even after a short walk, and an hour outside her room, she was exhausted. It had been her first outing. And after she had lunch and took a nap, she felt better.

Timmie was feeling more like her old self again when Jean-Charles came for his daily visit, and he noticed immediately that her color had improved. She told him she had gone for a short walk on the Avenue Montaigne, without mentioning her little shopping venture. She was planning to give him the watch on her last day in Paris, when he came to see her for the last time.

His cell phone rang several times while he was visiting her, and it was obvious he had several very sick patients. He told her he couldn't stay and chat that day. He called her that evening to check on her again. She assured him she was fine. And by the next morning, she felt it. She was improving noticeably day by day. She actually did take a walk down the Avenue Montaigne that day, and then came back to the hotel to rest again. Her little outing was a major improvement. Even Jean-Charles was pleased when he saw her that afternoon. He didn't even scold her for how far she'd ventured when she told him.

"If you walk even a little farther tomorrow, I think you'll feel strong enough to fly home on Thursday," which was what they had planned.

In spite of the surgery that had kept her there for an extra week, Timmie was genuinely sad to be leaving Paris, although it had been a hard way to extend her visit, and not the reason she would have wanted. But she had also enjoyed getting to know the doctor better, and she was more than slightly intrigued about his marriage. He had obviously made compromises in his life, for his children—which he thought justified. Having gleaned that from some of his comments during his visit to her on Sunday, she was now fairly convinced that he was unhappily married, and intended to stay that way forever. She thought it was foolish of him, but it was no worse than what she was doing, settling for brief relationships with men who were clearly not worthy of her, out of loneliness and convenience.

His whole face lit up when he talked about his children, and that touched her. Deeply at times. Despite that, nothing inappropriate had passed between them, not a look, not a glance, not even a slight double entendre. He wasn't trying to pick her up or seduce her. He was just a hardworking, sometimes lonely, thoroughly dedicated doctor. Timmie felt sure he not only liked her as a patient, but enjoyed talking to her as well, on a multitude of subjects and levels.

He came to see her for the last time on Wednesday at five o'clock. He had his doctor's bag in his hand, and was wearing gray slacks and a blazer, and a very good-looking Hermès tie. He looked serious and professional, and his eyes were sad as he looked at her. She didn't know if something had upset him that day, or if he was as saddened at her leaving as she was herself to be saying goodbye to him and leaving Paris.

"When are you coming to Paris again?" he asked, as they sat on the couch in her suite. Her gift for him was on the table, but neither of them commented on it. They had wrapped it in simple dark blue paper, with a curly gold paper ribbon that held the wrapping paper together.

"Not until February," she said in answer to his question. "We come back for the ready to wear shows again then. But that time I'm only going to Paris and Milan, and New York of course. I'm skipping London. My reps there can handle it for me. Four cities is just too much. This trip damn near killed me, even before my appendix burst."

"I hope our paths cross again sometime," he said formally, and she felt sad. He was already slightly different. He seemed stiff somehow, awkward alone in the suite with her, and somewhat distracted, as though he had other things on his mind. She didn't know him well enough to ask him what they were.

They chatted amiably for nearly an hour, until he finally said he had to leave. He had a patient waiting for him at his office, and he was already late after lingering with her. She hated to say goodbye to him. And she knew that when she saw him again, things would be even more different between them. Their ease with each other now had been caused in great part by her solitude in Paris and her illness. It had allowed them the opportunity to get to know each other, and even become friends.

She liked to think she was leaving a friend behind in Paris, but she wasn't entirely sure he was. He was her doctor, he had cared for her well, and been kind to her. And she would have liked to have him as a friend. She hoped that in February they could once again pick up the threads of the bond that had begun to form between them, but she had no idea if that appealed to him as well, or if this had been only a passing moment, between doctor and patient, never to occur again.

As he started toward the door, she handed the blue wrapped box to him. He stopped, looking startled, and glanced at her awkwardly.

"What's that?"

"A thank-you for being so kind to me," she said softly. She had shared with him things she had never told anyone else before. She had come to trust him, both as doctor and friend. But he had expected nothing from her, other than the time they had shared. It had been gift enough to talk to her. The box she handed him came as a big surprise to him, and he hesitated for a moment before taking it from her hand.

"I wasn't kind," he said quietly. "I was doing my work." But to Timmie, he had done more than that. He had been a source of enormous support, and had quietly nurtured her in ways no one else ever had. She had felt an overwhelming sense of warmth and humanity from him, and she had wanted to thank him for it, with a gift to remind him of the deep exchanges they had shared. "I'm very touched," he said, putting the gift in the same hand as his doctor's bag, and then he extended a hand to her and shook hers.

"Thank you," Timmie said softly, "for listening, and for being there . . . for holding my hand when I was scared." She had been through so much worse that he couldn't imagine he had made a real difference, even if it had seemed important to her at the time. But to him, it was nothing. And surely not worthy of a gift.

"Be careful," he said with a smile. "Rest. Don't do too much when you go back. You will still be tired for a while." He was back to being just her doctor, and he looked troubled. He didn't like goodbyes, and her gift had thrown him. It was totally unexpected, though typical of Timmie, which he couldn't have known. "Take good care of yourself," he said, smiling at her finally. "Call if I can ever help you."

"Maybe I'll get sick when I'm here in February," she said hopefully, and then laughed.

"I hope not!" he said, and then pointed to the gift. "Thank you for this. You didn't have to."

"I wanted to. You were very kind."

He imagined it was a silver pen, or the sort of thing he got often from patients. He was in for a surprise.

And then, without warning, she leaned over and hugged him. She kissed him on both cheeks, and he smiled. *"Bon voyage,* Madame O'Neill," he said as he saluted her, and then opened the door and walked out of the suite. She stood in the doorway and watched him head toward the elevator and press the button. It was there in an instant, and he got in as two Japanese guests got out. He gave her a last wave and then disappeared, as Timmie walked back into her familiar suite and felt a lump rise in her throat. She had always hated goodbyes. When she said goodbye to people she liked, and saw them leave, even now, after all these years, she always felt abandoned. Watching him go, she felt a familiar pang of sorrow, which even she knew was silly. He was only a French doctor after all, not her lover. And in her experience all good things, even friendships, came to an end.

Chapter 5

Timmie packed her bags that night, and called Zack when she got up the next morning, to tell him she was coming home that afternoon. It was still Wednesday night for him, and Thursday morning for her. The flight back to Los Angeles would take eleven hours, with a nine-hour time difference in her favor. It would be early afternoon when she got there, and noon when she left Paris.

"Hi," she said casually when he answered. He sounded relaxed, and as though he was in bed, but said he wasn't sleeping. "I'm coming back today, I thought I'd call and see if you want to come over." She hadn't seen him in four weeks, but they had kept in reasonably regular contact, although he hadn't knocked himself out to call her when she was sick. He had called a few times, tried to be funny, and said he was looking forward to seeing her. She knew enough not to expect more from him, although it would have been nice if he'd surprised her, and had been more attentive. He didn't have it in him. Their relationship had never been more than superficial. It was, in great part, why she was with him, and had made a ten-year habit of others like him. She had reminded herself of that the night before, after she said goodbye to Jean-Charles. Zack was an entirely different breed. He wasn't deep, of thought or intention, and had never pretended to be. All he wanted was a good time, which was in fact all Timmie wanted from him. She reminded herself not to lose sight of that now. And the holidays were coming. It would be a lot more pleasant spending them with Zack than alone.

"Sorry, Timmie, I can't make it," Zack said, sounding vague, in response to her invitation that he drop by that night after she got home. His answer reminded her again of their separate, independent lives. He was not a devoted boyfriend, desperate for her to come home. He had a life of his own. And so did she.

"That's too bad," Timmie said calmly. She was used to answers like that from him. They saw each other when it suited them, and they were free. And Zack had been spoiled by women who pursued him constantly. He rarely put himself out for anyone, although the relationship with Timmie was ego food for him. He liked telling people he was dating Timmie O'Neill.

"I'm going to San Francisco to see a guy I was in a play with a few years ago," he explained. "He just called me. I didn't know you were coming home." She hadn't called him earlier to make plans with him. She had intended to call him when she got home. And he didn't offer to cancel his San Francisco trip for her. She suspected it was his small revenge for her not taking him to Europe with her. He had to make the point.

"That's too bad. It sounds like we'll just miss each other. Maybe I'll see you in the airport," she said light-heartedly. She didn't take his rejection seriously. She wasn't desperate to see him either. It just would have been nice after four weeks.

As she listened to him, she was aware of the difference between her conversations with him, and those she'd had recently with Jean-

Charles. It wasn't just a difference in intelligence, but in interest in each other and common ground. Even after dating Zack for several months, and sleeping with him, there was no deep connection between them, and probably never would be. She already felt far more connected to Jean-Charles, which seemed odd to her.

"I'll see you when I get back," Zack said breezily. "I'm just going for two days. What are you doing this weekend? Going to Malibu?"

"Maybe. Depends how I feel. I just got out of the hospital a few days ago," she reminded him. It was like talking to a stranger after a month away, and in many ways he was.

"Call me if you go out there. I'm coming back Saturday. You can get me on my cell phone. I'll be driving back from San Francisco. Let me know your plans." She knew he'd be less enthusiastic about seeing her if she was in Bel Air. She knew all of that about him. He loved weekends at the beach with her, and he knew she hated going there alone.

"Have a safe trip home," he said easily.

"You too," she said, feeling sad as she hung up. Sometimes, in spite of her resolve not to get too deeply involved, she couldn't help wishing Zack was more. It would have been nice to come home to someone who loved her and really cared.

She finished dressing and left the hotel a few minutes later, half-hoping that Jean-Charles would call to say goodbye again, but of course he didn't. There was no reason for him to do that. He had said goodbye to her the night before, and discharged her as a patient. She wondered if he had opened the gift by then, and if he liked it. She hoped he did.

She left tips at the concierge's desk, tipped the bellmen and doormen as she left, and then Gilles sped her through Thursday-morning Paris traffic on the way to Charles de Gaulle. He checked her bags for her when they got to the airport, something David always did for her when they traveled together, and she got a rolling cart for her heavy bag. After her recent hospital stay, the walk through the terminal seemed unusually long, but she wasn't in pain. She was just a little more tired than usual, and a VIP ground attendant found her at the gate and escorted her onto the plane and to her seat in first class. Everything had gone well.

She settled into her seat, took out a book to read, accepted some magazines from the flight attendant, laid her head back against her seat, and closed her eyes. She felt as though she had been gone for years. The unexpected surgery had only added a few days to the trip, but she had actually been in Paris for more than two weeks. As much as she loved it there, when she wasn't sick, it was going to be good to get home. She was sure there were stacks of work waiting for her in her office. She had a million decisions to make about the following year's lines. They were talking about introducing yet another fragrance, and she had some new cosmetic ideas. Her mind was whirling as the plane took off, and half an hour later, she fell asleep, and slept for the first five hours of the trip.

When she woke up, they served her dinner, and she watched a movie, turned her seat into a bed, snuggled under the comforter, and slept the rest of the way to L.A. The purser woke her as they were about to land.

"Madame O'Neill?" He gently touched her shoulder, and when she heard the male French voice, for a moment she thought she was back in the hospital and it was Jean-Charles. And then she saw where she was. He asked her to put her seatback in an upright position, and she saw through the window that they were coming in to LAX.

She went to the bathroom, brushed her teeth, washed her face, and combed her hair, and got back to her seat just in time for them to land. As soon as they were at the gate, she was one of the first off the plane, with her heavy alligator bag in hand. A VIP service agent took it from her as she stepped off the plane. She passed through immigration quickly with nothing to declare. The few things she had bought had gone home with Jade, or been sent straight to L.A. She hated wasting time in customs, so rarely brought anything in with her.

As she came through the doors from immigration, she saw Jade waiting for her. Timmie's driver was outside. Jade took the heavy alligator bag from the agent, and escorted her through the airport, explaining that David would have come but he had too much work.

"I don't need two of you to get me home." Timmie smiled at her, after giving her a hug.

"How do you feel?" Jade had noticed that she looked slightly thinner, and very pale. Suddenly her fair skin seemed almost translucent in contrast to the red hair.

"I feel okay," Timmie said, surprised herself at how well she felt, and how wide awake after the long trip. But she had slept most of the way. She almost always did.

"I felt so terrible that you got sick. I really wanted to come back."

"You didn't need to. I was fine. I had a very good doctor, and they took great care of me at the American Hospital. After the initial shock, it was a pretty decent rest, although not exactly what I had in mind." She looked like her old self as she strode across the airport with her assistant at her side.

"You're so brave," Jade said admiringly. "I would have totally freaked out, getting sick in a foreign country, and having to have emergency surgery. I'm about two years old when I get sick," Jade said sympathetically, looking slightly embarrassed as Timmie laughed. She was happy to see Jade again, and be back in her familiar surroundings and routine. It was actually going to feel good to be in her own bed in Bel

Air, despite the luxuries of the Plaza Athénée. This was home, and it was great to be back.

"I was about five," Timmie confessed. "I don't think anyone loves getting sick away from home. All things considered, it went okay. The doctor was excellent. He held my hand." She smiled.

"They would have had to sedate me for the whole ten days," Jade said, as they crawled through packed freeways. The traffic was fierce, which was familiar too.

"So what do we have planned?" Timmie asked, and Jade told her about the meetings she'd scheduled for her for the following week. She had tried to go easy on her since Timmie had been sick. By normal standards, and to ordinary mortals, the schedule she'd planned would have sounded like way too much. To Timmie, it was a breeze, or usually anyway. She had the energy of ten people when she was in top shape, and she hoped she'd be back there soon. She couldn't tell after the long flight. For her, on Paris time, it was after midnight. It was going to take a few days to get over the distance, the surgery, and the trip. But she felt surprisingly well. She was planning to catch up on her desk the next day, and go to Malibu for the weekend, more than likely with a stack of work.

They chatted easily the rest of the way into L.A., and at the last minute, Timmie decided to stop at the office first, before going home. There was no one waiting for her there, and she wanted to get a look at her desk, to size up the force of the avalanche waiting for her return.

"Are you sure you should?" Jade asked with a look of concern. "Shouldn't you rest?" But this was Timmie they were talking about. No mere human, who would want to go home, shower, unpack, and go back to sleep. The dynamo that was Timmie O'Neill, and who had been taking it easy for ten days, was about to leap to her feet. Jade could smell it, as Timmie laughed and insisted she was fine. She looked it, and was obviously in good spirits.

The office complex that housed the headquarters of Timmie O was in the fashion district in downtown L.A., and encompassed five buildings and a warehouse, where they cleared imports before shipping them out. There were additional warehouses several blocks away, a factory in New Jersey, and textile mills and factories she had bought abroad years before, mostly in Malaysia and Taiwan. She was negotiating to buy another plant in India. And as they drove up in front of the building that housed Timmie's offices, she looked around her and beamed.

"Welcome home," Timmie said softly to herself, glad to be back to her normal life. She felt strong and solid here. She always knew what she was dealing with, had a firm hand on all aspects of her empire, and enjoyed running the show. In the past dozen years, it had replaced all else in her life, and she knew without a moment's doubt that this was what she did best. There was great comfort in knowing this was something she did well. Running her vast conglomerate of lines, labels, and companies never frightened her, in fact it made her feel safe. It was the rest of her life that had always brought her pain. This never had. Right from the beginning, Timmie had discovered herself and her own capabilities and immense talent through her work. In recent years, the personal side of her life had always been lacking and never failed to hurt. She no longer allowed herself to think of it anymore. As long as she stayed focused on work, she was fine. Jade could almost see her come to life as she walked through the door, like a flower that had been watered. She seemed to grow as she took the elevator to the third floor. They weren't expecting her officially, but they had been warned. David had told them she would probably come in on the way home, and as usual, he was right.

Timmie walked into his office a moment later with a broad grin. "So, did you miss me?" she said as she gave him a warm hug, and he did the same, with a broad grin. Like Jade, he had been worried about her. But they had followed her orders, and stayed on to complete the meetings in New York.

"I sure did," he said, as he stepped out from his desk. "That's the last time we leave you anywhere. You had us worried sick."

"It was no big deal," she said, brushing it off, and suddenly Paris seemed like it was on another planet, as did her surgery, and even Jean-Charles Vernier. He didn't even cross her mind, although she had seen him constantly for nine days. Now all that was gone. She was back in the magic kingdom of Timmie O, which she ran so well, and for which she lived. She had become, once again, the person he had met when she first got sick, the one he didn't approve of, who lived only for her work, and was willing to sacrifice all for it, including her health, even if finally at great price. This was who she was.

"Don't give me that," David scolded her. "A ruptured appendix is a big deal. You could have died."

"No such luck," she teased. "I'm too mean to do something like that. So what's hot? I haven't seen my desk. Warn me, before I have a heart attack when I walk in."

"Nothing much actually," he reassured her. "I put out a lot of fires today, but even they were small. We have a problem at the factory in Taiwan, I gave you a report on it, and you should have it on your e-mail, but even that's no big deal. I think I worked it out. You can read it tonight. The fabrics we ordered from Beijing all came in, so did the knits from Italy. They're already in New Jersey. Actually, I can't think of a thing for you to worry about, although I know you'll find something," he laughed at her, happy to see her again. She was like a big sister to him, a mentor, and the person he admired most in the world.

He admired everything she did, and had for the past six years, since she had discovered him and taken him under her wing. She had taught him everything he knew about the business. She was a perfectionist, meticulous about every detail, had her finger in every pie, was a genius at marketing, knew her audiences, and had a design sense that just wouldn't quit and never had. It was no small wonder that she was the most important woman in the industry. All that really mattered to her was her work. The world of Timmie O was now her child, and she groomed it, loved it, fixed it, scolded it, protected it, and held it dear to her heart.

"I'll be back in a minute," Timmie said as she left David's office for her own. Jade was waiting for her there, with a cup of tea, and her work and messages in neat stacks. There were files, brochures, faxes, sample boxes, and a thousand other things on her desk. And like a Chinese puzzle she loved to do, she sat down and began sorting it out. She was still sitting there at seven o'clock, with Jade next to her. They had gone through nearly everything by then, and there was a huge stack she was planning to take home and read that night. It was as though she had never left. Timmie had never looked happier. She was back in her element. And work was her favorite sport. She was Olympic class.

An hour later, Timmie was still at her desk, with her assistants near at hand. "I don't want to be rude," Jade said cautiously, shortly after eight o'clock. She didn't mind working late with Timmie, she almost always did, except when she had something special happening, like an important date, then Timmie let her go home. But Timmie almost always lost track of time when she was at her desk. She looked up at

Jade then, as though slowly floating back to earth when her assistant spoke. "It's nearly five in the morning for you. Maybe you should go home." She had had surgery after all and Jade was concerned. Timmie acted as though she had forgotten, which for the past several hours, she had.

"Yeah... sure...," she said, looking distracted, pulling something out of a fabric sample book that had caught her eye. "I slept on the flight."

"You've probably been up for close to twenty-four hours. You need to go home and rest." Jade often mothered her, instead of the reverse, and it touched Timmie's heart.

"I know... I know... I'll be through in a minute... I just want to look through one more file." She was like a child who wouldn't leave a game to be dragged off to dinner, or bed, or the bathtub. Her work was addictive for her, and always had been. Once she started, she couldn't stop. But she finally put the last file in the stack at eight-thirty, gathered them up in her arms, and Jade followed her out of the building. Timmie's driver was still waiting, and had been there for five hours. He was used to it, he drove her often, although she was extremely independent, and drove herself most of the time. But for airport runs, big parties, and major public events, she generally used a driver.

They dropped Jade off on the way, although she had offered to go home with Timmie. And at nine-fifteen Timmie was home, at the house in Bel Air. The driver carried her bags upstairs for her after she turned off the alarm. She turned on the lights and looked around. She felt as though she had been gone for ages, and the house looked prettier to her than she remembered. Her living room was beige, stark, and extremely open and airy, with striking modern paintings on the walls. She had a de Kooning, a Pollock, and an Oliveira. She had one of the early Calder mobiles, and a Louise Bourgeois sculpture in the corner. The room was simple, elegant, and very soothing. Her bedroom was white, and the kitchen was blue and yellow.

She had bought the house when Derek left her. She had wanted to put the past behind her, and successfully had for the most part. There was a photograph of her son on the bookcase, and she never explained it to people who came to the house and didn't know her well. It was rare that anyone asked her about it. Her assistants knew not to, the men who came and went in her life had little interest in a photograph of a four-year-old. They were more interested in the oval pool, the hot tub, and the sauna. She had a full gym set up in an upstairs bedroom and seldom used it. She got her exercise walking on the beach in Malibu, and hunting for shells. The gym always seemed too sterile to her, but others used it. Zack did whenever he stayed with her. And she had a big deck outside the kitchen where she liked to eat breakfast. It was the perfect house for her. She had an office, a dining room, a guest bedroom, a fabulous sound system, and enormous closets. She walked out to the kitchen now, opened the fridge, and stared inside it. The housekeeper had stocked it when Jade called her. Timmie realized she was too tired to eat, closed the door, and poured herself a glass of water. She took a shower, put on her nightgown, went to bed, and then lay there, wide awake. It was eight in the morning in Paris, time for breakfast. And for the first time since she'd left, she thought of Jean-Charles and wondered what he was doing. She wondered if he'd liked the watch, or would exchange it for something else.

She was awake for hours, and then started reading the files and reports she had brought home from the office. By the time she fell asleep, it was noon in Paris. Her work was done. It was three o'clock in the morning in L.A., and her bed seemed suddenly enormous. It seemed to have grown while she was away, as she lay staring at the ceiling, wondering why Zack had gone to San Francisco the day she got back. She wondered if it was truly a coincidence or if he'd done it on purpose, if he was still angry that she hadn't taken him to Europe. She finally decided it didn't matter as she drifted off to sleep, her mind a blank, her red hair fanned out on the pillow. Her eyes closed, and the last thought that wandered through her head as she fell asleep was of Jean-Charles Vernier in Paris. And for a strange, fleeting instant, she could feel his hand in hers. It was a warm, comfortable sensation, imagining him in the room beside her, even here, back in L.A. She wondered if she'd ever see him again. It seemed unlikely now that she was home, back in her own world.

Chapter 6

In spite of the late hour she'd fallen asleep the night before, Timmie woke up early. She made herself toast, ate half a yogurt, and had a cup of tea before she showered, dressed, and met up with her driver to take her to the office. She had been annoyed when Jean-Charles told her she couldn't drive for a month after surgery. But she made the best of it, and used the time to make calls to New York, and read the last of her correspondence. She was bringing all the files back to the office with a stack of notes for Jade. She handed them to her when she walked in as David looked at her, amazed.

"You finished them? All of them?" She nodded and grinned at him as he shook his head. "Why am I not surprised? Did you get any sleep at all last night?"

"A little," she said, as she glanced at something on his computer. She had slept for four hours, which was nearly enough for her. She rarely slept more than five, and could still function on three. She was a human powerhouse, and never seemed to run out of energy, although by late Friday afternoon, the jet lag got her, and at four o'clock, she was about to fall asleep at her desk. She had forgotten all about her recent surgery and convalescence. She was back to working at full speed, but by five o'clock she decided to call it a day. It was the weekend after all. She didn't even need to take work home, she had caught up on almost everything, and the rest could wait till Monday. She was afraid she might have to go to Taiwan to settle problems there.

With the traffic on the Santa Monica Freeway, she got home at six o'clock, and decided to go to Malibu that night. Zack hadn't called from San Francisco, and she didn't call him either. She'd been too busy and she knew she'd hear from him when he got back to the city. She had the driver take her out to Malibu at eight o'clock, after the traffic slowed down. He left her there, and she promised to call him on Sunday, when she wanted to go back to Bel Air, unless Zack drove her back. And by nine o'clock, she was standing on her deck, looking out at the ocean, and smelling the sea air, as the wind whipped through her hair. She loved being there. The house was done in blues and whites, with bleached floors, and stark white Chinese porcelains. She had a white marble coffee table, and oversize white furniture. The ceiling was painted the color of sky. Everything about the Malibu house reminded one of summer. She had a big white four-poster bed draped in white linen. It was a place she always enjoyed, and one of the few where she relaxed.

She couldn't wait to wake up and go for a walk on the beach in the morning. She had just decided she didn't mind being there alone, when the phone rang. It was Zack, he was on his way home, a day early.

"You're already at the beach?" He sounded surprised. "I didn't think you'd go out till the morning. I'm just driving past Bakersfield, I should be back in a couple of hours. Do you want me to come out there tonight?" She hesitated and then decided she might enjoy it. As she listened to him, she realized it would be nice to see him, although she had expected to spend the night alone.

"Sure. Why don't you come out?" she said easily. It was one of the things about him she liked most. He was an easy companion on weekends, and she never had to make a fuss for him. He came and went, and didn't expect her to do anything special for him, which was particularly nice when she was tired, or had a long week. He just liked to hang out, and be at the beach. Sometimes they didn't even talk for hours.

"I should be there around midnight. If you're tired, just go to bed, and leave the door open."

"I might," she said with a yawn. "I'm beat. I worked all day, and I'm still on Paris time." Although she hated to rub it in.

"I'll let myself in." He sounded like he was in good spirits.

She had a bath in her pristine white granite bathroom, with a view of the ocean from the bathtub. She was going to try to wait up for him, but left the kitchen door unlocked just in case, and long before midnight she was sound asleep in the canopied bed. She never heard him come in, and as he often did, he slipped quietly into bed, and fell asleep next to her. Their relationship was more companionship than sexual. He was the proverbial warm body, literally sometimes, and when she woke up early the next morning, she saw him lying beside her, his long blond hair tousled on her pillow, like a child's. He looked like a large beautiful boy as he slept, and she lay watching him for a few minutes and smiled. He was an exceptionally handsome man. She was never sure exactly what she felt for him, but it didn't really matter. There was nothing to analyze about their relationship. He was just there, for now. She didn't need or expect more than that from him.

She moved carefully out of the bed then, so as not to wake him up, and walked barefoot into her kitchen and out onto the deck. It was a glorious late October day. In fact, she realized with a start, it was Halloween. There was a soft breeze, and it was unseasonably warm. She couldn't wait to put on her jeans and walk down to the beach. The ocean was flat and still, the sand immaculate and smooth. It felt more like spring than fall.

She poured herself a cup of tea, and made coffee for Zack, and then sat down in the October sunshine. It was nine o'clock. She lay on a deck chair in the sun, and an hour later, looking handsome and tousled, Zack appeared. He looked like a movie star, or a Calvin Klein ad, with his exquisite body, as he walked out on the deck in his briefs.

"Hi there," Timmie said, smiling up at him from her deck chair. "I'm sorry I was asleep when you got here. What time did you get in?" He made no move to kiss her, just stood across the deck from her, smiling sleepily, and stretched lazily with a yawn. He wasn't a cuddly person, but he looked happy to see her, and she realized it was nice to see him too.

"I don't know, probably close to one. I stopped to get something to eat. I figured you'd be asleep. You look good, Tim. You don't look like you've been sick."

They were like two friends or roommates meeting after a long time, running into each other casually somewhere. He wasn't a particularly affectionate person. They were two entirely separate people on parallel tracks, which intersected from time to time, but rarely touched. If she hadn't had other relationships like it before, she would have found it very strange. Zack was neither passionate nor affectionate with her. Sometimes she felt as though they were more friends than anything else. He was friendly, but never really warm, and he liked hanging out with her. And once in a while, when the mood struck both of them, they made love. But sex was never of particular interest to Zack.

Looking at him, one would have expected him to be fabulous in bed, but he wasn't. He was very beautiful, but never terribly interested in anyone else, mostly himself. He lay down on the deck chair next to hers, and closed his eyes in the morning sun. He didn't lean over to kiss her. It never even occurred to him, after not seeing her for a month, but he was happy to be there. He was exactly what he looked like, a beautiful male model with a fabulous body, sometimes a huge spoiled brat, as he had been when she left for Europe, and at other times, he was actually fun. It was hard to predict which he would be at any given time. It depended on whatever mood he was in. This morning he looked sleepy and relaxed, and beautiful as always. He turned to her with a smile then, and opened one eye in the bright sun.

"I don't suppose you're in the mood to make me breakfast?" he asked, and then finally leaned over to kiss her. It was the merest peck on the lips. His own were tightly closed.

"I could be," she said, smiling at him. "It's nice to see you." It had been a month since she left. "Maybe you should cook for me," she teased. If they depended on his cooking, she knew they'd starve.

"I missed you," he said, his big blue eyes looking into her green ones. It was a rare admission for him. "Too bad you got sick. How do you feel?" Questions about her health were rare too. He was in unusually good form. He acted more like a twenty-five-year-old than a man of forty-one. All his reactions were those of a younger man. And most of the time, he hung out with people half his age.

"I'm fine. I felt lousy for a while in Paris. I'm okay now. Just tired from the trip. How was San Francisco?"

"Not too exciting. That's why I came back." She was sure that that was true. If it had been more interesting, he would have been in no rush to see her. She had no illusions about that. "I got two commercials this week. Big ones. National TV." He looked pleased with himself, and liked talking to her about it. She had given him good advice about his work.

"Sounds good." They talked about his career a lot, and rarely hers. But that was her choice, not his. He wasn't someone she could discuss her problems with, nor did she want to. He was just easy company and beautiful to look at. She realized full well that she paid a high price for how handsome he was. Men who looked like him were rarely attentive to their women. They expected the women in their immediate circle to take care of them, and to a small degree, Timmie did. "What do you want to eat?" she asked as she stood up. She liked making breakfast for him on weekends. It made her feel domestic. They rarely saw each other during the week. She was too busy, and with his easy lifestyle, he got underfoot, either when she was rushing in the morning, or when she came home exhausted at night. It worked much better when they met for weekends at the beach.

"Orange juice, two eggs over easy, bacon, toast, coffee. The usual." He rarely offered to make breakfast for her, but she didn't care about that either. He was a lousy cook, and for her, it was actually fun cooking for him, and hanging out together on the weekends, lying in the sun and walking on the beach hand in hand. It was friendly, easy, and warm. The only time she didn't enjoy his company was when he complained that she wasn't doing enough for him, like getting modeling jobs or taking him to parties. But he wasn't going there yet. She'd just gotten back, and he was still half asleep.

She disappeared to the kitchen to make him breakfast, and twenty minutes later, she came back with his breakfast on a tray. "Deck service, Your Highness," she teased him, and he sat up with a grin and took the tray from her. It was fun for her to have someone to pamper once in a while. She had put it all on white plates with seashells on them, with a linen placemat and napkin on the tray. She liked playing house at the beach, it was a side of her she rarely had time to indulge. And surely not during the week.

Over breakfast, he told her about some modeling go-sees he'd been on, and acting auditions, and brought her up to date on the dramas in his world. She told him about the ready to wear shows in Europe, and this time he made no comment about not coming along. After breakfast, they went for a long walk on the beach. He told her some funny stories, they picked up shells, and waded at the water's edge, and then he ran down the beach while she walked at an easy pace. But even the walking made her recently healed incision begin to hurt, so she sat down on the sand, while he continued running in the shallow water in the October sunshine. He was beautiful to watch, and from the distance he looked like a kid. He caught up with her on the way back. They went back to the house shortly after, and lay on the deck again. She was tired after the walk.

It was an easy, lazy day. They napped, and dozed. They made lunch together, and he barbecued steaks for them that night. They had no serious conversations, made no attempt to solve the problems of the world. He watched sports on TV, and she fell asleep on the deck reading a book. That night, they watched a video, and by ten o'clock, they were both in bed, sound asleep. He had made no attempt to make love to her, but fell asleep with his arm around her, and it gave her some warmth and comfort. Companionship was the hallmark of their relationship. Although when they woke up in the morning, he wanted to make love to her, and she told him she couldn't yet. Her surgery was too fresh. He was good-humored about it, and told her to make him breakfast instead, which she did. It was all easy and comfortable for both of them. They spent the day on the deck, although the air had gotten colder, and at six o'clock he drove her back to Bel Air. He used the gym and hot tub, while she checked her e-mails from work.

He didn't stay for dinner, he rarely did on Sunday nights. He usually made plans with his friends, and Timmie stayed home and worked, getting ready for the week ahead.

"What are you doing this week?" he asked her casually before he left. He liked knowing if she had some important event to go to. He was always angling for invitations to parties where he might be seen, but Timmie rarely went. She usually worked late every night. She had missed Barbara Davis's illustrious Carousel Ball while she was in Europe, and she hadn't paid much attention to the invitations Jade had left on her desk. They weren't nearly as important to Timmie as they were to Zack.

"Nothing much, I think," she said, watching him put his gym clothes back in his bag. "I'll check. I have a lot of work to do after being away for a month." He had never fully understood the volume of work she did, nor the pressure that was a daily fact of life for her.

"Let me know," he said, and she knew that if she didn't include him in her major social invitations, he'd have one of his tantrums. He was only pleasant as long as he felt he wasn't missing anything. She didn't always indulge him. When she did go out, she went to most events by herself. She didn't like advertising her relationships. She preferred staying private about it, which had never suited Zack. He hadn't had much luck getting her out, and he always said she worked too hard, which was correct, she readily admitted, and not something she intended to change. And surely not for Zack.

Even if he was pleasant company at the beach, he offered little else. The limitations of their relationship were even more obvious to her now after a month apart. It also struck her again how deceiving looks were. Anyone looking at him would have assumed he was fabulous in bed. Instead, he was boring and selfish. There was no fire and few sparks. There was something about his looks that captivated her nonetheless. His physical beauty was his main asset. He was beautiful to look at above all.

"I'll call you," Zack promised as he gave her another peck on the mouth as he left on Sunday night. "Thanks for a good weekend." It had been that at least. Good, and peaceful, although she felt empty when he left.

He hadn't been bratty, and they didn't fight. And it had been nice sleeping next to him, it almost always was. It kept her warm, both body and soul. It was amazing how things like that mattered when you were alone. Sex had become less important to her than hugs, or human touch. Sometimes it was just nice to sleep next to another human being. Without Zack staying with her on weekends, she would have been starved for human warmth. There was no one else in her life to sleep with or touch. Sometimes she thought she'd have been willing to sell her soul for a hug. Loneliness had become a huge factor in her life in recent years. Zack was an antidote to that.

The door closed softly behind him, and she heard him drive away in his battered ten-year-old Porsche, as she walked upstairs to her office. Two nights with him had been enough. She noticed as she thought about him that she felt more disconnected from him than she had before she left. Eventually, relationships like theirs died a natural death.

She was answering e-mails when Jade called her late that night.

"How was your weekend?" Jade asked easily. She wanted to make sure Timmie was feeling all right. She often called on Sunday nights.

"It was nice actually," Timmie answered, "relaxed and easy. I went out to the beach, and Zack came out."

"How was that? Was he still pissed off about Europe?"

"We didn't talk about it. I think he got over it, although I think he went to San Francisco just so he could make a point of not being here when I got back. It worked out. He came out to the beach on Friday night." Jade didn't say it, although she had before when they discussed it, but she wished Timmie wanted more than that. She deserved so much more. They had had that conversation a hundred times. Timmie said, and sincerely believed, that women like her were "unsalable" in the current market. The right men wanted younger women. The good ones were married. And even the wrong ones were hard to find, at her age. And these days, even Jade was finding interesting men to date hard to come by. She was still threatening to check out Match.com when she had time, despite Timmie's warnings to be careful. But for someone like Timmie, it was that much harder. She could hardly put her picture up on an online dating service. She'd have wound up in the tabloids in no time. So she contented herself with Zack.

"I had a blind date last night," Jade confessed with a sigh, as Timmie smiled. In the year since she'd left her married boyfriend, she'd had dozens of blind dates that hadn't worked out, but at least she tried. Timmie had to give her credit for that.

"How was it?" Timmie asked with interest. She was truly fond of her two assistants.

"It sucked. As always. He acted like he never got out of college. He took me to a sports bar, hit on the waitress, and got blind drunk, and I took a cab home without saying goodbye. David's going to help me do the computer dating thing next week. It can't be worse than this."

"Oh yes, it could," Timmie said, laughing. "One of these days the right guy will turn up, and you'll wind up married, and living in Des Moines with six kids."

"I'd settle for L.A. and two kids, or even one," she said sadly, and then was sorry she'd said anything to Timmie. Sometimes she forgot about Mark. Timmie never talked about him, but Jade had come to work for her just after he died. It had been a terrible time in Timmie's life, and Derek's leaving six months later had intensified her grief and made it that much worse. Jade remembered those days only too well, and the agony in Timmie's eyes. It was still there sometimes, which was what made Jade say very little about Zack. She knew as well as anyone that you did what you had to, to get by. She didn't like him for Timmie, but she knew why Timmie kept the relationship going. In her twelve years in Timmie's life, she had seen several Zacks.

"It'll happen," Timmie reassured her. She was always encouraging, and had been deeply sympathetic when Jade broke up with her married man. Jade had been heartbroken over it for the better part of a year, and unhappy long before.

It was hard to believe even now that Jade had stayed with him for ten years. He had continued to promise he would leave his wife, right up till the end. There was always some stumbling block or problem, some reason why he couldn't move out. Sick kids, his chronically dying mother, his wife's health and psychiatric problems, financial worries, a failing business, a child with juvenile diabetes who couldn't take the shock of his leaving, his wife's depression. It had gone on for years, until Jade finally gave up. Timmie knew from David that he still called her, but Jade wouldn't take his calls. He had been like a drug to her, but she had finally managed to give him up. She had wasted ten years of her life, and was afraid now that she had lost her chance to have kids. It wasn't too late yet, but she was getting there, and Timmie felt for her. Jade couldn't afford to play with men like Zack, she needed someone real who wanted to get married and have kids. "When you least expect it, the right guy will walk in. You'll see."

"Yeah, right," Jade said cynically, and then changed the subject to the appointments they had for the coming week. Timmie was moving back up to full speed, and after the weekend, she felt up to it. Her week of convalescence in Paris was history. She felt fine again, and had gotten some color over the weekend. The weather had felt like spring.

They wished each other good night and hung up, and Timmie thought of Zack when she went to bed that night. Her bed always seemed empty to her on Sunday nights, but by Monday she was used to it again. It was a familiar routine to her.

And on Monday morning, she was off and running, at her usual pace. She had a million phone calls, a thousand appointments, interviews, reps, people to see. She had meetings with her design assistants, solved endless problems with the spring line, averted a series of crises, managed to solve the factory problem without going to Taiwan, and by midweek it was hard to believe she'd ever had surgery or been sick. She looked better than ever, and was functioning, as always, on minimal sleep. Zack had called her on Tuesday and had wanted to come by that night, but she didn't get home till midnight, and when she called him, he was sound asleep. She was thinking about calling him on Thursday, when Jade handed her her mail, and she noticed a letter with French stamps on it, and saw that it was from Jean-Charles Vernier. She had no idea why, but she waited until Jade left the room to open it. She always opened her personal mail herself. She sat staring at the envelope for a minute, tore it open, and was surprised by the stationery he'd used. She had expected to find a letter with his professional letterhead, and instead there was a postcard, with a sunset on it, over an expanse of ocean. When she turned the card over, she saw that the photograph had been taken in Normandy. It seemed uncharacteristic of him, and when she read the card, the message was brief. He had reverted to a formal greeting, which surprised her too. Everything about the letter was surprising, and she didn't know what to think, if anything. It was courteous, and succinct, yet it had the quality of a message in a bottle that had been sent to her from Paris, or wherever he had been when he mailed it, and felt as though it had reached her by accident. She felt strange as she read it, thinking of him. He had written in his precise, careful hand.

Dear Madame O'Neill,

I was quite startled by your extravagant present. It is a most handsome, although entirely undeserved, gift. I am very pleased that your surgery went well, and hope that your convalescence is proceeding without problem. I will think of you when I wear the watch, which I most certainly do not merit, but shall enjoy nonetheless. I hope that you are well.

Very truly yours,
Jean-Charles Vernier.

It seemed so formal, and she was pleased that he had liked the watch. She almost couldn't tell if some of the formality was simply language or intended. The letter was so much stiffer than their many conversations as he sat in her room at the hospital, or when he dropped in on her after dinner parties. She remembered the things he had said about his marriage. His insistence that resigning oneself to "differences" and disappointments was always the right thing. She had wanted to argue with him about it, but couldn't. She didn't know him well enough. But she knew him better than this. She had told him her entire history, about Mark, and Derek, and her heartbreaking years in the orphanage as a child. She had told him all of it, and she didn't expect him to refer to it in his letter. But this felt so different somehow. She almost wanted to read between the lines to guess what he'd been thinking when he wrote it. Was she just a rich American who'd gotten sick and had surgery in Paris, and had given him an expensive gift that meant little to him? Or had the confidences mattered? She felt foolish for even thinking it, and for being disappointed that the letter wasn't warmer. What had she expected? She reminded herself that she had no right to expect anything from him. He was her doctor, and what's more, he was married. She wondered suddenly if she had given him the watch to woo him, or to thank him. She no longer trusted herself, or her feelings for him. Perhaps her motives hadn't been as pure as she intended. But if so, she knew she was barking up the wrong tree. Jean-Charles Vernier had no romantic interest in her. That much was clear. But had she expected him to, or wanted him to? She was no longer sure, as she questioned herself intently. Jean-Charles was handsome, proper, elegant, intelligent, and married with three children, in a country where people seldom got divorced, and he particularly did not believe in it. He may have held her hand before and during the surgery, and listened to her life story and sorrows, but in the end he was a married French doctor, who had sent her a formal thank-you note with a sunset on it. It meant nothing, and wasn't supposed to.

In the end, she was a patient, nothing more. It was just that she had thought their exchanges were unusual and profound. But even if they were, Jean-Charles had not lost his head. She told herself that he had intended to thank her with his letter, and he had done that. She had no idea why, but she wanted to answer it. She set the card on her desk and stared at it, as though it were speaking to her, and saying something Jean-Charles had not dared write to her, and never would. What was she thinking, she asked herself. It was a thank-you note. That's all it was. It was embarrassing to realize she had a crush on her

French doctor, if she did. She hadn't admitted that to herself when he was coming to visit her every day, and spent hours talking to her. But she was suddenly fully aware that for her, it had been more than that, and shouldn't have been. It was absolutely nothing. A fantasy. A girlish crush. And he had acknowledged her gift correctly. The only thing that seemed odd to her was the card he had used. A sunset over the ocean, as though it were calling to her, which she knew was entirely her imagination. It had to be. Wishful thinking.

There was no way she could write to him, nor should she. It would have been inappropriate and embarrassing if she responded to him, and he would probably think she was crazy. She had given him the watch. He had thanked her. The card was pretty, but so what? It meant nothing. It was not a message in a bottle. It was a formal thank-you note from a French doctor who had taken care of her in Paris. She read the card one last time, saw nothing between the lines, and knew there shouldn't be. Then with one last look at the sunset in the photograph, she told herself she was ridiculous, and threw it in the wastebasket. She had been thanked, properly and formally. Whatever she had felt for him, even without knowing it, was as healed as her incision. She nearly laughed at how stupid she had been, and hoped he hadn't thought she was flirting with him. And what if she was? How stupid would that be? Very, she told herself, as Jade walked into the room and saw her confused expression.

"Is something wrong?" She knew her well.

"No, not at all," Timmie insisted, as much to convince herself as her assistant.

"Your next appointment is here. The marketing people you asked David to set you up with. They're five minutes early. Do you want me to hold them, or are you ready to see them?"

Timmie hesitated, resisting an overwhelming urge to fish the card with the sunset on it out of the garbage. She was being ridiculous and she knew it. She couldn't allow herself to even think about him, and she wouldn't. But for an insane moment, she felt a pang of missing him, and all the time they'd spent talking to each other. It was crazy. She left the card in the wastebasket and looked straight at Jade with a serious expression, trying to focus on what she was saying. "Send them in," Timmie said, as Jade turned and left the room, and Timmie thought again about the note he'd written her. It was just a thank-you note from a French doctor. That was all it had ever been, or ever could be. And above all, she was absolutely certain it meant nothing, neither to him, nor to her.

Chapter 7

Timmie spent the next two weekends with Zack, and had a surprisingly good time with him. They went to an art fair, and to a movie preview she'd gotten tickets to, where he got his photograph taken with her, which always meant a lot to him. They went to the opening of a restaurant, spent time at the beach, and once in the course of each weekend, they made love, which was a lot for them. And they went back to their own lives, as always, on Sunday night. The rest of what happened in her life, she could handle herself. She had Jade and David to support her on business issues, department heads, managing consultants, advisers, and attorneys. All she needed from Zack was exactly what he was providing, a warm body in her bed on weekends, someone to share popcorn with at the movies, and a friend to make her laugh. She expected little of him. Too little, as far as Jade was concerned. She loved and admired Timmie profoundly and hated to see her settle for as little as Zack offered. She thought Zack was selfish, an opportunist, and a spoiled brat. Jade kept her mouth shut about it with Timmie, but was candid with David about it whenever the subject came up.

"He drives me nuts," Jade said honestly one afternoon, when they were both eating deli takeout in David's office at three o'clock. They hadn't had five minutes to stop before that. Timmie had finally gotten out of the building to meet with lawyers and their CFO downtown, about making some changes in their pension fund. "I hate the fact that she's willing to settle for a guy like Zack," Jade said with a mouth full of her egg salad sandwich, while David devoured his pastrami on rye. He was starving, but hadn't had a minute to stop to eat all day until Timmie left. She just kept fielding balls at him that never stopped, but it was what he loved best about his job. He knew he was learning things and getting opportunities he would never have had otherwise, even if he had to go at two hundred miles per hour most of the time to keep up with Timmie, who went twice as fast.

"The guy is such an asshole, such a zero." Jade continued her perennial list of complaints about Zack.

"Come on, Jadie. Don't be so tough on him. He's not a bad guy, he's just not a genius. Look, he's an actor and a model, a pretty face with a great body, that's why she likes him. What do you expect?"

"I'd like to see her with a man with brains and a heart, and maybe even balls. She needs a mensch, and he's just not."

David smiled at the Yiddish expression. Although Jade's origins were Asian, she had picked up a lot of Jewish expressions when she worked on Seventh Avenue in New York, where Timmie had met and hired her. She loved saying they were in the "schmatta" business, the rag trade. David always said Jade knew more Yiddish than his grandmother, who had grown up in Pasadena and married an Episcopalian. But he knew what Jade meant by a "mensch." She wanted Timmie to be with a man who had spine, heart, integrity, and guts. Zack didn't fit the bill, but David thought he was harmless, and Timmie had few illusions about him, if any, although he and Jade both agreed that Zack was out for what he could get. He wanted publicity and social and professional opportunities, and was always hitting Timmie up to be seen with him in places where his association with her, personal or otherwise, would do him some good. His ambitions on that score were fairly up-front. But Timmie protected herself well. She knew the type.

"At least he doesn't hit her up for money, or try to get her to set him up in business." They both knew the last one had. He had wanted Timmie to finance an art gallery for him, so he could sell his own art. She had gracefully bowed out, and spent the next year and a half alone, until Zack came along.

At first Zack had been funny, charming, handsome, and showered her with flowers and small gifts until she'd finally agreed to go out with him, and now they'd been a weekend item for nearly five months. If this relationship followed the course of her others, both David and Jade knew it wouldn't last for long. Sooner or later he'd push his luck, become too obvious in his manipulations, put too much pressure on her, or cheat on her with someone else, and she would quietly move on, unless he did first. They had none of the real glue that held people together, the deep respect, the understanding, the solid building of a foundation that would support them through good times and storms. All they had was fun sometimes. She no longer wanted to count on anyone but herself.

"I don't know why she can't find a real one, someone her own age, whose life is more like hers and who's worthy of her." None of her entourage thought much of Zack.

"Come on," David said, finishing the pickles that had come with his pastrami, and reaching for one of hers. He always ate her pickles, in exchange for some of his chips. It was their standard trade. "We'd all like to find that. So would I. Who has time? We work fifteen-to-twenty-hour days, put out forest fires, travel all over the world. Shit, I haven't had a girlfriend in two years, and the minute I meet someone, Timmie sends me to Malaysia for a month, or I wind up in New York solving problems for our ad agency, and then I'm running around Paris and Milan, chasing models with their tits exposed on and off runways, and helping them do their hair. And I'm straight, for chrissake. What 'equal' woman is going to put up with that? They want me around to take them out to dinner on Friday night, and go skiing with them on weekends. I haven't been skiing since I left college, although I made reservations at Tahoe six times last year, and had to cancel every time. I haven't had a vacation in three years. And Timmie works ten times harder than either of us. What guy is going to put up with that? The guys she should be with have their own female Zacks, for exactly the same reasons. A pretty face, a great body, and a hassle-free weekend when they have time. I think it just looks worse when it's a guy. We're not shocked when we see women like that. If Timmie were a man, and Zack were a woman, I don't think it would bother you at all."

"Yes, it would," Jade persisted. "She's so much better than that. You know it too. I just don't like what Zack stands for, and the fact that he's totally out for himself. I didn't ask her, but I'll bet you my Christmas bonus, he didn't even call her in Paris when she was sick. He wasn't around when she got home. He doesn't give a shit about anyone but himself." David didn't disagree, as he watched Jade eat his chips.

"It's the nature of the beast. None of us has a shot at meeting great people when you work as hard as this. Real people want more than we have to give. I don't have the time or the energy, and I'm thirty-two years old. Just how much do you think Timmie has to give a man in her life? She knows it, I know it, so do you. Maybe that's why you wound up with a married guy for ten years. A real one would have expected to see you more than once a week, when he could sneak out." He had hit a nerve, and Jade was silent for a minute, thinking about it, and then shook her head.

"That's not what it was about for me with Stanley. I loved him. He lied to me. Worse yet, he lied to himself. He kept promising me he'd get out of his marriage. He didn't, and then his wife got sick. Both his daughters became bulimic and wound up on antidepressants when he said he wanted a divorce. His father had open-heart surgery, and his son went to rehab for a year. His business went to shit. Everything went wrong, and it still is. One of his daughters is on drugs, and now his wife has cervical cancer and had a hysterectomy. They've all been living in hospitals for the past ten years, and he kept asking me to wait for one crisis after another. How the hell could I compete with that? Maybe if I'd stuck it out . . . I don't know . . ." She still got tears in her eyes when she thought about it. She had nearly committed suicide over him the last time he'd told her he couldn't leave his family and his wife. Her latest shrink had finally helped her get out. Even she knew she had to by then, to save her own skin and sanity. Ten years was long enough. And David had agreed. As much as he believed Stan loved her, he was never going to get out. But he also knew what he'd have been getting with Jade, and David suspected it hadn't been enough for him. She said she wanted a husband and babies, but she also wanted a career. Stanley wanted a full-time wife, and stayed with the one he had.

"So when are we going to get you on the Internet?" David sat back in his desk chair with a grin, changing the subject from the ever-painful topic of Stanley. Jade had been bitter ever since, and was always ready and willing to launch on a tirade about the evils of married men. According to her, one woman in a million got the guy in the end, the rest wasted years of their lives, and missed all the opportunities to meet the right guy while they lavished their time on a man who was never going to leave his wife.

"I'm ready when you are," she said about the Internet with a nervous smile, and then she frowned. "How do we know they're not married, and lying about being single?" She trusted no one now, although Stanley had never lied to her about that. He hadn't even promised for certain that he'd get out. He had just said he'd try. And she had been willing to take the risk. She'd forgotten that part over the years. But she was no longer willing to take that chance, which David thought was wise.

"You just have to check them out, and trust your instincts. That's all any of us can do. You can run a check on him later, if it makes you feel better. You can hire a PI. Some people do. But at least Internet dating broadens the pool." She glanced at her watch in answer to what he had just said.

"Okay. Show me." She pointed at his computer with a mischievous grin. She was ready. The time was now.

"Now? Are you serious?" David looked a little shocked.

"Yes, I am. Timmie won't be back till five o'clock, and she won't care. We cleared her desk before she left. I have three letters she doesn't need me to do till tomorrow. Okay, Maestro, introduce me to Internet dating. What the hell, it can't be any worse than what I dig up on my own. If I get fixed up on another blind date with a lemon, I may throw up."

He smiled as he turned to his computer and brought one of the better-known matchmaking services up on his screen. It was the one he had previously used, although he hadn't bothered to use it in about a year, for all the reasons he had mentioned over lunch. Mostly, no time. He had actually corresponded with a woman he had met through the personals section in the Harvard alumni magazine. She had just graduated from business school, and lived in San Francisco. They had met once, but as he put it after they met, she was "too granola" for him, although the smartest girl he'd ever met. She had moved to Berkeley shortly after that, had written to him, and said she was now in a committed relationship with a woman. Clearly, she had not been his destiny, nor he hers. He had written her back and wished her the best of luck, and had been too busy to think about it, or pursue others since. He was in no rush to find a relationship, although he wanted to get married and have kids eventually. He preferred the Jewish Internet dating service, because in his heart of hearts, he wanted to meet a nice Jewish girl. But he chose a service with a broader client base for Jade, and asked her several specific questions about age preference, and geographical location.

"What do you mean?" She looked momentarily confused. The process seemed exciting, but still somewhat scary to her. "Like what city?"

"More specific," David said as he waited to type it in. "How close to where you live? How wide a radius? Same city, same zip code, ten miles from where you live, five, one? Same state? Anywhere in the country? Major cities?"

"Shit, I don't know. What about the Greater L.A. area? Is that too broad?" The possibilities appeared to be endless. She was more interested in educational background and profession. She admitted to being a job snob, and had gone to U.C. Berkeley herself.

"That's up to you. I like same zip code, because I'm lazy about sitting around in gridlock on the freeway, and I don't want to spend an hour picking up a date. But I'm not exactly committed to the project either. I just do it to keep my hand in, so I don't forget how to date. And I haven't done it in a while."

"Let's stick with Greater L.A.," she said, feeling as though she were ordering from Groceries Express, which was how she got her food delivered. She ordered it by phone from the office, and had her doorman put it in her fridge when it arrived. The world was set up for busy people who no longer had time to attend to the menial tasks of life, between demanding jobs, travel, weekend projects, and whatever time was left over spent at the gym.

After typing in what she wanted, along with an age range of thirty-five to fifty-two, a series of photographs came up, almost like a menu, and David motioned to her to bring her chair closer so she could check out what was on his screen. There were long rows of photographs of men, some funny-looking, some handsome, and some in between, with descriptions they had written of themselves. Some sounded embarrassingly stupid, to the point of being absurd. "Hot Sexy Dad" made Jade groan as David explained that some of their answers and descriptions were formulated by checking off a box. When she liked one of the photos and brief descriptions, they pulled up a more detailed profile, which stated their religious preference, sexual habits, previous marital history, number of children, what sports they spent time doing, whether or not they had tattoos or piercings, and what they were looking for in a woman. Some wanted the same religion, Olympic-class athletic prowess, or made reference to sexual fantasies. They mentioned their professions, and some referred to salary range, again selected by clicking a box, if one chose to, and educational background. And then they wrote a brief paragraph about themselves, most of which made Jade wince. But there were six she liked from what she'd seen. They looked nice, sounded sane, had decent jobs and educations, two were divorced with young kids, which wasn't her preference but was acceptable to her, and all six said they were looking for a professional woman in her age range, liked to travel, were looking for committed relationships, and said they wanted to marry eventually and have kids. One said he preferred Asian women, which she considered a yellow flag but not a red one, in case he had illusions about finding someone submissive. One had even graduated from Berkeley the same year she had, but his photograph didn't look familiar, and with a student body of nearly forty thousand at U.C. Berkeley, that was hardly surprising. He was an architect and lived in Beverly Hills.

"What's wrong with all these people that they can't find dates?" Jade asked David, looking suspicious, and he laughed at her.

"Who was it who said any club that would have me, I wouldn't want to belong to? It was either Woody Allen, or Mark Twain, I think. Look, they're all in the same boat we are. We work our asses off, don't have time, are sick of the weirdos our friends fix us up with, we don't have relatives who fix us up with their friends' sons or daughters, and if we do, we wish they wouldn't. What do I know? This seems to work for a lot of people. It's worth a shot. I've hit a couple of lemons when I tried it, but most of the women I met through Internet dating were actually very nice. One or two of them might have been serious options, I just didn't have the time, or the inclination to get serious. But I had a nice time with the women I went out with. You follow the rules. You contact them through their box on the Internet, you don't give them your home address or phone number, or even the office at first. You meet in a public place a few times, you feel them out, follow your instincts, and don't put yourself in any scary or potentially dangerous situations. And you see how it shakes out. What have you got to lose?"

"Not much, I guess," Jade said, still unsure, but definitely intrigued. Enough so to check it out.

"Do you want to write to any of the six guys? You can do that on my account. But if you want to do this seriously, you need to put your own picture and profile up. You can do it in a protected way, where only the people you want to give it to can check it out. You don't have to put your photo up on the main lists. So do you want to write to these guys?"

She nodded, looking pensive. So far, from his description, she liked the architect best. He said he was divorced, had been married for six years, and had no kids. He lived in Beverly Hills. His passion was European literature and art, which she had majored in at school. And his favorite cities were Paris, Venice, and New York, which hit two out of three for her. It definitely narrowed the field. Far more than her friends had been able to do. His favorite weekends were skiing, camping, theater, movies, or cooking with the woman he went out with, or even for her if she couldn't cook, which Jade said was a good thing. Her culinary skills were limited to Cup A Soup and Top Ramen or salads she brought home from Safeway. And Hostess Twinkies when no one was looking. She always kept one in her desk for emergencies, along with a bag of M&Ms, when she didn't have time to eat. Health food, as she called it. All six men sounded interesting to her, and she slid her chair over closer to David, and answered each of them with a brief message about herself. She realized that she had to subscribe to the dating service herself, and open her own account, in order to provide them with a profile and pictures, but she wanted to see what kind of responses she got before she did.

She had just finished sending off the last e-mail, and was both nervous and excited as David grinned and she giggled, when Timmie walked in.

"What are you two kids up to?" she asked. She had seen the mischievous look on the faces of both of her assistants. She was sure that whatever it was, it was harmless. And it did them good to take a break when she was out, once in a while. There were no major crises at the moment, and she looked relaxed too. Her legal meetings about the pension fund had been informative and had gone well. "Okay, fess up. You look like two cats who ate the canary," she said, smiling at them.

"Not one canary. Six," Jade confessed. She knew Timmie was leery of dating services, Internet or otherwise, but Jade had no secrets from her.

"Explain that," Timmie said, and then saw what was on the screen. There were rows of photographs of men with a few lines of description, and she looked at both of them with a motherly expression. "Watch out, you two! No ax murderers, please. I need you both."

Jade wanted to tell her to try it too, but she knew Timmie couldn't. Even if she didn't give her real name, her face was known all over the world, and she was a very distinctive-looking woman. The long red hair and green eyes would have given her away anywhere, and her face had appeared in articles and ads for years. She was a success story in business schools everywhere, and an icon in the fashion world. She would have wound up in the tabloids in about ten minutes if she put her photograph up on an Internet dating service, or even discreetly with a matchmaker, which were becoming the rage too.

The era of mail-order brides had been modernized and come into its own again, which only proved how hard it was for anyone to meet a mate these days, no matter how young, good-looking, or successful you were. The men Jade had written to all fit into that category and all claimed they were looking for long-term relationships and obviously hadn't been able to find them on their own. Timmie was not unique in her inability to find an equal partner, although her limitations were more specific, due to age and fame. She had a handicap, and had to settle for what she could find on her own, which wasn't much, as witnessed by the likes of Zack and the men who had come before him in the past eleven years. And Timmie hadn't been willing to go on blind dates for years. She said they were too humiliating and too much trouble.

"Just be careful," Timmie reminded her, and then went back to her own office, as Jade followed her.

David had promised to let Jade know if any responses came in. He said he'd check his e-mail over the weekend. Jade grinned excitedly as she went to go over some notes with Timmie, who seemed in good spirits too.

She left the office at six o'clock, which was early for her, and Zack showed up around seven. It was the week before Thanksgiving, and they had a quiet weekend planned. She had plans the following day, even though it was Saturday, and Zack was good-natured about it. He knew that roughly once or twice a month she had commitments that kept her busy on Saturday mornings and into the early afternoon. She said it was related to work, and it gave him a chance to go to the gym, or work out at her place, and have lunch with friends.

They had dinner at the Little Door that night, which was one of her favorite places, and went to a movie afterward. They saw a thriller Zack had wanted to see. Timmie didn't love it, and on the way out afterward she teased him that the popcorn had been good at least. She didn't mind how bad the movie was, it was fun being out with him. And they were both in a good mood. He had gotten a minor acting job that week, and was waiting to hear about a major national commercial that could open other doors to him. He was always happy when he got work, and depressed when he got passed over. It was the nature of what he did. He was lucky he looked as young as he did, and she knew he'd gotten help with that. He had had his eyes done several years earlier, and got Botox shots regularly. He had had collagen shots, and lightened his hair. He wasn't quite as naturally blond as he looked, and he was far vainer than she was. She had never done any of that to herself, nor would she. She was far more willing to age gracefully, and her work didn't depend on it as his did.

Timmie was up at seven o'clock on Saturday morning. She worked out in the gym for half an hour, showered, and made herself a light breakfast of yogurt, cereal, and tea, and she was just about to leave the house when Zack came downstairs with a towel around him. He kissed her lightly on the lips, picked up the newspaper, and headed for the kitchen. It was a peaceful little domestic scene, which gave her the illusion of intimacy with him, which was more fantasy than fact.

"I left you a pot of coffee," she called back to him.

"Thanks. What time will you be finished?"

"I should be back here by three," she answered.

"I'll meet you here," he said easily. He knew where the key was, and she closed the front door gently behind her. It always intrigued her that he never asked her what she did on the Saturday mornings she didn't spend with him. He figured it was her business. He didn't tell her everything he did either. The time she was gone never seemed that long to him. He didn't mind her being busy.

She had left the house in jeans, sneakers, and an old sweater with a denim jacket over it, her hair pulled back in a ponytail. She wore no makeup, and looked surprisingly good, given the hour of the morning. She rarely worried about her looks, and as a result looked beautiful and real, despite her age.

She drove to Santa Monica, listening to music and smiling to herself. She felt good. She loved the mornings she spent like this, and looked forward to them for weeks. She didn't have time to do it often, but she carved out time whenever she could. It fed her soul, and was something she wanted to give back to the world, although it gave just as much to her, sometimes more. She knew this was something she could never give up, for anyone. It touched the deepest part of her heart.

Twenty minutes after she left Bel Air, she pulled up in front of a freshly painted building. It was a Victorian house that had obviously been renovated and enlarged. It had an old-fashioned front porch, and a bicycle rack out front, well stocked with bright new bikes. There was a handsome climbing structure in back. It was obviously a house inhabited by kids, and she smiled as she let herself in through the unlocked front door. Two women with weathered faces, kind eyes, and short hair were talking in the front hall, and another sat at a desk.

"Good morning, sisters," Timmie said easily. The two women talking to each other were considerably older than she was, while the one at the desk looked like a kid herself. All three were nuns, although nothing about their dress would have suggested it. They were wearing sweatshirts and jeans. They looked up with broad smiles as Timmie walked in. "How's everyone?"

"We thought you'd come today," the oldest of the three women said. She had been in a Carmelite order in her youth, and had left them to join the Dominicans, and work in Watts. She had worked with underprivileged inner-city kids for forty years, first in Chicago, then in Alabama and Mississippi, and finally in L.A. She ran the house they called St. Cecilia's.

It was a home for children who had been orphaned but for one reason or another, often health issues or age, were ineligible or inappropriate for adoption, or had been unsuccessful in being adopted out of the system, and had also not done well in foster care. It had been Sister Anne's idea from the beginning, and having heard of Timmie's charitable bent and soft spot for children years before, she had come to present her dream to her. She had never expected what had happened next. Without a word of explanation or argument, Timmie had written a million-dollar check and handed it across her desk, to buy the house, staff it, and run it. That had been ten years before, and she had supported it ever since. St. Cecilia's existed on the benevolence of Timmie O'Neill, although that fact was kept strictly confidential. Only David and Jade knew of her involvement with them. Timmie didn't like recognition for the charitable works she did.

The house was run by six nuns, and inhabited by anywhere from eighteen to twenty-five kids. There were twenty-one there at the moment, and she knew that two more were due in within the next few weeks. They ranged in age from five to eighteen. The balance of sexes was always about equal, as was the racial balance. It varied, and some of the children had been there for as long as five years. Their goal was always to place the children, if possible, but by the very nature of the situations that brought them there, most stayed at St. Cecilia's for several years. Their longest-term resident had been a blind girl who had been with them for seven years, and had graduated and been accepted at USC on a scholarship the year before, with Timmie's help. She had been impossible to place through the system, and St. Cecilia's had been a haven and godsend for her, as it was for the others. There were three children who had juvenile diabetes, which made them equally difficult to place, and another with emotional problems as a result of severe abuse. Several had been chronic bed-wetters when they arrived, for similar reasons, and had stopped wetting their beds within months. Some just weren't attractive children, others had been oppositional. Several had stolen from their foster parents and been sent to juvenile hall. Some were just extremely shy, or didn't get along with their foster families' natural kids. Whatever their reasons, they had been rejected again and again, and sent back like fish thrown into a pond of rejects, and one by one the sisters who ran the house had lovingly fished them out. They provided the children who lived there love, safety, and a good home.

Timmie loved coming to visit, and did so at every opportunity, almost always on Saturday mornings. The children all called her Timmie, and even they had no idea what her connection to the house was, or that she was in fact providing all the bounty that came to them, and their home.

"We heard you had your appendix out in Paris," Sister Margaret said with a look of concern. She was the twenty-five-year-old nun at the front desk. She had gone into religious orders at eighteen, which was rare these days, and had only recently taken final vows. She had called Timmie's office to talk to Jade and check on when she was coming back from Europe, and they had all been worried and frightened to hear that she was sick. "How are you feeling?"

"Fine," Timmie said with a broad smile. "As good as new. Although it was a little scary when it happened. I'm okay now." She had forgotten about it entirely in the past two weeks. It was as though it had never happened. "Anyone new?" she asked with interest. She loved knowing which children were there, and why. She took a deep personal interest in each case. St. Cecilia's was dear to her heart, for reasons most people never knew, although years before she had told her own story to Sister Anne, as they worked side by side, restoring the house. She had helped them put the place together, only two years after her own son had died, and the year after Derek left. She readily admitted it had saved her life.

"We're still waiting for the two new kids to arrive, but I don't think they'll be here till next week. There's been some sort of technical delay in the system. We're trying to get them here by Thanksgiving." The holiday was only five days away. They fought hard to pull kids out of the system, and give them a home that could potentially change their lives, and almost always did. Once in a while, it was too late, and the children sent to them were too hardened, too damaged, or too sick, and had to be placed in medical facilities that offered either medical or psychiatric treatment that they could not. St. Cecilia's wasn't a jail or a hospital or a psych ward for children, it was in fact a loving home, provided for them by Timmie, where the children who lived there could thrive and enjoy opportunities, both educational and emotional, that they would never have had otherwise. It was what she wished she had had forty years before, and would have altered the course of her life at the time.

As she always did, she wandered through the house all morning, stopped and talked to the children who were familiar to her, and tried to become acquainted with those who had arrived in the past month or two, whom she had seen, but not yet talked to. She approached them all with respect and caution, and gave them the choice as to whether they wanted to open up to her or not. And after that, she sat on the porch with the nuns, and watched the younger ones play in the back garden, while the older ones went off to visit friends or do weekend jobs. It was just like having twenty-one children, with all the work, patience, and understanding that entailed, and love.

Just before lunchtime, one of the children she knew well came and talked to her. He was nine years old, an African American boy with one arm. His father had beaten him so badly, and then shot him and his mother, that the child had lost his arm. The mother had died, and the father had gone to prison for life. Jacob had been with them since he was five, and managed extremely well with one arm. He had come to them straight from the hospital after the shooting. The social workers in foster care had felt it was pointless to try and place him through them. He was unable to be adopted, as his father refused to sign the relinquishment papers, but he would have been nearly impossible to place anyway. The nuns of St. Cecilia's had been quick to embrace him and bring him home. He handed Timmie a drawing he had made, of a cat with purple hair and a big smile. Those who had been at St. Cecilia's for a long time were, for the most part, happy kids. You could easily see the ones who were recently arrived, who still looked frightened, and had wounded eyes. It took time for them to understand that they were safe, after the terrors many of them had survived.

"Thank you, Jacob," Timmie said, smiling at him, holding the drawing. "Does the cat have a name?"

"Harry," Jacob said, looking pleased. "He's a magic cat. He speaks French."

"Really? I was just in France last month. In Paris. I had my appendix out," she informed him, and he nodded, with a serious expression.

"I know. Did it hurt when they took it out?"

"No, they put me to sleep. And then it just hurt for a few days after that. They were very nice to me in the hospital. And everyone spoke English, so it was okay. I wasn't scared." He nodded, satisfied with the information, and then went back to play.

Timmie stayed through lunch, and chatted with the nuns, whose company she had enjoyed over the years. Some had moved on to other positions and programs elsewhere, but most had stayed. One had gone to South America to work with Indian children in Peru the year before, and one had gone to Ethiopia shortly after they started, but other than that, the nuns at St. Cecilia's loved the children and the work, and had been there for years.

It was two o'clock when she left and drove back to Bel Air. She felt happy and peaceful as she always did when she visited them. Zack was watching a video when she got back. He didn't ask and she didn't tell him where she'd been. It was a private joy for her that she never shared. She wanted no publicity for it, no attention, no awards, no recognition, no kudos. It was just something she did, that meant the world to her.

"I called you on your cell phone. They're having a sale at Fred Segal's. I wanted to know if you wanted to meet me there."

"I turned off my phone," she said, smiling at him. She always did when she went to visit the children. She didn't want any interruptions when she was there. She liked giving them her full attention. "I'm sorry. Do you want to go now, or head to the beach?" She was his for the rest of the weekend, and didn't really care what they did. It was cold in the city, and she knew it would be windy and chilly at the beach.

"Let's go to the sale," he said, looking pleased. He turned off the movie, while she went to get a drink of water, and five minutes later they were in her Mercedes heading for Fred Segal. She never said it, but she thought his ancient Porsche was a death trap, and he kept it in poor repair since he couldn't afford to do otherwise. He liked driving her car. It was the latest sports car. She had treated herself to it that summer. It handled beautifully as they headed down Melrose. And when they got there, Fred Segal was a zoo. It always was when they had sales, but Zack managed to find a stack of things he liked, and Timmie found some things too, some cashmere sweaters with hoods for the beach, a gold Marni jacket she could wear with jeans to the office, and two pairs of shoes. They both looked delighted as they headed to the car with their spoils. He had paid for most of his own, except a leather jacket that he fell in love with and couldn't afford, so she got it for him. He was thrilled with the gift. She had also bought some coffee table books, and they had gotten takeout pasta at the deli so they didn't have to cook dinner that night. It had been a perfect afternoon. Zack settled back in front of the TV to finish his movie as soon as he got home, while Timmie read several copies of *The Wall Street Journal* she'd been saving all week. She liked catching up on her reading on weekends.

As the movie ended, Zack looked over at her and laughed. "Shit, Timmie, I love you, but you really are a guy." He didn't mean it quite the way it sounded, and she looked up at him in surprise. It didn't sound like a compliment to her.

"What does that mean?"

"How many women do you know who read *The Wall Street Journal?*"

"A lot actually," she said, trying not to wince at the sexist comment. In addition to which, how many women ran corporations the size of hers? In many ways, she was one of a kind. And the morning she had spent with the children at St. Cecilia's made her even more special, but he had no idea about that. She wondered after his somewhat unflattering comment if his viewing her "as a guy" was why they so rarely made love. It suddenly made her feel insecure about herself. "Why does reading *The Wall Street Journal* make me 'a guy'?"

"Look at you, you're a business mogul. You have about a million employees in I don't know how many countries, and you're a household name. How many women ever come close to that? They stay home and have kids, or work as secretaries, or get their tits redone. Women just don't think like you do, or act like you do, or work like you do. Don't get me wrong, I like it. But it would scare the shit out of most guys," he said honestly as she sighed, and looked sad. What he had just said confirmed what she had believed for years. Apparently she was right.

"It always has," she said mournfully. "I guess they don't get it, that you can be successful and work your ass off in a man's world, and still be a woman. I don't see why it has to be either-or."

"You wouldn't. That's what I mean. You're a guy." It was depressing to hear, although not news to her. She was sure most men who met her felt that way, although they didn't say it out loud, like Zack. "It's okay," he reassured her, "I like you just as you are." But he didn't love her. That was the whole point. Men never had, and never would. Her husband had left with another man, and all the men she'd met since either tried to take advantage of her, or ran like hell. Or felt like Zack, that she was nice, but Zack was as likely to fall head over heels in love with her as he was to grow wings and fly. She didn't want him to anyway, she reminded herself. And a little while later she put the pasta they had bought in the microwave. His comment had upset her considerably, and hurt her feelings, although she didn't point it out to him. She didn't like showing him her vulnerable side. Instead, she asked him what he was doing for Thanksgiving, and he surprised her by saying he was leaving town. It hadn't occurred to her to ask him before. She had assumed he'd be around, and she had nowhere to go.

"You are? You didn't tell me that." She tried not to look hurt, but was. She forgot sometimes how unattached they were to each other, and how limited their relationship was. In effect, it was a five-month two-night stand.

"You didn't ask. I'm flying up to Seattle, and having Thanksgiving at my aunt's. I go up there every year, unless I have something to do here. You never said anything, so I figured you had plans." She noticed that he didn't invite her to come to Seattle. And in fact, she had no plans of her own. She had no family at all, just friends and work.

"Are you doing something special?" he asked with a look of interest. He might have been willing to forgo Thanksgiving at his aunt's for a holiday meal with one of her celebrity friends.

"Actually, I'm not," she said simply. Holidays were always painful for her, for obvious reasons, and she tried not to think of them till the last minute, when the inevitable had to be faced. This year had been no different, and she'd been too busy to think about it for the past few weeks. Denial was a wonderful thing. She had somehow assumed that since they had a weekend relationship, she'd be with him on Thanksgiving. It wasn't entirely his fault that she hadn't mentioned it and he'd made other plans, although it would have been nice if he'd said something to her. They had been together for the past three weekends and he never said a word. "I don't usually do anything too exciting for Thanksgiving or Christmas. I'm not too keen on the holidays anymore." She didn't go into further detail, and in this case, less was more. He hadn't been in her life the year before, so he didn't know what her habits were.

"I don't like them much either, which is why I always go up to my aunt's." He didn't ask if she had anywhere else to go, and assumed she did. He couldn't imagine her enjoying Thanksgiving at his aunt's. She lived in a retirement community in Bellevue, outside Seattle, and her husband was a prison guard. It wasn't exactly high end, and he couldn't imagine Timmie participating in that, or how they would react to her. It was easier not to ask. "I probably won't come back till Monday. I hang out with my cousins when I'm up there. I hope you figure out something to do."

"Thanks," she said, trying not to look annoyed. In fact, she wasn't angry at him. She was saddened and slightly hurt. He hadn't even offered to come back for the weekend, after spending Thanksgiving with them. It told her a lot about what the relationship meant to him, and didn't. But if she was honest with herself, it didn't mean much more to her. It was just depressing to be alone on Thanksgiving. It wasn't his fault, or even hers. She should have thought of it sooner and made other plans.

The rest of the weekend was easy and peaceful. He went back to the TV while she did the dishes. They went to bed early that night, and he left the next morning after breakfast. He was going out with friends. It often happened that way when they didn't go to the beach. He usually left early, and made arrangements that didn't include her. It was yet another reminder of all they didn't share. Most of his friends were in their twenties and thirties, and Timmie had figured out early on that she and they had nothing in common. Zack was the only common link they shared, and he was far more at ease with them. It was an open secret between them that she didn't like his friends. They drugged, they drank, most of them were models and actors, working as waiters and bartenders in Hollywood, waiting for their big break. Even Zack was long of tooth to be in their midst, although he looked no older than they. He had long since invested considerable energy in remaining one of them. The forever Peter Pan. Being around them made Timmie feel old, and bored her to tears.

He called on Wednesday night before he left for Seattle, to wish her a happy Thanksgiving, which was nice at least, and she didn't tell him she had been unable to come up with anything to do. Everyone she knew was either busy or away. She'd had an extremely hectic week, and didn't have time to think of it or deal with it to any great extent. She said nothing to David or Jade either, as she knew they went to their families every year, and she didn't want to intrude. It was just going to be one of those off years.

Jade had been in high spirits in the office all week. She had heard from four of the six men she'd written to on the Internet. The other two hadn't picked up their e-mail yet. But four had answered, including the one she was convinced she would like most, the architect who had graduated from U.C. Berkeley the same year she had. She had a date with him the following week, for coffee at Starbucks, so they could check each other out, as David had suggested to her. And two more were asking to have lunch with her. She was having fun, for the first time in a while.

When Thanksgiving morning rolled around, Timmie lay in her bed, wide awake and staring at the ceiling. There was something very revealing about spending Thanksgiving alone. It reminded her of where her life had gone, and what she'd been doing with it recently. She'd been spending time with men who didn't care about her, weren't attached or connected to her, any more than she was to them, and without her office to go to, she had nothing to do. She didn't want to go to Malibu alone.

She dressed and put on jeans and a sweatshirt, while trying to figure out what to do with herself. There was a simple solution that came to her finally, as she sat watching the Macy's parade on TV alone in her living room, which seemed pathetic, even to her. She kept her gaze averted from the photograph of Mark on her bookcase, and from remembering that he would have been sixteen years old by now. Holidays always made her heart ache again with a vengeance, and she was determined not to let that happen, or to indulge herself by feeling sorry for herself. She picked up her bag and denim jacket and went out the door. She knew exactly where to go, and should have thought of it before.

She arrived just in time for Thanksgiving lunch at St. Cecilia's. The nuns looked surprised to see her, but gave her a warm welcome. She had never shared Thanksgiving with them before, but they were thrilled to see her, as were the children. She went home at five

o'clock, filled with turkey and stuffing, cranberry jelly, and sweet potatoes covered in marshmallow topping. It had been the perfect way
to spend the holiday. She was still coasting on the warm feelings of it
when she got home, and decided to call Zack on his cell phone to
wish him a happy Thanksgiving. He answered on the first ring, and
she could hear people talking and laughing in the background. He
told her they were at dinner, and he would call her later that evening.
He never did, nor for the rest of the weekend.

It was a statement about him, her life, and the decisions and
choices she had made for the last eleven years. It was something she
needed to see and think about. She wasn't sure what she should do
differently in the future, but she knew there was a message in it, and
it was a wake-up call to her. There was nothing malicious about Zack.
He just didn't care a lot about her. Nor she about him. Which made
her question what she was doing with him, and how many years she
was going to waste with men like him.

She spent the weekend cleaning out closets, reading *The Wall
Street Journal,* going over papers she had brought home with her, and
doing sketches for their summer line. All worthwhile activities, without question, and it was how she was going to spend the rest of her
life, if she didn't make some major changes soon. The question that
kept running through her mind was how. She wasn't even sure what
her options were, or if she had any. She spent a lot of time thinking
about it over the weekend, particularly when she realized again on
Sunday night that Zack had never called. His silence was deafening
and eloquent over the holiday weekend.

Chapter 8

It was Thursday, a full week after Thanksgiving, before Zack called. It was a clear message to Timmie. Several of them in fact. The first one was that he wasn't all that crazy about her, which was hardly a news flash, particularly if he thought of her as a "guy." And the other was that if she didn't actively do something about it, Christmas was going to look a lot like Thanksgiving, and she wanted to do whatever she could to avoid that. She broached the subject with Zack on Saturday afternoon in Malibu, where they were spending the weekend. He made no reference to the fact that he hadn't called her over Thanksgiving, nor did she. In fact, he never even bothered to ask her what she did. He obviously felt that her holidays were not his problem, nor did he feel any inclination to include her in his. It was a powerful statement to her.

"What are you doing over Christmas?" Timmie asked him, as they started thinking about dinner. It was raining so they couldn't barbecue, and she had offered to cook pasta for him, which he declined. He was dieting and said he didn't want to eat carbs, so he offered to make a big salad for both of them, which suited her. She wasn't hungry anyway.

"I don't know. I haven't made plans yet," he said in answer to her question. "Why? What did you have in mind?" He made it sound like he was open to the best offer, but she didn't care how he viewed it. She had no intention of spending Christmas alone. Her whole purpose in being involved with him was to avoid solitude at crucial times, like Christmas and Thanksgiving. For the moment, her plan was not going well.

"I always get sick in Mexico," she said as she followed him into the kitchen, "and the Caribbean is a hell of a long way and hard to get to from the West Coast. The weather is unreliable in Florida this time of year, although South Beach is fun. What do you think of Hawaii?"

"Is that an invitation?" He looked up at her, pleased, as he took three kinds of lettuce and a bag of tomatoes out of the fridge.

"I think it is. How does that sound to you? We can leave on the twenty-third, and my office is closed till the third of January. That gives us eleven days. We could go to the Four Seasons on the Big Island, if I can get a room. Or maybe the Mauna Kea. The rooms aren't as up-to-date, but they have a terrific beach. I actually like it better there. You're never in the room anyway. It would be nice to get away."

"It sure would," he said, leaning over to kiss her. "Are you sure you wouldn't be missing something exciting here?"

"Nothing I know of, or care about. What about you?"

"I'm free as a bird." He looked delighted, and she was pleased. Christmas was going to be a lot better than Thanksgiving. This was exactly why she was going out with him. He wasn't the man of her dreams, but he was an antidote to solitude. And not being alone over the holidays was important to her, particularly given the painful memories she tried to dodge every year, which was challenging at best.

"I'll see what I can reserve this week." She was planning to give the project to Jade.

"You know, I just had an idea," he said casually, as he put the lettuce in a colander to wash it. "What about St. Bart's, in the Caribbean? So what if it takes us two days to get there. I hear it's great, and we've got eleven days. What do you think?"

"Too far to go," she said practically. "I've been there. We'd have to spend a night in Miami each way, and I hate the little plane you have to take. It's the only way to fly in to St. Bart's, and it scares the shit out of me. The weather's not that reliable in the Caribbean this time of year either. I vote Hawaii." She didn't point out to him that since she was paying, and inviting him, she had the only legal vote. She didn't want to be rude to him. But in fact that was the deal. Her credit card, her choice.

"Maybe you should check it out," he persisted, as he spun the lettuce to dry it. "That's where everybody who's anybody goes." He was still pushing for St. Bart's.

Timmie laughed at what he said, not sensing how serious he was about it. "That sounds like a great reason not to go. I don't want to run into everyone I know from L.A., which is exactly what happened the last time I was there. St. Bart's is actually a lot more fun if you're on a boat, and can escape." But there was no way she was going to charter a yacht, and spend exorbitant amounts of money for a brief vacation with him. For a honeymoon maybe, but not eleven days over the holidays with Zack, who hadn't even bothered to call her on Thanksgiving. She hadn't completely lost her mind. All she wanted was a nice, easy trip.

"Are any of your friends going to be there on yachts?" He clearly had a serious interest in St. Bart's, or whoever would be there. Timmie knew a lot of fancy movie people went to St. Bart's. It was definitely one of the hot spots in the world.

"Probably," she said quietly. "But I have no desire to get trapped on a boat with a bunch of movie stars from L.A. I can't think of anything worse." Nor he of anything better. But he couldn't figure out a way to convince her to fly in to St. Bart's over the Christmas holidays, and he backed down gracefully when Timmie continued not to warm to the idea.

"It's going to be great," he said to her, as they ate their salad. She was actually looking forward to the trip with him, and agreed. He was fun when you spoiled him a little and indulged him. And he was very nice about thanking her while they did the dishes together, and he made love to her that night. Clearly, he liked the plan, and was touched that she had suggested it to him.

Timmie told Jade about it the next day, and asked her to see what she could do about a reservation at the Four Seasons on the Kona Coast. An hour later, Jade told her they had plane reservations on the twenty-third, direct to Kona, and a suite at the Four Seasons. It wasn't their best one, but they had told her it was very nice, with a view of the ocean.

"That was easy," Timmie said, looking pleased, and she called Zack on his cell phone to tell him. "We're all set. Four Seasons. Hawaii. Eleven days of sunshine, rest, and great weather. We leave on the twenty-third. I can't wait."

"Me too," he said, sounding delighted, and she was relieved he didn't bring up St. Bart's again. She had no desire to go all that way, nor to fly in on the tiny plane that scared her to death. Hawaii was perfect. Wonderful weather, and easy to get to. Nothing better. They were leaving in three weeks, and she could avoid Christmas entirely by being somewhere where she didn't even have to look at Christmas trees, although she wanted to get Zack a gift, in addition to the trip.

She bought him a good-looking rubber and stainless-steel diving watch at Cartier, which would be great for the trip and thereafter.

"He's a lucky guy," Jade said drily when she saw the watch.

"Don't be such a sourball. It's Christmas," Timmie said, teasing her. "How was your date, by the way?" She hadn't heard the latest bulletin since the week before. The coffee date at Starbucks with the architect had gone well, and so had lunch with two of the others. She had eliminated the fourth one because she thought he sounded weird on the phone, and the other two had dropped out of sight, or actually never appeared. David said the ratio was about right. He said you had to contact five or six, or sometimes even seven, to find one you liked. So far so good.

"It was great," Jade said, beaming, and she refrained from commenting that she didn't think Zack deserved all that Timmie was doing for him. She was her boss after all. And at least Timmie wouldn't be alone over the holidays, which Jade knew would have been hard for her. But she and David talked about it after Timmie left the office that night.

"Look, it's a tough dilemma for her," David said compassionately. "It's something we all deal with at some point. Do you sit home like the Virgin Mary, waiting for Prince Charming to come along? Or do you go out with Prince Not-So-Charming, and at least get out of the house and have some fun while you wait for the right guy to come along?"

"And what if he never does?" Jade said, looking worried about their boss again.

"That, my dear, is why God created Internet dating. It'll improve your chances immeasurably. Ours anyway. Timmie's in a tough spot.

She just has to hope she gets lucky one day, and that the right guy will fall out of the sky into her lap." But like Timmie, neither of them expected it to happen. Timmie had been alone for too long. And she had nearly convinced them both that Mr. Right would never come along.

"It doesn't happen like that," Jade said sadly. She had been afraid for years now that Timmie would wind up alone. She worried about it more than Timmie, who said she had resigned herself years ago to ending her days alone. "I'm not even sure she cares anymore. She says she doesn't. But I hate thinking of her like that. No one deserves a nice person in their life more than she does. She takes care of everyone else, all of us, all those orphans she supports. Why the hell can't some intelligent guy see who she is and fall in love with her? He'd be one lucky man."

David looked pensive as he pondered the question. They were in complete agreement about the good luck Timmie deserved but hadn't had, either in regard to her husband or her son. She was lucky in business and with money, but not much else. "Maybe she needs to give up the guys like Zack in her life, to make room for the right one," David said, looking thoughtful. "Maybe guys like him take up valuable real estate in her life. There's no room for the right one to land." They both believed that if the right guy turned up, she'd dump Zack in a hot second. But meanwhile, she continued to hang on, no matter how inadequate Zack continued to prove he was. The threat of solitude, particularly over the holidays, was still worse, in Timmie's eyes. She knew that if she wound up alone over Christmas, she would be seriously depressed and she was willing to go to major lengths to avoid it, and even take Zack to Hawaii.

Timmie and Zack left for Hawaii the morning of December 23. The flight was short and smooth. They arrived in Kona four and a half hours later, and Jade had arranged for a car and driver to take them to the hotel. The suite was beautiful. It had big open spaces, a view of the ocean, and a terrace called a lanai. She and Zack sat and watched the sunset on the first day, and the air was cool. It was chillier than Timmie had expected it to be, but it was comfortable and romantic and relaxed. She suggested they have room service that night, but Zack wanted to go to the restaurant, to see who was there. Timmie didn't care. She hadn't come to Hawaii to see people, only to relax and be with him. But she indulged him, and they went out for dinner.

She wore a periwinkle-blue dress that was one of her own designs, with a matching cashmere shawl and gold sandals, long gold and diamond earrings, her hair down, and a gardenia behind her ear. She looked tropical and beautiful. Zack was wearing a red Hawaiian shirt, flip-flops, and white jeans, and looked sexier than ever. He was a striking-looking man, and would look even better in a day or two with a deep tan. It was an easy, pleasant evening, and they both went to bed early. Zack was disappointed he hadn't seen anyone important in the restaurant, and she suggested that more people would probably come just after Christmas or for New Year's.

The next day was brilliantly sunny, and there was a surprisingly strong wind. The pool attendants couldn't put the umbrellas up because of it, and Timmie braided her hair to keep it from flying all over the place. They had lunch at the golf restaurant, and Zack thought he recognized a well-known producer, but he disappeared again before they had finished lunch. And finally, they went back to their room to rest. It was the afternoon of Christmas Eve, and after dinner that night, Timmie gave him his gifts. She had given him a stack of their men's sportswear, and two beautiful medium-weight suits that he could wear in L.A. all year. And the Cartier diving watch, which he was crazy about. He thanked her profusely for her generosity and then handed her a small box. It was a beautiful simple gold bangle he had gotten for her at Maxfield's. It was the kind of thing she would wear constantly. They wished each other a Merry Christmas, and then sat on the lanai, looking at the moonlight on the ocean, and drinking champagne.

"This is perfect," Zack said happily. "Thanks for bringing me," he said, and sounded as though he meant it.

"It's a nice Christmas for me this way too," she said, smiling at him. He was easy to travel with, seemed grateful for the things she did for him, and she enjoyed his company. She knew she would have been miserable alone at home, engulfed in memories, solitary, and depressed for days. Coming to Hawaii had been the perfect idea.

They spent Christmas Day at the pool, and went to Waimea, up the mountain, to dinner at Merriman's that night. And they were talking about going to the beach at the Mauna Kea the next day, unless the surf was too rough. The wind had been strong for two days. And when they woke the next morning, they were disappointed to see that the sky was gray, and it started raining by late afternoon. It rained for the next three days. They stayed in their room, read, talked, watched TV, and ordered room service. Timmie didn't feel like going to the restaurant. They were cozy in their room.

The weather finally cleared the day before New Year's Eve, the wind died down, and the ocean was finally smooth. They took a cab to the Mauna Kea hotel, and lay on the beach. And at the restaurant at lunchtime, Timmie saw three major movie stars she knew. She casually said hello to them, introduced Zack, and then walked back to their chairs on the beach. She noticed when they sat down again, he looked seriously annoyed. She had no idea why he was suddenly in a bad mood.

"Is something wrong?" she asked innocently. He clearly had a problem.

Smoke was nearly coming out of his ears. "Why didn't you want to have lunch with them? They invited us to sit down," Zack said, looking petulant and irritated.

Timmie looked surprised both by his tone, and the look on his face. "We already ate. And I didn't want to intrude. They were just being polite. And I don't know them that well."

"They acted like you were old friends. They all kissed you, for chrissake. And one of them is producing a movie. He said so when you asked him what he's been doing."

"I kiss a lot of people, and I know a lot of people producing movies. That doesn't mean I want to have lunch with them. They're on vacation, Zack. So are we. I'd rather be with you than sit around for two hours watching them drink mai tais when we could be lying on the beach."

"I'd rather have had lunch with them. It may be no big deal to you, but it is to me." He looked furious, and as though she had robbed him of a golden opportunity. He didn't speak to her for the rest of the afternoon, and he went swimming by himself without asking if she wanted to come in. And afterward, he went snorkeling alone. He was still cool with her that afternoon when they went back to their hotel. It was not the first time, but it was a revelation of what mattered most to him. Meeting important people, showing off, and being seen. None of which mattered to her. But she knew that about him.

"Look, I'm sorry, Zack," she finally broached the subject with him again. "I like staying to myself on vacation. I don't need to see a lot of people, I just want to be with you." He didn't look impressed. It was in fact a compliment to him, that she preferred his company to that of other people she knew.

"Is that why you didn't want to go to St. Bart's?" he asked angrily. "Because that's where all the right people go. The people who want to see and be seen. This place is a dump," he said angrily. "There's no one here except fat suburbanites and their kids." Timmie looked shocked at what he said, and seriously annoyed. He was pushing his luck. She was willing to accept the fact that they had separate lives and liked different things, but she was not willing to put up with his being flat-out rude.

"Are you here for a vacation?" she asked him, "or are you looking to be discovered at the pool?" There was an edge to her voice as she said it, which he noticed and angered him even more.

"Maybe both," he said honestly. "What's wrong with that? You have a lot of opportunities to meet people that I don't. I have to use whatever chance I get. Networking is very important to me. Something major could have happened if we'd had lunch with those three guys today." She didn't tell him that if something major were going to happen to him, it would have happened a long time ago. He was already too old. At forty-one, he wasn't going to be discovered, and she didn't want him "networking" by using her to make connections on the beach. He was prying her eyes open to his motives, whether she wanted him to or not. What he was saying to her, and who he was showing himself to be, was impossible to ignore.

"Zack, nothing would have happened," she said quietly. "They're on vacation. So are we. Half the universe tries to take advantage of people like that. They don't want people working them, any more than I do. I hate it when people do that to me."

"Oh right, this is a special little club, isn't it? How could I forget? A secret society of famous people who protect each other and keep out riff-raff like me. Well, *pardon* me." He was shouting, and Timmie looked upset. She didn't like any of what he had just said. None of it was respectful or even polite. She had brought him on vacation, and he was using her. That much was obvious even to her. He had done it on a smaller scale before, though he had never been as blunt.

"That's a rotten thing to say, Zack. This isn't a special club. Sometimes successful or famous people come here, and famous people don't want to be used. No one does." And then she added softly, "Neither do I."

His eyes blazed. "Is that what you think I'm doing here? Using you? Hell, if I'm using you, I'm sure not getting a lot out of it, am I? Except a suntan and a few days on the beach. For chrissake, if you weren't such a fucking recluse, and so discreet all the time, and so afraid to be who you are, we could be in St. Bart's, having a hell of a lot more fun." She was shocked by everything he said. It was a major slap in her face, but maybe better to know what he thought of her. Apparently, not much.

"What did you expect to get out of this vacation," she asked him bluntly, "other than a suntan? Because frankly, that's all I had in mind. I didn't invite you here to be discovered, or network, or make contacts on the beach. I invited you to spend some time here with me, so we could relax and have some fun. Or is that too boring for you, since apparently you think I'm a recluse?" She was hurt by everything he had said. She knew he wasn't in love with her, she had no illusions on that score, nor was she in love with him. But everything he had said to her showed a blatant lack of kindness, affection, or respect.

"For chrissake, Timmie, you damn near are a recluse. You never go to anything you're invited to. You turn down practically every premiere, unless you think you have to go because Timmie O did the clothes. You never go to parties. You think you're too old to go to clubs and bars, which is utter crap. I'm practically your age, and I go all the time. All you do is hide in both your houses, and work your ass off. And now you want to sit in your room and hide here, instead of getting out, seeing who's here, and working the crowd a bit."

"I don't want to work the crowd, Zack," she pointed out to him.

"I'm one of the people who get worked, which is exactly why I don't go out very often. I'm not interested in showing off or being in the press. I've been there, done that. There's nothing in it for me. I have PR people to get my company in the press. I don't need to be in it my-self. Why? What's the point? They just say shit about me I don't like. If you want to work the crowd, as you put it, maybe you should be with someone else. Or pay your own way to St. Bart's." She knew the last was a low blow, below the belt, but she had had enough. It made it sound as though she had to make it worth his while to be there, or why bother being with her. She hated everything he had said. It was everything she was not. He had completely missed the point about who she was, and how she lived. Or maybe he hadn't. Actually, he had gotten some of it fairly accurately, but he had been vicious about the way he threw it at her. She felt as though she'd been slapped, and al-most wanted to do the same to him.

"Look, it was nice of you to bring me," he said, calming down a lit-tle. "I appreciate it. It's just that this isn't me. It may be you, but this place feels like a cemetery to me. And the only three people we met that I wanted to talk to, you blew off, and wouldn't sit down to lunch with them. Did you do that to screw me over, or prove how powerful you are, or did you honestly not figure out what a lunch like that could mean to my career?"

"What career?" she asked angrily. "You do commercials, and you're a model. You're forty-one years old, no matter how good you look. It's too late, Zack. No one is going to make you a big star."

"You don't know that," he said, even angrier than he'd been before. He didn't want to hear the truth from her. In his own eyes, he was still a boy.

"Yes, I do," Timmie said firmly. "I know Hollywood a lot better than you do."

"Like hell you do," he said angrily. "You're so dead and over the hill, you wouldn't know what they do in Hollywood if it bit you on the ass."

"That's enough," she said in a shaking tone, and walked back into their room from the lanai. It was half an hour later when he finally wandered in, and by then her bags were packed. He looked startled when he saw what she'd done. She had packed his bags as well. She had already called the desk. They were booked on the red-eye out of Honolulu that night. She wasn't staying with him after everything he had said, about her, and her way of life, and his reasons for being there. She had finally heard enough. There was no way to pretend now that he was even her friend. He wasn't. She knew he wasn't in love with her. But as it turned out, he didn't even like her. He was using her, which seemed to be his only reason for being with her at all, and he was furious that she hadn't helped him do it. She realized then that the past six months must have been not only boring, but frustrating for him.

"What are you doing?" he asked with a look of surprise. He was still wearing his wet bathing suit and a towel. She had left out jeans, a shirt, underwear, and flip-flops for him.

"We're leaving tonight," she said, heading for the bathroom to get dressed.

"Why?" He looked stunned.

"Are you kidding? Do you think I'm going to sit here and listen to that kind of shit from you, and stick around? You'll be back in L.A. tomorrow morning. You can still catch a flight to St. Bart's."

"You know I'm not going to St. Bart's." They both knew he couldn't afford the ticket. He had been mouthing off at her expense. And he had been cruel, and rude. And disrespectful. She had no intention whatsoever of staying there with him. Their relationship had been limited and never a dream come true for either of them, but he had never openly admitted to her before the degree to which he was using her, for connections, exposure, and future work. It was just too blatant for her now. She was done. There were no illusions left about what he was doing with her or why he stuck around.

"Whether you go to St. Bart's or not is up to you. I'm going home, and so are you."

"Don't make it such a big deal," he said, trying to cool her off. He clearly didn't want to cut the vacation short, but it was too late for that. And there were a lot of things about her he liked. The relationship offered him more than it did her. It always had.

"It may not be a big deal to you, but it is to me. You don't have to pretend you're madly in love with me, to hang around in my life. But you have to at least like me, and not just use me. And I don't think you ever did like me. And I'm even less sure now that I like you. Actually, right now I don't. You had a brat fit when I didn't take you to Europe, which I didn't owe you, by the way. We had been dating for exactly four months, and I didn't owe it to you to drag you through half the fancy hotels in Europe while I worked my ass off. You didn't call me in Paris when I was sick. And when I called you, you said you were glad I was, that it was what I deserved because I hadn't taken you along. You saw to it that you were out of town when I got home, just to prove a point. And now you're pissed off that I brought you to Hawaii and the people here aren't fancy enough for you, and I'm not helping you work the crowd on the beach. Well, guess what? I'm not going to help you do that. And frankly, I'd rather be home alone. You're my antidote to loneliness, because I'm too fucking scared and lonely to spend the weekends alone. Well, to hell with it, I'd rather be by myself than be used. So we, my dear, are going home. You can work someone else over next year and have them take you to St. Bart's. Frankly, I don't give a damn. We're leaving the hotel in half an hour." And with that, she walked into her bathroom and slammed the door.

There was another one in the suite for him to use. She hadn't been this angry in a long time, and for once, although it was rare for her, her temper matched her hair. He had just proven everything that Jade said about him. He really was a using little shit, and he had been trying to take advantage of her. She had been aware of the inequities in the relationship all along, and chose to turn a blind eye to them. But in Hawaii he had crammed the obvious down her throat. She might have been more forgiving if she'd been in love with him. But she wasn't. The relationship was easy and comfortable for both of them, but no more than that. And she wasn't willing to be used as blatantly as he had just tried to do. It was the end of the road for her.

The only good news was that all he had really gotten out of her was a Cartier watch and a trip to Hawaii. It was no big deal, except that her feelings were hurt and she felt exploited. That was always the trouble with getting involved with men like Zack. Eventually, they went too far, and he just had. It was always a matter of time before it fell apart.

She came out of the bathroom twenty minutes later, in jeans, a T-shirt, a denim jacket, and a shawl. She was wearing sandals, and had wet hair. She had just stepped out of the shower. Zack was sitting in a chair brooding, in his Hawaiian shirt and jeans that she had left out for him. He didn't say a word to her, as he followed her out of the room. He was well aware that he had crossed the line, and didn't want to make things worse. As they walked toward the lobby, he asked her if she was sure she didn't want to stay. He didn't say he was sorry, but it was obvious that he felt uncomfortable and nervous. He had just blown a golden opportunity and four more days in Hawaii, however dull he thought the place was. It was still a free Hawaiian vacation, and she was still Timmie O.

"I'm absolutely sure I don't want to stay," she said as they reached the desk. What he didn't understand, and probably never would, was that she was not angry as much as hurt. No one, particularly in her position, wanted to feel like a pathetic old cow that was being milked, and apparently that had been his only intention all along. And he was complaining because the milk wasn't quite sweet or plentiful enough for him, instead of enjoying what he got.

Timmie checked them out of the hotel, and a cab took them to the airport. They didn't say a word to each other on the ride there. There was nothing left to say. He had said it all, and so had she. And he knew there was no way to backtrack now. The opportunity had been blown. They flew to Honolulu on Aloha Airlines, and had a two-hour layover there. Zack walked away from her and used his cell phone, and she wandered aimlessly through the airport shops, trying to avoid him, and asking herself if she'd been too harsh. She didn't think she had been. She had hated everything he'd said to her, and even if it had been said in anger, it had an ugly ring of truth to it, and she suspected he had meant everything he had said. He was furious that she hadn't given him more opportunities to network at her expense than she had. He may not have been her Prince Charming, but he had definitely just exposed himself as Prince Shit. By the time she got back to the gate, she knew she had done the right thing.

They checked in at the gate for a full flight, and she was relieved to discover that they had been seated apart in first class. She had no desire whatsoever to sit next to him. They were seated in different rows on separate sides of the plane. And they made no effort to rearrange their seats or trade with anyone. The seating arrangements suited her just fine. She did her best to sleep on the flight, with little success. The man seated next to her fell asleep right after takeoff, and snored loudly for the entire flight. The air conditioning was ice cold. And she was too upset to sleep. She couldn't see Zack from where she sat, and didn't see him again until they got off in L.A. He walked over to talk to her, as they waited for their bags. Theirs were among the first ones off, which was something of a relief. At least they didn't have to stand there awkwardly, waiting for them. It was just after six in the morning, L.A. time.

"I'm sorry about the way things worked out," he muttered under his breath, and didn't meet her eyes, although she was looking squarely at him, wondering who he had been all along. Apparently no one very nice. She had never thought he was a hero, and she had always known he enjoyed the perks she could offer him, but she had never thought his intentions were quite as blatant as they were. He had given her a lot to swallow in Hawaii, and she had decided on the flight home that it was for the best. He had done her a favor showing his hand. It was time anyway, she told herself. The Zacks in her life never lasted more than six months. His time was up. And maybe this was the last Zack she'd have. She didn't want to do this again. What was the point? It was an utter and total waste of time, and a lot of the time it hadn't been fun, or even good sex. Maybe it really was better having nothing at all, if not love. She was tired of being with the wrong guy, one she didn't even care about, and who cared nothing about her. Maybe the era of Zacks had come to an end. She was feeling that that might be the case. Maybe being alone, instead of with the wrong man, wouldn't be so bad after all. It had taken her eleven years since her divorce to get to this point. She was ready to face life alone at last, without a husband, or a man.

"I'm sorry too," she said as she picked up her bag. "Good luck," she said, and he didn't answer, as she walked out to the sidewalk to hail a cab. There was one waiting at the curb and she got in. She didn't turn back to see Zack, nor did she offer him a ride. He had had all he was going to get from her. She gave the driver her address in Bel Air and rode home, free at last.

Chapter 9

After sleeping for a few hours, Timmie drove to Malibu on the afternoon of New Year's Eve. She didn't call anyone to say she'd come back. She was sure all of her friends had plans by then. And she knew David and Jade both had dates. She didn't want to be with them. All she wanted now was to be alone. She didn't even need to lick her wounds. There were none. She felt free and more alive than she had in years. She had no regrets about ending the relationship with Zack. All she felt was freedom and relief, and a sense of her own power. Zack had hit hard, but maybe it was what she needed to hear, she told herself, as she drove out to the beach. He had done her a favor after all, rather than lingering for the next several months, trying to take advantage of her and angry that he couldn't. She had even been thinking of taking him to the spring ready to wear shows, just to keep the relationship going for a few more months. It would have been incredibly stupid, but she hadn't wanted a scene like the one before, and she knew what it would take to keep him around, if that was what she wanted. In any case, he had solved that problem in Hawaii. She didn't have to worry about it anymore. She felt cured of the breed forever, or maybe any man. She could sense that she was about to embark on one of her long spells of celibacy, and she didn't regret it at all. She was glad she hadn't stayed with him in Hawaii, and that she'd had the guts to end it and come home.

She spent New Year's Eve alone in front of the fire in her living room in Malibu. It was crisp and clear, and she stood on the deck in the darkness and looked at the moon, grateful for her life, and suddenly no longer afraid to be alone. There was something a lot cleaner about it that way, being with men like Zack just dragged her down. She was suddenly convinced she'd be happier alone. For the first time ever she felt totally independent and strong.

She woke at nine o'clock on New Year's Day, and went for a long walk on the beach. It was a beautiful winter day, and she spent the rest of the weekend quiet and solitary, enjoying her house in Malibu. She felt surprisingly good, and totally at peace. Predictably, Zack never called, and she didn't think he would again. She had been through this before. Men like him vanished into thin air when the ride was over. Thank you, bye, it's been nice, or not so nice, and they were gone. Once in a while, they stayed friends, but not often. Men like Zack were incapable of real friendship with anyone, and surely not with her.

She stayed at the beach until Sunday morning, and then stopped at St. Cecilia's for a while, to wish them a happy New Year on the way home. She had lunch with the sisters and the kids, and then went back to Bel Air, where she worked until she went to bed. She was at her office at eight the next morning. Jade was startled when she got in and saw her there. Timmie looked businesslike and busy, and had already made all her morning calls to New York. She smiled as she handed Jade a stack of files. Jade noticed instantly that Timmie looked happy and relaxed.

"Happy New Year," Timmie said with a smile.

"How was Hawaii?" Jade could see something in Timmie's eyes, but she wasn't sure what it was. Whatever it was she looked happier than she had in a long time.

"Short," Timmie said cryptically in answer to her question. But Jade had gotten the message in the single word.

"You came home early?" Timmie nodded. "When?"

"On the thirty-first. In the morning. We took the red-eye from Honolulu the night before." Timmie didn't look upset about it. For the first time ever, a relationship had ended, and she was glad.

"Uh-oh. What happened?" She was almost afraid to ask, but Timmie looked fine. In fact, she hadn't looked as well in a long time.

"Apparently, Zack wasn't getting the networking opportunities with me he thought he needed and deserved. So I gave him the opportunity to move on." She looked at Jade and smiled. "I'm done. I think he was the last of the breed. I think I'd rather join a convent than do one of those again. I felt like a complete fool when he told me how boring I am. He's right, I guess. But I'm not about to go to every premiere I get invited to, to please him, or start hanging out in clubs and bars with his sleazy twelve-year-old friends." Jade grinned as she listened. Whatever else Timmie did from now on, Jade was glad he was gone. He wasn't worthy of her, and had never been. David stuck his head in the door as they were talking about it, and saw the intent look on Timmie's face as she told Jade what had happened.

"What's up? Something in New York?" Jade shook her head, and Timmie looked at him with a smile.

"No more Zack. We blew up in Hawaii."

"I hope you blew him up and not the reverse," David said, looking worried, and Timmie laughed.

"I guess you could say that. He dropped a bomb, and I dropped a bigger one. We had a nice week before that, so it was fine. His time was up anyway," she said ruefully. "His six-month visa had expired."

"I hope you took away his passport as he left the magic kingdom." David grinned.

"Who knows. I guess he'll find someone else like me who'll parade him around and give him what he wants. All I felt was stupid when it was over. It was a waste of time," she said honestly. She was never afraid to admit her mistakes or frailties to them, which was one of the things they both admired about her. Timmie was never afraid to be humble or wrong.

"Better stupid than sad, or seriously depressed," David said sensibly, and then glanced at Jade with a look of interest. "How was New Year's Eve?"

"Hot," Jade said as she beamed. She had gone out with the architect again. They had had several dates in the past few weeks, and he had given her a beautiful Gucci bag for Christmas. She had given him a cashmere sweater from Timmie O's top line. They had both loved their gifts, and things were starting to get hot and heavy with them, which David and Timmie had both warned her was a little too soon, but she seemed happy, and she reported that the architect was too. They had gone skiing over the New Year weekend. And David had had a date with a new girl. So all was well in their world, and at least peaceful in Timmie's. More than anything, she felt relieved.

The three of them worked hard for the rest of the day, and for the next week. They had a lot of work to do related to the spring and summer lines. In February they were presenting their collection at the ready to wear shows in New York, and going back to Milan and Paris immediately after. Jade was busy setting up the trip. And this time, they were giving a fancy dinner party at the Plaza Athénée. They couldn't get off the hook again.

Jade and Timmie were going over the details for it in early January, and Jade handed her the guest list to see if anyone should be deleted or added. All the local fashion press was on the list, along with several editors from *Vogue,* major buyers, some important textile people, and a few important clients. And then for no apparent reason, Timmie frowned.

"Something wrong? Did I forget someone?" Jade looked worried. As long as they caught it now, it wasn't a disaster at least. They had once forgotten the most important fashion editor in the French press.

"I was just thinking," Timmie said, gnawing on the end of her pen, and then traded it for one of the lollipops she loved. They gave her energy when she was tired.

"Someone you want to take off, or someone you want to add?" Jade looked puzzled by her expression. She was lost in deep thought.

"I'm not sure. It doesn't really fit, but it might be nice, as kind of a gesture. I'll think about it and let you know." Jade nodded and they continued down their list of details. Timmie didn't do anything about it till the following week. She left a note for Jade, and then went back and tore it up. She still wasn't sure, but decided to make the call herself. It seemed insulting somehow, or impersonal at least, to have an assistant do it. Europeans never understood that unless they were in the business too, and this one wasn't. She went back and forth, and then finally made the call from home late Sunday night. It was Monday morning in Paris, as good a time as any to call. She hadn't wanted to call over the weekend, and still wasn't sure she would. She had sat in her office at home for half an hour, trying to decide what to do, and then took a scrap of paper out of her address book, grabbed the phone, and dialed.

The cell phone at the other end rang several times, and she was about to chicken out and hang up, when he finally answered. It was Jean-Charles Vernier, the French doctor in Paris.

"Allo?" he said, sounding official and busy.

"Bonjour," she said, feeling silly. She knew her accent was awful. No matter how many times she went to Paris and stayed at the Plaza Athénée, or dealt with French textile houses, she had only learned a few words of the language. They always spoke to her in English.

"Yes?" He had heard the American accent, but didn't recognize the voice. Why should he? He had only known her for ten days, and hadn't spoken to her in two and a half months since.

"Hello, doctor. It's Timmie O'Neill."

"What a pleasant surprise," he said, sounding genuinely pleased. "Are you in Paris? Are you sick?"

"No on both counts." She smiled as she held the phone, sitting in her office at home in her nightgown. It was after midnight in L.A., and just after nine in the morning for him. "I'm in L.A. But I'm coming to town next month for the ready to wear shows again, and I was wondering . . . I don't know if this would appeal to you or not . . . but I thought . . . we're giving a dinner for press and buyers, at the Plaza Athénée." She took a breath, feeling awkward suddenly, and slightly embarrassed to have called him. "I was wondering if you and your wife would like to come. It's a business dinner, but it's an eclectic group and it might be fun." She had no idea if they'd come or not, but she thought it might be nice to see him again, after all their lengthy talks the previous October. It was a good excuse to see him without having to get sick. She hoped she'd manage not to do that this time.

"How nice of you to think of me," he said, sounding genuinely pleased, which made her feel slightly less stupid for having called him. For a minute she'd been afraid that he'd really think she was nuts, or pursuing him, which she wasn't.

In the past two weeks since she'd ended it with Zack, she had come to the conclusion, emphatically in fact, that she was happier alone. She had entered what Jade called one of her ice queen phases. She swore she'd never get involved with another man again. She was actually loving her time at the beach on her own, and Zack had never called again. Weekends alone no longer scared her at all. The relationship with Zack was definitely over, and Timmie swore there would never be another Zack again, nor anyone else. She had announced victoriously only days before that she was through with men. Her invitation to Dr. Vernier and his wife was purely social, with no ulterior motive whatsoever. She told herself emphatically that was the case.

"I'm afraid I have a problem," he explained cautiously, although she had not told him the date yet, except that she was coming to town in February, and it was obviously going to be then. So there was no way for him to know if he had a conflict on that date, unless he had a hard-and-fast rule not to accept dinner invitations from patients. "My problem is that I assume you want a couple, since you were kind enough to invite my wife and me to your dinner just now. But I'm afraid that she and I have had a parting of the ways, I think you call it. A fork in the road. Or an end to diplomatic relations would probably be more exact." She had forgotten how formal he was at times, until she listened to him, frowning, not sure what he was saying. "Our marriage is on the rocks, as you say in America. We are no longer going out socially together. We are selling our apartment. And I imagine that having a single man at your dinner would be awkward. So if you wanted a couple, I'm afraid I must decline. And if you don't mind a man alone, then I would be delighted to come. But please don't feel obligated to have me." She digested what he had just said to her and found it interesting. Very interesting. She didn't want it to, but it had caused her a minor flutter, which she reminded herself instantly was stupid. She was through with men for good, and he was technically still married, but he would make a very nice dinner guest, and she was happy to hear he was willing to come.

"That's perfectly fine if you come alone," she reassured him. "There are actually no couples coming. All the press come singly, as do the buyers and clients. I hope it won't be too boring for you, it's the whole fashion scene and a few other people mixed in. But sometimes those dinners can be a lot of fun. I'd love to have you come. It's February thirteenth. I hope you're not superstitious."

"Not at all," he laughed, and made a note of it. "I'll be delighted. What time?"

"Eight-thirty. At the Plaza, in a private dining room."

"It's not black tie, is it?" he inquired politely.

"Oh God, no!" Timmie laughed at the suggestion. "The press will come in jeans. We might have a model or two, and they'll come half naked. The buyers and clients will wear dark suits. You can wear any-thing you like, slacks and blazer or suit. The people responsible for putting fashion together are almost never decently dressed," she said, pleased that he'd said he would come, and wanting very much to put him at ease.

"With the exception of you, Madame O'Neill," he said politely, and she wasn't sure if he was teasing.

"What happened to 'Timmie'? I liked that better." She remembered then that his thank-you note had also addressed her as Madame O'Neill. During their long talks in the hospital and at the hotel he had called her Timmie. She missed the intimacy of that now.

"I didn't want to be presumptuous. You were my patient then, and now you're a very important woman."

"I am not," she said, sounding indignant, and then laughed at herself. "All right, maybe I am, but so what? I thought we were friends, or at least I thought so in October. Thank you for your nice note, by the way." She remembered the sunset on the card perfectly and so did he.

"Thank you for the extravagant watch, Madame...Timmie..." He said cautiously, and sounded shy for a moment. "I was very embarrassed when I saw it. You didn't need to do that."

"You were very nice to me when I had my appendix out. And I was very scared," she said honestly.

"I remember. You're well now?" He sounded cautious and a little shy.

"I'm fine. Though I probably won't be when I get to Paris. Those road shows are exhausting."

"I remember that as well. You refused to go to the hospital until after the show."

"Yes, and you were right about my appendix bursting. It's hard to stop what you're doing in the middle of those shows."

"You must pay attention to your health," he said quietly.

"I'm sorry about your marriage," she said bravely, not sure how he would feel about her comment.

"These things happen," he said, sounding momentarily somber. "Thank you for letting me come alone. I appreciate the invitation. When are you coming to Paris?" She thought it interesting that he asked her. It changed things somewhat between them now, knowing that he was getting divorced.

"We arrive on the eighth. Five days before the show. And I'm staying at the Plaza, as always." As soon as she said it, she felt stupid. It was as though she was throwing a lure out to him, and she didn't want it to look that way to him. They hardly knew each other, except as doctor and patient. And he obviously had his own problems to work out. She didn't want to seem like some desperate man-hungry

American woman who was chasing after him now. At least she had extended the invitation to him and his wife, so he knew she hadn't been putting the make on him when she called. And why would he think that anyway? She suddenly felt awkward for having called, but was glad she had. After all, why not? She felt like a kid talking to him now. He sounded so serious and grown up, and as she recalled, he was, although he had a nice sense of humor too. They had been so at ease with each other three months before.

"Well, I shall see you on the thirteenth at the Plaza Athénée," he said solemnly. He had been extremely decorous with her during the entire call. Not warm, but very correct, as he had been with her at the beginning before.

"See you on the thirteenth," she confirmed.

"Thank you for your call," he said politely again, and then they both hung up, and she sat staring into space in her tiny office. It had been nice talking to him again.

She sat thinking about the call for a few minutes after that, and his surprising piece of news, which had actually startled her, given his somewhat archaic and extremely European Catholic views on marriage. It had been nice of him to offer not to come, if she didn't want a single man. But it would work fine the way it was, although she would have been curious to meet his wife. That was obviously not going to happen, and she hoped he'd have a decent time with the motley crew that came to those events. But in any case, it would be nice to see him again. She yawned, stood up, and then went across the hall to her room, and went to bed. She forced herself not to think of Jean-Charles Vernier, or even their previous talks in Paris. She assured herself that neither that nor the news of his divorce meant anything to her at all. He was a nice man, and at most potentially a friend. And nothing more. She was sure of that now.

Chapter 10

The next day, Timmie gave Jade Jean-Charles Vernier's name for the guest list for the Paris dinner party, and had her send him a fax as a confirmation. And for the next week, their lives were insane at the office. So much so that Timmie forgot about him completely. She went to Malibu on Friday night and stopped at St. Cecilia's for dinner on the way. The children were in good spirits, and two new residents had arrived, a little girl who had been in twelve foster homes unsuccessfully, and molested by a sibling in the last one. She was quiet and reserved, and fourteen years old. The nuns explained her situation to Timmie in detail after dinner, and were somewhat distressed to find that she had been aggressive with some of the other children since she'd arrived. It wasn't surprising given what she'd been through, and the other children were being patient with her, although two of the girls had gotten in an argument with her in the bathroom that morning and claimed she had stolen their toothbrushes and combs. She was hoarding everything she could lay hands on under her bed, and one of the nuns was afraid she was planning to run away. They knew, as Timmie did, that her adjustment to new surroundings would take time, maybe even a long time in her case. She had been severely beaten in her original home by her natural mother, and raped by an uncle, and several of the mother's boyfriends. Her father was in jail, as many of the children's fathers were. Her history was a nightmare.

The second new resident at St. Cecilia's had come in only two days before. One of the sisters had mentioned him to her in passing as they went in to dinner, to warn her not to be surprised if he exhibited un-usual behavior. So far, he had sat under the table, rather than at it, and had spoken to no one. They had been told by the social worker during his intake that in his mother's home, he had been fed scraps on the floor like a dog. He had bright red hair, the same color as Timmie's, and he was six years old. Timmie noticed him immediately as she followed the children in to dinner, and she saw him slip silently under the table, just as she had been warned he would. He had been living in a small apartment in Hollywood, with his mother, and she had just gone to jail for dealing drugs. She claimed the father was un-known. The boy's name was Blake, and the mother claimed as well that he never spoke. He had been tested for autism, but didn't meet the criteria. His psychiatric evaluation in juvenile hall, when the po-lice brought him there, said that their assessment was that he had been traumatized at some point, and stopped speaking as a result. He had full comprehension of what was said to him, but offered no re-sponse. His eyes were big and bright. The psychiatrist at juvenile hall suspected both physical and sexual abuse. His mother was twenty-two years old. She had given birth to him while addicted to crystal meth and crack cocaine. She had added heroin to the mix since, and was likely to go to prison for a long time. The current one was her fourth offense, and the DA wanted prison.

There were no known relatives, and he had nowhere else to go. They had called St. Cecilia's from juvenile hall as soon as his evaluation was done. They thought it was the perfect placement for him, he was in no shape for foster care, didn't belong in juvenile hall, and he was the profile of the kind of children the nuns at St. Cecilia's welcomed with open arms. Timmie's heart went out to him the minute she saw him, and even the nuns commented on how much he looked like her. He could have been her son, and for a moment she wished he was. His mother had refused to relinquish him for adoption, and said she wanted him back when she got out of jail, which was likely to be a very long time. Possibly as long as ten years. Very probably he would be emancipated, or even on drugs himself by the time she got out. The nuns had every intention of doing all they could to change the course of his life. And if the other nearly impossible cases they had worked with successfully were any example, they had a good chance of helping Blake.

Timmie could feel his little body curled up near her feet under the table, but she made no sign of having noticed, as she talked to the other children laughing and chatting around her. They loved it when she joined them for dinner, as did the nuns. Most of the children called her Aunt Timmie. They were halfway through their hamburgers with macaroni and cheese, when she felt Blake lean against her, and rest his head on her legs. Without thinking, she reached under the table, and stroked his silky hair, as she met one of the nuns' eyes. She would have liked to tell her what was happening, but didn't dare. And a moment later, she quietly slipped a piece of hamburger to him wrapped in a paper napkin. He took it without a sound. She handed him another little bit shortly after, and continued to do so until he had eaten almost a full burger. She never looked under the table at him, and when he was finished, he tugged at her skirt and handed her the napkins. She took them, with tears in her eyes. There was something so agonizingly wounded about him. She handed him a Popsicle for dessert, and he ate it all. He didn't emerge when the others left the table. Timmie continued to sit there, as the nuns and children disappeared, and finally he came out and looked at her with his enormous eyes. She handed him a glass of milk and a cookie, and he devoured both, and then set the glass down neatly on the table in front of her.

"You ate a very good dinner, Blake," she said quietly, praising him, with no response from him. She thought she saw him nod almost imperceptibly, but she wasn't sure. "It's too bad you missed the macaroni and cheese. Would you like some now?" He hesitated and then nodded, and Timmie went out to the kitchen to get him a bowl of the leftover macaroni, and set it down in front of him at the table. He took it and set it down on the floor and then sat down next to it and ate it with his fingers. Timmie said nothing as one of the nuns walked by, nodded, and smiled. She was doing a good job with him. She felt an odd bond with this boy, maybe because he looked like her. He was locked in a prison of silence, which made her heart ache thinking about how he had gotten there. God only knew what had really happened to him while he lived with his mother, at her hands, or those of her friends. He was the ultimate casualty of her lifestyle, even more than she was herself. It was hard to imagine. He had been born in San Francisco, while she was on the streets of the Haight-Ashbury at sixteen. She had already been on the streets for two years by then. And she had moved to L.A. shortly after that, and begun her career of arrests. He had been in foster care for the first time at six months. Before that, she had left him with friends, and with her drug dealer the last time she went to jail. Blake had had a checkered career and a disastrous life by the time he was six. He ate all the macaroni Timmie had put in the bowl, and then looked at her and smiled.

"Well, you won't be hungry after that," Timmie said, smiling at him. "More?" He shook his head and smiled back. It was a very, very small smile, but it was one nonetheless. She reached out to touch his hand, and he shrank back. "I'm sorry. I didn't mean to scare you," she said, as though having a conversation with him, which in a way she was. "My name is Timmie. And I know you're Blake." His eyes didn't acknowledge what she had said, he just stared at her, and then backed away. She didn't want to move on him too fast. He had had enough contact for one night, and apparently all he could tolerate. He went to sit in a corner of the dining room, on the floor, and continued to watch her, and one of the nuns who had come out of the kitchen to sponge the table. Timmie chatted with her for a few moments, and then turned to Blake again. "Would you like to come upstairs and listen to a story?" Timmie invited him. She wanted to get to Malibu, but she couldn't tear herself away. She felt suddenly anchored to him, more than she had to any child who had come to the house previously. There was something agonizing for her about this one boy. She wasn't sure what it was, but for a moment she felt as though destiny had brought them together. She wondered if her son Mark had had a hand in it from somewhere in Heaven. It would have been nice if that were the case. There had been an agonizing void in her heart in the twelve years since he had died. She didn't expect anyone else to fill it, and surely not this child, but for a moment the empty place in her heart didn't ache, except for Blake. She asked him about storytime again, and he shook his head. He continued to sit silently in the corner, watching them, and looking afraid. But at least he had been decently fed. He was seriously underweight and rail thin, as many of the children were when they came in, suffering from neglect and malnutrition, particularly if they came from their parents' homes. They looked far better coming out of foster care, where they were usually decently fed. Blake clearly hadn't been, and he had devoured every-thing Timmie had given him. He had eaten more dinner than she had. She turned and smiled at him again.

"I'm going to go soon, Blake. Do you want me to take you upstairs to your room?" It would be bedtime for them soon, after storytime and showers. She would have liked to give him a nice warm bubble bath, as she had when Mark was little, but baths were impractical here, with so many children to bathe. They had to give the children showers. He shook his head in answer to her question, and made no move to approach her again. Timmie looked at him and smiled and then left the room with the nuns. They said in a whisper that he would follow them upstairs on his own soon. He had done that after every meal so far. He was keeping his distance from them, and did from Timmie too, except while he had rested his head against her legs during the meal, and allowed her to stroke his hair. It was the only physical touch he had tolerated so far, so at least they knew he was able to endure being touched, which some of them weren't. She told them about it when they left the room, and she followed them up-stairs to the playroom where the children were playing games and do-ing puzzles, and watching a movie on TV before their showers.

"I guess I'd better go," she said reluctantly. She hated to leave. Her time with them meant so much to her, and particularly tonight, with Blake.

"You did a good job with him. He hasn't eaten much since he's been here."

"Do you think he'll speak again?" Timmie asked, looking worried. She had seen others come in, in worse condition, but there was some-thing about him that suggested greater damage even than what they could see. She could sense it in her soul. All she wanted was to put her arms around him and hold him tight, and make everything right for him. It had never been right in his entire life, from everything she'd heard.

"Probably, in time," Sister Anne said, in answer to her question about his speech. "We've seen others like him before, and so have you," she said wisely. "Many worse. It takes time. One day they feel comfortable and start to open up. You got a long way with him tonight. Come back and visit him again. It'll do you both good." She smiled. She thought Timmie looked well these days, although she worked too hard, as they all knew. There was an openness and peace about her eyes suddenly, as though a burden had been lifted from her. Timmie wasn't aware of it, or that it was visible, but ending the relationship with Zack had been good for her. She looked younger and happier than she had in a long time. What had started as a plus for her had ended up weighing on her in the end. Zack took more than he gave. It had only been a week since she ended it, but Jade and David had noticed too that she looked better every day.

"Maybe I'll come by on Sunday, on my way home from the beach," Timmie said, and a moment later they saw Blake scurry past the door to the living room and run upstairs. Timmie watched him go, and didn't follow him. He obviously wanted to be alone, and was still frightened of all of them. He was only six after all, and a lot of scary things had happened to him in the past few days. St. Cecilia's was new to him, and he wasn't sure yet if he was safe. He had never been before.

She left a few minutes later, after saying good night to the children and the nuns, and an hour later she was sitting on her deck at the beach, bundled up in a cashmere blanket, looking out at the water and the moon. It was a beautiful star-filled night, and she felt peaceful and alive. As she sat there, listening to the waves, all she could think of was Blake. She felt as though she'd been hit by a train. She was already longing to go back and see him again. Something had happened between them that night, or to her at least. He was the first child she had ever desperately wanted to take home with her. She ached to hold him in her arms.

She went back to St. Cecilia's on Sunday afternoon, after a relaxing weekend at the beach. She hadn't been able to get Blake out of her head, with his enormous terrified green eyes, and beautiful little face. He looked like a child in a fairy tale, and she realized now that he looked a lot like Mark. She wondered if this was the hand of God at work, or fate.

She mentioned wanting to take him home, to Sister Anne, when she went back, and the older nun looked at her with interest.

"And why is that, Timmie? Why him? Because he looks like you?" She seemed to be questioning Timmie's motives, which wasn't a bad thing. She'd questioned them herself all weekend. Was it just some form of narcissism that was drawing her to him, because he looked like her, or like Mark? Or was it something more? Was it about Blake himself, or her? Or maybe to fill a void in her life that was aeons old, and had never filled. She had no idea.

"I don't know. Something about him just pulls at my heart and won't let go. I thought about him all weekend. Do you suppose I could take him home sometime? Just for a meal and a bath, or the night? I could take him to the beach. It might be fun for him." She was groping for ideas, and for a way to fill a need, a need for him, and someone to love. This was so much better than a man, and she could do him some good and give him a better life. She couldn't believe she was thinking as she was. Sister Anne didn't look surprised.

"And then what, Timmie?" she asked quietly. "Where are you going with this?"

"I don't know ... I'm not sure ..." She looked troubled, tortured by the same questions she had asked herself all weekend, and had no answers to yet. She hadn't expected this when she had come to visit on Friday night. She had been haunted ever since, by this small, redheaded, silent, deeply troubled boy. It would be a lot to take on, if she did. And then what? She couldn't adopt him, his mother hadn't relinquished him, and said she wouldn't. Did she really want a foster child? She had always said that foster care was a recipe for heartbreak, children you love as your own, and can lose at any time. It was the last thing she needed, with a history of loss and abandonment like her own. And yet, here she was, thinking of just that. Why? She didn't know, and neither did Sister Anne.

"It's good that you come to visit him," Sister Anne said quietly. "But if you take him home with you for a day or a night, then what? You bring him back, he still lives here, and he feels abandoned, just as you did as a child. He still has a lot of adjusting to do. Emotional trauma of any kind could set him back. And it might not be good for you either," she said gently. "It may bring up a lot of old memories for you." She knew something of Timmie's history, although not all of it, and that it was why Timmie had started the house. She didn't want her to perpetuate the same agony for Blake that she had experienced again and again herself as a child, of always being sent back. Even if in this case it was well meant. But it might do more harm than good, for them both.

It was something to think about. No decisions had to be made yet, about anything. Blake wasn't going anywhere. He had just arrived. Yet Timmie had a sense of urgency about it, as though she wanted to sweep him under her wing immediately, and make him feel safe as fast as she could. She hated knowing all the terror he must be feeling now. She wanted to make it instantly better for him, and the reality was that she couldn't. It was going to take a long time, no matter what happened.

"Why don't you visit him here for a while, and see how it goes?"

Sister Anne said sensibly. "See how you feel. He's not going into foster care, for now anyway. He's staying here. He's the poster child for what we do, thanks to you." She smiled at Timmie, and gave her a warm hug.

For the rest of the afternoon and evening, Timmie sat near Blake, smiling at him occasionally, and playing with the other children. He sat at her feet again at dinner, and she fed him chicken and mashed potatoes and carrots from a bowl she set down under the table. He ate it all. She left an empty chair next to her, for him, in case he wanted to join them at the table, but he never left where he was sitting, next to her legs. And once again she stroked his hair, as he leaned on her, and rested his head against her knees. He seemed more peaceful to her than he had two days before, and he smiled broadly at her this time, at the end of the meal, when she handed him a bowl of ice cream and a cookie. The other children were making s'mores, but he refused to approach or join them, or even eat one. He was still extremely cautious about approaching the other children, and looked frightened. And because he wouldn't speak to them, the other children ignored him. Even the nuns gave him a wide berth. Timmie was the only one who spoke to him directly, and he made eye contact with her several times before she left on Sunday night. She would have loved to hug him, but didn't dare.

As she had been on Friday night and all weekend, she was haunted by him again on Sunday. She lay awake all that night, thinking about him, and on Monday before she left for work, she called Sister Anne at St. Cecilia's. Timmie sounded breathless when the nun answered.

"I want to adopt him," she said without preamble. She knew she had to, it was all she could think about and all she wanted. She wanted to make a difference for Blake, and she was sure he had been brought to her for a reason. And for the briefest instant, Sister Anne sounded slightly startled. She had sensed that Timmie was heading that way, but she thought it would take her a long time to get there. Timmie had already arrived.

"He's not available for adoption, Timmie. You know that. His mother won't relinquish."

"Won't she lose her rights or something, if she goes to prison for a long time?"

"She could, but that's not a quick or easy process. It could be in the courts, and with social services, for a long time, depending on what they recommend. And we're not sure there are no other living relatives. I know they're doing some investigative work on that now. At best, he might be eligible for foster care, once he's in better shape than he is now. But even that won't be for quite a while. That could be a good thing," she said quietly. "It would give you time to really make up your mind." She had never known Timmie to behave impulsively, and the decision she had made the night before was more than a little unusual for her. Timmie had seen many children come through St. Cecilia's over the years, many of them in far worse shape than Blake, and some so adorable that they were impossible to resist falling in love with. But this was the first time she had lost her heart to a child, since her own son had died, and she suddenly felt her destiny was somehow intertwined with Blake's. She knew she was doing the right thing, and she was falling head over heels in love with a silent, six-year-old redheaded little boy.

"I think I've made up my mind," Timmie said, sounding certain, and Sister Anne was impressed, but cautious anyway.

"Let's give it some time, and see how you two relate. It would be nice to get him talking again, and see how it feels then." He didn't seem like a hostile or aggressive child, just one who, like so many others they saw, had been neglected, abused, and badly hurt, in many ways. "There's no rush on this, Timmie. He's not going anywhere."

"What if they turn up relatives somewhere? They could be as bad as his mother, and take him away. What do we do then?"

"Let's see how things unfold. It all takes time. You're not going to have a problem prevailing over a natural father in prison somewhere, or grandparents who deal drugs," which was usually what turned up in searches for relatives, who didn't want to be burdened with their children or grandchildren in any case. Their own lives were complicated enough. Very few children they saw ever went to live with relatives, they were either given up for adoption, or went into group homes or foster care. Timmie was not going to have a problem competing with any of that. "Why don't you come and visit him whenever you can? Maybe you'll get him talking one of these days. And given what you have in mind, maybe you can take him home for a day or two after he settles in here." Timmie knew she would do everything she could to help. The nun who ran St. Cecilia's was not only good at what she did, but she had become a friend. And she was impressed by what she was hearing from Timmie now. She had always wondered if Timmie would wind up taking one of the children home with her for good one day. She wasn't entirely surprised, given her own history, and everything that had motivated her to start St. Cecilia's. But this was clearly the first time Timmie had fallen head over heels in love with a child. More than that, she seemed to feel compelled. And if it was meant to be, Sister Anne felt sure it would all happen in good time.

Timmie was absolutely glowing when she got to work that day. David saw it the moment she walked in, and Jade looked worried as Timmie smiled ecstatically at her.

"Uh-oh." David was the first to comment on it, as she set her handbag down on his desk and beamed at him. "Don't tell me. You're in love."

"How did you know?" she asked with a four-thousand-watt smile.

"Are you kidding? I could see it from fifty miles away. What happened?" The ice queen phase had ended quickly this time. He had never seen her look like that before, nor had Jade.

"Who is it?" Jade asked, looking panicked. She hated to see Timmie fall for the wrong guy again. And this time she looked as though she had fallen head over heels in love. She had. With Blake.

"His name is Blake." Timmie played with them for a minute. "He's absolutely gorgeous, he has red hair and green eyes. He's younger than I am, but that's never been a problem before." Jade felt her stomach sink. It was one of them again. Another replay of Zack. But at least she wasn't hiding it, and was telling them. She always did in the end.

"How young?" David asked cautiously, as worried about her as Jade. She was one of the smartest women he knew, yet she had a vulnerable side to her that left her wide open sometimes to the wrong guys. He hated to see it happen again.

"Very young this time," she said, looking mischievous, as both her assistants tried not to groan. She waited an interminable length of time to answer him, and then finally smiled, with a sigh, and said, "Six."

"Six what?" David looked confused.

"He's six." She smiled even more widely than before.

"Six? As in six years old?"

"I'm afraid so. Blake is six. We met on Friday night, at St. Cecilia's. His mother is going to prison, for the next hundred years, I hope. I think Mark sent him to me. It was love at first sight."

David leaned back in his chair with a broad grin, and laughed out loud. "Well, I'll be damned. In that case, I approve. When do I get to meet him?" He was happy for her, and like Sister Anne, he wasn't surprised. He had expected something like that to happen years before, and was surprised it never had.

"You're adopting him?" Jade looked shocked. She didn't look nearly as enthusiastic as David. She knew how busy Timmie was, she couldn't imagine her taking on a child, although David could. He thought it was a great idea.

"Not yet," Timmie answered Jade's question. "He's not up for adoption at the moment. His mother won't relinquish him, or at least not yet. We'll see what happens. They're doing a search for other relatives now. But from the sound of it, no one is likely to turn up. No one worth worrying about anyway. The kid's mother sounds like a total mess. She had him when she was homeless on the streets in San Francisco at sixteen, and he's been kicked around in her drug life ever since." Her eyes grew sad as she thought about it and then added, "Right now he doesn't speak."

"That's a lot for you to take on," Jade said, looking worried. "What if he's too damaged and he turns out to be an ax murderer, or a drug addict like his mother? You don't know what's in his genes." Timmie looked sadder still as she heard the words.

"I know what's in his eyes. I don't want him to have a life like I did, living in an orphanage all his life. I was a year younger than he was when my parents died. The least I can do, or maybe the best I can do, is spare him that. What else am I going to do with the rest of my life?" She said it as though the obvious conclusion was that she devote the rest of her life to Blake. It didn't even occur to her not to step up to the plate. In Timmie's mind, he was already hers.

"I can think of a few things you might do to keep you busy for the next few years," David said with a cautious smile. He loved the look of love and joy in her eyes, but he was also worried about her. "What if his mother doesn't give him up?" He didn't want her heartbroken if something went wrong and his mother got out of prison and took him back. Things like that happened, and she had already thrown her heart over the wall for this child. It was written all over her, Timmie wore her heart on her sleeve. She had already lost one child, he didn't want her to go through the heartbreak of losing another one, even if for different reasons. She gave her heart so totally when she did, and he could see that she already had in just two days. There was a bond between her and the boy that had formed the moment she laid eyes on him and that was getting stronger by the hour. She could hardly wait to take him home with her, and had already decided on her way to work what room to put him in when he came to visit, and then came home for good. It was a guest bedroom she used as an office, right next to hers. "I'm very happy for you," David said warmly, "if this is what you want." In his mind, it was better than some guy who would take advantage of her for a while and then disappear out of her life, as all the others had. At least this would change someone else's life for the better, as well as hers. It was an incredible way for her to give back all the good things that had happened to her. And so typical of Timmie to do something like this, without reservation, or even fear. She had no doubt whatsoever about what she was doing. Blake was one lucky little boy, as far as David was concerned.

"I hope it turns out all right," Jade said, looking worried. She was always the devil's advocate, and the voice of doom and fear. But it was hard to deny the look of love and excitement on Timmie's face.

Timmie went to visit him again that night. She fed him from the dinner table again, and then sat in the dining room with him afterward for a long time, after everyone else left. While he looked at her anxiously, sitting in the corner again, she told him that she had grown up in a place like this, and that she wanted to be his friend. She didn't dare tell him she wanted to be his mom. That would have been frightening to him. No matter how bad his own mother was, she was familiar to him, and he had only known Timmie for a few days. He ran past her finally, and up to his room. She went upstairs, stood in the doorway, and blew him a kiss before she left. That time, he still said nothing, but smiled shyly at her, and then turned away. She was getting there, slowly but surely.

She had too much to do at the office on Tuesday to get to St. Cecilia's again. They were busy preparing for the February ready to wear shows, and they only had a few weeks left. She went back to see him on Wednesday night, and this time, he came out from under the table at the end of the meal and stood beside her chair. She didn't say anything, and didn't try to touch him. She didn't want to frighten him, but there were tears running down her cheeks as she smiled at Sister Anne, and she choked on a sob, when for the merest instant, she felt his tiny fingers like butterflies on her arm, and then he ran away. Sister Anne nodded her approval, and afterward Blake followed Timmie upstairs. And when she said goodbye to him from the doorway this time, his eyes bored into hers and he waved.

By Thursday, he owned her heart as though he had been in her life for years. It was not unlike a newborn who arrived, and suddenly you could no longer imagine what your life had been like without him. All of Timmie's plans in her head were suddenly made around Blake. She was worried about her upcoming trip, and how he would feel when she disappeared. She was becoming a daily presence in his life, and she spent several hours with him on Friday afternoon, before leaving for the beach. She was reading a story to him when Sister Anne walked into the room, and motioned for Timmie to come with her. Timmie went to find her in her office as soon as she finished reading the book to Blake. She promised to come back to him in a few minutes.

"Is everything okay?" Timmie asked, looking worried. She didn't like the look on the older nun's face.

"Probably," she said cryptically. "I had a call from Social Services a few minutes ago. Blake's grandparents contacted them. Apparently, they've been looking for him for weeks. They're flying in from Chicago this weekend. They've requested a hearing Monday afternoon." It was all she knew. But to Timmie, it did not sound good.

"What kind of hearing?" She felt panic run up and down her spine.

"Temporary custody, and permission to take him out of the state. They live in a suburb of Chicago, and apparently they've been trying to get custody of him for years. Every time they tried, their daughter would clean up for a few weeks, and the judge wouldn't take Blake away from her. They're pretty adamant about kids staying with their natural parents, even in circumstances that horrify the rest of us. You know how that is. I don't know how the judge will feel now about letting him out of the state. But unquestionably, his mother will be gone for a long time. I told his social worker about you." It had all happened so quickly that Timmie hadn't done anything official about it yet. She thought she had plenty of time, and now there was a hearing on Monday afternoon, against people she didn't know, but who were blood relations of Blake's.

"Can I go to the hearing too?"

"I thought that's what you'd want, so I asked the social worker about it, and she said it would be okay. I didn't expect there to be a custody battle over him. This is pretty unusual stuff for one of our kids." Usually no one wanted them, now there were going to be two families, or two camps, fighting for him. And Timmie didn't intend to lose.

"Can I bring an attorney?"

"Maybe you should. I'm not sure the judge will let you speak. The hearing is really about them, and the petition they're going to make. But I told the social worker who you are, and that you're serious about him. I'm afraid that I had to explain that you're the force behind St. Cecilia's. I wanted to give it all the weight I could," she said apologetically, and Timmie looked relieved.

"I'm glad you did." She was a single woman after all, and not as young as most foster and adoptive parents, although she certainly had the means to provide him a wonderful life. "Do you know anything about the grandparents?" Timmie asked, looking terrified. She felt as though someone were trying to take away her own child. He had become that in her mind in the past week.

"He's a doctor in a suburb of Chicago, she's a housewife. They have three other kids, all in college, I think a boy, and a set of twin girls. He's forty-six, and she's forty-two. They sound like solid citizens, and Blake's mother is the black sheep. That's all I know. The social worker said all three of their other kids go to Ivy League schools. I think one of them is at Harvard, and the twins are at Stanford and Yale."

"Smart kids," Timmie said, even more terrified than she had been before she knew.

"It could be a tough fight," Sister Anne said softly, wishing she could spare her this. But they all had to hope for the best outcome for Blake, whatever that might be. His grandparents didn't sound like easy people to dismiss. She was worried for Timmie's sake.

The weekend passed for her like a blur. She spent Sunday afternoon and evening with Blake. He never made it into the chair at dinner, but he poked his head out several times from under the table and smiled at her. She fed him ravioli and meatballs from a bowl with a spoon, and he kept popping up for more. She stayed with him until he went to bed that night, and speaking softly to him, she tucked him in, as Sister Anne drifted by, and watched them for a minute. She looked worried. Not only had Timmie bonded tightly with the child, but he was obviously becoming attached to her. If his grandparents won their petition, it would traumatize him again. Sister Anne hoped they wouldn't, she felt certain Timmie would be a wonderful mother to him. She was seeing a side of her she had never before seen to that degree. Timmie already loved Blake, almost as much as if he had been her own. It worried her for her friend. It was going to come as a terrible blow to her if Blake's grandparents took him away. She knew Timmie had already lost a son. This was different, but if it didn't go well at the hearing on Monday afternoon, it was going to be very hard, for both Timmie and Blake. All they could do now was pray.

Timmie couldn't sleep as she thought of it on Sunday night. She kept running it through her head again and again, worrying about what would happen in court the next day. In the end, she stayed home from work on Monday, and didn't go to see him that day. She somehow knew she couldn't, until she saw how things turned out. She was already so attached to him, she couldn't imagine losing him now, but knew she could. She tried not to think about it as she dressed for court in a black suit and high heels. She pulled her red hair straight back in a ponytail down her back. The hearing was set for two. She had called her lawyer over the weekend, and explained the circumstances. There was not much they could do. It was not so much a case of Timmie versus the grandparents. It was a question of whether or not the judge would grant their petition for custody of him, even temporarily. If not, the way was open for Timmie. But their rights had to be evaluated first, and their suitability. After that,

Timmie was free to pursue fostering Blake. But it didn't hurt to have the judge know that Timmie was waiting in the wings, and cared enough to be there.

She met her attorney on the courthouse steps at a quarter to two, and they quietly took their place in the courtroom. Blake's grandparents were already there, they looked like nice, wholesome, solid, respectable people from the Midwest. His grandmother was wearing a skirt and blouse, which Timmie realized was from one of her lines, and his grandfather looked like a doctor in a blazer, tie, and slacks, with well-polished shoes. They both looked neat and trim, and younger than they were. Timmie realized as she thought about it that they were younger than she was, and they were married. In some ways, they were better candidates than she, and they were blood relations. All she could offer him was love, herself, and a very good life that might have been beyond their means. But they looked as though they were doing well too.

The judge walked in promptly at two, and Blake's file was on his desk. He had looked at it in chambers that morning, and had read the grandparents' petition and request. Everything was in order, and there were a slew of references and testimonials from solid people in their community. There was little to object to about them. The social worker had also sent him a letter describing the circumstances around Timmie's interest in the child as well, and who she was. He had been duly impressed, particularly to learn about her association with St. Cecilia's, which he knew well, and where he had sent many children over the past few years. He thought her interest in it admirable, and in this child as well.

The judge spoke to both grandparents at some length. Blake's grandmother cried when she talked about her daughter's ongoing problems with drugs and the law since her early teens. It was a night-

mare to listen to. In contrast, all her other children were stars and doing extremely well. He spoke to the grandfather after that, and between them briefly acknowledged Timmie's presence in the room. He
spoke to her with a warm smile, which she returned, although there
was a knot in her stomach the size of her head, and her palms were
soaking wet. She thanked the judge for his kind words, when he
praised St. Cecilia's and her for her involvement with it. He clearly
had a great deal of respect for what they did. And then he turned his
attention to Blake's grandfather, who was impressive on the stand. He
was a quiet, well-spoken, sensible, obviously trustworthy man, an up-
standing citizen in every way, and both were deeply committed to
their family, community, and church. There was absolutely nothing
wrong with them, or with Timmie either. The problem was that she
wasn't in the running, and there was no doubt in the judge's mind
where the boy belonged as the hearing came to an end. He needed to
be back with his own family, where he could grow up with his grandparents and aunts and uncle, and they could nurse him back to physical and psychological health.

The judge looked at Timmie again briefly at the end of it, and said
he was sure that Timmie would understand. Although her interest in
the boy was admirable and deeply touching, he was sure that she too
would want him returned to the family in which he belonged, and
who were so anxious to make a home for him, the home he had never
had. Timmie nodded, as tears ran down her cheeks. She felt as
though she'd been shot. It was obviously the right thing, but it hurt so
incredibly much. She tried to be gracious to the grandparents when
the hearing was over, and Blake's grandmother gave her a hug as
tears flowed down her cheeks too. Everyone was crying, the grandfather, Timmie's lawyer, and the judge's eyes looked damp as well. He
had been particularly moved to hear the condition Blake was in, and

that he didn't speak. He hoped that with the right care, and love from his family, Blake would talk sometime soon. The boy had been traumatized beyond belief by his life with his mother.

They all walked out of the courtroom together, with the social worker, and they proceeded to St. Cecilia's in three separate cars. Timmie's lawyer left her at the courthouse, and told her how sorry he was. He felt terrible for her, but there was nothing he could do. His hands were tied, and he too thought the child probably belonged with his grandparents, although he could see what a blow it was for Timmie. She had fallen utterly and totally in love with the child in the short time she'd known him. The floodgates of her heart had opened and let him in. Now she had to face the agony of letting him go. She was going to St. Cecilia's with them to say goodbye. The judge had signed the order in the courtroom, and his grandparents were flying him to Chicago with them that night. Their mission had been accomplished. A permanent order for custody would be confirmed to them in six months. And it was unlikely Timmie would ever see him again. She didn't intend to follow him into his new life, she knew it would be too confusing for him. She was just a loving person who had been there for him for a few days, before he went off to his life with them. But she wanted to see him one last time.

His eyes lit up when he saw her, and he looked at his grandparents suspiciously. He had never seen them before, and they were total strangers to him. The social worker told Sister Anne what had happened, why they were there, and she instantly looked at Timmie with deep compassion and put her arms around her. She knew what a blow this was going to be for her, to see Blake go. She would have loved to spare Timmie this agony, but there was no way to do that. Timmie was going to have to live with losing one more person she loved from her life. There was just no way out.

As Blake watched one of the nuns pack his bag, he looked suddenly worried. His eyes flew to Timmie's, as though asking for some explanation, and she spoke to him as she would any other child, and explained to him that these were his grandparents and they had come to take him home. He shook his head no, as tears bulged in his eyes, and he flew into Timmie's arms. It was the first time he had done that, and it made it that much harder for her. She nearly sobbed, as she held him, but she had to retain her composure for his sake. She told him he was going to go on a big airplane with them, and have a wonderful life in Chicago. Both his grandparents were crying then, and trying to talk to him, to reassure him. They saw that this was not going to be easy, and hardest of all for the child. They felt like monsters suddenly taking him from Timmie, but they wanted to take him home. The judge was probably right, Timmie knew, they looked like nice people, but she wished she were dead, as Blake clung to her and started crying. She held him tightly in her arms, loving him, and trying to comfort him as best she could this one last time.

The hideous moment finally came when he had to leave for the airport with them. He was crying loudly, and as they reached the door to St. Cecilia's and he clung to Timmie's hand, he suddenly turned and faced them all and shouted "No!" It was the first word he had said since he'd been there, and with that, Timmie held him close to her as they both cried, and she knelt down to look at him, trying to give him courage.

"It's okay, Blake. It's going to be fine. You'll be happy there. I promise. They love you, and they're going to be good to you. I love you too, but you have to go with them. You'll like it."

He said "No!" another dozen times, as he cried uncontrollably, and finally his grandfather picked him up in his arms and walked out the door, with a look of apology to Timmie. "I'm sorry," he muttered.

"I love you, Blake," Timmie called after him, knowing that in years to come he would no longer remember. It didn't matter. He would have a good life, and the woman who had loved him for a few days didn't need to be remembered. She knew that she would never forget him or the agony of this moment.

She stayed at St. Cecilia's with Sister Anne for several hours, sobbing in her arms, and aching for the child who had almost been hers, and never would be now. The one she thought Mark had sent her. He had slipped right through her fingers and her heart as Mark had years before. Apparently it was not her destiny to be Blake's mother, or anyone's. She felt as though Mark had died again when she went home that night. She could remember no other pain quite as agonizing as this one. The intolerable loss of a child, whether hers or not. And just for a minute, she had loved him.

She drove home alone that night, remembering the little face, so like her own and Mark's. She prayed for his happiness and safety, and then she prayed for her lost son, as she did sometimes. She felt as though a part of her had died that night when they carried Blake out, and he had looked back at her with those big green eyes that begged her to save him, and she couldn't. She lay in her bed and sobbed that night until nearly morning. It was two days before she could go into the office.

The lawyer had told David and Jade what had happened, and they very wisely said nothing when they saw her. She couldn't have borne it. Now all she had to do was live the rest of her life without him.

Chapter 11

Timmie was painfully quiet the following week in the midst of the final preparations for their trip, and she looked absolutely awful. Jade and David were worried about her, but continued to say nothing about what had happened. Sister Anne had called Jade several times to see how she was, and she wasn't surprised that Timmie was devastated. She had opened her heart to the child totally, and digging him out again was like taking a bullet out of her soul. She was still bleeding profusely, but doing so in silence. And given her history, losing one more person in her life was a far greater blow than it would have been for most people. For the remainder of the week, until they left, she didn't go near St. Cecilia's. For now, she couldn't. Sister Anne understood that.

They left for New York a week after Blake's hearing. She was relieved to get out of town for a while. The show went well in New York, and the trip to Milan after that. They arrived in Paris on schedule, and for the first time in weeks, Timmie looked a little better. Jade and David were relieved to see it.

They were landing at Charles de Gaulle as Timmie mentioned

Jean-Charles Vernier to Jade casually. She had been thinking of him on the flight. She felt silly mentioning him to Jade. Everything seemed unimportant to her now, in comparison to losing Blake. It was going to take her time to recover.

"Do you remember the doctor on the list?" Timmie asked, staring blankly out the window, as the landing gear came down.

"The one who took care of you when your appendix ruptured?" Timmie nodded. "What about him? Did he cancel? Should I take him off the list?" Jade had a thousand details to keep track of, and as usual, by the time they got to Paris, they were all stressed and exhausted, but Milan had gone well, and so had New York.

"No, he's coming." She hesitated for a moment, and then went on. "He's getting divorced." She added no further comment, and Jade stared at her.

"Are you telling me something?" Jade looked puzzled. "Do you like him?"

"He was very nice to me when I was sick. And yes, I like him. But not like that. I'm perfectly happy on my own. He'll probably be a mess for a while anyway." And so was she, after losing Blake. She felt like the walking wounded. She kept wondering how he was.

"That sounds to me like you like this doctor, Timmie." Jade smiled at her, wondering how long the ice queen phase would last. Timmie was capable of holding out for a long time, and often had, convinced she would never go out with a man again. She was firmly entrenched in that point of view now. But eventually, that always changed.

"I told him we were coming to Paris today. He asked. I wonder if I'll hear from him." She looked at Jade cautiously as she said it, and her assistant was intrigued. There was something about the way she talked about him that was sending up flares for Jade. It was good to hear her talk about normal pursuits, rather than mourning the child.

"You might," Jade said vaguely, and then decided to warn her. "Beware of married men, Timmie. Even if he says he's getting divorced, it could take him years." After her own bitter experience with her married lover, Jade was extremely sensitive on the subject, and somewhat paranoid. Timmie only nodded. She wasn't worried about Jean-Charles. There was nothing between them anyway. And she was in no mood for romance.

"I'm not going out with him. He's just coming to dinner," Timmie said vaguely, deciding silently that if he called her, he might be interested. And if he didn't call before the dinner party, he obviously wasn't. It would be interesting to see. There had never been anything flirtatious between them during her surgery and convalescence, but she had liked talking to him. There was something about him that she trusted, and made her feel safe whenever he was near.

The plane landed on the runway then, and she didn't mention him again. She was too busy to think about him, but the day of the show and dinner party afterward, it occurred to her that he hadn't called. The message was clear. No interest. Oh well. It was no big deal. The good news was that she was so busy, she had also had less time to think of Blake, although her heart still ached whenever she did.

They were as crazed as ever, before and during the show, but it went off brilliantly. The press loved it, the buyers were already placing orders. And by late that afternoon, before the dinner, Timmie felt as though she'd been on her feet for years. She was exhausted but elated, as she always was after a show, and wished she could lie down for a few minutes and get some sleep. But Jade had scheduled two interviews back-to-back before dinner. Timmie barely had time to change her clothes, and then run down to the private dining room to greet her guests. The press was late as always, the buyers came in a block, two of their biggest clients had just walked in, and then right behind them, she saw Jean-Charles, waiting politely to enter. She had been talking to their biggest client, when she broke away and went to greet him. As she had seen him dressed before, when he came to visit her after dinner parties, he was wearing a well-tailored dark blue suit, he was even taller than she remembered, and his eyes were an even brighter blue. She was wearing a black cocktail dress and high heels, with her hair pulled back, and diamonds on her ears. She looked elegant and simply dressed, and the dress was shorter than she liked, but it had a youthful, sexy look that appealed to her. It was one of her own dresses from that season, and had been a big hit.

"Good evening," the doctor said politely, but his eyes lit up when he saw her. Despite the warmth in his eyes, among the unfamiliar guests around him, he looked a little stiff.

"Thank you so much for coming," she said with a warm smile. She was disappointed that he hadn't called her during the week, but there was no reason why he should. And he was only a dinner guest that night, not a date.

"I hear the show was a big success," he complimented her, and she looked surprised.

"How did you hear that?"

"One of your guests was saying it on the way in. He said it was your best one yet." She looked pleased at his kind words, and introduced him to several guests before she left him again. He was going to have to fend for himself. She had thirty people to say hello to.

She didn't see him again until they were ready to be seated at the table. She had no idea where Jade had seated him. She had all the most important clients and buyers seated close to her, and Jade had done the rest. She noticed him taking his place at the other end of the table, and their eyes met, just as she sat down. He smiled at her, and then went on chatting to the woman seated next to him, a buyer from a department store chain based in New York. The press were seated at either end, with the *Vogue* editors closer to her.

It was an evening of work for Timmie, and she was sorry she couldn't talk to him, but she had to be the ambassador and spokesperson for Timmie O. She had a job to do, and she didn't get a chance to speak to him again until he was ready to leave, and came to say good night to her.

"You were very kind to invite me," he said warmly.

"I'm sorry we didn't get a chance to talk," she said sincerely. "These evenings are always work for me. I hope you had a decent time." The food and wines had been delicious, although she knew he didn't drink much. But at least the dinner had been good, and everyone seemed pleased. The atmosphere of the room was elegant and intimate and there had been a profusion of flowers on the table, low enough so people could talk across the table. Jean-Charles mentioned how pretty the flowers were.

"I was wondering if . . . perhaps . . . When are you leaving Paris?"

"Day after tomorrow," she said, surprised that he asked her, since she hadn't heard from him all week.

"Would you like to have a drink tomorrow? I'm afraid I'm not free for lunch or dinner. Are you free for drinks?" he asked, looking nervous and cautious. Timmie was startled. She hadn't expected to see him again after that night. And she was completely free the following day. They had set aside one day to wrap up. This time she had no time to spend a few days on her own in Paris, as she almost always did. They had important meetings in New York before they went back to L.A.

"I'd like that very much," she said in answer to his invitation. It would be nice to sit and talk to him again, without a flock of people around. It had been a busy night for her. "What time?"

"Six o'clock?" he asked, and she nodded.

"The bar?" He hesitated, and she realized that he might be nervous about being seen with a woman during the awkwardness of ending his marriage. "Would you prefer my suite?" He had been there before, and it seemed more discreet for him.

"That sounds very good. I'll see you then," he said, shook her hand, and left.

She didn't mention his invitation to Jade that night. They were both too tired to discuss anything except the obvious success of the party. Both Jade and David had to get up early the next morning, to make sure that everything got packed. Timmie was planning to make her final round of phone calls until noon.

It was late the afternoon of the next day, when Jade asked Timmie what she wanted to do for dinner, that Timmie mentioned that she was having a drink with Jean-Charles Vernier.

"You are?" Jade looked almost as surprised as Timmie had when he had asked her.

"Yeah," Timmie said casually. "No biggie. It was nice of him to ask." Jade had never seen him before the dinner the night before, and was willing to concede that he was a good-looking man. "Do you want to have dinner in my room afterward, or would you rather go out?" Timmie would have taken them if they wanted to, but both David and Jade looked wiped out. They had been working like dogs for hours, and she was tired herself after the grueling week.

"Do you mind doing room service?" Jade asked apologetically, and with a look of relief Timmie said it would be fine.

She left them then to brush her hair and put on decent shoes, and wash her face, before her drink with the doctor. She wasn't sure why he had asked her. He obviously wasn't interested in dating her, after not contacting her all week, and he had been very circumspect at the dinner. She was sure he was just being friendly, which was fine with her. They had enjoyed so many conversations when she was sick. She put on black pants and a black sweater, high heels, and brushed her long red hair with a bright green clip on one side. She looked elegant but sexy and casual, as the bell rang and she opened the door. He looked extremely serious for a moment when she first saw him, and then he smiled. His eyes always lit up when he did. She remembered that from four months before. He had kind, gentle, warm blue eyes. And this time he was wearing a blue shirt, blazer and slacks, and a serious dark tie. She noticed too as he walked in that his shoes were freshly shined.

"Good evening, Timmie," he said cautiously as he walked in. She thought he looked nervous, which was unusual for him. He never had before. "Did you work hard today?" he asked, as they both sat down and she asked him what he wanted to drink. He asked for champagne, since he was off duty. She had a glass of mineral water, as she sat on the couch across from him.

"Yes, I did work hard today," she said with a smile. "The day after the show is always a lot of work. Thank you for coming to the dinner party last night." She had seen that he'd been sitting between two intelligent women, and hoped he'd had a decent time.

"It was very nice." He smiled warmly, and she caught a glimpse of his friendly, kind expression, familiar from the hours they'd talked in the hospital four months before. "You were nice to include me."

She was dying to ask about the state of his marriage, but didn't dare. Instead, she inquired about his kids, and he said they were fine.

"Thank you for your card last fall," she said with a shy smile. "I almost answered it and then thought that was silly." He pulled his shirt-sleeve back then with a broad smile, and she saw the watch.

"It was a very handsome gift. You were very bad to do that," he scolded her.

"I like being bad." She laughed. "You were very good to me when I was sick." It seemed aeons ago now. She suspected that other patients had given him similar gifts before her, but it was always a little touchy as a single woman, giving a gift to a man, particularly if he was married, which seemed to be no longer the case now, given what he'd said on the phone when she called to invite him several weeks before.

"You're going to New York tomorrow?" She nodded. "For business or pleasure?" he inquired, and she laughed again, as he began to relax. She looked beautiful when she laughed.

"There is only business in my life, doctor. I don't have pleasure. I just work. I believe that was our first argument before my appendix exploded. I told you I couldn't deal with it until after the show." They both remembered it perfectly, and she recalled how annoyed he was, and the speech he'd made her that there were some things in life that were more important than work, like her health. And she hadn't listened to him, of course.

"That was very foolish," he scolded her, "and you paid a big price for it, I'm afraid." She nodded, thinking about it, and their eyes met as he set down the glass. "You've been well since I last saw you?" He looked at her as though it mattered to him, and she was touched. He was a kind man. She remembered thinking that she was sorry he was married, when she first noticed his wedding band. She looked again, and saw with some surprise that it was still there. He saw her glance, and nodded.

"It's hard to give up old habits. I'm not sure I'm ready to be perceived as a single man." It was an honest admission, and a big change for him, she knew, after twenty-seven years of marriage. He had been so adamant four months before that people needed to stay married,

despite diverging paths, separate interests, and whatever other challenges they had to face, particularly if they had children. She wondered what had changed to finally make him give up the opinions he
had then.

"I wore my wedding band for a long time too," she said gently, and
then decided to ask him. "What happened?"

He sighed and looked at her, as though facing the mystery of the
ages. "To be honest with you, Timmie, I'm not sure. I just couldn't do it
anymore. We had the same arguments we always did, and I woke up
one day, and I knew that if I did this for another year, it would kill me.
We had become total strangers. I have great respect for her, and she's
the mother of my children after all. But our lives have been separate for
years. We're not even friends. We were beginning to hate each other. I
don't want to live like that anymore. I don't want to be that person. I realized that I'm dead inside. Or at least I thought I was. Now I realize
that the marriage was dead, not I. I'm not looking for anyone else. I just
don't want to hurt or feel that way anymore. I knew I had to get out."

Timmie knew it was the sort of thing that did most marriages in,
the vast rift that happened sometimes when people were too different,
and only got worse if they forced themselves to stay together. They
continued to drift further apart day by day. "Our marriage died somewhere along the way," Jean-Charles continued very openly with her,
"and everything we ever felt for each other died with it. I knew we had
to finally bury it. It was cruel to both of us, and even our children, not
to. It's a terrible thing to end a marriage, but perhaps it's worse to live
that way." It was almost exactly what she had said to him four months
before. He hadn't been ready to hear it then. And now she was amazed
to hear him say it, given how normally proper, formal, and reticent he
was about his personal life.

"How are the children taking it?" She knew divorce was far less common in France. In the States it was an ordinary occurrence, here it wasn't as much so, and their reaction was likely to be stronger and different than what one would expect from kids in the States.

"We told them a few weeks ago. It was terrible. And I'm not entirely sure they believe us. My wife asked me to stay until the end of the school year, and I agreed to do it. We are selling our apartment, which will also be a big change for the children. Or my daughters anyway, both of them are still at home. My son is in medical school, so we rarely see him. It's not an easy time for any of us."

Timmie could tell just from looking at him that he felt extremely guilty. He had chosen his own relief and eventual happiness over theirs, and she knew from everything he had said to her before that it went against the grain of everything he believed in for him to do that. He was the last person she had expected to get divorced. And she knew he must truly have felt that his own survival was at stake to make such a serious decision. She sensed correctly that the last four months must have been rough, or simply the last straw. "I hope that eventually my daughters will forgive me. My son is older and a little bit more understanding. This was very hard on my wife and the girls." She was suddenly reminded of Jade and all the agony her married boyfriend had gone through.

"They'll adjust in time. Children always do. They love you. I'm sure this is very hard on you too. It's a big change for all of you. When did you make the decision?"

"Just after Christmas. The holidays were a nightmare. I decided I just couldn't do that again. So after agonizing a great deal over it, I decided not to stay. It was a terribly hard decision." His eyes told her that it was. It was all very new, for all of them. Christmas had only been seven weeks before. Not even two months yet. He must have been struggling with planning to tell his children when she called him the month before. It was a hard time for him, of loss, adjustment, and change. An enormous change for them all.

"I'm so sorry," she said, looking at him gently. She could see how difficult this was for him, and her heart went out to him. Their eyes met and held for a long silent moment.

"The marriage has been dead for years," he said hoarsely.

"I sensed that," she said carefully, "when we talked about it last October. But you had very different views about it then. I didn't agree with you about staying in a bad marriage, but everyone has to come to these decisions on their own. I never had a chance to make the choice. My husband just hit me over the head with the news, and then left." The news that he was leaving her, that he was gay, that he had a male lover he was madly in love with. And all of it just months after Mark's death. Even now, she could hardly think of the trauma it had been for her without wanting to cry, and she could see that there were tears in Jean-Charles's eyes. And without thinking, she reached out and took his hand in her own, just as he had once done for her when she was scared. "It's going to be all right, you know. The children will get used to it. Your wife will be okay. You'll find your feet again. It's just a very hard time right now. But people adjust to these things. The pain and the frightening part don't go on forever. Eventually, you won't even feel guilty," she said, smiling gently at him, as he nodded, grateful for her kindness, and even the warm gesture of her hand, which he hung on to. He didn't want to let it go, and neither did Timmie. They were rediscovering their bond of four months before, and it was subtly different now. They were not patient and doctor, but woman and man. It was a more level playing field, for both of them, but there were no masks or roles to hide behind.

"It's hard to imagine," he said softly. "Thank you."

Jade walked into the room then, to ask her something, saw that they were holding hands, and realized it was an awkward moment. She backed out of the room as quickly as she had come in, without saying anything, and closed the door.

"I'm sorry," he said apologetically. "You must be busy."

"Not at all," she said in a comforting tone. Timmie had always been a very nurturing person. With her son gone for the past twelve years, and no man of importance in her life, she had lavished her time and affection on her employees, who loved her all the more for it. And now, listening to her, and the comforting things she had said to him, he could see the depth of her character and the warmth of her love, as he hadn't been able to see in October, when she herself was so frightened. He could see now that she was on her feet again. Timmie was not only warm and giving, but rock solid. The traumas of her own past rarely showed, except in the compassion she felt for others. "We got everything done today. My assistants are just used to having access to me at all hours of the night and day," she said, acknowledging Jade's sudden appearance without knocking a moment before.

"They're very lucky to have you to rely on." He could see now what a tower of strength she was. She was not just powerful in the world, she was strong in her heart and soul and being. She would have had to be in order to survive all that she had gone through, from her son's death to her husband's betrayal, and all the horrors of her orphaned childhood. He remembered every detail of what she had told him, and admired her all the more for it. Now he could see where it had brought her, to a place of gentleness and kindness. Even though he had liked her before, he could see that he had underestimated her. She was truly a remarkable woman with a heart of gold.

"I'm very lucky to have them," Timmie said about her employees.

"They're like my family. We spend an enormous amount of time together. They're wonderful people."

"So are you," he said quietly. "I was very impressed by what you told me in the hospital last October. I haven't forgotten it. I don't know many people who have faced such enormous challenges, and who have still accomplished all that you have."

"Don't be too impressed," she smiled. "Remember what a mess I was with my burst appendix. When bad things happen like that, I turn into a terrified five-year-old in about five minutes. Maybe we all do. I hate to admit it, but I don't have the resilience I once had. Nowadays, the things that frighten me hit me much harder. Eventually the blows you've suffered take a toll."

"I feel that way myself sometimes, about the erosion of time and life. I think the disappointments of our marriage wore me down more than I thought. I was so tired of the constant criticisms and accusations. I was tired of feeling I was never enough. The day we told our children that we're getting divorced, I thought I would die when I saw them cry. I felt like I had killed them. It was a terrible thing to do to them. But in spite of that, I can't stay." He looked devastated as he said it, as Timmie's eyes held his.

"You didn't kill them," she said sympathetically. "They just don't know that yet. All they really need to know is that you still love them. That's not going to change. Once they understand that, they'll calm down, and everyone will feel better. They'll get used to the change in time. And they'll have their own lives. You have a right to yours."

"I keep worrying that they'll never forgive me," he said sadly, with worried eyes.

"Children always forgive parents who love them." She smiled then, and the light in her eyes touched his heart. "I even forgave mine for dying." The agony her parents' death had brought her had turned her childhood into a nightmare, and doomed her to a life in institutions and among strangers until she was an adult. But in the end it had made her a deeper, more caring person, and given her compassion for others' failings, tragedies, and ills, just as she felt now for his.

"Thank you for listening to me. I don't know why, but I knew you would understand . . . or maybe I do know why. You are a very strong woman with a kind heart," Jean-Charles said quietly as they continued to hold hands.

"I'm no stronger than you are, Jean-Charles. This is all very recent. You made a very big decision, and your whole life is in an upheaval. I promise you, it will all settle down again." She looked reassuring and calm, and he found himself soaking up the comfort of all she said.

He smiled looking at her, his eyes a deep vibrant blue. Hers were green and crystal clear. "Why is it that I believe you? You are a very soothing woman. And at the same time very convincing." Everything about Timmie exuded strength.

"I think beyond the fear and guilt, you know what I'm saying is true."

"Do you always speak the truth?" he asked her. It was an interesting question, which deserved an honest answer from her.

"As often as I can." She smiled more broadly then. "Most of the time, people don't like to hear it." She remembered her last meeting with Zack as she said it. It was six weeks before, and she had never heard from him again, and knew she never would. Much to her own surprise, it no longer mattered. It was as though he had never existed in her life, and in fact, he hadn't. All he had ever been was a convenience and an illusion. Jean-Charles was a deeply loving, caring man. She could see it in his eyes, and had known it since the previous October. She had viewed him differently then. He belonged to someone else. Now he seemed to be floating in space, trying desperately to find his footing. He wasn't used to being on such slippery ground, and he was finding it hard to live with. Just talking to Timmie helped, more than he had ever expected. His intention when he asked to meet her for a drink was simply to spend an hour or two in her very charming company. Now, much to his own astonishment, he was finding it was something else. He had no idea what, but something about her stirred him deeply, and he felt a powerful, inexplicable, almost irresistible link to her.

"Thank you for listening," Jean-Charles said, feeling vulnerable and slightly foolish. Four months before, he had provided strength and comfort for her, and now the tables had turned, and she was doing the same for him. More than he realized just then, it was a fair exchange. "What a shame you're not staying a few days longer. But then, I don't suppose it's very amusing for you, sitting here and listening to me tell you my troubles."

"We all go through hard times. I've had mine too. We all do. Don't feel guilty about yours. In the end, that's what makes us human." He realized again as he looked at her what an exceptional woman she was, to have come so far, had so much pain, still retain her compassion and humanity, and have come out the other end. And as he was thinking that, she was having almost the identical thoughts about him. "I'm sorry I'm not staying for a few extra days this time too. I hate leaving Paris. I don't even speak the language, but it has always been the city of my heart. I love coming here every chance I get."

"It's a beautiful city," he said, smiling at her. "I still appreciate it, even though I've lived here all my life."

"Are you originally from Paris?"

"I am, although my family came from Lyon. I still have cousins there, and in Dordogne. That's a lovely part of the country too. It's horse country for us," he said, trying to lighten the moment after his heartfelt confessions to her. He had bared his soul, and it embarrassed him somewhat.

"I've actually been there once, to visit friends," Timmie said. And then for no reason in particular she told him about Blake, how she had fallen instantly in love with him, wanted to adopt him, and lost him within days. Listening to her, his heart went out to her again. It was one more loss for her. "I'm so sorry that happened," he said sympathetically, his big eyes deep into hers.

"It was worth loving him, even if only for a few days. He was a lovely little boy." Jean-Charles found himself admiring her again for her huge heart.

He glanced at his watch then, and saw that he had to leave. He hated to leave her now, it had made him feel so much better talking to her. He was sorry that they didn't live in the same city and could be friends. They always had so much to say.

As though reading his mind, she looked at him with a smile as he stood up. "You should come to California sometime. Maybe now that you're free, you will." It might give him something to look forward to, and a brief change of scene, although it was so far away for him.

"Perhaps. I haven't been there in a long time. I go mostly to New York."

"That's not nearly as much fun," she chided him, and walked to where he stood, and then, as though an electric current had gone through both of them, she stood looking up at him. And as he looked down at her, he said not a word. She had a moment of brief, total insanity, and almost found herself drifting into his arms. She had to stop herself and resist a nearly irresistible pull, and she wondered if he felt it too. Surely not, she told herself, as he took a step back and looked at her. Just as she had felt it, he looked as though he had just been shaken by an electric shock. For a long moment, neither of them knew what to say. And then, feeling foolish, he thanked her for the champagne.

"Have a safe trip back to California," he said, groping for something to say on the way out. They had said so much, and now he could no longer find the right words.

"I'm actually going to New York for a few days. I won't be back in California till next week," she said, feeling dazed. They were both filling the air with empty words. There was something much bigger and deeper happening between them. If Timmie had believed in it, she would have called it love at first sight, but she had long since given up romantic notions like that. And so had he. This had to be something else. Perhaps a deep and unspoken admiring bond, which would evolve into a real friendship one day. She tried to tell herself it was that. "Take good care of yourself, Jean-Charles," she said, searching his eyes again, as though the answer to her questions was there. But all she saw was her own confusion mirrored in his.

"And you as well," he said. "Call me if I can ever do anything for you, like medical advice." It was all he could offer her now. But this was entirely different from the exchanges they had shared before. This was far deeper and more powerful than that. It had the force of a tidal wave.

He walked to the doorway and she followed him, and then just before he left he gave her a card with all his numbers, address, and e-mail on it, "in case she needed him," and asked her for hers. She jotted them down on a piece of paper and handed them to him, and gave him a hug as though they were old friends. *"Au revoir,"* she said, and he smiled.

"Merci, Timmie," he said in his deliciously French-accented words. And then without saying anything more to her, he left, and she stood staring at the door he had gently closed, as Jade walked into the room, and looked at her. Timmie turned to stare at her with wide, stunned eyes.

"Are you okay?" Jade asked, glancing at her in disbelief. In twelve years, she had never seen Timmie look like that. Nor had Timmie ever felt anything even remotely like it. Not even in October when she had met him before. Everything had been different this time, as were they.

"I'm fine," Timmie said, turning away, pretending to tidy up the room. She had to do something to keep from running after him. Whatever had just happened had confused her totally. It was dizzying. She felt as though the roof had just fallen on her head.

And then Jade looked at her again. "Oh my God, did he kiss you?" She couldn't think of any other explanation for why Timmie looked like that.

"Of course not," Timmie said in a strong, clear voice. "We just talked." She felt fiercely protective of all they'd said, and offered no more explanation than that.

"About what?" Jade asked, instantly suspicious, since technically, he was still a married man.

"Everything. Life. Children. His divorce."

"Jesus, I remember all that." She was so grateful now to be with a single man. "Has he moved out yet?" She knew all the questions to ask, as David wandered into the room.

"Has who moved out yet?" David looked confused.

"The French doctor. Timmie just had a drink with him."

"He seems nice."

"He'll be a lot nicer after he's divorced," Jade said tartly, and Timmie said nothing at all, while her assistants talked, unaware of the state she was in. Timmie could hardly breathe or think.

"Don't be so paranoid," David scolded her. "Give the guy a chance."

"I don't want the same thing to happen to Timmie that happened to me," Jade said, glancing at her boss. Timmie was standing there, looking thunderstruck.

"Are you okay?" David asked her, far more gently than Jade had. He could see that something earth-shattering had happened to her.

"I don't know," Timmie said honestly. "Something weird just happened to me." It was almost frightening, the feeling was so strong.

"Maybe it happened to him too," David said hopefully. "He looks like a mensch to me. I approve." Timmie smiled.

"Not so fast," Jade added, and then David beamed.

"Do you know what day this is?" David asked them both and they looked blank.

"Thursday?" Timmie offered, looking vague.

"That would be correct. But better than that, February fourteenth. Valentine's Day. Maybe Cupid struck."

Timmie smiled and shook her head. "I'm past all that. He's just a friend," she insisted, and after that they ordered room service and had dinner together. She never mentioned Jean-Charles again, but couldn't help wondering if he'd call that night. He didn't, and she had already gone to bed, when she heard an e-mail come in, in the living room of her suite. She couldn't resist getting up to see who it was from.

Her heart pounded when she saw it was from him. She clicked it open and stared at what he'd written, devouring every word.

"I am deeply troubled after seeing you today. I had a wonderful time, and now I can't get you out of my mind. You looked beautiful.

Thank you for talking to me. You are so very wise and kind. Have I gone mad, or are you as troubled as I? J-C."

She instantly sat down to write, with shaking hands, wondering how much she should say, and then decided to be as honest with him as she had told him that she was. All of Jade's warnings meant nothing to her.

"Yes, I am troubled too. And I also loved seeing you. I think the building fell on my head. I have no idea what it means. What do you think? Is insanity contagious? Do I need medical advice? If so, please answer immediately. Thinking of you. T." It was actually more than she intended to say, but she sent it before she could stop herself or take it back. He answered her immediately.

"Insanity is contagious. Extremely dangerous medical condition. Be careful. Perhaps we have both fallen ill. Whatever this is, clearly very serious case. When are you coming back? J-C."

"I don't know. Happy Valentine's Day. T."

"Oh my God . . . that explains everything. The work of Cupidon? I will call you in New York. *Bon voyage. Je t'embrasse.* J-C."

She could easily guess that Cupidon was Cupid in French, and she knew that *Je t'embrasse* meant "I kiss you." So Jade was right after all. He had kissed her . . . and her heart pounded harder still at the thought of his calling her on her cell in New York. She wanted to resist, she knew she had to. This was truly insanity. She lived in Los Angeles and he lived here. He wasn't even divorced yet. And sane adults did not fall in love at first sight. It just didn't happen, she told herself. She wouldn't let it. But even as she thought the words, she knew she had never been so taken with anyone in her life. The seed had been planted months before. Maybe his thank-you note with the sunset had been a message in a bottle after all. And now, on

Valentine's Day, the roof had caved in on them both. And the oddest thing of all was that it had happened to both of them at exactly the same time. All she could do now was hope he would call her in New York as he said he would. And then what would they do? She had absolutely no idea.

Chapter 12

The flight to New York seemed endless to her. Timmie hardly spoke to David and Jade, and this time she couldn't sleep, as she always did. She couldn't even work, or read.

All she did was think of Jean-Charles. She still didn't understand what had happened to both of them the night before. It was all very nice to say it was the work of "Cupidon," but what the hell had hit them, and why? She couldn't help wondering if it had actually occurred four months before. She didn't even know what had happened. But it had been obvious to both of them that something had. Whatever it was.

They went through customs in New York, and she declared the few things she had bought. David went outside to find their limousine, while Jade looked for a porter, and by habit, Timmie turned her cell phone on as she followed David outside so she could smoke. The moment she turned her phone on, it rang. It was Jean-Charles.

"Hello?" She had just walked through the door, as David motioned to her. He had found their car. She signaled to him and got in, as David went back inside for their bags.

"How was your trip?" He sounded very French and very sexy on the phone. She smiled just listening to him.

"Very long," she admitted. "I was thinking about you."

"So was I. Where are you now? At the hotel?"

"No. I just got off the plane. Your timing was perfect. I just turned on my phone, and there you were."

"I thought about you all day," he confessed. It was nine o'clock at night for him, and had been a very long day. He had just seen his last patient at the hospital, he told her, and was in his car, on his way home. "Timmie, what happened yesterday?" He sounded as thunderstruck as she was, and as confused.

"I don't know," she said softly. "It was Valentine's Day. Maybe that explains everything." She couldn't believe she was saying that to him. She had protected her heart for years, and had promised herself celibacy again, and now she was falling all over him, and talking about Valentine's Day. Maybe she truly had gone insane. But if so, he sounded as crazy as she did, and she loved that he had called her. It made her feel like a kid again. And then she thought of something she wanted to ask him. "Was there some hidden message in the thank-you note you sent me last fall? The one with the sunset in Normandy on it?" She was dying to know.

"I didn't think so then. But maybe there was. Now I think there must have been. I bought that card for you, and I thought a long time about what I wrote to you. First, I didn't want to make mistakes in English." She smiled at the admission. Everything about him touched her now. She loved the combination of his strength and vulnerability, his compassion and good heart, his concern about his children, his confusion about what they were doing, which mirrored her own. There was absolutely nothing about him she didn't like. "But I was also being very careful about what I said to you. I didn't want to say too much or too little. I was so touched by the beautiful watch you gave me. I've had gifts from patients, but never one as wonderful as that. And it meant so much to me because it was from you." He melted her heart with what he said. "It was a very sweet thing for you to do." He had been wearing it ever since, and told her that a minute later, and then Jade and David came out to the car with their bags. She didn't want to talk in front of them, and asked if she could call him an hour later from the hotel. He told her to call on his cell phone and he'd be waiting. They hung up then, and she chatted with David and Jade on the way into the city. They found her unusually animated, but had no idea what was going on. Neither did she. All she knew was that she was incredibly attracted to him, totally distracted, and suddenly obsessed with him. She felt like she was losing her mind, but if so, it was a very pleasant sensation, and she had no desire to stop it. All she wanted to do was speak to him again.

She called him back from the hotel as soon as she got to her room, and he stunned her by asking if she would wait for him in New York the following week. If so, he would come for a few days, spend some time with her, take her to dinner. He sounded desperate to see her again, and she wanted to too. But she couldn't the following week. She had just agreed to fly to Taiwan a few days after she got back, to deal with a crisis in their factory there. He sounded disappointed when she told him. But she still had her empire to run, even if something remarkable had happened to them the day before.

"You work very hard, Timmie," he commented, and she didn't deny it. She couldn't. He already knew her too well, and had seen it for himself. She wouldn't have denied it to him anyway. She wanted him to know who she truly was, and she wanted to know more about him. What his life had been like growing up, where he went to school, what his family had been like, did he have brothers and sisters, what were his children like, what were his dreams, his secret terrors, and what did he want from her? She wanted to know it all. He already knew her deepest secrets, and the most important things about her.

"What are we going to do?" Timmie asked him as she lay on her bed in the hotel. It was five o'clock in the afternoon for her, eleven o'clock at night for him. They were three thousand miles apart, and soon they would be twice as far. And she knew that if she had any sense at all, she would listen to Jade, and wait till he got out of his marriage, or at least moved out of his apartment, before getting too involved with him. But something was happening to both of them, and she was losing her head over him. She was so overwhelmed by her feelings for him that it had dulled the terrible ache of losing Blake.

"I don't know what we're going to do," he answered her honestly. "We need to take some time to find out," he said carefully. "This is all very new for me. I've never felt like this before." He was fifty-seven years old, and she was nine years younger, and she couldn't remember feeling like this before either. Not even with Derek when she fell in love with him. And surely not with anyone since. This was a unique experience in her life, and apparently his as well. "I'd like to spend some time with you. When are you coming back from Taiwan?"

"I'll only be there for a few days, I hope. I'm going on Wednesday, and I should be back on the weekend."

"Maybe I can come out to California after that," he said quietly, as a shiver of excitement ran down her spine. This was all happening so fast. She had no idea what to make of it, or how to defend herself against it, or if she even needed to. She needed time to figure it out, and so did he. He had already told her he wasn't moving out until June. That was four months away. And what if he changed his mind and didn't, as Jade's friend had done? What if he just stayed there forever, dangling her, once she was attached to him? But she could already hear herself throwing caution to the winds as she talked to him. She wanted him to come to California to see her as soon as he could. They both needed to find out what this was. "My marriage has been dead for years," he explained to her, as he had before. But she had understood that in October, perhaps even more than he had. His heart had been unfettered for a long time, he had just forgotten where it was and how to use it. And now it was coming alive like Rip Van Winkle, and everything in Timmie was turning to mush in response. This was no little crush, she felt sure of that. It was something huge happening, like a tidal wave that was pulling them both loose from their moorings, and they were both being swept away, while clinging to each other for dear life. And worse yet, neither of them had life jackets on, and they knew it. She was well aware of it as they talked.

They talked for an hour, until just after midnight his time, and then she lay on her bed in the hotel and thought about him for a long time. She thought about him later, when she knew he was sleeping, and at three o'clock in the morning in Paris, when she thought he was asleep, she heard an e-mail come in. She had just finished dinner with David and Jade, and they had gone back to their own rooms. She was alone when his e-mail came in.

"Dearest Timmie, I am thinking of you, and can't sleep. I am thinking of all that has happened to us in the past two days. I have no idea what it is either, but whatever it is, it is the most wonderful thing that has ever happened to me. I already know that with my entire being. You are the most exceptional woman, and I have no idea why I have suddenly been so lucky. Sleep well. You will be in my dreams. *Je t'embrasse fort.* J-C." Now he was kissing her "hard." She knew that was what *fort* meant. And the rest turned her topsy-turvy. She felt more dazed than ever as she read his e-mail again and again. She had never read anything more romantic in her life. They were like two children sending each other lovesick notes in class. She answered him immediately again.

"Dearest J-C, I miss you. How is it possible to miss someone you barely know? But I do. I have been thinking of you constantly again tonight. Come to California soon, whenever you can. Much to talk about, I think. *Je t'embrasse fort* too. T." She couldn't help asking herself as she sent the e-mail if she would sleep with him when he came to California, if he did. She didn't think she should. Maybe not until he left his house in June. That seemed the sensible thing to do. Because with a man as exciting as he was, she could easily be swept away. And once she slept with him, he would own her, in her heart and spirit. She felt sure of it as she went to bed that night. And no matter how smitten with him she was, she was determined to keep this chaste. She was going to tell him that before he came out. In the end, she said it to him in another exchange of e-mails later that night. By then it was morning for him, and he said he had watched the sun come up and thought of her. This was getting more serious and more passionate by the minute. But in spite of that, he agreed that they shouldn't sleep with each other when he came out to see her. He was treating her with great respect. And listening to how she felt. No one had done that for her before either. He truly was a remarkable man. She couldn't understand how his wife would let him go, nor how she had allowed herself to lose him, or why she had wanted to go separate ways for all those years before. Timmie couldn't help thinking that if she had been married to a man like him, she would never let him go. Not in a million years. He made men like Zack look embarrassingly inadequate, and her brief relationships with him and men like him seemed even more absurd to her now.

She was tired when she woke up in the morning, but still went to their factory in New Jersey anyway. She met with the plant manager, and they discussed all the problems they had there. She had a lot on her plate these days.

For the entire time she was in New York, Jean-Charles called and e-mailed her, and she felt as though she was returning to L.A. with a rare treasure. She had gone to Paris on business, and had fallen in love with a remarkable man.

She discussed it with Jade again on the way home. Jade was still leery of him, based on her own past experience, and admitted it. She didn't want Timmie to get hurt as she had, and she pointed out to her again that she could.

"Just try to stay sane," Jade admonished her, as though speaking to a kid sister instead of a woman who was ten years older, and wise in the ways of the world, although she had never gone out with a married man, and had to remind herself constantly to go slow. *Slow* was definitely not the operative word. They were anything but. And by the time she left for California four days later, he was even more enamored with her than before.

Timmie slept all the way back on the flight to California, and when she walked into the house in Bel Air, she felt as though everything had changed. A lightning bolt had struck her life in Paris in the form of Jean-Charles Vernier. He was on the phone to her now constantly, calling at all hours, speaking tenderly about his feelings for her. Neither of them could figure out what had happened, or why, but whatever it was, it was lighting up their world, like a beacon shining brightly in the dark. They were talking, laughing, sharing confidences, explaining about things they did, people they cared about, their lives as they grew up. He was the oldest of five children, took care of his parents, felt responsible for his brothers and sisters, saw them as often as possible, and seemed to feel a mantle of responsibility for everyone in his world. He was very French in his points of view, somewhat old-fashioned, extremely proper, and was suffering considerably from guilt and embarrassment that his would be the first divorce in their family, previously unthinkable, and finally inevitable. Even more so now with Timmie suddenly the object of his affections. By the time she left for Taiwan on Wednesday, they were talking several times a day, and admitting to each other that they were falling in love, based on the conversations they were having, their constant e-mails to each other, their confessions and admissions, and what they were discovering about each other. Timmie felt dazed.

"These things don't happen," she said to him, trying to hold on to the last wisp of sanity, the night before she left for Taipei.

"Apparently they do," Jean-Charles said calmly. Most of the time he was as disoriented as she was now. He said he had nearly asked a female patient the day before how her prostate was, as he carefully perused the wrong file. He had been planning to refer her to an ophthalmologist for cataract surgery. And neither of them had slept or eaten properly in days. She had no interest whatsoever in their factory disasters in Taipei. She was completely distracted, and whenever Jade or David talked to her, she looked happy and vague.

"I think I'm losing my mind," she said to Jean-Charles on the phone, sounding concerned. In fact, they had both lost their minds at the Plaza Athénée in Paris on Valentine's Day. "I always thought people who did this kind of thing were nuts. Whenever someone told me they had fallen in love at first sight, I thought they belonged in a straitjacket. And now it's happening to me." They were both grateful that he had been the doctor her friend referred for emergencies in Paris.

"Only happening?" Jean-Charles asked, sounding disappointed. "Falling in love with you has already happened to me. I thought it had to you too."

"You know it has," she said softly. A week before they had both been sane people, with careers that mattered to them and that they conducted efficiently. They were masters of their own worlds. Now he chafed at the burden of seeing patients, and she didn't give a damn about the next year's summer or winter lines. Fashion had become instantly unimportant to her, or at least far less interesting to her than Jean-Charles. And he had to force himself to pay attention to his patients, his appointments, house calls, and hospital visits. The only patient he wanted to talk to was Timmie, and she was no longer a patient, or at least not for the moment. He told his best friend in Paris, a radiologist who found his discomfort vastly amusing, that he was beginning to think Timmie was the love of his life. He had no idea how he had lived without her until that moment, nor could she imagine what her life had been before the constant phone calls and e-mails that told her how taken he was with her, how important she was to him, and how wonderful she was. It was an avalanche of emotions for both of them that bathed all in beauty and wonder and gave them both what they had lost years before, the gift of hope. Suddenly life was new and different. She couldn't even imagine how they would work out the distance between them, if they could ever blend two demanding careers. He had three children he loved in Paris. They had responsibilities and duties, he had a large family he was deeply attached to, and he wasn't even divorced. There was no question in either of their minds, it was utterly insane, or challenging at best.

But Timmie recognized that it was the sweetest insanity she had ever indulged in. When she married Derek, they had worked together for two years on the men's line, and their love was a slow evolution of their friendship and a shared interest in the business. This was a sharp clap of thunder in a summer sky, a lightning bolt that had electrified both of them to their very cores. Everything they'd ever known as solid reference points in their lives had suddenly shifted and changed. He had even begun to have bouts of panic about her safety and well-being, and was concerned about her traveling so far away. She had gone to Taipei with David, while Jade stayed in the office to field problems there. And as she had in New York and Los Angeles, she spoke to Jean-Charles several times a day from Taipei.

She flew back to Los Angeles on Saturday, and David brought up the subject on the long flight back. The trip had gone well, and they had managed to solve most of their problems, salvage the integrity of the factory, and replace two key employees, who they were convinced were stealing from them. But all of that seemed to pale in her mind in comparison to her conversations with Jean-Charles.

"Seems like you have a very serious case for the French doctor," David teased her over dinner on the flight. They both knew how Jade felt about it, that Timmie shouldn't even think about him until after his divorce was final. But David was well aware that sometimes real life didn't work that way. Timing was not in one's own hands, but in the control of the gods, no matter how reasonable one intended to be. It hadn't gone unnoticed on the trip that her cell phone rang constantly. And now, instead of looking irritated when she answered it, annoyed by the interruption, she beamed from ear to ear, and walked away to talk privately, even when in meetings, or in earnest discussions about some crucial issue. The woman of iron who ran the empire of Timmie O looked like a schoolgirl and giggled when she was on the phone. She seemed to have blossomed like a flower in the days since their trip to Paris, and her encounter with Jean-Charles at the Plaza Athénée on Valentine's Day. Their feelings for each other were growing exponentially day by day.

David liked everything he was seeing, and the softness it gave her. This was exactly the kind of companion he had hoped she would find one day. Kind, intelligent, trustworthy, responsible, a man of substance and morals, respected in his own world, and hopefully able to deal with hers, without petty jealousy or ulterior motives, like all the unworthy men who had come before him, and with whom Timmie had sought refuge in order to avoid loneliness and solitude.

The only fly in the ointment David could see so far was the wife he had not yet divorced, but said he was planning to. And David felt in his gut that if this man said he was going to free himself of the bonds of his marriage, he was certain that he would. Not so for Jade, who trusted no one still legally married, and was absolutely certain he would jerk Timmie around without mercy, break her heart, and dump her on her head.

"What's the worst that could happen?" David said philosophically as they finished dinner on the plane. "You could end up dumped, duped, and distraught. So what? You've lived through worse, much worse. It's worth taking a chance. From everything you've said about how he took care of you in October, and how crazy he is about you now, I trust this guy. Don't ask me why, but I do. My gut tells me you'll be okay."

"Tell that to Jade," Timmie sighed. She was trying to say as little as possible to her, or to anyone for the moment. But traveling with David, it had been obvious to him what was happening, and since he was so enthusiastic, she had been fairly open with him in the past few days. "I think what scares me is that it's happening so fast. I've never trusted things that happen that way. I always thought the right things took time, even a lot of time." But her business didn't always happen that way either. Sometimes her best decisions had come to her like lightning bolts, just like her sudden romance in Paris. The whole thing had arrived in their lives, ready to go and fully formed. There was no infant stage.

"I think it happens this way sometimes," David said quietly, looking at her with a warm smile. "I hope it works. I think it will. I'm happy for you, Timmie. You deserve it. No one can shoulder the load forever all alone. Life is too hard that way. You've been pushing boulders up-hill alone for a hell of a long time. I don't know how you do it. And you make it seem effortless most of the time. I think I'd have given up years ago in your shoes," particularly after the hard blows that had happened to her, losing her son, and then her husband in such a shocking way. It would have been enough to knock lesser people off their feet, and dishearten them completely. It had decimated Timmie too, but she had gone on anyway, on sheer grit, with the kind of dogged determination and strength that made her who she was. Her blessings had been hard earned. "I know it's early days yet, very early days. But I trust this for you."

"I know it sounds crazy," she said quietly, "but so do I. It's hard to explain it to anyone sane though. If I told anyone I had fallen in love at first sight at the Plaza Athénée, they'd have me committed. And if someone told me that, I'd probably think they were crazy too. But this feels right to both of us, or as though it could be. And I haven't even kissed the man, or gone to bed with him."

"That'll give you something to look forward to," David teased her.

"I'm not even sure I will. Not for a while anyway. I think I want to wait to sleep with him, until he moves out in June. Just to be on the safe side, and make sure he makes it out of enemy territory." It was the sensible thing to do, and she had said as much to Jean-Charles again on the phone the night before, and he agreed. He wanted to do what was right for her, and he respected her wishes. But they had both laughed and were in complete agreement that it was going to be a long four months till June.

"I know whatever happens, you'll do the right thing," David reassured her. "And don't be too tough on yourself if you change your mind and wind up in bed with him before June. Worse things could happen. Sometimes it's hard to slow down that train. Maybe you don't even need to slow it down, if you really love each other." He had enormous respect for her judgment, her wisdom, her integrity as a human being, and the fact that she was throwing her heart over the wall for Jean-Charles told David a lot about him. He had never seen her do that before, and had never expected her to. She wouldn't have done it for just anyone. He had to be a very special man for Timmie to feel this way. Timmie felt sure he was. She had no doubts about him whatsoever, and trusted her instincts unfailingly this time. She was sure she was right about who he was.

It was a long flight home, and finally she slept. She dropped David off at his apartment on her way back to Bel Air, and her driver carried her bags in for her. Her phone rang almost the instant she got home. She picked it up, expecting it to be Jean-Charles, and instead it was Jade.

"How was the trip?"

"Long," Timmie said. It felt good to be back, and it would be better yet to sleep in her own bed. She felt as though she'd been traveling forever, after the weeks in Europe, and now the trip to Taipei. "But good." She told her about the problems she and David had resolved. It had gone better than either of them had hoped.

"I hate to do this to you, but you've got to go to New York tomorrow. The union struck the factory in New Jersey while you were on the plane. They want you there for the negotiations. You may be able to solve it quickly, but if not, we're going to miss all our deliveries for spring. I hate like hell to tell you that. I told the lawyers you couldn't do it, and they say you have to."

"Shit," Timmie said, and sat down. "I haven't been back for ten minutes. When do I have to go?"

"I've got you on a noon flight tomorrow. Something could change in the morning. But it didn't look like it at six o'clock tonight. I'll call them at seven from my house. You may not have to stay for more than a day or two. I just called David, he said he'll go with you. You must feel like you're traveling through outer space these days. I tried to get you out of this trip, but I just couldn't." She knew Timmie was exhausted. Timmie looked at her suitcase when she hung up. There was no point unpacking. She would just take all the same things to New York. And as she contemplated getting on a plane again, her cell phone rang. It was Jean-Charles. She told him about the trip to New York, and the reason for it, and there was a long silence at his end. He was thinking. She was ready to cry, she was suddenly so tired. And she hated dealing with unions. They were always so damn unreasonable, and she couldn't afford to miss all her spring deliveries. It just wasn't fair.

"What if I meet you there?" he asked gently, afraid to intrude on the running of her business. But he was dying to see her, and suddenly saw the hand of providence offering them a gift.

"Are you serious?" She smiled, and felt something in her stomach do a small, neat flip, like a tiny gymnast doing somersaults. She had wanted some time to get used to the idea of what they were saying to each other, and make sure that it was real. Seeing him again so soon in New York was going to be extremely real, and maybe more than she could deal with just yet. She wasn't sure. But her desire to see him again and see what this was was stronger than the fear.

"I am. Unless you think it would be an intrusion, with the problems you have to deal with there."

"I probably need a day or two to sit down with the union lawyers and see how bad it is. But . . . I'd like to see you . . . ," she said softly, remembering what she had said to him, that she wouldn't sleep with him, or even date him, until he moved out in June. It seemed the wisest course to her, and a better way to start, to wait for him to move out before they began a relationship, even if they were falling head over heels with each other. Sensible people could wait, and if this was real, it would. He had agreed.

"When are you going?" Jean-Charles asked cautiously. He would have to cancel his patients, and find someone to cover for him, not always an easy task.

"Tomorrow at noon," Timmie said with a sigh. All she had time to do was get a good night's sleep and walk out the door again. She no longer had any idea what time zone she was in. She felt like she was in outer space. But part of that too was the excitement of what she was feeling for Jean-Charles. That had disoriented her too, but in the nicest way.

"They don't give you any time to breathe, do they?" he said sympathetically. "Must you do all of this yourself?" he asked, sounding worried about her. "Is there no one who can take some of this off your shoulders for you?"

"Not really." They both knew she was too much of a perfectionist to let any of it go. She liked overseeing it all herself, and having her finger in every pie. It was part of the legend of Timmie O. She did damn near everything herself, from designing their collections to running the whole show. She was a magician of sorts, a high-wire act that dazzled the crowd, with no net under her most of the time, except the faithful employees she kept close. But the responsibilities of making the entire operation run rested on her. Jean-Charles had begun to see that now, as he called her all over the world.

"Why don't I come to New York on Thursday?" he suggested. "That will give you time to deal with the problems in New Jersey. Can you take a few days off? It would do you good." And him as well.

"I'll try," she said, her mind racing over all she had to do. She felt as though she were falling behind, and then suddenly she took a breath, and realized what he was offering her. The opportunity to love and be loved, a glimpse of a whole new world. "No," she said, sounding stronger, and different. Her priorities had already begun to shift ephemerally in the past two weeks. "I will." She held her breath, thinking of him. This was terrifying and wonderful, something she had never expected, a dream she had never in a million years thought would happen to her. "Can you really come to New York?" She felt like a child waiting for Christmas as she thought of it. Now waiting even a few days to see him seemed too long. Fate had handed them an opportunity, and neither of them was going to miss it. It was time to reach for the brass ring as the merry-go-round went round and round. The prospect of catching it was dizzying for both of them.

"Of course I can come," Jean-Charles said reassuringly. "How could I not, Timmie?" he said, sounding so loving, it nearly made her cry. "I'm doing this for myself as much as I am for you. I want to see you." They both wanted to see now if this was real, even if they still had to wait several months until he was physically free. "Do you want me to stay in a different hotel?" he asked sensibly. "I don't want to cause any problems for you, or embarrass you."

"I think we can behave ourselves," she said, sounding confident. "Why don't you stay at the Four Seasons too? It would be silly if you didn't."

"I'll make a reservation for Thursday . . . and Timmie . . . thank you for meeting me . . . and letting me come . . ." He sounded moved, and so did she. She was so tired that all her emotions were close to the surface, but they had been for two weeks, and perhaps even before. She was beginning to think that this had been brewing since her ruptured appendix in October, without either of them knowing, or wanting to admit it to themselves.

"Thank you for coming to New York," she said gently. She could hardly wait to see him, and he sounded as excited as she.

"I'll take the night flight back to Paris on Sunday. That will give us three and a half days, nearly four. I'll take an early flight on Thursday morning, and with the time difference, I could be at the hotel by noon."

"I can't wait," she said softly, although she was frightened now. They were both taking a step into the future, which would either take them one step closer to their dreams, or dash them forever. And then she forced herself to remember this was only a weekend, a string of days to spend with him, and discover who he really was, while he did the same with her. It was an exploratory mission between two people who had been struck by lightning. What they needed to know now was whether or not to go forward. Perhaps they would see each other and realize how foolish they had been for the past two weeks. It was still possible that it was only an illusion. True or false? Dream or real? All either of them knew was that they would find out in New York.

"I'll see you in New York on Thursday," he said gently. "Now get some sleep. I'll talk to you tomorrow." She said good night to him, and realized as she hung up that she had almost said she loved him. How could she love this man she scarcely knew, so soon, and what were they doing? All either of them knew was that they would find the answers, some of them at least, in New York. Timmie stood looking around her bedroom, feeling thunderstruck again, and suddenly frightened, as Jean-Charles sat staring out the window in his office in Paris, thinking of her, and smiling. He had never been as happy in his life.

Chapter 13

Miraculously, after ten hours a day at the bargaining table, negotiating with a fleet of lawyers beside her, Timmie was able to resolve the strike at the factory in New Jersey. It had cost them dearly, but it was worth it. The factory opened again on Wednesday night, with new overtime rates, new benefit packages, and a higher wage for all their workers. Sometimes you had to know when to be tough, and when to give in. Timmie had a good sense of what it took to keep her business running. She felt relieved, if not victorious, when the union backed off and the employees went back to work. David shook her hand in open admiration, and booked a seat on the last flight to L.A. out of Newark, and was surprised when Timmie said she was staying in New York.

"God, I would think you'd be as anxious to get back as I am." This was why he hadn't had a serious relationship in nearly two years. Who could find the time when they were flying between Paris, New York, L.A., Taipei, and back to New York again? It was hard to believe, but Timmie didn't even look tired. She liked to say she had the constitution of an ox. She seemed like Superwoman to him.

"I'm taking a few days off," she said quietly.

"Why here?" He looked puzzled. It was freezing cold, and had snowed three times in two days. All he wanted was to get out and go back to L.A. She was obviously in no hurry to go back, and he guessed that she just wanted to disconnect after the many trips and complicated negotiations. He could hardly blame her, and maybe she could do it better in New York, three thousand miles from her office, although her business and the demands it made on her followed her everywhere, even here.

"I just want to take it easy," she explained, as they left the last of the negotiations, with the lawyers following behind them, congratulating each other. "I want to sleep, go to some plays, and shop." It never occurred to him that she was meeting Jean-Charles in New York, and she wanted to keep it to herself. Like a newborn baby, she wanted to protect the fledgling feelings they had for each other. For this first time anyway, she just wanted to disappear with him, and see what happened. They had already agreed what wouldn't, the rest remained to be seen, and didn't need to be observed, or even acknowledged, by anyone else.

She went back to the hotel that night and slept for hours. It was too late to call Jean-Charles when she got back from Newark. And when he left Paris the next morning, it would be too early for her. Due to the time difference, there would be silence between them until he arrived. He had told her not to meet him at the airport. He would meet her at the hotel, and call her as soon as he arrived. As it turned out, she went to bed so early, and slept so deeply, that she woke up just after six o'clock in the morning. She had plenty of time to bathe, dress, have breakfast, and meet him at the airport. She had his flight number, and called her driver at seven o'clock. She told him to meet her downstairs at nine. Jean-Charles's flight was arriving at ten A.M. She just hoped she wouldn't miss him as he came out of customs, which was always a zoo in New York.

She was pensive on the way to the airport, thinking about him, and all they had said to each other in the past two weeks. They had both allowed themselves to go to the edge of reason. What if in the clear light of day, it was a total bust? They were both well aware that that could happen. She couldn't wait to see him and find out, although it was scaring her to death. It seemed crazy to have these adolescent feelings at her age.

As his plane landed at Kennedy Airport, Jean-Charles was having the same thoughts. What if it had been his imagination? Or hers? A wild flight of fancy, a mad infatuation that would evaporate instantly the moment they saw each other? They were about to find out. He was glad he still had some time to compose himself, going through customs, and the long cab ride into the city. He wanted to shave and shower before he saw her. And as the plane touched the ground, he saw that it was snowing. Big graceful flakes that were falling slowly from the sky. There was a blanket of snow, added to what had fallen earlier that week. There was a magical quality to it as they taxied down the runway toward the terminal, stopped, and the jetway was attached to the plane.

He was one of the first to leave the aircraft, with the carry-on he had brought with him. He had no bags to claim, all he needed was a stamp in his passport at immigration, and he would be on his way. His heart nearly pounded as he stood in line, got his passport stamped, and walked into the terminal with his head down, thinking about her, and the fateful meeting, and ensuing days, that were about to happen at the Four Seasons in New York.

Timmie was standing just outside the doors leading from customs, leaning against a pillar and intently watching the people coming out.

She was suddenly afraid that she would miss him, or perhaps already had. But the flashing sign said his flight was still in customs. She was watching the doors, as she suddenly saw him come out, with his head down, in a navy blue topcoat, and his bag in his hand. She smiled the minute she saw him, and felt her heart leap, as he walked toward her, never knowing she was there. She had no doubt in her mind or heart as she saw him walk toward her. She knew that what she was seeing was her destiny, in the form of this one man.

He was only a few feet away from her, when instinctively, he looked up and saw her. His breath caught, and he stopped, smiling slowly. She took two long steps toward him, as he let go of his bag, and he put his arms around her. People swirled around them, like water in a stream, as Jean-Charles held Timmie tightly in his arms, and forgetting everything around them, he kissed her, and she felt everything in her soul dissolve into his. They stood there for what felt like an eternity as he held her, and could barely pull away from each other, until at last he looked down at her and smiled.

"*Bonjour,* Madame O'Neill," he said gently as she smiled up at him.

"*Bonjour, docteur,*" she whispered back, and felt an overwhelming urge again to tell him she loved him. And instead, she just smiled at him, and everything she felt for him showed in her eyes. "I'm so happy to see you." Every fiber of her being trembled as she said it. She had never been as happy to see anyone in her life. She had the feeling as she stood and looked at him that a great love story was beginning.

Slowly, with his arm around her, they walked out of the airport, and she found her driver. Jean-Charles kissed her again the moment they got in the car, and they talked quietly all the way into the city. She explained to him about the union negotiations she had been doing, and all the intricacies involved, as he listened with fascination. They talked about his work, his patients, and above all, they talked about how excited they were to see each other, which was obvious just looking at them both.

He checked into the hotel and she followed him to his room, which was on the same floor as hers. They were both on the forty-eighth floor with a spectacular view of the city. And again in his room, he set down his bag, and took her in his arms, as they both became aware that sticking to their plan of abstinence was going to be a greater challenge than expected. Timmie was beginning to wonder if they had been somewhat optimistic about their ability to resist each other. What they were both aware of now was that after their confidences of months before, their many phone calls in the past weeks, and their irresistible attraction to each other, they felt totally at ease in each other's company, as though they were picking up the threads of an existing, or even long-term, relationship, not a meeting between strangers. They felt like two halves of a single whole that fit seamlessly together. The result was a sense of unity and love that astounded them both, and took Timmie's breath away, as he held her in his arms again and kissed her. Even after the brief time they had shared, there was no question in her mind that she loved him. And she could see in his eyes that what she felt for him was the mirror image of everything he was experiencing toward her.

They went back to her suite so she could check her messages, and decided to take a walk in the park to get some air. They walked down the snow-covered path in Central Park, with drifts on either side of them, and everything was blanketed in pristine beauty. She threw a snowball at him, which left powdery marks on his dark blue coat, and he gently tossed a handful of the sugary loose snow at her bright red hair. She wanted to run through the snow with him, to be a child again, to share all the joy that neither of them had ever before known until they found each other.

Their faces were bright with the cold, as they walked back toward the hotel, and then on a spur-of-the-moment impulse, he hired a horse-drawn hansom cab to drive them through the park in the winter wonderland all around them. They sat in the cab, with a heavy blanket over their laps, snuggled next to each other like happy children. And afterward, they went to lunch at the Pierre. It was mid-afternoon by then, and they wandered through assorted stores on the way back, and finally got back to her suite, looking happy and relaxed. They hadn't stopped talking all afternoon, and had held hands throughout like high school lovers. Timmie felt fifteen years old again, and Jean-Charles said he felt twenty. And for her, it was a far happier fifteen than she had ever known or dreamed of. For this infinitely precious moment in time, life was perfect, with him.

"Where would you like to go to dinner, my darling?" he asked her, as they relaxed in the living room of her suite. He suggested Café Boulud or La Grenouille, which were the only restaurants he knew well in New York. She knew a variety of more fashionable options in SoHo and the West Village. In the end, they decided on a tiny restaurant she knew, which was warm and cozy. They had days to decide where else to go, to show off, to indulge themselves, and to discover each other.

He left her so she could dress, and went back to his own room to shower and change. She beamed at him when she opened the door to him again an hour later. He looked impeccable and elegant as always, and he was struck yet again by how beautiful she was, with her big green eyes, long red hair, and lithe youthful body. She was glowing. He kissed her the moment he saw her, and followed her slowly into the suite, with his arms tight around her. She was dizzy when they stopped, and her voice was soft with dusky passion. Suddenly, their dinner plans seemed of no interest whatsoever, to either of them, as he stood there kissing and holding her, unable to resist her.

"I'm sorry...I can't stop...," he said hoarsely, as she smiled shyly at him. She didn't want to stop either, and without saying a word to him, she kissed him again, and slowly took off his jacket and began unbuttoning his shirt. It was a not-so-subtle message, and he pulled away to look at her with a question in his eyes. He didn't want to do anything she would regret later, and he knew how strongly she felt about his intermediate situation, on the way out of his marriage. "Timmie, what are you doing?" he asked gently.

"I love you," she said softly.

"I love you too," he whispered to her, and then said it in French, which felt so much more natural to him, and more real than anything he could say to her in English. *"Je t'aime...tellement...* so much..." She could see in his eyes that he meant it. It seemed stupid now to follow rules and plans that had made sense in the beginning, and made no sense now in the face of how deeply they were falling in love with each other. The boundaries were rapidly dissolving between them. "I don't want you to do anything that you will be sorry about later. I don't want to hurt you."

"Will you hurt me, Jean-Charles?" she asked, looking at him sadly. She was asking if he would betray her, if he would never leave his wife, or abandon her one day. Promises that were as fragile as butterfly wings, and could not always be protected. They both knew there were no guarantees in the world, only hopes and dreams and good intentions. They were both people of honesty, integrity, and goodwill. Perhaps it was all one could hope for.

"I hope never," he said honestly, and she could see that he meant it as she nodded. "And you?"

"I love you...I will never betray you, and hope I never hurt you." They were the only vows they could exchange at this point in their lives, the promise to do the best they could to stand side by side and protect each other. It was enough for Timmie, and for now it was enough for Jean-Charles as well. No one could see into the future and predict the challenges or pain that would come later. The only question was if they were willing to risk the uncertainty of life, to weather whatever storms came, together.

She said not a word to him then, and walked him slowly into her bedroom, where she unbuttoned his shirt, undid his belt buckle, and gently slid off his trousers, as he undressed her, and within moments, their clothes lay in a heap on the floor, tangled together, and they slid under the sheets together, her long smooth ivory body entwined in his powerful male one. The room was dark, and she could feel the force of his passion for her throbbing next to her, as she ached for him to be inside her.

"Timmie, *je t'aime . . . ,*" he moaned softly, as she almost purred with desire for him, and told him she loved him too. And then suddenly their passion overwhelmed them, irresistible, beyond measure or reason, a tidal wave of desire that swept them both away with such overwhelming force that neither of them could have stopped it, nor wanted to. Timmie gave herself to him completely, her hopes, her dreams, her heart, her body, and he took her with him on a journey of such love and passion that they both knew without question that wherever it led them, they had no choice now but to be together. They both sensed as they lay in each other's arms that it was destined.

And later, as they lay clinging to each other peacefully, two bodies seeming one, they dozed peacefully, and their dinner plans were forgotten. What had happened was so much better. They had crossed the bridge from uncertainty into a sure love for each other. The tides of passion had brought them there, and what they found now in each other's arms was a love that had irreversibly bound them together. With luck, and the blessing of the gods, hopefully forever.

Chapter 14

The days Timmie and Jean-Charles shared in New York were magic. They took long walks in the park, went to art galleries, and stopped in funny little restaurants for coffee, or pizza when they were starving. They walked all over SoHo, enjoying its charms and delights, and between times and all night long, they fell into each other's arms with insatiable passion. Timmie had never made love so often in her life, and Jean-Charles rediscovered youthful powers he had long since thought were forgotten. They made love for hours. They were both in odd time zones from their travels, dozed and slept, woke to make love, took naps in the afternoon once they were sated, and called room service for enormous breakfasts at four in the morning. One night they left the hotel on foot as it began snowing again, and found a truck stop on the West Side, where they ate steak and hash browns at five in the morning.

There was an incredible surreality to it, a sense that they were dreaming. And yet again and again, as they woke up and saw each other, they smiled broadly, and then laughed with the sheer joy of the miracle they were sharing. On Sunday, as Timmie packed her bags, she looked bereft, as he lay in bed and watched her.

"I don't want to leave you," she said sadly. After living with him for only four days, she could no longer imagine a life without him. This was dangerous, heady stuff, and they were both becoming rapidly addicted to it. He was just as besotted as she was, and just as sad to leave her.

"Nor I," he said, looking somber. "I don't want to go back to Paris." But they both had lives they had to return to. "I will come to California to see you."

"Do you promise?" She felt like a frightened child as she said it. What if she never saw him again? If he changed his mind, or abandoned her, how would she survive it? She had lost so many people she had loved before that she could no longer bear the thought of that happening to her again. And he understood what he was seeing. Her panic mirrored his own, just as their love for each other was an identical reflection of what each felt for the other. They were perfectly matched in their passion, feelings, and terror.

"I don't want to lose you either," he said gently, coming to put his arms around her, as he pulled her slowly back to their bed. "And of course I will come to California. I will not be able to live for long without you." He had a dramatic bent to him, which she was discovering was the flip side of his immense love for her, and she liked it.

And then she turned to him with an unexpected question, as she lay in his arms. "When are you moving out of your apartment?"

He looked upset when she asked him. He hated to think of that now. This was the only life he wanted. His past life no longer existed. It had been dead for years, and the ashes of it had gently dispersed as his bond to Timmie grew stronger. She was not taking him away from anyone, she was welcoming him into her arms, soul, and life, just as she had into her body, with overwhelming love and gentle passion.

"I told you before. In June. I told my children I would stay until the end of the school year. I hope we will sell the apartment by then. But if not, I will move out over the summer." It seemed a long time to Timmie, but she had only just arrived in his life, and didn't feel right pressing him about it. She wanted to be fair...but if he didn't move...if Jade was right, or he prolonged it for years...what then? "Please don't look so worried," he said, pulling her tightly into his arms to reassure her.

"I am," she said honestly, "it scares me." She had held nothing back from him, no part of herself. She had left herself wide open to be wounded, if for some reason he chose not to join her on the journey of a lifetime. What frightened her, as it always did, was the prospect of being abandoned on the shore, terrified and alone. "What if you never leave her?" She looked panicked.

"We left each other years ago," he said simply and honestly. It was, in his view, a correct assessment of the situation. "I am there for my daughters, not for her. It is a promise I made them," he said solemnly. "I owe that to my children." And what would he owe her? She knew she could not compete with the love he had for his children, nor did she want to. She didn't want to tear him apart, or pull him away. She wanted him to willingly come with her.

"What if your daughters beg you not to leave in June? What if..." The agonies of the unknown always plagued her. The past had always been so much worse than she expected, and never better. It was always hard for her to believe that the future would be different.

"Then we'll deal with it then," he said calmly, which did not entirely reassure her. He was not saying that he would leave no matter what. He was leaving the door open, to see what came later. She would have much preferred a firm promise, a vow sworn in blood, but she knew that now she had to trust him. She had cast her lot with his, for better or worse, whatever happened. "I love you. I am not going to hurt you or abandon you." He knew her history, he had seen her raw terror the night of her appendectomy. He was mindful of her fears, and willing to reassure her. "I love you. I need you now, just as you do me. I am not going to walk away from you, Timmie. I promise."

She sighed at the comfort of his words, as she lay with her back against his chest. He was pressed tightly against her with his arms around her, and she felt safe and protected. "I hope not." She turned to kiss him, and although the time was growing short, they made love for a last time, and then afterward sat in the bathtub together as they had many times that weekend, talking and laughing and teasing, and enjoying their last moments together.

When the time came, it was nearly impossible for Timmie to tear herself from their room. She wanted to stay there, lock the door, and cling to him forever. She didn't want to leave him, or fly thousands of miles from him, while he flew just as far in the opposite direction. He saw all the agony of what she felt in her eyes as he held her.

"We will be together again soon. I promise." She loved the way he reassured her, and everything about him made her believe him. She had never thought herself capable of trusting anyone again, and yet she trusted him now. Completely. She just prayed she was right to do so. But in any case, she had no choice. For better or worse, she was his now. And with the grace of God, he was hers.

They rode to the airport in her limousine, and he took her to the terminal for her flight. Hers was leaving first, and he had to leave her at the security checkpoint. They were barely able to leave each other, and she looked devastated as she stood at the other side of the security lines, waving at him as he watched her. He felt as though he were watching a small child he loved being taken away. All he wanted was to cross the lines and take her in his arms again to reassure her. And as soon as she vanished from sight, he felt bereft himself.

He called her on her cell phone as she walked to the gate.

"I miss you too much," he said miserably. "Perhaps we must run away together."

"Okay," she said, smiling. She was so happy to hear him. "When do you want to go?"

"Now." He was smiling too, as he got out of the car at the international terminal, to catch his flight to Paris.

"Thank you for the most wonderful weekend of my life," she said softly.

"You made my dreams come true," he said gently, as moved as she was. And then he laughed. "And you have certainly reinspired my lost youth." They hadn't stopped making love day and night, and both had claimed they had never before experienced anything like it. They were a red-hot dazzling combination. Like fire on dynamite. Each time they touched it was an explosion. "I'll call you as soon as I arrive," he promised. She knew he would. Jean-Charles was a man who kept his promises, which she loved about him. She hated to think of him going home to the apartment he still shared with his wife, but even that worried her less now than it had at the beginning. He just needed time to work it out, and live up to the agreement he had made with his children. She believed him. And a passion like theirs couldn't be resisted. She had a feeling now that it would all work out in the end.

She boarded the plane and took her seat in first class. Thinking of him, and the wonders they had shared for four days, she closed her eyes, and slept all the way back to L.A.

When she got home, she couldn't stay awake long enough to call him. She had to stay up till midnight, in order to call him in his office in the morning. She was sound asleep long before that, and then awake at five A.M. It was sad waking up without him, and the days in New York already seemed like a distant dream. It was two o'clock in the afternoon for him when she called him at five A.M. in L.A. He was just coming back from lunch, and was delighted when he heard Timmie's sleepy voice in his ear.

"I miss you," she said sadly, and he smiled the moment she said it.

"So do I. I was awake all night looking for you. I want to come and see you soon. I feel like an addict without his drug." He sounded as miserable as she was.

"Me too," she said happily. She loved knowing that he missed her, and hadn't simply returned to his normal life, without a backward glance, after spending four days with her. For her, their days in New York had changed her life, hopefully forever, and it felt wonderful to know that he was experiencing exactly the same thing.

"I will come to California soon," he promised, and then had to see patients. He promised to call her at the end of his workday, which would be late in the morning for her. She thought of going back to sleep after talking to him, but couldn't. She tossed and turned, thinking about him, and the nights they'd shared, and then she lay on her back and smiled, remembering everything he'd said to her then, and on the phone. She finally got up and got dressed at six, and was in her office at seven-thirty. She often went in early when she had jet lag or couldn't sleep. It was a wonderful time of day to get things done. New York and Europe were already up and at full speed.

She had already done a stack of work when Jade came in at eight-thirty. She was happy to see Timmie again, not particularly surprised to see her at work, and asked her how her weekend in New York had been.

"Fantastic!" Timmie said instantly, with a broad grin. She gave herself away with the dreamy look in her eye, and the abundance of happiness that was seeping through her pores. Jade narrowed her eyes and frowned at her. She knew Timmie too well to think that she could look like that after a weekend of museums and shopping on her own. Timmie rapidly looked away, shuffling through papers on her desk, but Jade had already guessed what must have happened in New York, and more than likely whom she had been with.

"I smell a rat," she said suspiciously, as Timmie chuckled.

"I hope not," Timmie said, trying to look innocent with little success. "Maybe it's our new perfume."

"Don't give me that," Jade said, resting on twelve years of hard work and friendship. She often allowed herself to say things to Timmie that others wouldn't have. And Timmie was always a good sport about it. Today was no different. "You spent the weekend with the French doctor, didn't you?" she accused her with a knowing look, and Timmie nodded. She was excited about what was happening, and proud to be his woman. They had to be discreet for a while, but here at least she could let her joy and excitement show.

"As a matter of fact, I did," Timmie said, looking like the cat that had swallowed the canary. In truth, she looked more like the lioness that had devoured a bald eagle. Happiness radiated from her so powerfully that she could have lit up the entire room.

"I hope you didn't sleep with him," Jade said sternly. "You said you wouldn't do that until he moves out of his family's apartment in June."

"Absolutely," Timmie lied through her teeth, and looked at her assistant with a thoroughly innocent grin. She knew exactly what she had said, but suddenly everything was different. She was madly in love with him, and there was no way she could have resisted him for all four days, given what they both felt. She was happy they had done exactly what they did. She had never in her entire life spent such a passionate weekend, and whatever dire fate Jade was predicting for her, at Jean-Charles's hands, it was impossible to believe now that he wouldn't do exactly what he had said he would in June. There wasn't a shadow of a doubt in Timmie's mind that he would move out. What had happened to Jade was sad, but very different. Timmie was no longer worried about him, and she didn't want to have to defend him or their passionate affair to Jade or anyone else.

"Why is it that I don't believe you?" Jade said, vibrating with suspicion. "You look too good. You look disgustingly happy. You're more beautiful than ever. You absolutely exude an aura of a woman who spent a whole weekend in bed with her lover. I think you're lying to me, Timmie." And then in a worried tone, she added, "I just hope you're not lying to yourself, or that he's being dishonest with you."

"I don't think he is," Timmie said calmly. "I think he's an honest man who'll do what he says, when he said he would. I think he's just concerned about his children."

"Then you did sleep with him!" Jade accused her. Timmie felt like a naughty teenager who was being accused of "going all the way" with her boyfriend. The thought of it made her laugh out loud just as David walked in.

"What's going on here? What am I missing?"

"Not a thing," Timmie reassured him with a grin. "Jade is making some very unfair accusations." It amused her no end. And she felt totally sure of Jean-Charles, no matter how traumatic Jade's previous experience had been.

"She spent the weekend with the French doctor," Jade filled him in while Timmie smiled benevolently at them both. She enjoyed the good-humored bantering relationship the three of them shared. And when necessary, both of her assistants knew when to back off. Timmie hadn't reached that point as Jade grilled her about her weekend. It was all in good fun, and well meant, born of their concern and love for her.

"So that's what you stayed to do in New York," David said with a look of admiration and interest. "Good for you. I hope you had fun!" he said generously. He liked everything he'd heard about the French doctor, and wasn't nearly as worried about him as Jade.

"A little too much fun, if you ask me," Jade commented, as Timmie picked up the phone. It was time to get to work.

Jade mentioned it to David again over lunch that afternoon, as they made the usual trade of potato chips for pickles. "I'm worried about her," she said honestly. "That's exactly what happened to me. First, you think everything is fabulous and you're the luckiest woman in the world. You've never been so in love in your life, and then these guys start killing you by inches. They cancel dates, they back out of dinners, they have to change plans for vacations. The weekends they promised you don't happen because they have to be at home with their kids. Their wives get sick, their children get hysterical. You spend holidays alone. They keep you in the closet. And eventually, you don't have a goddamned thing except a lot of broken hopes and dreams. They're still living at home ten years later with their wives and kids. And if you hang around long enough, it's too late for you to have your own kids. I don't want that to happen to her. Not that she wants kids at her age. I just don't want her to get her heart broken over him."

"None of us do," David said seriously. "But that's what happened to you. That's not necessarily what's going to happen to her. He seems like a good guy. He's a doctor and a responsible person. He didn't know she was going to come along so soon. I think it's reasonable for him to honor the commitments he made before they fell in love."

"That's what I thought too. It's not about commitments, it's about fear. Bottom line, in the end, they're too damn scared and cowardly to leave, so they never do."

"I hope that won't be true," he said calmly. "I think we need to just support her and see where this goes. He may do everything he's promised her he would. I hope he does. We don't have any reason to disbelieve him yet. Let's give the guy a chance."

"I hope he does what he said he would too. But I wouldn't bet money on it. I've heard too many stories like mine from other women. That's why it's not a good idea to go out with married men."

"I don't think he's exactly married, from the sound of it. I think he's a man who's getting divorced. That can be messy for a few months. And Timmie doesn't seem to be suffering yet. I've never seen her happier in all these years."

"Neither have I," Jade conceded. "That's what scares me, because if things go wrong, and he doesn't leave, he'll break her heart. I know."

"Let's not worry about it yet. Let's see what he does. I'm backing him." David held his ground.

Jade shook her head, deeply cynical about it. "I hope you're right."

"We all do," David said as he threw the rest of his lunch away. "How's your architect, by the way? Why don't you worry about him, instead of Timmie's French doctor? She's a big girl and can take care of herself. Count on it, she'll do all the right things. And hopefully, so will he. So tell me about your guy." David expertly guided her off the subject, and she told him how wonderful her new architect friend was. She thought that Internet dating was the best thing since sliced bread.

And while they were discussing her love life, Timmie was in her office, talking to Jean-Charles. It was eleven o'clock at night for him, two in the afternoon for her.

"I missed you terribly all day," he said, sounding unhappy.

"So do I," she said, smiling. It was nice to know he missed her, and amazing to think that only the day before, they had been in each other's arms in New York. It already felt as though it had been weeks before. "I can't wait for you to come to visit."

"I'm trying to work it out here. I have to make sure I'm covered. My assistant said he'd let me know in the next day or two."

It was hard for her to believe that Jean-Charles was coming to California to see her. This all still seemed miraculous to her.

She asked him about the patients he'd seen that day, then told him about the things she was going to do that afternoon. She told him about her house in Malibu, and he said he couldn't wait to see it and stay there with her. It all seemed like a dream. This totally kind, loving, passionate, sexy, wonderful doctor in Paris had fallen in love with her, and she with him. They had just spent four days in New York together, in the throes of intense passion. And now he was coming all the way to Los Angeles to see her. It was utterly and totally amazing. And as she thought about it, after they hung up, looking out the window, she thought about the unexpected surprises in life, the unexpected gifts of hope that made all the difference. Jean-Charles was that for her now, a gift from God fallen from the sky. It made her think about the blessings in her life, and just how sweet they could be. As sweet as Jean-Charles.

Chapter 15

Jean-Charles's assistant came through, as promised, in two days, and agreed to cover him for a week in mid-March. Miraculously it was only two weeks away, and Jean-Charles called Timmie immediately to give her the news. He had already made his reservation when he called her. He could hardly wait to come out, and sounded like a kid at Christmas, and so did she. The timing had worked out perfectly. She had design deadlines before that, and she was going to work like a dog to get things done. She wanted to devote the entire week to him. She was going to take the week off, and spend the time doing whatever he wanted to do, and hopefully at least a few days in Malibu. All Timmie wanted was to be with him, which was his dream too.

The next two weeks ticked by interminably. Each day felt like a thousand years to her, and just as long to him. She was grateful that she had her work to keep her busy. She took work home with her at night, and spent weekends working on designs, and straightening up her houses. She wanted things to look fresh and pretty, and started throwing things out that looked old and tired or faded. She bought new houseplants at a nursery, ordered fresh new towels, and took new sheets out to Malibu. She was fluffing up her nest for him, although he kept telling her that all he cared about was her. The day before he came, she bought new CDs, for the city and the beach. She had checked out every detail, bought things she thought he liked to eat. She bought French magazines and left them on the coffee table. She arranged a big bowl of flowers for him the morning he was to arrive. She wanted everything to be perfect for him. Even the weather cooperated. It was a brilliantly sunny balmy day, without a cloud or a breeze. It felt like spring. She knew it had been freezing in Paris that week, so this would be a rare treat for him.

She wore beige slacks and a matching sweater, with her hair full and loose. She wore beige alligator flats, and carried a vintage Kelly bag she'd bought in Paris in a soft yellow. She looked like she'd stepped out of a magazine when she got out of her car at the airport. She hadn't gone to her office that morning. She'd been too busy at the house, arranging final details for him. Her bed was made with perfectly pressed brand-new Pratesi sheets, and she'd bought new ones for the beach too, in sky blue, with little seashells on them. She didn't know if he'd notice the details, but even if he didn't, she had wanted to do it for him. And she had told her office not to expect her all week. She had told them why she was taking the time off, and had completed the last of her work over the weekend. Jade had refrained from comment this time, with David's encouragement, as Timmie had left the office the day before, but she had given her a dark look, and then called to apologize for it later. She was just worried, and Timmie said she understood. David had wished her luck, and a fabulous time with Jean-Charles. She felt as though she were going on her honeymoon. And in a way she was. This was a whole new life for them, a continuation of what they'd started in New York. It was hard to imagine that their time together could be as good as that again, but Timmie wasn't worried about it, nor was he. He said all he wanted was to see her. He had called her late the night before, as he got on the plane, before he had to turn his cell phone off. They were as excited as two kids. It was an eleven-hour flight for him, and as she drove to the airport, she knew he'd be landing soon. She was sure he was as excited as she was, sitting on the plane, approaching L.A. This time she could hardly contain herself as she waited for him to come through customs.

She was standing outside immigration when the doors opened, and she saw him stride through in slacks and a sweater, carrying his blazer over his shoulder, with a blue-collared shirt open at his neck, and a red tie hanging out of his blazer pocket. He looked casual and handsome and very French, as he strode toward her, and she toward him, beaming. A moment later, she was in his arms, and he was holding her so tightly she could hardly breathe as he kissed her. There were no words at first to tell each other how happy they were to be together again. They didn't need words, it was written all over their faces.

"I missed you so much," she said breathlessly, holding him around his waist. It had only been two weeks but felt like an eternity to both of them. They kissed so often, they could hardly make it out of the airport.

"So did I," he said happily. "I thought the plane would never get here. It took forever." It was an incredibly long flight, but he had made it.

"Are you exhausted?" She was dying to fuss over him, to cuddle and spoil him, and he loved it.

"Not at all." He beamed at her. "I slept on the flight. I watched two movies, and had a very good dinner." She knew that on Air France, they served caviar in first class. "What are we going to do today?" he asked with interest. There was one thing he wanted to do first, and as they got into her car, he kissed her and gently touched her breast. He had been starving for her body since he last saw her. And it was so exciting to be with her now in California.

"I'm so happy you're here," she said, beaming. She couldn't wait to show him all her favorite places, her house in Bel Air, the one at the beach, to walk down the street with him, cook dinner for him, go out with him, show off with him, laugh with him, sleep with him, make love with him. It was all a rainbow of delicious pleasures, and the love they had for each other was the pot of gold at the end of the rainbow, and they both knew it.

They drove to Bel Air on the Santa Monica Freeway in fairly light traffic for once. They chatted about a thousand things, and Jean-Charles told her again how much it meant to him to be there with her, in her own surroundings. He wanted to learn everything about her, and share the world that she lived in. The time passed quickly as they talked, and they were at her house less than an hour after she picked him up.

She let herself into the house, and he followed her inside, impressed at how tasteful her surroundings were, how soothing and peaceful the living room was, how well the art went with all of it. He walked around discovering everything, admiring all she'd done, and then, as though he had been drawn to it, and it was meant to be, he stopped at the bookcase, and stood staring at the photograph of Mark. He knew who it was at once, as Timmie silently watched him, and Jean-Charles held it and looked at the child's eyes.

"This is your boy, isn't it?" he asked softly, as he read all the loss and pain of a lifetime in her eyes as she nodded.

"Yes. That's Mark."

"He was a beautiful child," he said gently, as he set it down, and

went to put his arms around her. "I'm sorry, my darling...so sorry...
I wish it would never have happened." She nodded again as he held
her. She didn't cry, she just stood there, remembering Mark and loving
Jean-Charles. It was as though the two great loves converged as one
in that moment. And although sad, it was a peaceful feeling. She
pulled away then to smile at him, and he kissed her again. He filled
her soul to the brim with tenderness and joy.

"Are you hungry?" she asked, as they walked into the kitchen, and
he took her in his arms again. He couldn't keep his hands off her for
more than a few moments at a time. He laughed at her question.

"Only for you, my love. I've been starving for you since you left
me." She smiled happily at him, and hugged him back.

"I meant for food." She had bought everything she could think of
that he might like to eat, including a long baguette of French bread,
which she had noticed in New York he ate at every meal. "I ate all the
way here on the plane. I don't need food right now. All I need is you,"
he said, and kissed her, and she felt like she was in a romantic, sexy
French movie.

She showed him the rest of the house then, and they wandered
into her bedroom. The curtains were opened wide as sun streamed
into the room, the bed was immaculately made, and she had a huge
bowl of flowers on the low table in front of the couch, and as Jean-
Charles looked around the room, he smiled.

"This is all so pretty, Timmie. I love your house." He loved seeing
her here, it all suited her perfectly. It was casual, elegant, sleek, welcoming, warm, artistic, creative, all the things she was herself. It
seemed the perfect house for her. And before she could thank him for
what he said, he swept her off her feet in a single gallant gesture, and
walked her slowly to her bed. "I'm very tired now," he said mischie-

vously. "I think I need a nap." She laughed as he deposited her gently onto her bed, and she held her arms out to him.

"Come here, my love," she said with all the love she felt for him in her eyes. He melted into her arms, and lay down on the bed beside her, and moments later, their clothes had vanished and were lying on the floor next to her bed. Their long naked bodies, so hungry for each other, were once again passionately entwined, just as they had been in New York. And in the warmth and comfort of her own environment, this was even better. She felt as though she belonged to him, and always would, and he felt like he had come home at last.

It was dark when they got out of bed again, after alternately sleeping and making love for hours. She couldn't get enough of him, nor he of her. It was an endless give-and-take, and sharing of their minds, their hearts, their bodies. Jean-Charles said at one point, as he held her close, that their hearts had merged into one, and she felt the same way he did. It was as perfect as it had been since the beginning, and only seemed to get better every time they met.

After nightfall, they went downstairs to the kitchen, naked in bathrobes, and she made him an omelette and a salad, and served him a wedge of Brie with the baguette he loved so much. It was the perfect snack before they went back to bed and made love again, and then sat for two hours in the bathtub, talking. Each time they were together, it was as though they disappeared to another planet, with no time zones, no responsibilities, no obligations, no time they were supposed to do anything, no meals they had to eat at any set hour. They did exactly what they wanted, and everything they did was done together. There was not a moment of the time they spent together when they were apart. And whereas normally, Timmie would have chafed at such constant companionship, and he would have as well, they both noticed that the intimacy they shared was so easy and comfortable that it only made them want more of the same. It was heady stuff, and totally addictive. They were both hooked. They were each the other's drug of choice.

It was far into the night when they finally fell asleep. It was afternoon for him, but he didn't seem to care. They slept until ten in the morning, and the moment he woke up, Jean-Charles said he was starved. He looked at his watch and ascertained that it was dinnertime for him. This time she made him a steak, and then reluctantly, they showered and dressed. It was another spectacular spring day, and they were going to the beach.

It was noon before they left the house, and she drove him slowly up the Pacific Coast Highway, while he admired her and the view.

"This is beautiful, Timmie. And so are you." He had never seen a day so perfect, or been so happy in his life. And when he saw her beach house, he nearly cried. "This is so wonderful," he exclaimed as he looked around. He loved the way she had decorated it, the airy blue and white, the handsome deck, the beach, the view. They went straight down to the beach to take a walk, ankle deep in the surf, and walked as far as they could, and then finally turned around and came back. "I could stay here forever," he said happily.

"I wish you would," she said softly. But they both knew that wasn't possible. He had a life in Paris, a medical practice he had invested years in, and children he loved. And she had a business to run here. They both knew that if they were to stay together, they would have to do what they were doing, travel to see each other as often as possible, and survive without each other in between. But after only two visits together, they were both already finding it excruciating to be apart. Jean-Charles wanted to be with her every day, as he was now, and it suited Timmie to perfection, far more than she had expected.

They lay around on the deck for hours that afternoon, soaking up the sun and talking. He dozed for a while, still on his Paris schedule and time zone, and she lay near him, watching him sleep, like a lion stretched out beside her. She could almost hear him purr. And as the air got chilly in the late afternoon, she covered him with a cashmere blanket until the sun went down, and then she woke him up and they went inside and lit a fire. They sat in the living room and talked. And Timmie tried to stay off the subject of their future, or when he would leave his wife. She didn't want to pressure him about what he was going to do, or when he was going to do it. She trusted him completely. She asked him to tell her about his children.

"Julianne is very elegant and reserved, she's very cool actually. She's like her mother. She's not as close to me as I'd like her to be. She's like a cat. She's a very aloof person. She watches everything and she observes. She sees it all. She's seventeen and very wise for her years. She's very close to her mother and sister, and not so close to Xavier. He's six years older than she is, and he always thought the girls were a terrible nuisance when he was a little boy. They got into his things and broke everything, or made a mess in his room when they went in to play. And they always teased him when he brought girls to the house. He finally stopped bringing them there at all, which was probably a good decision.

"Sophie is fifteen and very cozy. She's young for her age, in some ways, I think. Julianne is more sophisticated. She likes to dress up and wear pretty clothes. Sophie is more of a tomboy, sometimes, and at other times, she is all girl and female wiles when she winds me around her finger. She thinks Xavier is a hero, and I can do no wrong. But she and her mother don't get along as well. I think it's of the age. Julianne didn't get along with her mother at fifteen either. Now they are conspirators, usually against me." He smiled as he said it. It was obvious how much he loved his family, and how close he was to his children. Timmie loved him all the more for it, and was sorry she wasn't younger. Had he come along earlier, she realized, she would have loved to have his baby one day, once they settled down with each other. It was an amazing thought she'd never had before, and she shared it with him that night when they were in bed. He said it touched him to the core. He would have loved to have their baby.

He looked at her tenderly then and asked her a question. "Is it still possible?" he asked gently, with interest and some concern.

"Possible, but not likely. I can't imagine that would happen easily at my age. In fact, I'm almost sure it wouldn't." It made her sad, though, that she had wasted the last dozen years since Mark's death. It had never occurred to her to have another child, until she met Jean-Charles. "Sometimes I used to think about adopting." She told him about St. Cecilia's then, and he was enormously impressed by all she did, and the obvious love she had for the orphans she was housing and supporting. "I think I haven't done it," she explained to herself as much as to him, "because I've been afraid to love anyone again. Not just a child, but even a man. It's been easier to keep my distance."

"And now?" he asked, as he held her close to him. "Are you still afraid?"

She took a moment to answer and pulled him closer to her, "No, I'm not. I'm not afraid of anything when I'm with you," she said tenderly, "except losing you. I don't ever want to lose anyone I love again."

"None of us wants that." Still, they both knew that most people had more resilience in that area than she did. She had been through a lot in her life.

They talked about his children again, and other things. As they had before, they wandered through a variety of subjects, and always wound up making love, and then sleeping, and making love again. It never seemed to stop, and at four that morning, she teased him about it, when he wanted to make love again. She told him that he had obviously been lying and was a lot younger than he'd said. No man his age could possibly make love as often as he did. But apparently, he could. She accused him of having magical powers, which pleased him. And after they made love that time, they walked out onto the deck in bathrobes she had brought from the city. They lay on the deck chairs, holding hands, and looked up at the stars. It was the most perfect moment she could remember in a very long time, maybe in her entire life.

And then at last they fell asleep in each other's arms again, and this time slept until nearly noon. She made tea and croissants for them, and then they took a long walk down the beach.

In the end, they stayed in Malibu for four days. Jean-Charles loved it so much that he didn't want to leave. He was having a wonderful, peaceful, loving time in Timmie's world. He felt like he was in a cocoon, and had never been as comfortable in his life. He almost hated to go back to Bel Air, but he wanted to get at least a little feel of her L.A. life too. So they went to restaurants and antiques shops, went on long walks, and had cappuccino at a coffeehouse she knew. And they swam in her pool. They also sat in the hot tub for hours, and in her gigantic marble tub at night. They seemed to be spending most of their time either in bed, or in some form of water, almost like the womb. They had become twins of the soul.

And as it had the last time they got together, the last night came too soon. They lay in her big comfortable bed, talking about what a good time they'd had and when they were going to get together again. It was even more amazing for them to realize that their passionate love affair had only begun a month before. It already felt to both of them as though they had been together forever. They had

talked about everything from their childhood fears and griefs, to having babies, to their future. The babies weren't going to happen, but
they both hoped the future was. All in due time, as Jean-Charles said
to her whenever the subject came up.

She drove him to the airport the day he left, and they both looked
somber. The week had allowed them to become even more attached
to each other. They had developed a daily routine of things they liked
to do. She knew what he liked to eat for breakfast and lovingly fixed it
for him. They spent hours making love, and giving each other endless
pleasure. They were learning each other's needs and habits, secrets,
histories, tender spots, and private ancient terrors. There seemed to
be almost nothing left that they didn't know about each other. They
had come incredibly far in a very short time. And now they had to
part again, and learn to live without each other until they met again.
It was like learning to live without a limb, or the use of both hands.
Just as it had been last time, they suspected it was going to be a huge
adjustment again, after they left each other, and neither of them was
looking forward to it. It was so painful being apart. Their love for
each other in the last week had been plentiful and lavish. The time
they had spent together had been a gift they both believed came
from God.

The only unreality in the time they shared was that while Jean-
Charles was there, Timmie never even called her office. Her instruc-
tions to them had been not to call her unless the building had burned
down. For anything short of that, she didn't want to be bothered. She
wanted her every waking moment to be his. So he had no real sense
of how hard she worked or what she did with her time when he
wasn't there. But Timmie thought it was better that way. She wanted
her entire being and all her time focused on him while he was with

her, and he loved it. So did she. She didn't want to be the CEO of Timmie O while she was with him. All she wanted to be with Jean-Charles was the woman who loved him. And that suited him just fine. In fact, it pleased them both. She felt like more of a woman with him than she had ever felt in her entire life.

Watching him check his bags in at the Air France counter, and get his boarding pass, was agonizing. She looked at him mournfully as he put his passport away. They lingered in the terminal together, and then went back outside for a few minutes. And finally, they had no choice. He had to thread his way through the security lines, and pass through the checkpoint to go to the gate. And she couldn't go with him. He stood and held her for a long, long time, kissing her, holding her, loving her, and hating to leave her. As always when she said goodbye to someone she loved, and more so than had ever been the case before, since her childhood, she felt like a child that was being abandoned. Even though she knew she would see him again, hopefully soon, it felt like a tragedy to her each time he left her. There was always a silent voice of terror asking herself how she would survive it if he didn't come back. He knew that about her now, and promised her again and again that he would. She believed it, but seeing him leave hurt anyway.

"I love you," he whispered for a last time, just before he went through the X-ray machine that would separate him from her. Even though she could still see him, she would no longer be able to touch him. Their inexorable separation had begun.

"I love you so much too...let's get together again soon..." She didn't see how he could come back to California. It was hard for him to be able to take a week off from his practice. This had been a rare gift, and they both knew it.

"When can you come back to Paris?" he asked, feeling almost the same panic she did at leaving each other. His life without her was so bereft and empty. He could hardly bear it.

"I'll try to come back soon," she promised, and meant it. She could easily find some excuse. And in truth, she didn't need one. All she had to do was shift her schedule around and get on a plane. The problem in Paris was that he had not yet moved out of the apartment he shared with his children and wife, so Timmie could obviously not stay with him. And he felt awkward staying at the hotel with her, in case some-one recognized them and he compromised her reputation, since he wasn't separated yet. They had talked about finding some other solu-tion, like a borrowed apartment, until he moved out and got a place of his own. It wouldn't be long. They had vowed to figure out some-thing. And suddenly he wanted her as part of his everyday life, hence wanting her in Paris.

"We'll see," she said, and then he kissed her again, and finally they managed to pull away with a nearly superhuman effort, and he walked through the X-ray machine with a grim expression. And when he got to the other side, he stood smiling at her. She knew it was silly, but it touched her to note that they both had tears in their eyes. They were both wonderfully silly, sentimental, and romantic. But they were perfectly matched in that too. They seemed to be perfectly matched in everything they thought, or touched, or did. It was truly amazing. They were both convinced there was God's hand in this, which, as she pointed out to him, was much better than computer dating. This choice, they both felt sure, had been made for them by God.

He waved to her as he walked away, and shouted back to her that he loved her, and she did the same. And then he had to turn down a hall, which would lead him to his gate, and she could no longer see him. He was gone. It was a feeling of loss and emptiness beyond be-lief, almost beyond bearing.

Once he was gone, she walked back to the garage, and got in her car, and just sat there for a long moment. She could still smell his af-tershave in the air, and feel his skin on hers, almost as though he were a ghost of some kind who would not leave her. And then slowly, thinking of all they had shared in the past week, she started her car. And drove home to the house that had been their nest for a week, the bed that had been their cocoon and where they had made love. Everything about her house seemed permeated by him now. She had no idea when he would come back again, but she knew perfectly, without question, that she was his, and this was home for both of them. Jean-Charles had put his own special stamp on her house, just as he had on her, since they fell in love in Paris. She was his woman now.

Chapter 16

Three weeks passed while Timmie and Jean-Charles called each other constantly, said how much they loved each other, and sent many e-mails a day. They still had no firm plan to meet again, and both of them were going crazy, like hungry lions in a cage with no set dinner plans.

Jade and David had noticed easily how unhappy she was these days, how anxious to spend time on the phone, or write to him. When Jade or David told her he was on the line, she flew. All her attention was directed toward him. Her only goal now was to see him. And at the same time, just as she was desperately lonely without him, she also had the comfort of knowing that he adored her, and was just as anxious to work it out as she was. Timmie felt in her bones that they would. They just hadn't figured it out yet. But they were both sure they would find a way to be together a good part of the time, once he moved out in June.

In the meantime, they were both living for their next visit. There had been a very serious epidemic of some kind of flu in Paris, suppos-edly a strain that had come from North Africa, and Jean-Charles had his hands full with countless patients who were sick. They talked morning and night, and she was still trying to figure out how to get away, when problems erupted in the factory in New Jersey again. The union was threatening a wildcat walkout, and many of her employees wanted her to dump the union. She was tempted, although it would give them dangerous ammunition to use against her, which she didn't like. She preferred to try to pour oil on troubled waters again, even if it cost them. And while she was figuring out a negotiating plan, along with her lawyers, one of the biggest department stores they sold to wanted to triple their orders, which presented yet another problem with production.

She finally decided she had to go to New York to sort it all out in person. It had been three weeks since her last visit with Jean-Charles by then, and both of them were going crazy. And then she realized that her problems on the East Coast were an unexpected blessing, although her time there might be harried or even stressful. She called to tell him about her unexpected trip. She was flying to New York the next morning. She also knew how hard it was for him to leave his practice on short notice.

"I'll probably have to be there for three or four days," she explained, which would take them to the weekend. "Do you think there's any chance you could come for a couple of days?" Until then, she had been trapped in California, dealing with a different set of problems on the West Coast, and he had been completely swamped in Paris, and his primary assistant who usually covered for him had broken his leg skiing. But Jean-Charles had just recently reported that he was on the mend.

Jean-Charles was instantly delighted to learn that she was coming East. It was theoretically easier to meet her in New York, which was only a six-hour flight, than go all the way to California on an eleven-hour flight, and where he lost a day traveling each way. New York was a great deal simpler for him.

"I'll do everything I can. My assistant is back to work again, and he can get around in his cast." It had been a nightmare for Jean-Charles when the younger man had been flat on his back, and unable to work. "I'll call you tonight," he promised. She told him he could let her know at the last minute. She was hoping to stay in New York, and spend the weekend with him. It had been obvious for several weeks now that they both needed it. Staying apart too long depressed them both, and made them both anxious and unhappy. This trip was good news for both of them. It had been an agonizingly long three weeks, without physical contact with each other, although they talked constantly, and e-mailed many times daily, to report on events in their lives, and say they loved each other. He was the most affectionate man she had ever known.

He called her back at midnight that night—nine o'clock the next morning for him—and he had worked it out. He was leaving Paris after work on Thursday night. There was an eight P.M. flight he could be on, which would land him in New York at almost the same time, local time, and he could stay with her till Sunday night and take the red-eye back. His assistant had agreed to work a three-day weekend, despite the broken leg and the cast. Jean-Charles was elated. And so was Timmie. It would give her much to look forward to as she met the challenges of the week, which would surely not be easy. But the reward at the end of it would be great, for both of them.

She slept fitfully that night, thinking of the week ahead, and the excitement of another visit with him. She took the first flight to New York the next morning, which meant she had to get up at an ungodly hour to leave for the airport at five A.M. It was a businessman's flight, and she was one of two women in first class. The rest were all men who looked extremely corporate, and as always David came with her, while this time once again, Jade stayed home to hold down the fort. And once again, she, David, and their attorneys managed to resolve their union problems, which were always a powder keg ready to go off. There was no quick or permanent fix to their problems, but she thought they had bought a year or two of peace with the compromises they made. They even figured out how to cover their tripled orders by increasing production in Taiwan, and adding more employees. By the time Jean-Charles arrived on Thursday night, Timmie had her business life in order, although she looked exhausted and he was worried about her. She had lost weight since he'd last seen her, and he made her eat frequently while he was with her. She always relaxed when she was with him, and this time was no different. They made love the moment he got to the hotel, and although they went out to dinner every night, they spent an inordinate amount of time in their room as well. It rained hard for all three days, and all Timmie wanted to do was lie in bed with him, cuddle, and make love, which suited him perfectly, since it was what he needed from her as well. Aside from the excitement of the sex they shared, and the generosity of their loving, they also gave each other enormous comfort, which shored them up for the days alone and buoyed them. She was relieved to know that he would be moving out of his apartment in two months by then. He said he thought his daughters were resigned to it now, and they had several potential purchasers of the apartment circling over them. Jean-Charles continued to believe he would have his domestic situation worked out in early June, and Timmie could hardly wait. It meant that they could stay together in Paris, once he was living alone, and he wanted her to help him find an apartment, and decorate it with him. He wanted her in every aspect of his life now, and hoped to introduce her to his children within the next few months. It all sounded good to her.

On Saturday night, they canceled a dinner reservation at Cipriani, and stayed in bed at the hotel instead. It was pouring rain, and they were both relaxed and unwinding, making the most of the days they had together. Timmie didn't want to get dressed up and go to a fancy restaurant, she said. So they stayed home in their little cocoon, dozing and talking, and when they made love that night, Timmie felt a closeness to him that even they had never felt before. Theirs was such a passionate love story, but every now and then, they seemed to reach heights that were almost frightening, their feelings for each other were so profound. It was as though for a span of time, not only their bodies merged, but their minds did, and their hearts and souls. He felt it too that night, and there were tears in her eyes after they made love. She had never felt anything like it with anyone before. What they did together defined making love, and afterward when she lay spent in his arms, she felt as though her whole soul had opened up to him and would never separate from him again. Each time they made love was different and better than the time before. And this time, she lay in his arms all night, pressed tightly against him, his arms around her. She drifted off into a deep sleep, as he looked at her sleeping, and his heart melted again. She touched places in him that he hadn't known existed, and she had done that that night. She had given him a gift of herself and taken something from him that he offered. And all night long as she slept in the safe circle of his arms, she dreamed that they were one.

Before they woke in the morning, they lay sleeping, facing each other, and smiled when they first saw each other the moment they woke up. Their noses were touching, and almost their lips. He kissed her, and they lay for a long time before either of them got up. She hadn't moved from where she lay the night before. He ordered breakfast for them, and even then she didn't want to get up. She just wanted to lie there forever in his arms and doze. She got up finally to have breakfast with him, and did him the honor of brushing her teeth and combing her hair. She looked beautiful as she sat down to breakfast with him. They each read sections of the Sunday newspaper, and discussed what they'd read. She always devoured the business section, and he liked the supplements on science. It made for intriguing breakfast conversation and an interesting shared life.

They went to the Metropolitan Museum that afternoon, and then went back to the hotel in the rain. She was profoundly happy and sated. They made love for a last time before they had to get up to leave, and Timmie still looked sleepy. She had been so tired when they met this time that she never quite caught up on her sleep. She dozed as she lay against him in the cab going to the airport, and he held her tightly. She loved it when he did that. And then they did the agonizing dance of saying goodbye to each other again. She promised that she would come to Paris in a few weeks. She was going to try and shake up some of their textile mills so she could do business there as well. But even if not, nothing pleased her more than Paris in spring. It was April now, but she was hoping to get to Paris to see him by the first of May, which would be even better. And once there, there would only be one more month left in his somewhat absurd living arrangement. But she wasn't even thinking of that now. She was drifting, floating beside him. And when he kissed her goodbye this time, she felt slightly less sad. What she felt instead was total harmony with him, total synchronicity of thought and movement. She felt as though the two strong, independent people they were had finally become one.

She still felt that way when she got back to California. She was feeling strangely peaceful, and more in love with him than ever, although even days after they left each other, she still hadn't been able to organize the trip to Paris, but she was working on it. She was determined to have a reason to get there, although he was reason enough. She wanted to kill two birds with one stone. She was going to Paris, or wanted to, for their romance, but she also wanted to address the local business issues wherever she was. And it would give her something to do while he was busy working.

She had just set up a series of meetings with a new textile mill outside Paris, and was waiting for confirmation, three weeks after his last visit, when she got violently ill one afternoon. Jade had ordered them all sushi for lunch, and it was obvious to Timmie that whatever she'd eaten hadn't been good. She had rarely been so sick in her life, or been so frightened by how ill she was. She called Jean-Charles to discuss it with him, and he suggested she go to the emergency room. He wanted her to get an IV for dehydration, but she hated hospitals so much she waited, and she felt better by that night, so didn't go. But she still felt weak the next morning, and was annoyed that the textile mill had sent no confirmation. It was the first of May, and she wanted to come to Paris to see him. Their months of waiting were almost over. He was moving out in a month, when the school year ended, and he was starting to look at apartments. Everything was beginning to happen, and then she got sick again. She felt ill in rolling waves, and she called him again to say how sick she was. He said it sounded more like a gallbladder attack than food poisoning, or maybe some virulent kind of flu. And this time, she finally called her doctor and met him in the emergency room. She was so pale when she got there, she looked translucent, and he decided to run a series of tests on her. She didn't want them, but Jean-Charles insisted she have them, as she was throwing up again.

She had spent a truly miserable two days, and then Jade called her at the hospital on her cell phone to say that the textile mill had finally confirmed. She had appointments with them the following week, and Timmie was pleased to report it to Jean-Charles. But he was far more worried about her health.

"Never mind the textile mill," he scolded her, "just get the tests your doctor ordered. Do you want me to talk to him?"

"No," she said, sounding calmer. "I'm feeling better. I think it really is the flu. I feel stupid having a bunch of tests for nothing. I'm sure I'm fine."

"Thank you for the diagnosis, doctor. Just get the tests. And we'll talk after you get the results." Jean-Charles wanted her to make sure she didn't have something like hepatitis. She drove herself so hard and traveled so much that it could have been anything, including an ulcer. So she let them do whatever they wanted. They took samples of blood and urine, and by then she felt better anyway, so she went home, feeling slightly stupid for having made such a fuss over what was probably nothing. But she was touched by how concerned Jean-Charles was about her. He still wanted to talk to her doctor when the results came in, if anything significant turned up.

"Stop worrying. I'm fine." She went home and went to bed, and fell asleep, exhausted. The next morning, she was slightly queasy, but infinitely better, and she was back in her office, feeling decent again when the doctor called. Jade told her he was on the line, and Timmie took the call. She was looking distracted, and had convinced herself that she was fine. Whatever it had been in any case was gone.

"Hello, Timmie," her doctor said pleasantly when she took the call. "How are you feeling now?"

"Fine," she said, sounding faintly embarrassed. "A little queasy, but I think I got it out of my system. I don't know if it was food poisoning or the flu, but I can tell you I won't be eating sushi again anytime soon." She had never felt as sick in her life, except maybe when her appendix ruptured. This had been nearly as bad, though not quite.

"I'm not completely convinced you got it out of your system. I'd like you to come in this afternoon, so we can go over some of your tests."

"Is something wrong?" Timmie sounded suddenly worried.

"Not at all. I just don't like giving results over the phone. I thought if you had some time this afternoon, you could come in. Or tomorrow morning. It can wait. Everything is fine." It didn't sound right to her. If it was so fine, why did he want to see her? She was instantly concerned.

In fact, she had two appointments waiting for her, and unless she canceled them and sent them home, there was no way she could get free. But after what he had just said to her, she was tempted to skip her appointments and go in.

"Is it anything serious?" She was beginning to panic.

"Timmie," he said, trying to reassure her. He had been her doctor for years. "I agree with your diagnosis. I think you had food poisoning. But some of your blood levels were high here and there, in the panels we did. I'd be irresponsible if I didn't go over them with you." He made it sound simpler than she had first feared, and she started to calm down.

"It's not cancer or anything, is it?" She always assumed the worst.

"Of course not. It was just a good idea to get those tests, given how sick you were two days ago. And as I recall, you haven't had a checkup in a while. It's time for you to come in."

"I've been busy and traveling a lot," she gave him as an excuse, and it was true.

"That's also why it's a good idea to check on things. Doing these blood panels was a good idea. You could pick up a number of things on your trips."

"I was in Taiwan a couple of months ago. But I never drink the local water when I travel, and I'm careful what I eat. I didn't pick up something disgusting, did I?" He laughed, and she could hear that he didn't sound worried, which was a relief.

"No, you didn't. Stop worrying. Take it easy. Watch what you eat for the next few days. And come in tomorrow, if you have time." He sounded almost casual about it now, which greatly relieved her mind.

"What time?" She couldn't cancel her appointments for that afternoon, but she was willing to the following day. She wanted to hear what he had to say.

"How does ten o'clock work for you?"

"That'll work." She could make her New York calls from home, and come into the office late after her appointment at the doctor.

"See you then. Just don't go out for sushi tonight," he teased her.

"Don't worry, Brad, I won't. I'll see you tomorrow at ten." She sounded businesslike and unconcerned, which was not how she felt at all.

She hung up, and didn't have time to think about it after that. She had two appointments back-to-back, one with a design consultant she wanted to hire, and the other to look over ads for the winter line. They were always working six to nine months ahead. And by the time she thought of her conversation with her doctor again, she was on her way home. Whatever Brad Friedman had seen in her tests couldn't have been too serious, or she felt sure he would have insisted she come in that afternoon. She mentioned it to Jean-Charles that night. It was already the following morning for him.

"Did he say what was elevated?" he asked, sounding concerned.

"No, he didn't. He just told me to come in tomorrow."

"You might have an infection, or an allergy. I don't know why he didn't tell you on the phone." He was annoyed about the delay, and sounded worried.

"Doctors are always weird here about things like that. They never want to give you test results on the phone."

"I want you to call me as soon as you talk to him. And if he makes it confusing, I'll talk to him myself. It sounds like he's just trying to make himself important. I agree with you, if it was serious, I think he'd have had you come in right away." She was glad that Jean-Charles agreed with her, and she felt better after talking to him, and slept soundly that night.

Timmie was up early in the morning, made her New York calls, and had a cup of tea. Her stomach still felt somewhat delicate after the food poisoning, so all she had was a piece of toast for breakfast, skipped the yogurt, and got to Brad Friedman's office, after crawling through traffic, at ten-fifteen. The nurse took her into his office immediately. They never made her wait to see him. Even if he was busy, they put her in his private office. At the doctor's office, just as everywhere else, she was treated like a VIP. And she didn't have long to wait to see him. He walked into the room five minutes after she sat down. She was beginning to feel nervous again. What if it really was something serious, and he had only been trying to reassure her until he could get her in to give her the bad news in person, whatever it was.

"How are you feeling?" he asked breezily. He was a health nut, played a lot of tennis, had a second wife who was twenty years younger than he was, and he had three young kids.

"I'm fine," Timmie said, feeling anxious and looking suspicious.

"Never mind how I feel. Why don't you tell me how I am." He could see that she was worried.

"I wanted to ask you a few questions, which is why I had you come in. I haven't seen you in a while, and things change in people's lives, sometimes pretty radically. I assume that you're still single, you haven't advised us otherwise."

"What does that have to do with anything? Shit, have I picked up an STD?" It probably would have been Zack in that case, if it was one of those slow-cooking silent ones. She couldn't imagine that Jean-Charles would have given her an STD, although she had slept with him far more recently.

"No STDs. We checked for those too. What kind of relationship are you in at the moment?" he asked, watching her more carefully.

"Oh my God...AIDS or HIV?" He smiled and shook his head at that one. He had done an AIDS test on her, and didn't have the results yet, but he wasn't worried about that with her either. At her age, such as he knew her, she wasn't in a high-risk category for HIV. "No, we picked up something else, that came as a surprise to me, and may be a surprise to you. Or you may have forgotten to mention it to me. My lab tech is a little overzealous, she'd run prostate tests on women, and pregnancy tests on ninety-year-olds. I didn't ask her to, but when I asked her to order a complete blood panel on you in the emergency room, she must have checked off every box on the form. The level I mentioned to you that ran high was your HCG level, which was a little bit startling to me. So we ran a pregnancy test on your blood and urine. You came back positive on both, Timmie. Maybe you knew that already, but I wanted to get you in and discuss it with you, to see which way you're planning to go on this."

"You *what*?" Timmie stared at him in disbelief. "Wait, run that by me again. I'm pregnant? Are you kidding?" She couldn't be . . . but she could. She trusted him. They hadn't used condoms. They'd made love more than she ever had in her life. They'd had sex several times each day and night. She just didn't seriously think that she could get pregnant anymore at her age. She had said as much to Jean-Charles, and he didn't seem to think it was likely either. People had a hard enough time getting pregnant, at her age, she figured it would have taken a lot of effort, hormone support, and state-of-the-art assistance. Apparently that was not the case. It truly hadn't occurred to her that she'd get pregnant on her own, just making love with Jean-Charles, like people half their age.

"Do you still get your period regularly?" He didn't seem upset about it one way or the other. But that was because it wasn't happening to him. She was so shocked by what he had just told her, she had no idea what to think. She had no reaction to it at all, other than to be totally stunned.

"No, I don't. They're irregular, but I still get it. Maybe it's a mistake. Maybe you got someone else's tests confused with mine," she said, looking hopeful.

"No, it's not a mistake. And your elevated HCG levels say that your body is supporting the pregnancy, at least for now. How pregnant do you think you are?"

"I have no idea." She had slept with Jean-Charles in February, March, and April. And it was now early May. "At most slightly less than three months, at the least just about a month." She hadn't seen Jean-Charles now in nearly a month.

"My guess is that you're closer to a month, or six weeks the way we figure it from LMP." He was speaking jargon to her and she was feeling crazy. This couldn't be happening to her. And what would Jean-Charles say? She loved the idea, in theory, but the reality of a baby at this point in their relationship might be something else. He might not be pleased at all. And she had no idea what she felt. She was still too stunned to sort it out, although a part of her was thrilled, and she told herself that was insane. They weren't married, they lived six thousand miles apart, he was still living with his wife, and she was forty-eight years old.

"I think if you were more pregnant than that, you'd have noticed the signs by now. You've been pregnant before." He knew about her son. He had been her doctor when Mark died, and Derek left.

"Do you think that's why I got so sick?" She looked utterly amazed.

"Maybe. It probably was just bad sushi, but maybe you were more sensitive to it, and got sicker, because you're pregnant." She still couldn't absorb the words. "My question to you is what you want to do about it. I don't know how serious you are about the father. If this isn't a pregnancy you want to keep, you should probably opt for a termination now." Pregnancy. Termination. HCG. LMP. The words were flying around her head like birds. "You should see your gynecologist and make a decision fairly soon, particularly if you think you might be two months pregnant. I'd rather see you deal with it within the next month, and I'm sure so would you. Is this someone you're serious about?"

"Very," Timmie answered. "But he's fifty-seven years old, lives in Paris, and we've only been going out for three months, if that. Not quite." Not to mention the fact, which she didn't tell Brad Friedman, that Jean-Charles was still living with his wife, and wasn't due to move out for another month. Although admittedly, this might speed him along. Or blow him right out the door of her life. She was not entirely sure which. This was a lot to ask of any man, even Jean-Charles. "And my gynecologist just retired," she added, as though that made a difference, which it didn't. She didn't know what to think or say.

"I can give you a couple of names. That's not a problem," he said, looking sympathetic. "I don't know how you'd feel about having a baby at your age. Genetically, and physically, it could be fairly high risk. There are tests to handle the genetic issues, amnio and CVS. It's hard to assess the physical risk of a delivery at your age, but there are a number of women who do it these days. Some doctors now consider normal childbearing years up to fifty. I have other patients who've done it, and even sought it out. And you're in very good health. I don't think it would be a problem for you, as long as you cover your bases on the genetics. But you're also a very busy woman, with a major career. I figured that maybe something like this wasn't what you had in mind. I take it you didn't use condoms, or did it slip?"

"No, we didn't use any. He'd had a recent AIDS test for an insurance policy, and so had I." She had had one eight weeks after the last time she'd had sex with Zack, just to be sure. She had done it as a routine thing, and told Jean-Charles she had. And even though she had talked about a baby with him, she hadn't expected this to happen, or at least not yet. "I feel a little stupid at my age, calling a guy and telling him I'm pregnant."

"How do you think he'll react?" Brad looked sympathetic as he asked.

"I don't know," she said pensively. "We're crazy about each other. But his situation is complicated. He has kids, he lives in France, and he's getting a divorce. He has a lot on his plate."

"So do you," he said, and she nodded. She did, undeniably, and she hadn't expected to have a baby on it as well. She needed time to sort this out. And she wasn't going to tell Jean-Charles just yet. She needed time to digest it herself first.

Brad wrote down some names on a piece of paper and handed it to her. They were the names of three gynecologists he recommended, and he suggested to her that she see one of them soon, and that she make up her mind, either to go ahead with it and get prenatal care, or terminate the pregnancy if she decided not to proceed. He made the decision sound a lot easier than it was.

"Thank you," she said, slipping the piece of paper into her purse, and then she looked across the desk at him again. "Did you find anything else?"

"No." He smiled kindly at her. "Everything else was fine. I thought maybe this would be enough."

"Yeah," she said quietly, "it is." In fact, it was a lot. It was huge.

"Let me know what you decide."

"I will," she promised, and then left his office, feeling sad. This was such shit luck. It should have been something wonderful, and there was no question that she loved Jean-Charles, but this was an enormous burden to put on a relationship that was barely three months old. Even she knew that. But maybe God had other plans. It was amazing how that worked sometimes.

She called Jade from the car, and did something she never did. She told her she was sick and going home to bed. In fact, she was thinking of doing just that. She just wanted to crawl into her cave to think. It was Friday, and she was going out to the beach. Jade told her to take it easy, and she hoped she'd feel better by Monday. She was in good spirits herself, as she had a date with her architect friend lined up for the weekend.

Timmie had just hung up after calling her office, when Jean-Charles called on her cell phone in the car. He wanted to know what the doctor had said, what the tests had shown, and what part of her blood panel had been elevated. She listened to him with tears in her eyes, and held her breath. She hated lying to him, but she just wasn't ready to tell him the truth. She truly needed time to think and make her own decision. This was a major event in her life. And what if he didn't stick around, or never left his wife? Suddenly that mattered more than ever.

"It turned out it was just something silly," she lied. "The tests showed that I had some kind of allergy or something. He thinks I was allergic to the fish I ate. And aside from that, it was probably rotten. He thinks I have a stomach infection, and put me on antibiotics."

"I thought it was something like that. How stupid of him not to tell you on the phone. He was just trying to make himself important. I can't tell you how it annoys me when doctors do that." Jean-Charles sounded very official as he said it.

"Yeah, me too," she said, as tears rolled slowly down her cheeks.

"Are you all right, my darling? You sound funny. What kind of antibiotic did he put you on?"

She hesitated for a moment, not sure which one to say, and then took a wild guess. "Erythromycin. I'm allergic to most of the others."

"That might upset your stomach again. I wouldn't have made that choice." Probably Brad Friedman wouldn't have either, but she had no idea which one he'd use for a stomach infection. "Be sure to tell him, if it gives you a problem. Don't be afraid to call him over the weekend, particularly since he worried you for nothing." She wouldn't exactly call it nothing. And she was sure Jean-Charles wouldn't either. She loved him so much, and suddenly all she wanted was his baby. But she had to be intelligent about this and make the right decision. She was about to impact everybody's life. Hers, his, a baby's, even his other kids from his current marriage. And that was part of the problem. However much she loved him, his marriage was in fact still current, and he was married to and living with someone else. She had to take all of that into account. "Are you on your way to the office?" He sounded in good spirits, but she suspected he might not have been if he had just heard the news. She wondered just how much it would have upset him.

"Actually, I'm still feeling lousy. I'm going home to bed."

"My poor baby. I'm sorry I'm not there to take care of you and hold you in my arms."

"So am I," she said, and choked on a sob. "I'll call you from home."

"I'm actually going out to dinner with the children. I'll call you when I get back."

"Have a nice time," she said, sounding distracted, and then remembered to tell him that she loved him. She did. But that didn't mean she had a right to have his child or screw up his life. She cried all the rest of the way home after she hung up.

As promised, he called her later that afternoon, and late that night when he woke up on Saturday morning. He called her all through the weekend, as he always did. He was adorable and loving and worried about her stomach. He asked her several times if the antibiotic was giving her a problem, and she said it wasn't. But he could tell she wasn't feeling like herself. She made excuses for it all weekend, and whenever she wasn't talking to him, she lay in bed and cried. It was the most painful decision she had ever had to make, whether to have this baby or not, and without input from him. Did she have a right to deprive this child of a father, if for some reason the relationship with Jean-Charles broke up? Was she truly that committed to him? Much to her surprise and relief, she concluded that her answer to that was yes. What if it wasn't a healthy baby, because of her age? She was surprised to find that that wasn't a determining factor for her. She was willing to take her chances on that, and if she wanted to, she could always have amniocentesis or other tests. So what was the problem? She tortured herself about it all weekend, as she walked slowly down the beach, or lay on the deck. The problem was that Jean-Charles was

married, they had been in love for less than three months, and if for
whatever reason, he didn't leave his wife, she would be bringing up
this child alone. And worst of all, what if something terrible happened again, as it had to Mark? She didn't think she could live
through the agony of losing another child. Even one that had been in
her life as briefly as Blake. So what was the answer? Run away and
lose it before it was even born? How could she ever face that, or forgive herself? She wasn't deeply religious, but she was still Catholic
enough to believe that abortion was wrong, for her at least, particularly if she had the money to bring up a child, and provide for it hand-
somely, with or without a man. In the end, it became a moral issue for
her, and a lot more. It boiled down to how much she loved Jean-
Charles, and wanted his baby, even if it made no sense at all.

By Sunday morning, she felt utterly tortured, and all she could
think of was her late son. She was haunted by Mark as never before.
She was the mother of a child who had died, a boy she loved so much
who had been taken from her. And now, if God had chosen to give her
another one, however inconvenient or ill timed, how could she refuse
such a gift? In addition, she had grown up as an orphan. Her own parents had died when she was five. For years, she had devoted time and
energy to helping children like her, to make their lives a better place.
They were all children that no one wanted, and she was deeply committed to taking care of them. Given that, how could she refuse to
open her heart to this baby? How could she cast away yet another un-
wanted child, because his conception had been an accident? And
what if he or she was the greatest joy of her life? What right did she
have to refuse this child life?

And then there was the biggest issue of all. She loved this baby's
father, more than she had ever loved any man in her life. She wanted
a life with him, she had given her heart to him. She had opened her

life and soul and body to this man, and above all her heart. How could she turn away from the baby that was the evidence of their love? And what if he did leave his wife, and came to her after all, what if this was their one and only chance to have a child? She was no longer young enough to be able to count on it happening again. What if it never did? She knew that if she gave it up, she would forever regret what she had given up, out of fear and cowardice. She knew she would never forgive herself, and perhaps Jean-Charles wouldn't either. Suddenly, this baby seemed more important than either of them. She might lose it anyway, at her age. But if she didn't, in her eyes, this was a baby who deserved the chance to live. She couldn't deprive herself of that, nor Jean-Charles, or even the baby that was the fruit of their love. Their union wasn't based on sex, it was all about love.

In the end, it was Mark who made the decision, as she stood looking at his photograph when she went back to the house in Bel Air on Sunday night. She held his picture in her hands, and looked into his eyes. She could almost feel him next to her, and remembered the delicious silk of his hair, and his huge green eyes so like hers. She had lost him so many years before, and ached for him for so long. She still missed him every day. And now this new baby had come, not to take his place, but to give her a chance to love a child again. She couldn't have buried one child, and allowed herself to kill another. Just as Mark had been, this baby was a miracle in her life. Even more so, because she loved Jean-Charles, whether he left his wife or not. She hadn't told him about the baby yet because she didn't want to pressure him and needed to think it out herself.

As she went to bed that night, she knew the decision had been made. She could almost see Mark smiling at her, from wherever he was in Heaven. Not only did she feel as though he was at peace, but so was she. God had given her this baby, this one last chance to have a child, fathered by a man she loved so much. She knew she couldn't turn this gift of love away, any more than she could have turned away from its father. This baby was the outcome of their love. He called her just before she fell asleep, and for the first time in days she sounded like herself.

"I've been worried about you," he whispered, as she answered sleepily.

"I'm fine now. I love you." More than she could tell him or dared to say. "So much." He smiled at his end as he heard her words.

"I love you too. I'm so happy that I'm going to see you next week." In her upset and excitement over the baby, she had forgotten that. She was going to Paris to talk to the people at the textile mill. And now she would have to tell Jean-Charles about the baby. He had a right to know, and even to have a voice in this. He could toss her away because of this if he chose. But she knew he would never do anything like that. She hoped he would be happy about it too. And in a few weeks, he would leave his wife. "Sleep tight, my darling," he whispered, and she hung up after telling him again that she loved him. She drifted off to sleep with a smile on her face. She was going to tell him about their baby next week, when she went to Paris. With luck, it would all turn out okay.

Chapter 17

Timmie was already packed and ready for her Paris trip the next day, when she got a call from Jean-Charles at midnight, sounding seriously distressed. At first, she didn't even recognize his voice. He sounded near tears.

"What's wrong, *chéri*?" She was starting to pick up French words here and there, and kept promising herself to take a class at Berlitz. When she had time, whenever that would be. In another lifetime maybe, but she wanted to learn French for him.

"We have a serious problem," he said in an ominous tone, and her heart nearly stopped as he said it. For an instant, all she could think of was that he was dumping her. The baby she was carrying, and that he didn't know about, didn't even cross her mind. All she could think of was that he was about to tell her it was over, and her heart started to pound. Her breath came in short gasps. Terror struck at his tone. It was reflex for her. Visions of the orphanage again, and being sent back again and again, for years.

"What do you mean?" Timmie asked in a hoarse croak. She had never heard him sound like that before.

"My wife is sick. Very sick. She was diagnosed with cancer today."

"Oh my God. I'm so sorry." Timmie's thoughts turned instantly to her, without thinking of him, or herself. And then, more slowly, she began to realize the impact this could have on them. It sounded like it already had.

"She had a small lump in her breast. I thought it was nothing, so I didn't mention it to you. She worries about her health, and she's had these scares before. We got the results of the biopsy today. She has stage-two cancer. They will remove the lump, not the entire breast, but she will need chemotherapy and radiation. She's enormously upset, and so am I for her." He didn't sound cold to Timmie, only different. Very different. And she was terrified of what this meant for them, or could. "Timmie, she asked me to stay with her, and not move out in June. She's very frightened, and wants me with her for the treatments. She has several months of treatment ahead, anywhere from two to six, depending on how she responds. She will lose her hair, and possibly be quite sick. She's the mother of my children. I can't walk out on her right now, no matter how in love we are. And I love you very much," he reiterated, but Jade's voice was suddenly much louder in Timmie's head than his. Jade had warned of things just like this. She didn't think he was lying. But it was the first postponement of perhaps many more to come, if he ever left at all.

"I don't know what to say," Timmie said, sounding shaken and frightened. "I feel very sorry for her . . . and scared for me," she said honestly.

"Don't be scared," he said, sounding calmer than he had a minute ago. He had been desperately worried about what Timmie would say, and it had been a stressful day dealing with his wife, who was in a total panic, and his kids. Even his son was upset. Their mother was extremely ill. "This doesn't change anything. It's just a delay in our plans." Or the end of them. And right now, six months made a big difference to her. She hadn't been to the obstetrician yet, but she had been mildly nauseated all week. She was pregnant, and had no exact idea yet how much. Somewhere between one month and two. And she had been planning to tell him that week. Given what he was saying now, she would be six or seven months pregnant when he left his house, if his wife was even well enough then for him to leave, or he came up with some other excuse. Even though there was no denying that this one was valid. Timmie understood, but her own terrors were rearing their heads. She was scared stiff he'd never leave his house, or his wife. Maybe Jade was right. "You're very quiet. What are you thinking?" he asked, sounding worried about her now. "Timmie, I love you. Please know that, no matter what happens here."

"I'm scared," she said honestly. "I feel terrible for her. It's everyone's worst nightmare. I think of it every time I get a mammogram, or any other kind of test. And chemo sounds so awful. I don't blame her for wanting you there. I'd be scared too. I just wonder what it means for us." And what if she stayed sick for a long time, or got worse? He would never leave. "I know that sounds selfish, but I love you, and I don't want you to stay there forever."

"We're not talking forever. Just a few more months." He had originally wanted four. Now he wanted six more. To be with his wife. And what if her illness brought them closer together, or repaired the old wounds in their marriage? Where would Timmie be then? She'd be dumped, duped, and distraught, as David said. Heartbroken. Lost. Alone. Worse yet, now with his child. She didn't want that to be a factor for him. She was not going to pull him, or use it to entrap him, or manipulate him. She wanted him fair and square. Not a wife with cancer pulling one arm, a pregnant mistress yanking the other. If he came to her, she wanted it to be because he loved her, not because he felt he owed it to her, because of a baby, or anything else. She was not going to use it to manipulate him. She wanted him honestly, and only for her, not out of some sense of duty to a child he felt obligated to acknowledge and might not really want. Telling him about the baby now seemed manipulative to her, and she was not going to play that game with him. She was going to keep the news to herself for now, at least until things settled down in his life. But that could take a long time.

And then he hit her again. "I don't think you should come over tomorrow, Timmie, unless you really have to, for business. Things are very complicated for me here. I'm not sure I could get away, and that would be hard for both of us. I don't want to upset my wife just now. I hope you understand." There was silence at her end. She felt a sudden exquisite, overwhelming pain in her gut, as the air went out of her lungs. She felt it like a physical blow. He was abandoning her, even in some small degree. And this was not so small. Every fiber of her being reminded her that she had been here before, and it was not a good place to be. For her, it was the very worst place of all. Abandoned and alone, to whatever degree. The wounded five-year-old in her instantly woke up.

"I understand," she managed to squeeze out the words. "Let me know when things calm down."

"I'll call you tomorrow. I'm truly sorry," he said somberly. "This is no one's fault." He was right, not even his. But it pained her to become acutely aware that his primary allegiance was still to his wife, and not to her. His wife had history on her side, which was one of Timmie's worst fears. Her greatest terror was that his wife would win in the end. And she would lose. "I love you," he said softly.

"I love you too," Timmie answered, and then they hung up, both of them feeling drained.

As soon as the line disconnected, Timmie felt overwhelmed with panic. He did not want her to come to Paris. She had no idea when she would see him again, or even if. It was a horrifying thought to her, and she would not allow herself to go there. Instead she lay in bed, curled up in the fetal position, with her arms around her knees, and cried. What if he never saw her again? She asked herself if it changed her mind about the baby, but she knew there was no turning back. She was not only having this baby because of him, although he was the largest part of it, but she was also having it for herself, because of Mark, and thanks to God. But it meant the world to her because it was his. At her worst, as she lay there, she thought about his never knowing about it, and never seeing her again. She knew she was being dramatic, but it was hard not to be. Her situation with him was completely unstable. No matter how much she loved him, or he said he loved her, he was still a married man, living with his wife, who was now extremely sick and needed him. And he was staying with her for now. Everything about the situation was designed to arouse Timmie's worst fears. It couldn't get much worse for her, unless he ended it for good.

She lay in her bed and cried all night. And at six o'clock she finally got up and dressed. She sent e-mails to the people she had been planning to meet with in Paris, telling them that an emergency had arisen and she had to postpone her trip. She canceled her flight and reservation at the hotel, and sat in her kitchen, staring into a cup of tea, but not drinking it. Nothing had passed her lips since the night before, nor did she want it to. She finally took a sip, and then left for work. She was at her desk before eight, and appeared to be hard at work when Jade walked in, with a look of surprise.

"What are you doing here?"

Timmie avoided her gaze, trying to look important and busy at her desk. Neither of them was convinced. "Jean-Charles had an emergency. I postponed the trip. I'll probably go in a few days when things settle down."

"What kind of an emergency? Personal or professional?" Jade looked suspicious when she asked.

"A family thing." She didn't want to go into detail with Jade. It sounded too predictable now, and too much like the scenarios Jade had described. Timmie didn't want to give her that, or upset herself any more than she already was. She didn't need Jade hammering her as well. And Timmie knew she would. It would have been impossible for her to resist. Jade's feelings on the subject were still too raw. And in her mind, all married men were the same. Maybe they were. Timmie desperately wanted Jade to be wrong.

"Did something happen with his wife?" Jade persisted, and Timmie's eyes were stern when she looked up. Her message was clear: back off.

"It's too complicated to explain. Someone in the family is sick, so he's tied up."

"His wife, I'll bet. I heard that one before. Stanley's wife had Crohn's disease. Every time he looked like he was about to leave, she wound up in the hospital, sick as a dog. It got so I could predict it every time. What's this one got?" Shit. Cancer, Timmie thought to herself. That beat Crohn's disease, hands down. She wasn't encouraged by what Jade had just said.

"It doesn't matter," Timmie said smoothly. "I'll probably go over in a few days, when things calm down."

"I hope you're right," Jade said, and left the room, with a dark look in her eyes. She hated this for Timmie, but not half as much as Timmie hated it herself.

Timmie went to the bathroom, locked the door, and sat down and cried for a half-hour. After that, she threw up, which she knew was angst, not morning sickness. She always threw up when she was scared. And she was. Very, very, very scared. She wondered if maybe she'd have a miscarriage as a result. That would solve one problem at least, but as she thought it, she knew she didn't want that to happen. She wanted his baby, whether he ever came to her or not. She loved him that much, fool that she was.

Jean-Charles called her late that afternoon, at her office. It was nearly two in the morning for him, and she had felt sick over it all day. She should have been on the plane by then, only a few hours away from his arms. He sounded exhausted when he talked to her, told her again and again that he loved her, and that they just had to be patient and everything would work out.

"When is she starting treatment?" Timmie asked, sounding bleak. Everything was about his wife now, and not about her.

"She has to have the surgery first. They're doing it next week. They can't start chemotherapy until after that, once everything heals. They may decide to do radiation first." He was obviously completely en-meshed in the arrangements around her, and caught up in the hyste-ria that her ominous diagnosis had caused. Intellectually, Timmie understood it perfectly, and even felt sorry for her. Emotionally, she was a terrified child, and a total mess. A pregnant mess on top of it, with serious problems of her own, which he knew nothing about. She couldn't blame him for that. She couldn't have told him, if she wanted to. But the news that she was pregnant was the last thing he needed right now. Out of compassion for him, she had no intention of telling him until everything else settled down. The timing of his wife's breast cancer couldn't have been worse, for all of them. Timmie couldn't help wondering what would have happened if his wife had gotten sick after Jean-Charles had left. Would he have gone back? Maybe so. If so, it was better that it was now. That would have been even worse.

To have him come to her, set up an apartment and a life with her, and then go home again to care for his sick wife. There was no happy way of playing out the drama with which they were faced.

He told her before he hung up that he would call her whenever possible, but things were very tense and fairly chaotic at his end. He said his wife was being brave, but terrified. So was Timmie, about him. He had no idea how frightened she was. Total panic had followed his news of the night before, and her canceled trip.

She had kept to herself all day, and since everyone thought she was away, there were no calls. And she made none. She sat at her desk, valiantly trying to crawl through her work, and accomplishing virtually nothing. She couldn't concentrate, she threw all her sketches away, and all she did when the door was closed was cry. Jade had warned David that something was seriously wrong, and they both left her alone all day. David, with his usual optimism, said he was confident they'd work it out. He had great faith in Jean-Charles. Jade just hmphed loudly and stomped back to her desk, although privately, she was desperately worried and chagrined for their friend and boss. Timmie looked absolutely awful for the rest of the week.

She left her office around six on Friday, and went straight to the beach, without going home to pack a bag. She brought no work home that weekend, no book to read. She spent the entire weekend sleeping, crying, and walking on the beach. And when she wasn't worrying about him, she was thinking about their unborn child. She knew she had to get to a doctor one of these days. She had been planning to do it after Paris. She didn't really care how pregnant she was. All that mattered was that she was carrying his child. It was the sweetest secret of her life, no matter what his situation was. Although his current one made the reality of a baby somewhat terrifying for her. She had made the decision to have it, even if she was alone.

And she had never felt as alone as she did now. She found herself thinking a lot that weekend about Mark. How sweet he had been when he was born and how much she had loved him. How devastated when he died. She had almost wanted to die herself. And now, miraculously, God had given her this second chance, to have a baby with a man she loved so much. She couldn't think of anything more wonderful than having his child. She only wished she could have told him about it in Paris, if things had turned out differently than they had. And some of the time, she hoped he was right, that this was not an end to anything, but only a delay, a blip on the screen of time in their lives. Hopefully, in the next few months, his wife's treatment would be over, and he could finally leave their house. There was nothing Timmie could do now except wait and see, and believe what he said.

Jean-Charles was exceptionally loving with her when he called that weekend. He called her several times a day to reassure her, and apologized a thousand times for asking her to cancel her trip.

"I'm hoping that this will all calm down and be resolved in the next few months," he reassured her. "I'm hoping I may even be able to leave by the end of summer." Timmie hoped so too, but it was going to be a long summer, waiting for him to leave, as her belly grew. He said he hoped she could come over in the next few weeks. Maybe between his wife's surgery, while she recuperated, and before chemo began. He didn't see how he could get away right now at any other time. Timmie didn't comment. She had definitely taken a backseat now to his wife, her illness, his children, and their more pressing problems. She hadn't seen him in a month now, and had no idea when she would again. And what worried her even more, when she thought about it, was that she was a woman he had been in love with for three months, and had spent passionate visits with three times. They had spent exactly fourteen days together in all, end to end. How could she expect him to pit two weeks with her, or even three months if you counted e-mails and phone calls, against a woman he had spent nearly thirty years with? In Timmie's mind, you couldn't, and probably not in his mind either. She was nothing more than a fantasy to him, she told herself, a dream he was hoping would materialize, in a life that was still out of reach. Only the baby she was carrying was real. The rest was still nothing more than a dream, or the hope of a life she might share with him. But for the moment, realistically, he was still sharing his life with his family on a daily basis, living with them, no matter how in love with Timmie he claimed he was.

On Sunday, she went to St. Cecilia's to visit the children, on her way home, and ended up staying for dinner with them. Three new children had arrived, instead of the expected two. One of them was an adorable six-year-old boy, who had been rescued from foster care, after being seriously abused, not only by his family, but also by the foster family that had taken him in. It happened sometimes. He sat silent and wide-eyed all through dinner, and all of Timmie's attempts to engage him in conversation were fruitless. He reminded her agonizingly of Blake. She'd had a card from his grandparents saying he was doing well. She still missed him at times. He would always have a place in her heart.

Sister Anne explained that this child was suffering from post-traumatic stress and didn't speak, much like Blake. They had him in therapy. And when Timmie gently touched his head as she said good-bye, he raised an arm to protect himself, and flinched as he cowered away from her. It brought tears to her eyes, and a sense of reality about what these kids had been living with before they came to St. Cecilia's.

Jean-Charles called her again late that night, but said nothing about her coming over. He told her how much he loved her, but sounded exhausted. It was Monday morning for him, and people were waiting for him in the office. He said his wife's surgery was scheduled for Tuesday. It was all he could talk about these days, and most of the time, Timmie just listened. It was really all she could do for him, and she kept assuring him that she loved him and was there for him. He said she was the only thing keeping him going. She was dying to see him, particularly now, but didn't want to pressure him, so said nothing about it to him. She wanted to be understanding about what he was going through, and hoped it would be good for them in the long run if she at least tried to be supportive, but she was engulfed by waves of panic now much of the time. This was by no means an easy time for either of them. She loved him, but had absolutely no security with him. All she had really was the knowledge that they were madly in love with each other, and had been for three months. The only certainty in her life now was that she was going to have a baby the following winter, as long as nothing untoward happened in the meantime, which was always a possibility at her age. For a multitude of reasons, it seemed wisest to wait before she said anything, since she had decided to have it anyway. For her, the decision had been made.

Knowing that his baby was growing inside her, she loved him more than ever, and missed him terribly. She cried a lot these days. Both David and Jade had observed her somber mood at the office. Neither of them was asking her anything, and both were steering clear. They figured that if she wanted to say anything about it, she would. She was saying nothing to them about going to Paris, had made no arrangements since the trip she'd canceled. And nothing happened or changed in her life till late May.

Just before the Memorial Day weekend, she broached the subject of going to Paris with Jean-Charles again. His wife had had the lumpectomy, and was starting chemotherapy in two weeks. This was the break he had alluded to previously when he thought Timmie could come over. And she asked him about it just before she left for Malibu for the long weekend. She had finally seen her obstetrician about the baby that week. It was growing nicely, she had seen it on the sonogram, with its little heart beating, and she had cried when they showed it to her. She had carried the still photograph of it with her everywhere since. According to their computerized calculations and whatever information she could give them, she was nine weeks pregnant, and the baby was due at the beginning of January. The whole thing still had an aura of unreality for her, particularly since no one knew, not even him. It was her deepest and most tender secret, and one she cherished just as she did her love for him, and his for her, although they hadn't seen each other now since she'd seen him in New York in April, the fateful visit where she had conceived their baby. She was still waiting for an opportune time to tell him, and wanted to, but not over the phone, and preferably not in the midst of his crisis at home. She was waiting for things to calm down so she could tell him, and was hoping he'd let her come to Paris soon.

On the Friday afternoon of the Memorial Day weekend, she asked him how his schedule looked. There was a sigh, and then an immediate silence at the other end. He always sounded stressed and on edge these days, not specifically with her. But he felt pulled in a thousand directions, and he said both his daughters were terrified for their mother. It was a very hard time in his family. And not an easy one for Timmie either.

"I don't know, Timmie. I want to see you so badly. Every day I want to ask you to come over. I just can't get away right now. But even if you were in Paris, if there were a crisis here, or my children needed me in their anguish over their mother, I couldn't be with you the way

I'd want to. I don't want to do that to you, out of respect for you." She was sure he meant it kindly, but it felt like being put off to her. She almost told him that she didn't care how little she saw him, she was willing to come over anyway, but he wasn't encouraging about it, and asked her to wait a few more weeks, to see how the chemo went. Yet another delay, even if a valid excuse. How could she argue with cancer, or the terror of his children, or even his state of anxiety over it? She couldn't. But what about her? a small voice in her head asked. The truth was that there was no room in his life for her at the moment, except on the phone. And she needed more of him than that. Much, much more.

"What about getting away for a few days before she starts chemo? I could come over for a weekend." She had even hoped he would let her come this time, since Monday was a holiday for her. But she would have gone over anytime, and her doctor said she could. She herself felt that the comfort and joy of seeing him would counterbalance any stress the long flight put on her. She would have walked over hot coals to see him, which was not the case for him. He had all the hot coals he could handle these days at home. And in quiet moments, she felt genuinely sorry for him. At other times, she felt sorrier for herself. This was a tough situation for all.

"I don't know what to tell you, my darling. I think we should wait." Until what? Until his wife was desperately sick with chemo and her hair fell out? Then he would be even less able to get away. And his children would be even more upset. Timmie could see what lay ahead, and none of it looked good to her. And surely not to them either. His wife had a rough patch of road ahead. Timmie had seen it at close range with some of her friends. And so had he, with patients. "I'm so sorry to do this to you, and ask you to be patient. I know that by the end of summer, after her chemotherapy, things will be calmer again. Radiation is tiring, but not nearly so difficult as chemotherapy." Their whole life revolved around his wife's treatment now, because his did. And no matter how sympathetic Timmie was, she had some needs too, none of which were being met, other than knowing that a married man in Paris was in love with her, or said he was. But their romance was beginning to seem distant and unreal, to her certainly, and perhaps to him too. The only reality was their baby, which he knew nothing about, and until she saw him again, she intended to keep it that way. Knowing she was pregnant would just add to the general atmosphere of hysteria that was prevalent in his life these days. And she had no desire to contribute to that, for his sake, or even hers. It was a promise she had made herself, and which she intended to keep. She was not going to manipulate, beg, force, blackmail, or plead. She would only tell him about their baby when there was at least a chance he would view it as a gift, and not a threat. Meanwhile, he knew nothing about their unborn child.

"What are you saying to me?" she said sadly, when he offered no hope of seeing her for even a weekend if she came to Paris to see him. Their situation was getting more depressing every day, and so was his. They were the caboose on the train to misery that was currently his wife's.

"I'm saying that I have no idea what to do," he sighed. "I love you, but I don't know when I can see you again. My wife has cancer, my children are going crazy. I had to take our apartment off the market, because it made her hysterical to think that she might have to move in the middle of her treatment, so that was the least I could do for her. Timmie, what can I say?" Her stomach did a quiet double flip. It was the first she had heard of his taking their apartment off the market. "What would you like me to do, given everything that's happening here?" She would have liked him to leave anyway, and perhaps care for his wife while living in his own apartment. But the way he put it to her, it would have sounded cruel to say it, so she didn't. He had to figure it out for himself, and he wasn't. He was doing the right thing for his wife and kids, but not for her at the moment. Worse yet, she wasn't even sure she blamed him. She understood. But it was frightening for her anyway. And being pregnant now only made it that much worse. But she knew she would have been worried and upset even if she weren't. Her worst fear was always that he wouldn't leave his wife and come to her. It had become a far worse version of everything Jade had said, and cancer was so serious, there was no way she could argue with him.

"I don't know," Timmie said with tears in her eyes. She seemed to cry constantly these days. She missed him terribly. And he said he missed her just as much. There was no way to measure pain, to determine who was suffering most, or who had the most at stake. It was a tough spot for both of them, Timmie knew. She tried to make light of it for a minute, there was nothing else to do. "Maybe we should use the *Affair to Remember* solution."

"And what is that?" he asked, sounding offended. "I don't consider this an affair. I don't take this lightly, Timmie. You are the love of my life." And he was hers. But he hadn't come to her yet, and maybe never would. She couldn't lose sight of that anymore either. What was happening was too frightening for her to ignore the obvious risks. Nothing about their situation was secure.

"You are the love of my life too," she said, sounding serious, and then went on to explain. "*An Affair to Remember* is a movie, a very old one. A classic. With Cary Grant and Deborah Kerr. They meet on a ship and fall in love, both are engaged to other people, and they agree to meet six months later at the Empire State Building after they clean up their lives. They both need jobs, and need to wind out of their engagements. Anyway, they make a date at the Empire State Building, if they're both free. Cary Grant tells her that he won't hold it against her if she doesn't show up. She promises the same thing. The day comes. He's waiting for her, and she gets hit by a cab on the way to meet him, and she never gets there. She is in a wheelchair, and doesn't want him to see her that way, so she never calls him. I think he runs into her in a theater many months later, and he doesn't realize that her legs are paralyzed, and he's pretty mad at her. He does a painting of her, because he's an artist, and someone at the gallery tells him that a woman in a wheelchair bought the painting . . . and then he understands, and goes to find her . . ." She had tears in her eyes as she said it. "And they all live happily ever after. Even though she tries to lie to him when he finds her. But when he sees the painting in her bedroom, he realizes that she was the woman in the wheelchair, and he loves her anyway."

"That's quite a story," Jean-Charles said, touched though slightly amused at the comparison to the old movie. "I hope you're not planning to get run over by a car. And you're not going to wind up in a wheelchair, Timmie." It sounded a little melodramatic to him.

"No, I'm not. But what I meant was, maybe you want to make a date for a few months from now, and let this rest until then. You can't see me anyway, and I keep holding my breath and waiting for you to set a date for me to come over. Maybe we have to let that go for now." She was crying as she said it, and he sounded instantly upset.

"Is that what you want, Timmie?" He sounded as unhappy as she did, and somewhat panicked now himself. He didn't want to lose her, no matter what it took. But there was no question, currently his life was a mess, and his family needed him, to the exclusion of all else, even her. And he knew how unfair it was to Timmie. He had been feeling guilty about it constantly, and didn't know which way to turn, without letting other people down. He wondered if maybe she was right.

"No, it's not," she said honestly. "I want to see you. Now. Immediately. I love you. I miss you terribly. But it doesn't sound like that's possible for you, given your wife's situation. Maybe it would take the pressure off for you if we make a date, and promise ourselves to sort out everything by then, or as much as we can." She had nothing to sort out, he did, and he knew it. But there was something simpler about her plan. At least he wouldn't be disappointing her every day, when he failed to ask her to come to Paris, and couldn't fly over to see her himself.

"Would you still talk to me if we did that?" he asked, sounding worried.

"I don't know if we should . . ." And then she started to cry harder, and it nearly broke his heart. All he wanted was to take her in his arms and make everything better. He hated the fact that his wife had gotten cancer, for all of them, and that he was letting Timmie down now as a result. He was well aware of the damage he was doing her, and how terrified she must be, given her old fears of abandonment. The situation would have been hard for anyone, and was even more so for her. He hated doing that to her. "I don't know if I could survive months of not talking to you," Timmie said, sobbing. "I already miss you so much." Talking to him was getting her through the days and nights of loneliness and fear. Without that, it would be even harder, maybe too much so. Especially now that she was pregnant and needed his support, whether he knew about the baby or not.

"I couldn't do it either," he said firmly. "My darling, please try not to worry. I love you. We will be together again. Forever. I promise." But what if they weren't? Timmie thought it but didn't say it. "Perhaps you're right though. Perhaps we should forget trying to get together now, or even this summer. It will be the first of June on Monday. By September first, she will have finished chemo. Radiation will be far less traumatic. And I will have seen her through the worst by then. Neither she nor the children can reproach me for abandoning her during her illness. I would feel comfortable moving out in September. Timmie, if you give me that time, I will be forever grateful." Timmie couldn't help wondering what would happen if she got sicker instead of better, or if the children didn't see it the way he did. What if he didn't leave then either? But she didn't say it to him. She was trying to be decent about it, and he was too. She just hoped he wasn't being naïve with what he promised. "Shall we make a date at the Empire State Building on September first?" he said gently, and she laughed through her tears.

"It doesn't have to be there." And then she laughed again. "What about the Eiffel Tower? But if we're talking to each other, we'll know anyway if the other is going to show up or not."

"I will show up," he said, sounding serious. "It is a solemn promise I am making you. On September first, I will be yours forever, to do with what you wish. I love you, and I will be entirely yours from then on." She made a rapid calculation and realized she would be five months pregnant by then, or close to it. It would be a big surprise for him when they met. But she could wait. If he was promising a life with her, she could wait another three months. She had no doubt in her heart or mind that he was worth it. And she didn't want to put more pressure on him and tell him about the baby. She could manage on her own till then, or forever if she had to. Hopefully, this time the child she had would be hers forever. And with luck, so would Jean-Charles.

"All right, it's a date," she said sadly. She hated knowing she wouldn't see him for another three months, but it seemed to be the only way to do this, and for him to stay sane. "The Eiffel Tower on September first."

"I will meet you at the Jules Verne Restaurant," he said, feeling slightly silly. "And I will call you every day until then. That, I promise." They both sounded sad when they hung up. She felt as though she had lost something rather than gained, with their agreement. She had lost the opportunity for constant disappointment and broken promises. But she had also given up the hope of seeing him for the next three months. It was going to be very hard, for both of them. She just hoped the relationship would survive it. There was no way to tell. All she had now were her hopes, her dreams, her deep love for him, and the child she carried that he knew nothing about, and maybe never would. If he didn't show up on September 1, she had already promised herself that in that case, she would never tell him about their child. And if so, she would be alone with their baby for the rest of her life, with only memories of him to keep her warm. It was a frightening thought. And all she could hope was that he would show up, as promised, on September 1. All she could do now was pray, hope, trust, and wait.

Chapter 18

The next months were hard for her. She tried to be a good sport about it, but not seeing him was a bigger challenge than she had thought. Jean-Charles called her every day to report on the situation there. The chemotherapy was predictably horrible, and a week after it began, his wife had lost all her hair, and his children were beside themselves at the prospect of losing their mother. There was no way to tell yet if the chemotherapy would work. And Jean-Charles sounded drained each time they spoke. He kept assuring Timmie that he loved her, but he was becoming a disembodied voice to her now. It was hard to believe or remember that she had once been so happy in his arms. Her ever-growing belly was the only tangible proof of that.

As the summer got under way, she managed easily to keep her pregnancy from David and Jade. She was more tired than usual, and lay down when she went home. She was queasy at times, and had headaches now and then, but she shared none of her discomforts, or private hopes, agonies, or fears with them. She kept everything to herself, and as she was slim and tall, nothing showed. She wore looser shirts, and in July bought slightly bigger jeans, but she still looked as thin as ever.

There was no reason for anyone to suspect she was pregnant. It was the furthest thing from anyone's mind. Jade commented to David once that she thought Timmie had put on a little weight, but they both knew she was having a hard time. It was obvious that Jean-Charles had put her on the back burner of his life, and she had finally told them both that his wife had cancer, and they were putting things on hold until September. She made no further comments, although both her assistants knew that he was still calling. And David hadn't given up hope. Jade had no doubt whatsoever what would happen, but now she only shared her dark predictions with David.

"He's history," Jade said to him in July. Timmie hadn't seen him since New York in April, three months before. "He's not coming back. His wife will need him because she's sick, his kids would never forgive him if he left, even later. And for the next five or ten years, even if she gets cured, they're all going to be scared shitless she'll get sick again. Forget it," Jade said bluntly.

"Isn't it even remotely possible the guy is trying to do the right thing, and he'll still manage to get out? He's a decent guy, Jade. You've got to admire him for trying to get out clean."

"Bullshit. How much do you admire him for what he's doing to Timmie? Have you looked at her face lately? She looks like someone died. And she's right. She did. Believe me, I know what that feels like. She probably knows in her heart of hearts he's not coming back. She's just not ready to admit it to herself."

"Christ, you're pessimistic. I think they really love each other. Why don't we suspend judgment till September, as Timmie is? If he doesn't come back then, maybe I'll give you some leeway on your position. But even then, September is just a guess for him. Maybe he won't make it back into her life until November or December or January. But I think he'll be back. I'd bet my life on it. All my instincts tell me he's a good guy."

"You're just sticking up for your own sex. Believe me, he's not coming back."

"A thousand bucks says he is," David said with a smoldering look, as Jade looked at him with hard eyes.

"You're on," she said. "I need a new Chanel bag. What's our deadline?"

"October first. Let's give him thirty days slippage."

"September first."

"You're tough. And what happens if he comes back after and I was right?"

"I'll lend you my purse." She knew he was straight, and they both laughed.

"You drive a hard bargain. I say you sell the purse, and buy me some new golf clubs."

"All right, all right, if he comes back after September first, I'll take you out to an expensive dinner."

"You're on." They shook hands on it as Timmie walked in. She was going to Santa Barbara for the Fourth of July weekend the next day and didn't look enthused about it. She didn't look enthused about anything these days, and she was being more short-tempered than usual, although they knew that Jean-Charles was still calling her every day. She was always happy for a few minutes after he called her, and she put up a good front for him, and then her spirits plummeted again. Jade had rarely seen her as down, and David worried about her. They both did.

"What are you two up to?" She had seen them shake hands on their bet, and knew they were up to some kind of mischief. Jade was in good spirits these days. Her romance with the architect was blooming. And David was going out with three new women he had met on the Internet. She thought they were both silly, but whatever worked.

They were young, and deserved to have some fun. All she could focus on these days was her baby, although no one knew about it.

"Nothing." They both answered her in unison. "We just made a bet about whether or not David would score with the girl he just met on Match.com."

"You two are disgusting." She smiled. "The poor girl. Imagine if she knew that all she is is fodder for a bet. Do I want to know how much?"

David shook his head and laughed. "No, you don't." He handed her some reports, and she went back to her office. She was keeping to herself these days. In great part, because she didn't want to have to listen to Jade say "I told you so." And in any case, Jean-Charles was still being loving, and calling every day as he had promised. His wife was very sick, his kids were monumentally upset, and they still had a date for September 1, to meet at the Eiffel Tower. It was all she had to hold on to at the moment. It wasn't much, but it was all she had. And he had no suspicions about the baby. There was no reason why he would.

The only comment he had made was that he almost always woke her up now when he called her at midnight, when he called at nine A.M. Paris time from his office. When he had called her before at that hour, she was always working, or reading. Now she was almost always asleep. And he was worried that she might be depressed and sleeping more. It never occurred to him that it was because she was pregnant.

They still talked for hours on the phone, and shared what was happening in their lives. She told him about work, the things she did, the weekends in Malibu. She told him about everything but their baby, who was quietly growing inside her, a tribute to their love for each other. And it saddened her beyond belief when she thought sometimes, in her darkest hours, that he might never even know about their child. She was still determined not to tell him if he stayed with his wife. She only wanted him to know about the baby if he came back to her. If not, it was her responsibility and not his problem. She had no desire to be a burden to him, or to appear pathetic. She didn't want him out of pity, responsibility, or concern. She only wanted him as he had come to her in the first place, as they had conceived this child, out of the deepest love for each other. She wanted nothing less than that from him.

Her weekend in Santa Barbara was predictably boring, and for the rest of July, she worked, went to Malibu, and spent time with the children at St. Cecilia's. She felt faint there one day, on a particularly hot, airless, smoggy afternoon, and Sister Anne said she was worried about her.

"I'm fine. Just working too hard, as always." Timmie brushed off her concerns, and they chatted for a little while. The wise old nun saw through Timmie's front of ease and bravado. She knew something was wrong these days, and hoped that if Timmie needed to, she would talk to her about it, and encouraged her to do so. Timmie gave her a warm hug as she left with tears in her eyes. The nuns were taking all the children to Tahoe for two weeks, on a camping trip, and they had invited Timmie to come along, but she'd declined. She was tired, and camping with them for two weeks was more than she could handle at the moment. She said she might come up for a weekend, and did on the first weekend in August. Sister Anne was thrilled that she had come, and all the children cheered when she got out of her car and they saw her.

"I'm so glad you decided to join us," Sister Anne said, and gave her a warm hug. They had set up tents, and the children loved it, and all the nuns were there. The house in L.A. was locked up, alarmed, and empty.

"I haven't camped in years," Timmie said ruefully. "I'm not even sure I want to." She was the first to admit that she had gotten very spoiled over the years and liked her life that way.

"You'll love it!" Sister Anne reassured her. And she was right.

They had campfires every night, roasted marshmallows, and made s'mores, which Timmie proved to be an expert at, she had made them in the orphanage herself as a child. She went fishing with them, went on nature walks and hikes, ran in terror from a bear that lumbered by and never bothered them again. And finally, after swearing she never would, she dove into the lake with them on the last day. Predictably, it was as freezing cold as she had feared, but she had a wonderful time with them, and taught one of the children to swim, the little boy who had refused to speak when he arrived, and now never stopped talking. She taught them all songs at night around the campfire. And she was happy and breathless as she got out of the lake and wrapped herself in a towel. She noticed that Sister Anne was watching her with a warm smile. Her eyes met Timmie's, and the two women exchanged a peaceful, loving look.

She didn't say anything to Timmie until later that night, when the other nuns were putting the children to bed, despite arguments and protests. They had had a ball at the lake, and loved staying up late at night to tell ghost stories, which they were about to do now in their tents, scaring each other to death.

The two women sat side by side at the fire, as Timmie roasted one more stick of marshmallows and offered them to Sister Anne. She always enjoyed talking to her, and had enjoyed the time she had just spent with them. She was sorry to be leaving in the morning, but they were already busy in her office, preparing the October shows, even though they were still more than two months away. This was always a busy time for them.

"I'm glad you came up to join us, Timmie," Sister Anne said quietly. "You're an enormous blessing for these children. Not just because of what you do for them, but because of what you demonstrate to them. You show them that even if you had a hard beginning yourself, you've managed to have a wonderful life."

It didn't feel so wonderful to her these days, but she didn't say that to Sister Anne. And she hadn't talked to Jean-Charles in three days. Her cell phone didn't work in the mountains, and in some ways it was a relief. She didn't know what to say to him anymore. And she was tired of lying to him about the baby. They had four weeks left before their date at the Eiffel Tower, and she was beginning to doubt that he would make it, although his wife's chemo treatments were almost finished. But Timmie had begun to wonder if he'd ever get out. He was still so entrenched in his old life. Hope was beginning to wane, or maybe she was just bracing herself for disappointment, if he didn't show up. He might not. She knew that if she'd asked, Jade would have assured her that he wouldn't. And she was beginning to believe her.

She hadn't seen him in four months, which meant that she was four months pregnant. It didn't show, because no one suspected it was there. But if anyone had known, they would have noticed her gently protruding stomach. And she felt as though her bottom had doubled in size, although it really hadn't. She had just that week felt what she thought was the first flutter of movement, although she told herself it was her imagination. It had been as gentle as butterfly wings whispering past her heart, and she cried the first time she felt it. She wished she could have shared it with Jean-Charles when he called five minutes later and asked why she was crying. She had told him she'd been reading a sad book, and had long since sent him a copy of *An Affair to Remember,* which he said his wife and daughters had loved. She wasn't quite as thrilled to hear that piece of news as he had hoped. Sometimes even he didn't get the point, as much as he loved her, and as sweet as he still was.

Sister Anne was watching Timmie cautiously, as she licked her fingers, after eating the last of the marshmallows. She had a healthy appetite these days, and indulged herself more than she had in the past.

"Would I be totally out of line if I asked you a question?" Sister Anne asked her in a soft voice, as Timmie smiled.

"Never. You can ask me anything you want." She assumed that the nun who ran St. Cecilia's was about to ask her for more money for their budget, maybe so they could take more vacations like the one they'd all just enjoyed so much. "Fire away."

"I watched you after you were swimming today. And I'm no expert about these things, by any means." She smiled. "But it seems to me that I saw . . . a small bump . . . I could be wrong . . . but I was wondering if . . ." She had suddenly remembered Timmie's fainting spell the previous month. And had come up with her own suspicions, which were accurate, of course. "Is it possible that God has given you a gift?" she asked, and Timmie smiled. It was a nice way to look at it and she was touched. She hadn't wanted to tell anyone yet, but she knew Sister Anne would keep it to herself, if she chose to take her into her confidence. She trusted her completely. And eventually, everyone would see it anyway, but hopefully not for a while.

Timmie looked into the fire, and then into the old nun's eyes. All she saw was love there and support for her. Her eyes brimmed with tears as she nodded, and Sister Anne put her arms around her and told her how happy she was. Particularly since she knew Timmie had lost a son, and been so disappointed over Blake.

"You're not shocked?" Timmie asked in surprise.

"No, I'm not. I think you're very lucky. That's the only thing I've missed in the religious life, not having a child of my own. If I had it to do over again, maybe I'd do that, but I've had so many children over the years"—she smiled at Timmie—"that it doesn't really matter. But if I were you, I would be so grateful for this baby, and celebrate every moment of its life." The way she said it made Timmie cry. She told her then about Jean-Charles, about meeting him and falling in love with him, their plans and dreams, and his wife's cancer, and that they were supposed to meet in a few weeks at the Eiffel Tower. She assured her, as Jean-Charles had her, that his marriage had been long dead when she came on the scene. She would never have stolen a man out of a viable marriage. His decision to divorce had been his own, before their relationship began. And now the decision to delay leaving his wife was his as well.

"You know, Timmie, I don't know this man. But from everything you're telling me, I have confidence in him. He's just done the right thing for his wife and children. He sounds like a good man. I don't think he'll let you down."

"I wish I were as sure," Timmie said sadly. She had begun to have so many doubts in recent weeks. Four months without him had been an eternity, and she just couldn't see him walking away from his family now. "I never believed in love at first sight until I met him," she said with a sigh.

"I think it happens," the nun said wisely. "It never did to me." She laughed. "But I've heard plenty of stories where it did, and even if it was a little bumpy at first, it all worked out. I think this will too."

"Will you pray for us?" Timmie asked her. It was the first time Timmie had asked anyone to pray for her in years, since she was a child. But she had faith in Sister Anne's prayers. Timmie felt sure that she had the ear of God.

"Of course I will. And for the baby." She looked serious for a moment then. "I take it you haven't told him about the baby?" Timmie shook her head.

"I want him to walk out of there because he wants to and loves me. I don't want to pull him out with obligation and guilt. He just did the right thing for his wife. I don't want him just doing 'the right thing' for me. I want him to come back because he loves me."

"I'm sure he does," Sister Anne said quietly, "but it might be nice for him to know about the baby. It's his baby too, after all."

"I'll tell him when I see him at the Eiffel Tower. I didn't want to put pressure on him while he was going through all this. And if he doesn't show up, then he doesn't need to know. The last thing I want is to be a burden to him. I love him. I'm not going to force him to be with me, because I'm having his child. And I can always tell him about it later, after it's born. But I want things clear between us first. By September, I won't have to tell him anyway. I don't think I'm going to be able to hide it for much longer. He'll see it for himself . . . if he shows up."

"He will," Sister Anne said with a smile. Like David, she seemed to have no doubt. Timmie wasn't sure what she believed anymore. She ricocheted constantly between fear and love. She had managed to get through the past four months on trust. But it was finally starting to run out. Maybe Sister Anne's prayers would help. And it would all be fine if he showed up at the Eiffel Tower on September 1. "You'll have to call me from Paris," Sister Anne said happily, seemingly with no doubt at all that it would turn out right. "Or you can both come to visit when you get back. It's going to be so exciting to have a baby when you come to visit," she said, and Timmie smiled. It seemed so unreal to her, and talking to Sister Anne about it had given it some reality finally. And then she remembered what the nun had said about the example she had set for the kids.

"You know, I haven't done anything that impressive with my life. I run a successful business, and that's about it. I'm not married. I don't have kids. I have no family. All I've done worthy of respect is run Timmie O."

"The example you set," Sister Anne said quietly, "is by the kind of person you are. And that in spite of adversities in your life, you've never given up. That gives people hope. Sometimes we need hope more than love. In truth, we need both. You give these children something to hope for, by showing them they can do it, and to get them there, you give them love. There's no better gift than that."

As Timmie looked at the nun, what she saw was that that was exactly what Sister Anne had given her, and what she needed most. Sister Anne had given Timmie love and hope that Jean-Charles would come back. It was all she needed now, as she reached out and embraced the nun with a warm hug.

"Thank you," she said softly, as she looked at her again.

"It's all right, Timmie." The old nun patted her hand. "Trust God on this one. Jean-Charles will be back." Timmie nodded, and hoped that she was right.

Chapter 19

Timmie was saying goodbye to the children at the campsite the next day as a car drove up, and two priests got out. A young one had been driving, and an elderly priest in Roman collar with jeans followed him to where Timmie was standing with the children and the nuns. Sister Anne introduced them, as Timmie looked at the older priest strangely. There was something so familiar about him, but she wasn't sure what it was. He had a broad Irish face, a shock of white hair, and piercing blue eyes that danced when he smiled. He shook Timmie's hand as Sister Anne introduced them, and then he stared at her and frowned.

"Timmie O'Neill? . . . I don't suppose you were ever in a place called St. Clare's?" Timmie stared at him with wide eyes, and remembered instantly who he was. He had been the priest who heard confessions in the orphanage where she grew up. He always brought candy to the kids, and pretty hair clips for the little girls. She remembered he had once given her a big blue bow for her hair. She had never forgotten the kind gesture, and wore it until it was ragged. It was the only one she had ever had.

"Father Patrick?"

"I'm afraid so," he said with a broad grin. "One and the same. You had the boniest knees I've ever seen, and more freckles than I've ever counted on any one kid in my life. What have you been up to for all these years?" She laughed at the question, and so did Sister Anne. He was probably the only man or woman in the country, or half the world, who wasn't familiar with her name.

"I run a clothing company in L.A.," she said humbly, and he stared at her again.

"Oh my God, you're not *that* Timmie O, are you? I never made the connection in all these years. I always buy your jeans and dress shirts. You make very nice things," he complimented her in his heavy Irish accent. He'd been in the States for fifty years and still spoke with a thick brogue.

"Well, don't buy them anymore," Timmie scolded him. "I'll send you some things when you go back. I was just leaving. I'm so glad we met." He was one of the few decent memories she had of her childhood, and it touched her to see him. And within minutes, he, the young priest with him, the nuns, and all the children were trying to convince her to stay. She finally agreed to stay till after dinner. She needed to get back to San Francisco that night, and fly to L.A. She had work to do the next day, and meetings she couldn't get out of. But she loved the idea of spending the day with Father Pat, for old times' sake.

They sat and reminisced with the children over lunch, and she was touched to discover that he knew all about St. Cecilia's and had been there often. He and Sister Anne were old friends.

"You're doing some very fine work," he complimented Timmie. "It warms my heart when people who've suffered turn it into a blessing for others. These children need you, Timmie. Too many of them fall through the cracks in the system, just like you did, and never get adopted or placed in foster care. I remember how hard it was for you at St. Clare's. I could never understand why people didn't keep you. I think you were probably just too old by the time your parents left you. As I recall, they didn't sign the relinquishment papers for quite a while." She could tell he was getting old by the details he had forgotten. He had forgotten that her parents had died, but he remembered all the rest, and she was touched.

"Actually, my parents died, which is how I wound up at St. Clare's. I guess I wasn't all that charming. Maybe they didn't like knobby knees and freckles and red hair. Whatever it was, I always wound up back where I started. Right back at St. Clare's. I remember confessing to you once that I hated my foster parents for sending me back, and you told me not to worry about it, and gave me a Snickers bar, and didn't even tell me to say a Hail Mary for admitting how much I hated them."

"I didn't blame you one bit." He smiled, but his eyes looked troubled. The conversation moved on and centered on St. Cecilia's, and it was later that afternoon when he approached her, after she went for one last swim with the kids.

"Timmie," he said cautiously. He had discussed it with Sister Anne before saying anything to her, but they both thought she had a right to know, even if it was unorthodox for him to say something to her. But they both felt she was certainly old enough to hear it, and it might make some kind of difference to her, even now. "I'm not really supposed to say this to you, although the laws have changed in these matters. If you had decided to pursue it, they would be obligated to tell you. No one can hunt you down with information, but I thought you might like to know. Your parents didn't die, Timmie. They gave you up and went back to Ireland. I never met them, but I knew the story. They were both young and had run away together. They got

married and they had you, and then things started to go wrong. I
think they were both in their early twenties at the time. They had no
money, no jobs, they couldn't handle a baby. They put you up for
adoption, and went back to Ireland to their parents. I don't know if
they stayed together. And I remember that they took a while to sign
the papers, so they must have hesitated. I think they bit off more than
they could chew, so they gave you up and went back. They had a car
accident, I believe, you were with them, and you weren't hurt. They
had both been drinking and got in a head-on collision, and miraculously, no one was killed. For some reason, they made the decision
then and there. The ambulance took them to the hospital, and they
had you taken to St. Clare's. I think your mother broke her arm, and
your father banged his head a bit. They came to St. Clare's the next
day, but they didn't see you. Your mother said they weren't responsible enough to have a child and maybe she was right. You could have
been killed while they were joy-riding the night before. Thank God
you weren't." What he said brought back her memory of riding the
ambulance to St. Clare's. She had no recollection of being in the car
with them, or how they had been taken away, or what condition
they'd been in. She never saw them again and had always believed
the story that they died that night. "Your mother wanted us to tell you
that they died. She thought it would be easier for you to understand."

He looked troubled as he said it, and even now, all these years
later, hearing the story, Timmie was profoundly shocked. It was the
ultimate rejection, worse than their dying. They had just dumped her
in an orphanage, given her up for adoption, and gone home. And
even if the story was more complicated than that, that was what it
had translated to for her. They had solved their problems by letting
others care for her. And they had never come back. It had been her
greatest terror all her life, and now she knew why. Her worst night-

mares had been exactly what had happened to her, and even what she was so afraid of with Jean-Charles now. She had been abandoned by the parents she loved and who said they loved her. "Are you all right?" Father Patrick asked her when he saw the look on her face.

"I think so. Do you know where they are now?" He shook his head.

"Probably in Ireland. I'm sure there's no current information on them. They had no right to contact you, once they gave you up. But the diocese will have to give you the files, if you ask. You might find some clue to help you find them now, if that's what you want." He knew that others had, and claimed it had made a difference to them. He couldn't imagine that it made a difference to Timmie. She was so successful, and seemed relaxed and happy, but you never knew what ghosts tortured people, and he had felt compelled to tell her the truth when she mentioned her parents' death. He had somehow assumed that she knew the truth by now, but clearly she didn't, which was why he told her. He thought she had a right to know the truth, and not a lie. She had believed the lie of their dying all her life.

"Is O'Neill my real name?" she asked, still looking startled.

"I assume it is," he said kindly. And for the rest of the afternoon, she wandered around, feeling distracted, although no one could see how upset she was.

As promised, she left just after dinner, with all the nuns and children waving. The two priests had left just before she did, and she'd gotten Father Patrick's address, so she could send him something from Timmie O. She thanked him for the information he had shared with her. It was all she could think of on the drive back to San Francisco, and the flight back to L.A. She lay awake all night.

Jean-Charles was immensely relieved when he finally reached her early the next morning. He hadn't spoken to her in four days. She told him about the camping trip with the children, and then in a troubled voice she told him what Father Patrick had told her about her parents. Even all these years later, it was shocking for her. All her life, she had believed that she wound up in the orphanage because her parents died. It changed everything to know that they had left her there when they were alive. Knowing that made the abandonment so much worse.

"They just left me and went home, and never came back again." It was easy for him to figure out that their desertion had been the root of all her problems and terrors for an entire lifetime ever since. It even contributed now to her terrors about him, which he also understood. He could hear in her voice how upset she was.

"They must have been very frightened and very young," he said gently. "It's not so easy to be responsible for a child with no one to help you. They probably had no money, and didn't know what else to do."

"They could have taken me home with them. I wasn't a newborn they could dump on the church steps or in a trash can. I was five years old," she said with a sense of outrage that he could hear in her voice. But there was nothing she could do about it now. It had been forty-three years before, and they were long gone. The only thing she had left to remind her of them were the scars she had had on her soul ever since. They had no way of knowing what had happened to her once they signed the adoption papers, and apparently didn't care. It had been the ultimate abandonment, followed by so many others since.

"Timmie, you have to put it behind you now. There's nothing else you can do." He tried to distract her then by reminding her of their meeting at the Eiffel Tower. He said that everything was going well. His wife was feeling a little better, his children were calmer, and he was sure that in three weeks he'd be able to go. He said he could hardly wait. Timmie barely dared to hope. In three weeks, their life would begin. He said he was getting organized to leave, and planned to tell them in the next two weeks. "I'll be there," he said. It sounded silly and romantic. They would finally be together after five months of waiting for him.

"I have something to tell you when I see you," she said, smiling, and he was curious about what it was. They had so much to say and do and share. They had a whole life waiting for them, as soon as he got out. And Timmie was waiting for him with more love than she could tell him, and open arms. Life was going to begin for them in earnest on September 1. She had finally dared to hope again, and think that maybe Sister Anne was right.

She left for the office shortly after his phone call, and stewed about it all day. Not about what Jean-Charles had said to her, which was so encouraging and hopeful, but about what Father Patrick had shared with her the day before, and Jean-Charles's comments about it. She didn't agree with him. There was nothing she could do to change it now, but at least she had a right to discover everything there was to know about them. Not that seeing her file from the orphanage would explain to her why they'd left her. But it might tell her something.

She called St. Clare's herself at four-thirty, and asked them to send her all her records. She faxed them a release so they could do so, and she felt like the proverbial cat on a hot tin roof while she waited three days for them to arrive, and was disappointed when they did. There was not much there. Her parents' real names. Joseph and Mary O'Neill. Her mother had been twenty-two, her father twenty-three. Both were Irish, and said they were indigent, unemployed, and re-turning to Ireland, to live with their families. There was a copy of their marriage license, so she had been legitimate, not that it really mattered. It was very simple really, they just didn't want her, couldn't keep her, couldn't afford her. They had come to America in their teens, gotten married, had a baby, and when things didn't work out for them, they had dumped her and gone home. It had been their request to tell her that they had died, so she didn't feel too badly. There was a faded photograph of both of them. They looked about fourteen. She had her mother's features and her father's red hair. As Timmie sat and stared at the photograph of the people who had abandoned her forty-three years before, her hand shook, and tears poured down her cheeks. She wanted to hate them, but couldn't. All she wanted now was an explanation from them about why they did it, and if they had missed her after they left her. She wanted to know if they had loved her at all, and if they'd cared about giving her up for adoption. Had they been relieved or heartbroken? She wasn't sure why, but it mattered a great deal to her. Maybe all she really wanted to know, she realized, was if they'd ever loved her.

She sat there alone with the file for an hour, and then called Jade on the intercom.

"I want to find someone in Ireland," she said tersely. "Joseph and Mary O'Neill. In Dublin, I think. How do we do that? Do we call information or a PI?"

"I can do an Internet search for you if you want, and call Dublin information. It's a pretty common name, so I may come up with a few. If you give me more info, I can weed through them before I give it to you, so we know we've got the right ones. Relations of yours, I assume?" Jade asked. It didn't sound like a difficult request to her.

"Just give me whatever you find. I'll call them myself."

As it turned out, it was embarrassingly easy. There were three Joseph and Mary O'Neills in Dublin, at addresses that meant nothing to her. At first, she wasn't sure what to do next. Did she just call them and ask if they'd ever had a daughter named Timmie, and then say "Hi, how are you, I'm your daughter"? It seemed a little blunt. In the end, she decided to call them and pretend she was from St. Clare's. She got lucky, if you could call it that, on the second one. She said that they were closing out files from years ago, and wondered if they would like the records sent to them. Her mother had answered the phone.

"No, that's all right," the woman said in a thick brogue. "We still have ours. And it doesn't matter really. My husband died last year." Timmie wasn't sure what difference that made, but she doggedly pursued the conversation just so she could keep her on the phone. She tried to jog her memory to see if she remembered the voice, but she didn't. The woman sounded old. "I don't want you to send the records," the woman said firmly, which Timmie felt as yet another blow of rejection. They didn't even want the records of her brief existence in their lives.

"Why not?" she asked in a trembling voice, wanting to ask if they had ever loved her, and why they had walked away so long ago.

"I don't want our other children to see that, if anything ever happens to me. They never knew about her, and still don't."

It told Timmie that she had brothers and sisters that they had kept, but they hadn't loved her enough to keep her. She wanted to ask why. And how many of them were there? Why had they had other children, when they didn't keep their first one? None of it made sense. And how could they abandon her at five? They were the final and most important mysteries of Timmie's life. And then finally, the woman on the phone said something that touched Timmie's heart. "Is she all right? Is there anything about her in the file?" the woman asked in a sad voice. She sounded older than she was. According to Timmie's calculations, she was only sixty-five, but sounded much older, and as though she had had a hard life.

"We don't have recent records, of course," Timmie said, pursuing the masquerade she had begun to find out if this was her mother. "But as far as we know, she's fine."

"I'm glad," the woman said with a sigh of relief. "I always wondered who had adopted her, and if they were good people. We thought she'd be better off to leave her for other people. We were very young at the time." And heartless, and cowardly, and mean, Timmie thought to herself, as tears burned her eyes. She was suddenly angrier than she had ever been in her entire life. She was overwhelmed with sadness and anger. Unwittingly perhaps, these people had altered the course of her entire life, and caused her scars that had never healed and never would. All because they left her.

"Actually, no one adopted her," Timmie said cruelly. "She was a little too old when you left her. People want babies, you know. Five-year-olds are a lot harder to place. We placed her with a number of families, nine or ten I believe, but it never worked. And then we tried her in foster care for a number of years, but by then she was considerably older, and they always sent her back. She was a very nice child, but it's just one of those things that happen. She grew up at St. Clare's." There was an endless silence at the other end, as Timmie could hear the woman crying, and then felt guilty for what she'd done.

"Oh my God . . . we always thought she'd be adopted by rich people who would be good to her. If I'd known . . ." Yes, what? If you'd known, would you have kept me? Would you have taken me back to Dublin with you? Why the hell didn't you? Timmie wanted to scream, but couldn't as a sob caught in her throat, and she had to fight for composure so the woman at the other end didn't realize who she was. "You wouldn't have an address for her, would you? Maybe I can write her a letter, and try to explain things. Her father never forgave me for talking him into leaving her. I thought it would be best for her. We were so poor and so young."

"I'll see what I can find out," Timmie said vaguely, still reeling from all she'd heard. "I'll call you back and let you know."

"Thank you," she said, sounding shaken. "Thank you . . . and if you call . . . please don't talk to my children . . . just ask for me."

"I will. Thank you," Timmie said in a choked voice, and sat staring out her office window for a long time. And then, with her face pale, she picked up the phone, and made reservations on a flight to Dublin in the morning. She wanted to see her for herself. A phone call hadn't been enough. Maybe nothing would ever be enough. Maybe it truly was too late. But on the chance that it wasn't, that there was something she still needed from her, Timmie decided to see for herself. She had just hung up from the airlines when Jade walked into her office. "Cancel my appointments. I'm going away tomorrow, on family business," Timmie said brusquely.

"The O'Neills you had me look up in Dublin?" Timmie nodded. "Anything else I can do?" Timmie shook her head. "How long will you be gone?"

"Just a day or two, I think." She still had another three weeks before her date with Jean-Charles at the Eiffel Tower, and he obviously wasn't ready to do it any earlier than planned. She was not going to tell him she was in Europe. And she would not tell anyone why she went. She didn't know what would happen when she went there, or what she would find. But she knew with all her heart and soul that, whatever happened, this was a pilgrimage she had to make, not just to meet her mother, but to find herself and the piece of her that had been missing all her life.

Chapter 20

The flight from L.A. to London took eleven hours, and Timmie slept most of the way. She lay in her seat, and looked out the window, thinking of the woman who was her mother, and wondered what it would be like to meet her, and how upsetting it would be. Maybe she'd faint or have a heart attack, or throw her arms around Timmie. She had a lot of fantasies about it, and it was hard to guess which of them would be closest to the truth. Or maybe none at all. Maybe it would be boring and unemotional, although it hadn't sounded that way on the phone on the day before. At least the woman had had the grace to cry when Timmie told her she had never been adopted and grew up at St. Clare's.

They must have had all the childish illusions of poor people from Ireland, who imagined that there were diamonds in the pavement on the streets, and rich people on every corner, waiting to adopt freckle-faced little girls. The reality of Timmie's childhood had been light-years from that. And it was too late to change it now. Timmie just wanted to see her, and try to understand what had happened, and why it had gone so wrong for them, and then for her. Having had a child of her own, whom she had loved so much, she couldn't begin to imagine how they could have walked away. But they had had no money, no future, no family to help them. Maybe it had been different for them.

Even now, with this baby inside her, nothing on earth would have convinced her to give it up, or abandon it, no matter how poor or terrified she was, and she was alone. This was her flesh and blood and Jean-Charles's, she would have died to keep it, killed to protect it, and knew she would love it for the rest of her days. She just hoped that Jean-Charles would be there with her. That still remained to be seen. But first she had to see her own mother, to try to understand who she had been. It made a difference to her, and to her sense of history about herself. And maybe even to how she felt herself from now on. Maybe their abandoning her all those years ago had been about them, and not about her. She knew that, but somehow it had always felt like it was something wrong with her that she wound up an orphan. She needed to see it for herself now.

She had a two-hour layover in London, and then took the short flight to Dublin. She held the phone number in a shaking hand, and called her from the airport. She had a reservation at the Shelbourne Hotel, but she wanted to visit Mary O'Neill first. She wanted to get it over with, and see her now. As she had the day before, Timmie's mother answered the phone, and for a moment, this time, Timmie couldn't speak. This was much harder than she had expected. But she didn't feel it was right to surprise her, and ring her bell. There was always the possibility that her mother would refuse to see her at all.

"Hello?" The same tired voice answered as the day before.

"Mrs. O'Neill?" Timmie felt slightly breathless.

"Yes?"

"Mary O'Neill?" Timmie wanted to be sure before she went on, but

Mary O'Neill had already recognized the American voice at the other end as the one she had spoken to the day before.

"Yes. Are you calling from St. Clare's again?"

"Actually," Timmie said, trying to control the shaking in her voice as she stood in the pay phone at the airport with her carry-on beside her on the ground, "I'm calling from the airport. Not St. Clare's. The Dublin airport," she explained.

"Why are you doing that?" The woman sounded frightened, as though she thought they might come to punish her, or expose her, for abandoning her child.

"I'd like to see you," Timmie said gently, as the fury suddenly went out of her. This woman sounded so pathetic, so simple, and so old. "This is Timmie. I'm in Dublin. I came to see you. Would you see me for a few minutes?" She held her breath as her mother fell silent, and then Timmie could hear her crying again. This was hard for both of them.

"Do you hate me?" she asked bluntly, crying openly now.

"No," Timmie said sadly, "I don't hate you. I just don't understand. Maybe it would be nice to talk to each other. You don't ever have to see me again after this." She didn't want to invade her life. She just wanted to meet her once, and then go away in peace. Her mother owed her that at least. Maybe it was a gift they could give each other, in exchange for the love she hadn't had.

"We were so poor. We were starving. Your father went to jail for stealing us a sandwich and an apple. You cried all the time because you were hungry, and we could never find work. We had no education, no training, they couldn't understand us. Sometimes we slept in the park, and you were always catching cold or getting sick, and we couldn't afford to take you to a doctor. I thought you would die if we kept you. You could have been killed that night in the car, when we had the accident. We borrowed the car. Your father was driving drunk. He was just a boy. I knew then, you needed better parents than us. So I sent you to St. Clare's. The police offered to take you there." It had been as simple as that. For them. Not for her. A policeman's suggestion to a couple of kids driving drunk, and she was gone. Listening to her, a chill ran down Timmie's spine. What they had done had nearly destroyed her life.

Mary sobbed, remembering just how grim it had been for them nearly half a century before. To Timmie, it seemed hard to believe they were so unable to care for her, but maybe it was true. There was no reason for the woman to lie now. The damage was done, and had been long since. And in most ways, Timmie had recovered from it, and made herself a good life. Thanks to no one else, and surely not her parents.

"Why didn't you take me home to Dublin with you?" Timmie asked sadly.

"We couldn't afford to. Our parents didn't have the money for the tickets. We could only pay for two tickets home, and we couldn't have afforded to keep you here either. We didn't have children for ten years after we got home, and then we had two. Your father got TB then, and I worked as a charwoman for some fancy people. We've never had money, and I've always dreamed about you as our lucky little girl, living in fancy houses, with rich people, getting an education, and living like a swell." Her dream hadn't been far wrong, but thanks to no one but Timmie herself.

"I'm fine now," Timmie said sadly, brushing the tears off her cheeks. "I've been fine for a long time," she reassured her. "I've done well. But it wasn't easy back then." She had been miserable at St. Clare's, and for all of her childhood and youth.

"I'm sorry," her mother said, crying, and then softly, "Would you like to come round for tea, since you came all this way?" Mary wouldn't have chosen to see her, and wasn't sure she wanted to, in case Timmie was angry or hostile, but she sounded decent on the phone, so she decided to overcome her fears and meet her. She felt as though she at least owed her that.

"I'd like that very much." Timmie wrote down the address, and was there half an hour later. They lived in a dingy suburb of Dublin, in a battered-looking cottage that looked like it had been in disrepair for years, and had no hope of being salvaged anytime soon.

Timmie rang the doorbell. There was a long pause, and then a woman appeared. Timmie could see her through a window, and slowly she opened the door and stared at Timmie. She was as tall as her daughter and they had the same build, and similar features. She was wearing a housedress and slippers, and her hair was pulled back in a tight bun. She had defeated eyes, and hands crippled by arthritis. Her face was lined, and she looked like she'd had a hard life. She looked about eighty years old, not the sixty-five she was.

"Hello," Timmie said softly, "I'm Timmie." And then she gently took the woman in her arms and held her, comforting her for all she'd done and hadn't and should have, for the foolish cowardly lost girl she'd been at twenty-two, when she'd abandoned her five-year-old daughter. Timmie had vague memories of her, but like old photographs, most of them were faded. Mary O'Neill just stood there as her daughter held her, and then led her into the kitchen with an arm around her shoulders. Mary smiled at her with pleasure and said she had her father's red hair and her grandmother's good looks. It was hard to believe the two women were related, and in all the ways that mattered, they weren't. Destiny had taken them different ways. They were different people, and Mary would never have had the courage to face the things that Timmie had gone through. She knew it as she looked at her.

"You're beautiful," she said, and then laughed through her tears. "You look like a rich girl to me." She had noticed the diamond bracelet, the gold hoop earrings, and the expensive handbag, although Timmie was wearing a T-shirt and jeans. And then she noticed her protruding stomach. Timmie had worn a loose jacket on the plane, but in the heat in Dublin she had taken it off. She didn't care who saw her belly here. "Are you pregnant?" Her mother looked surprised as Timmie nodded. "Are you? Are you married? Have you other children?" There was a lot to catch up on, as they sat down to two mugs of strong tea.

"I was married. I've been divorced for eleven years. And I had a little boy who died twelve years ago of a brain tumor. I'm in love with a man in Paris, and this is his baby. I don't know if we'll get married. But I'm happy to have the baby. I don't have any other children, and I've been very sad since my son died." It was all she needed to know, and her mother nodded as she sipped her tea.

"I hope you have a healthy baby this time. My grandson died of leukemia a few years ago. These things happen. My daughter was very sad too." It was so strange to hear her talk about her daughter, and speak to Timmie as a stranger, which in fact she was. "You must have a good job." Even she could see that however casual, Timmie's jewelry and accessories were expensive.

"I do," Timmie said simply.

"I'm glad for you. Where do you live?"

"In Los Angeles." Her mother nodded. It was a lot of information to take in at once.

They steered clear of discussing Timmie's childhood, and she correctly sensed her mother didn't want to hear about it or know. Timmie was willing to accept that, it made no difference. She didn't need to beat her to death with it, she was just glad to be there, and see her. It filled in an empty place for her somehow. And halfway through their tea, a young woman came in with two children in tow. She looked as though she was in her late thirties, and she had the same red hair as Timmie, but they looked nothing alike otherwise. She was wearing jeans and flip-flops, and the children were very cute. The woman looked at Timmie with a broad smile, with no flash of recognition. Why would she? Timmie asked herself. She didn't exist as far as these people were concerned, and never had. She had been all but forgotten years ago, a dark secret they intended to take to their grave with them. Her mother looked at her with worried eyes, and Timmie nodded. She understood. She was not going to tell her sister who she was. She didn't need to know.

"I didn't know you had a visitor, Mum," the young woman said, and introduced herself to Timmie as Bridget. She helped herself to a cup of tea and sat down with them, while the children went outside and ran around in the untidy garden.

"She's the daughter of a friend in America, when your dad and I were there years ago. She looked me up when she got to Dublin. I hadn't heard from her mum in years. She died a long time ago," she added, as Timmie watched her face and realized it was true. The mother who had left her at the orphanage had disappeared forever, and might as well have been dead. And the child she had been to them was too. They had buried her when they left her at St. Clare's.

"Nice of you to look my mum up," Bridget said, smiling. "Having a holiday in Ireland, are you? You should spend some time on the Coast. It's lovely country," she said pleasantly, and then went outside to check on her kids, as Timmie stood up.

There was no point staying anymore. She had finished what she came to do. She had seen her mother, met her sister. She didn't know all the reasons why they had done what they did. But she knew enough. They had been young, ignorant, frightened kids who had a child, and ran off in the night, too afraid to do what they should. And in seeing her mother, Timmie had done what she needed to do for herself. Maybe in the end they had given her a gift, without ever meaning to. They had given her herself, and a strength she might never have had otherwise, to survive Mark's death, Derek's leaving, everything it took to build Timmie O, and now to stand beside Jean-Charles through all his problems and wait for him, and to love their child and be there for it forever. Without ever intending to, her parents had given her the strength they never had, and still didn't now.

Her mother didn't have the courage to tell her sister who she was, or why she was there. Timmie was passing through their lives, only for minutes, like a breath of air from a long-forgotten time that Mary O'Neill didn't have the strength to address or remember, and never had. Instead of anger or regret, Timmie only felt sorry for her. She stooped to kiss her cheek, and touch her shoulders as Bridget came back in with her boys.

"Goodbye," Timmie whispered softly, and gently touched her mother's hair, wondering if she had done that as a child, as Mary looked up at her with grateful eyes.

"God bless you," Mary said softly, as Timmie walked out of the kitchen, through the house, and out the front door to the cab still waiting for her outside. She got back in the taxi, and waved at Bridget as it pulled away and drove off, back toward the airport. She could still hear the sound of her mother's blessing, and realized that whatever had happened to her along the way, He already had. God had blessed her in so many ways, over the years, and was doing so again now. She knew she could better live with the present, and face the future, now that she had faced the ghosts of the past.

"Nice woman," Bridget commented before she left her mother. "Looks like a rich one. You must have known some fancy people when you were in the States, eh, Mum?" Her father had told a lot of tales over the years to impress his children. Mary had never said much. And she only nodded now, and looked away with tears in her eyes.

Chapter 21

Timmie called Jean-Charles from the airport, during her lay-over in London on the way back. He was in his office and sounded busy, and had no idea where she was. For a moment, she was tempted to tell him, and fly over to Paris to see him. It was only two weeks until their promised meeting, and she was aching to see him now.

"What are you doing?" she asked, sounding more relaxed than she had in a while. She felt freer, and suddenly lucky, and as though everything was going to turn out fine for them as well. Maybe Sister Anne's prayers had worked. And the baby felt like it was growing bigger and stronger by the hour. She had her loose easy jacket back on for the trip, so nothing showed.

"I'm just about to take my wife for her last treatment," he said, sounding frantic. He had a lot to do in the next two weeks, and his children to tell the following week. He was meeting them in Portofino for a little trip. Just he and his girls, and Xavier had promised to join them. He wanted some time alone with them, to share his plans with them, and then he would tell his wife that he was leaving for good. He would be around to help her through her illness, if she wanted him to do that. But if not, he knew she could handle the radiation on her own, and the girls would be there for her. He had stood by for the worst. "Why? Are you all right?" He sounded worried about Timmie. She sounded as though she had something on her mind. He was always so afraid that she would just throw in the towel and give up on him. He was so grateful she hadn't yet, and he was deeply appreciative of that, as he told her every chance he got. He thought she sounded happy on the phone.

"I don't know. I was just having a crazy moment, and wondering if you want to advance our date at the Eiffel Tower by a couple of weeks." If so, she would have flown to Paris then and there, and met him anywhere he wanted. She felt suddenly lighter than she had in years, and free. A huge burden had slipped from her shoulders in Dublin, and she wanted to share it with him.

"Timmie, I can't." He sounded anxious. "You know I need the next weeks with my kids. I really owe it to them." She tried not to feel as disappointed as she was. They only had a few more weeks to wait, and she could get through it, if he insisted on holding to their date on September 1. And as she listened to him, they called her plane.

"Gotta go," she said without comment on what he'd said. She wasn't going to argue with him. They had a date on September 1.

"Where are you?" he asked, sounding puzzled.

"Nowhere. I'm on my way home. I just thought I'd call." She didn't say from where, and when he called her back an hour later, her cell phone had been turned off. He wondered where she had been when she called, and he couldn't reach her again for nearly twenty-four hours. By then he was seriously worried about her, and afraid she was angry at him, but she had sounded fine.

She was getting more and more excited about their date at the Eiffel Tower. It had been four months since they'd seen each other, an eternity to both of them. They'd been to hell and back, with assorted detours in between. But they were still on track, steady on course, and very much in love. She felt blessed, and less scared these days, particularly after seeing her mother. The visit had lifted some sort of curse on her she'd always feared, that she was doomed to be abandoned. She didn't feel that anymore, and hadn't since her day in Dublin. They had abandoned her, but her mother had seemed so weak and defeated, Timmie wondered if they would have been capable of doing anything else.

She was in high spirits for the next two weeks. She had her plane reservation for Paris, and a room reserved at the Plaza Athénée. She was flying on August 31, so she'd be fresh when she saw him on September 1. She had even bought something to wear, which would conceal her stomach for the first few minutes. After that, it would be hard to hide from him, especially if they went to the hotel to make up for lost time. She was amazed that she had been able to conceal it so far from David and Jade. She wore a lot of long jackets and loose tops these days. She only wore clothes that revealed her stomach when she was alone at home.

Jade commented on her good mood to David two days before Timmie was scheduled to leave. He had been teasing her that she was going to owe him a thousand dollars very shortly on their bet on Jean-Charles showing up on September 1. There had been no message to the contrary so far, and he was calling her a lot.

"I told you he would come through," David said victoriously, as Jade raised an eyebrow and refused to concede. It was August 29.

"Don't be so sure. He hasn't shown up yet. If he's anything like Stanley, he'll call her to cancel the night before. It's more fun that way."

"Don't be such a cynic, for chrissake," David scolded her.

"We'll see. I hope I'm wrong. For her sake. I think if he was going to get out of that marriage, he would have done it months ago. The ones who wait never do. He's still taking care of his wife, not her."

"She had breast cancer, for Heaven's sake. He would have been a shit to leave." She nodded and went back to her desk. And Timmie left the office early the next day, to get her hair trimmed and her legs waxed before the trip. She waved happily at them both as she left. She was taking a week off to be with him, which was what they'd agreed on. She might even go to the South of France with him. She wasn't sure. Jade had reserved her usual suite at the Plaza Athénée for her for a week.

Timmie was packing last-minute things that night, when Jean-Charles called. She had everything organized, and had even bought several new outfits for the trip, from a maternity shop on Rodeo Drive, claiming they were for her niece, since she was well known. She was planning to come out of the closet about the baby as soon as Jean-Charles was back. And she was smiling happily when she picked up the phone. It had been the longest, hardest four months of her life, except for those after Mark had died. Those had been worse, but these were tough.

"Hi," she said, sounding elated, when she heard his voice. She was almost giddy thinking about their meeting at the Eiffel Tower. It was silly, but one of the most romantic things she'd ever done. He could just as easily have come to the hotel. "I'm just getting ready to close my bags." She was taking a noon flight the next day.

There was a strange silence at his end, and then she heard his choked voice. "Timmie, I can't come. The girls were staying with friends of their mother's in Sardinia. They went there after I left them in Portofino. Julianne just had a car accident. She's in the hospital with a broken pelvis and two broken legs, and a head injury of some kind. I'm flying there tonight." For a moment, she was too stunned to speak.

"Will she be all right?"

"I don't know. Her legs are very badly broken, but it sounds like she'll be fine eventually. She's going to be flat on her back for a long time. I'm taking a neurologist with me to Sardinia. I want to be sure her head is all right. But there's no way I'll be back day after tomorrow." He sounded as devastated as she felt.

"Boy, you guys don't play for small stakes, do you?" she said, letting her own terrors slip out.

"What do you mean?"

"Car accidents. Cancer. It's hard to compete with that." Although their baby might have, if he'd known. She was almost sorry she hadn't told him yet. She was getting tired of standing in line, behind other people's crises, and being the last priority on his list. It was wearing thin. And she was so disappointed about September 1, she felt like a child who had just been told Christmas had been canceled.

"This isn't a competition. And hopefully I'll be back in a week. At most two. I don't want to leave her there alone, and her mother is in no condition to go to her. She starts radiation next week anyway." All of a sudden it felt like too much to her. She felt overwhelmed. It was turning into more of a soap opera than a love affair, with him playing rescuing hero to everyone but her, while she stood by and waited for him, and tried to be understanding every time. It was getting old. She had waited a long time. "I'll call you as soon as I see what condition she's in." He sounded terse. Timmie hadn't been as sympathetic as he had hoped. In fact, almost not at all, which was unlike her. She felt stretched to her limits now. Maybe beyond them. She wasn't sure. It depended on what he did now, and how long he expected her to wait again. Or if he'd come up with another dramatic excuse. At least his excuses were good, if that's what they were. She didn't know what to believe anymore, except that she was sure it was all true. Just hard to live with it again. She had been counting the minutes for days, and she was so in love with him. "I'll call you from there," he said, and started to hang up, when she stopped him.

"Should I just fly to Paris, and wait at the hotel?" It might make more sense, rather than waiting for him in L.A. He hesitated at her question for what seemed like too long.

"No. Why waste your time here? Stay there, at least you can work. I'll let you know as soon as I'm coming back, and you can fly in then." His answer made her suspicious again. Why did he want her to wait in L.A.? What was going to be the next excuse or delay? Maybe he was planning one. All she could hear in her head now was Jade, with her constant predictions of doom. Maybe she was right. Maybe this was just a very bad joke he was playing on her.

Timmie took her suitcase off the bed and lay down. She stared at the ceiling, thinking of him, wondering if he was for real. Maybe Jade was right. Maybe he wasn't. Maybe he was just stringing this out, or couldn't bring himself to leave his family and didn't want to tell her. She didn't know what to think anymore. She didn't sleep all night. She just wandered around her house, looking dazed, waiting to hear from him. He called her twelve hours after the last call. Julianne's head was going to be okay. Her legs were not. Or not for a while. She had to stay in the hospital in Italy in traction for four weeks. He couldn't move her until then, and he couldn't leave her alone in a hospital there. She was totally panicked. And so was Timmie as she listened. She tried to be sympathetic, but knew she wasn't. She didn't have it in her anymore. She just told him to do what he had to do and call her when he was free. It was the best she could do.

She strode into her office the next day without a word. It was

September 1. David stared at Jade, who looked smug, and told him he'd better start writing her a thousand-dollar check. But beyond the bet, they were both upset for Timmie, who closed her office door and shut them out. She worked quietly on designs all morning and then explained that Jean-Charles's daughter had had an accident and was in a hospital in Italy for a month, with him stuck there with her. This time Jade said not a word. She was sorry for Timmie, and so was David. Timmie looked so upset that neither of them dared talk to her all day, and she left the office for the weekend without saying good-bye to them.

She went straight to Malibu, and Jean-Charles called her there several times over the weekend. She tried to be understanding to him, and sympathetic with Julianne's woes, but it was hard not telling him how upset she was, how disappointed and discouraged. She couldn't help wondering how many times this would happen, and if she'd ever see him again. She wanted to call Sister Anne and ask her to pray harder. Or maybe this was the answer to her prayers. Maybe Jean-Charles wasn't the man for her, and her prayers were exposing that. It was hard to know, and as she listened to him every day, she began to trust him less and less. How much longer would this go on? He swore to her no longer than a month, and she dragged through all of September believing him. She was still hiding their baby. She still hadn't told him. And her nerves were raw. Her temper was short. Her terrors were rampant and in full control. And there was nothing she could do but wait. Or give up, and she wasn't ready to do that yet. She wanted to believe in him, and she was hanging by a thread.

He got back to Paris with Julianne on the twenty-fifth of September, and Timmie made another reservation. She didn't care about the Eiffel Tower anymore. He could meet her at the Plaza Athénée, or anywhere he wanted. She just wanted to see him, and she told him so. And then he called the night he got back to tell her that Sophie said she would never see or speak to him again if he left the house for good and moved out, and his wife was having an adverse reaction to radiation. He sounded near tears when he called her, and Timmie sat staring into space, holding the phone, with a blank expression. She had heard it all by now, teenage tantrums, cancer, chemo, radiation, broken legs, car accidents, head injuries, what was left? A sick dog maybe, or the maid quitting, or their house burning to the ground and he had to stick around to rebuild it with his bare hands. How much longer did he expect her to wait for him, while he went nowhere? He obviously needed more to get out of his house and marriage than a woman who loved him. She was glad she hadn't told him about the baby, and it probably wouldn't have made any difference to him anyway. He was trapped there forever. She could see that now. All that remained was for her to have the guts to get up and leave him. And there was nothing to leave anyway. She hadn't seen him in over five months, and probably never would again. It was up to her now to do what he apparently couldn't, end it. He was giving her no other choice. She couldn't sit there like a fool forever, with his baby in her belly, believing he was coming back to her. Clearly, he wasn't. She wanted to believe him, but couldn't anymore. There were a thousand excuses, a million excellent reasons for him to stay right where he was forever. He was nothing more than an illusion, and a voice on her cell phone. He was a promise that was never going to happen, and she knew it now. Jade had been right all along, and had told her, warned her. She didn't want to listen, but it was all too clear to her now. She listened to what he was saying, with tears rolling down her face. They were tears of both sadness and anger, and as he pleaded with her to be reasonable, she snapped at him.

"What do you want from me? What am I supposed to do? I've been waiting for you for almost six months. I haven't seen you. I waited through your wife's cancer, and Julianne's accident. Now Sophie's threatening you, and your wife is having a reaction to radiation. You haven't moved out yet. We started in February. You asked me to wait till June. I did. Then September. Now it's almost October. And you need more time. If you wanted to get out, you would. You could be dealing with all of this from an apartment. You don't have to be living with them to be playing Red Cross to them night and day. You haven't even seen me since April, Jean-Charles." She almost slipped and mentioned their baby, and then caught herself in time. "I feel like a fool. I'm not even your mistress. I'm just someone you call, while you go on living with your family. Maybe you're embarrassed to tell me it's over. I guess it's been over for months anyway. You didn't have the balls to say it, and I didn't have the balls to hear it. It doesn't matter. I love you. I've never loved anyone as I do you. But I'm not going to play this game anymore. You don't need to come up with any more excuses. They can stop having accidents, and catching diseases. Sophie doesn't need to threaten to throw herself off the roof. I'm done." She was sobbing by then, and so hysterical she could hardly speak, and at his end, he was utterly stunned. He had always been afraid of losing her, but now he was shocked that she was telling him it was over. He just wanted a little more time, to solve a few more of their problems, and leave them in good shape when he finally left. Why couldn't she understand that? Unless she didn't love him. He was as upset as she was, and then she delivered the lethal blow. She wanted to be sure that if he heard about her baby, he wouldn't think it was his. It was over for her. She was never going to tell him the baby was his. And the only way to do that was to tell him it was someone else's, so she did, in so many words. "It doesn't matter, Jean-Charles," she said coldly. She forced herself to say the words, burning her last bridge behind her, so she couldn't go back to him. She wanted no more hope or promises from him. She knew now there were none. She didn't even know if he really loved her, and clearly not enough to leave his marriage for her anyway, a marriage he had claimed had been dead for years before she came along. Apparently, not as dead as he said, since he was still in it, and she was alone, carrying their baby. She was ending it with him now forever. She knew he'd never leave his home. He would have dragged it out forever. It was over. She knew it. And this time, she wasn't going to be abandoned again. She was walking out first. Head held high, no matter how heartbroken she was. "I've been seeing someone else anyway," she added, like a final lethal bomb she threw at him and everything they'd built for eight months. "Actually, I've been seeing him since April," she said, and winced as she heard a gasp at the other end of the phone. Her bomb had hit its mark, but it had to be. If there was someone else, and had been for that long, he'd know the baby wasn't his, if he ever heard about it, and he would. She'd be all over the papers and magazines when she had it. Timmie O having a baby as a single mom would be big news. So she was protecting herself from him now. She had to do it, no matter how much it hurt both of them, and it did.

"I see. I had no idea," he said with a shaking voice. "I know you don't believe me, but I have actually been trying to get out of this mess to be with you. I had no idea my wife would get cancer, or my daughter would be stupid enough to ride in a car in Italy with her boyfriend who was drunk, or even that my wife would have a reaction to radiation. And Sophie would have gotten over being angry with me, given a little time. You should have been honest with me that you were seeing someone, Timmie. It would have been nice. I guess Hollywood morals are different than mine. I would have had the decency to tell you if I had done something like that. I've been in love with you all this time, and the only reason I agreed not to see you this summer was so that I didn't drag you through this mess and drive you insane, while I tried to leave honestly and gracefully, and I'm very sorry I took longer to do it than I said I would. Sometimes things just take more time. I was doing my best," he said, as tears rolled down his cheeks too. "And I love you. Honestly. I had no idea that if I didn't move fast enough, you'd be sleeping with someone else. How long did you wait? A week? Two? I saw you in April, you must have started with this other person immediately. Not very nice of you," he said sadly. He sounded as though she had run a knife through his heart, and she had. But his constant excuses had done the same to her. It had become an imaginary romance with an invisible person, and she could only hold on for so long. Even if well meaning, he hadn't been fair to her. And now she had been intentionally cruel to him. There was fault on both sides, and immeasurable pain. Now there would also be a baby that he knew nothing about, with no father. Three people had gotten injured in this game.

"You never moved out when you said you would," she said hoarsely.

"I didn't have time to. I was planning to see three apartments next week, with you. Or whenever we got together," he said miserably.

"It would never have happened," she said. "You think it would. Maybe you believed it. But you would have come up with another thousand excuses to stay."

"Maybe you're right. Maybe I would have. I don't know anymore, Timmie. I'm sorry . . . good luck. I hope your other person brings you happiness. I want you to know that I loved you with my whole heart. I've never loved anyone as I did you, while you were playing around with someone else." He sounded devastated more than bitter, and she had said what she did to protect herself and her baby, even if it hurt him. He had no right now to know the baby was his after he never saw her again, and perhaps never would have. The baby was no longer his or theirs, it was hers. She wanted no pity from him. She would take care of it by herself. And if the child wanted to know who its father was one day, she would tell it, and he could decide what to do then. She was going to tell their child that its father had been a wonderful, honest, decent, loving man, whom she had loved more than life itself. And whom she had fallen in love with at first sight one day in Paris. It was the best she could do now. There was nothing else left to say.

"Take care. I love you," she said softly, and then hung up, feeling guilty for having hurt him and lied to him about the baby. But she felt she had no other choice. She would have waited for him forever and never seen him again. And one day he would have told her it was over, and he couldn't leave his wife or children. The handwriting was on the wall, and she had finally had the guts to read what it said and walk away.

She thought it would kill her losing him. She went to bed and cried for four days. She didn't go to her office or take calls from them. She didn't answer her cell phone when Jean-Charles called, which she saw he did three times. She looked like death when she finally went back to work. She said absolutely nothing to David or Jade. They were all leaving for New York, Milan, and Paris in two weeks, and she had a mountain of work to catch up on, after being at home for nearly a week.

There was a heat wave in Los Angeles that week, and their air conditioning broke. The office was stifling, in spite of the few windows they could open. And Timmie couldn't stand it anymore. She finally took off her big loose French smock that had become a uniform for her, almost like a burka, and she walked around her office in a T-shirt and jeans, with her belly sticking out. She was six months pregnant, and Jade stopped dead in her tracks and pointed when she saw her. Timmie would have laughed at her expression if she weren't still so devastated over Jean-Charles and the end of their relationship. In fact, it had ended in April when she conceived their baby, which was the last time she saw him. The rest had been just a string of excuses, lost hopes, broken dreams, and maybe even lies. She no longer knew, but she still cared, very much.

"What's *that*?" Jade asked, as she stared at her in disbelief.

"What's your best guess?" Timmie asked her with a sad smile, as David walked in and stared at her too. Her stomach looked enormous, and there was no hiding it now. Nor did she want to. It was time to come out of the closet, at least with them, if not the world. Yet. Eventually she'd have no choice, and couldn't hide it anymore. She was still hoping to keep it a secret through the ready to wear shows, to avoid gossip in the press.

"Oh my God!" David said, looking shocked. "Does he know?" There was no question whose it was, for any of them, and of course they were right. Timmie shook her head.

"No, he doesn't. And I don't want him to. I'm not going to be some pathetic woman he doesn't want, who had his baby. I deserve better than that. I was going to tell him when I saw him, but I never did. The last time he called with the new list of excuses as to why he couldn't see me, I told him I've been seeing someone else since April. If he reads about it, I don't want him to know that it's his."

"Why did you do this?" Jade asked her, looking horrified. She wasn't sure she wanted children, and surely not at Timmie's age, with a married man she was never going to see again. Jade couldn't think of anything worse.

"I'm having it because I love him," she said simply, "even if I never see him again, and he doesn't know. I loved him enough to want his baby. That doesn't change, just because he doesn't have the balls to leave his wife. And I did it because of Mark. I buried one child. I couldn't give up another one. This one is a gift. I'm keeping the gift, even if Jean-Charles is gone for good," she said as she wiped her eyes, and David gave her a hug.

"You have a lot of guts, Timmie," he said gently. He had always known that about her, and he was touched. "I think he should know. It's his kid too. I honestly think he loves you. It just took him longer to get out than it should have." He was willing to concede that, but not much more.

"Bullshit," Jade snapped. "He was never going to leave his wife. They never do."

"Some do," David said staunchly. But he had written her the check on their bet anyway. And she had bought the Chanel bag she wanted. She was wearing it every day. David was sorrier than ever that she had won. For Timmie's sake, not his own.

He gave her another hug, and they went back to their offices. Timmie went back to work at her desk. She had three more months till the baby was born. And an entire life to live without Jean-Charles. She couldn't imagine it. She knew she would never love anyone again as she had him, nor wanted to. He truly had been the love of her life. And now he was gone for good. It was her worst nightmare come true.

Chapter 22

For the two weeks before they left for Paris for the ready to wear shows, their offices were painfully quiet. Timmie rarely spoke, and they tiptoed around her. She worked late, kept her office door closed, and her houses felt like tombs. She went to Malibu once and couldn't stand it. She went to St. Cecilia's and told Sister Anne what had happened, and she told Timmie she would continue to pray for a happy resolution, and reminded her she had the baby to look forward to, which was beginning to seriously show. The nuns were excited for her, and the children patted her belly. They asked if the baby had a daddy, and she said it didn't, just like many of them, and they thought that was okay. Sister Anne hugged her when she left and said she'd be praying for her.

Timmie looked at her sadly and said it was too late for that, for Jean-Charles anyway.

"It's never too late for prayer," Sister Anne said cheerfully. Timmie just shook her head as she left.

She had Jade get a bunch of loose smocks for her, some big floppy unstructured jackets, and she designed a few herself, cleverly draped, so she could at least get through the shows without having news of her pregnancy hit the press. But she knew she wouldn't be able to hide it after that. It was hard enough now. She just had to hold out for a few more weeks, and then she could relax, and go into hiding in L.A. She was trying to keep this as quiet as she could. It wasn't going to help to have every fashion journalist on the planet trying to guess who the father was. She was grateful that no one knew about Jean-Charles. It turned out to be a blessing in the end. She was also nervous about running into him while they were in Paris, but there was no reason why she would. She'd be busy with her show, and would have no free time to go out, roaming around the city she had always loved.

David was still adamant that Timmie should call him herself and tell him about the baby. But she stonewalled him whenever he said it. He almost wished he had the guts to call him himself, but he had to respect the wishes of his employer, even if he thought she was wrong.

"The baby has a right to a father," he told her once, and she shook her head.

"I didn't. And I turned out okay."

"That's different. You had no choice."

"I don't want him in my life or the baby's because he feels sorry for us, or considers us a duty. If he'd gotten out of his marriage, that would be different. He didn't. So we're on our own. I'm not going to be some guy's cast-off mistress with an illegitimate kid. I have more pride than that." She bridled at the thought, and looked as miserable and bereft as she felt.

"May I remind you, he didn't cast you off? You cast him off. You even lied to him and told him there was someone else. You ended it. He didn't. And you packed a hell of a punch on the way out."

"He would have ended it eventually. He didn't want to see me. It was only a matter of time before he told me he wasn't getting out of his marriage." She was sure of that now, without a doubt. Jade had been right.

"You'll never know that now, will you?" David said harshly. But he got nowhere with Timmie, or even Jade, who insisted Timmie was doing the right thing, although she and her architect had just gotten engaged. She was all in favor of love, but not with married men. She said, and believed to her core, that they were all a dead end.

Their show went well in New York, and they went to Milan and London after that, as always. And when they got to Paris, David could see easily that Timmie was not only exhausted but depressed. Her usual excitement over being in Paris was nonexistent. She did what she had to do, to set up the show, was relentless about the fittings with the models, as always, but never left the hotel, and ate dinner in her room every night. She went nowhere, and was anxious not to be seen. She was still covering her secret with her smocks and draped tops, but it was getting harder and harder to conceal what was under them. The baby had grown visibly on the trip, and her belly looked huge to them whenever she was in her room in her jeans and took off the cleverly draped tops she had made, which still hid everything, though barely.

David had a feeling that she was afraid to run into Jean-Charles anywhere in Paris. And whenever she finished working, she scurried back to her room like a mouse. They suggested going out to dinner to her several times, and she always declined and told them to go out without her. She was tired anyway.

For some reason, the Paris show was more difficult than it usually was. Everything had gone smoothly before, but this time in Paris the moon was in feces, as Timmie put it. Everything that could go wrong did. Two models got sick, a third went to jail for getting caught selling cocaine at a party. Their florist in Paris screwed up and got their order wrong, and then couldn't produce what they needed. The runway had what looked like three speed bumps in it, and if they left it that way, the models would be breaking their necks in towering high heels on a slippery surface with bumps. Timmie said she didn't care what it took, or how much, they had to fix it by Tuesday. And last but not least, the lighting kept failing and blowing out everything in the room. While they were trying to fix it, a light bar fell, hit a technician, and broke his shoulder. It felt as though they were cursed.

"Shit," Timmie said with an exasperated look, as they waited for the models to show up for rehearsal. Five were late so far, and one had arrived drunk. And the seamstresses weren't through making the adjustments from the fittings. "Can anything else go wrong here? I'm expecting a herd of elephants to run through the room any minute."

"Some shows are like that," David said soothingly, but this one had been tough.

"Not in Paris, for chrissake. Oklahoma maybe. We can't look like fools in Paris. The press will kill us," Timmie said unhappily. She had looked miserable since they arrived. It was agony being in the same city with Jean-Charles and not seeing him. It ate at her night and day.

Their run-through the day before had looked like the Marx Brothers, and Timmie had insisted on a final rehearsal, even though the lighting wasn't right, and the speed bumps weren't out of the runway yet. They had managed to get rid of one, but there were two more to deal with. "What were those guys thinking when they built it? They must have been smoking crack," Timmie said, looking aggravated. She had been on everyone's back for days, and she could hardly wait for the show to be over. She wanted to go home and put her feet up. She hated being in Paris now. All she could think of was Jean-Charles, and when she walked into the living room of her suite where she had fallen in love with him eight months before, it made her cry. But she said nothing to the others. She didn't have to. They could see it. All she wanted was to get the show behind her and go home the minute it was over.

They were ready for the final rehearsal at four o'clock. The lighting was almost right, but not quite. Close enough to proceed, Timmie decided. All the models had turned up, and the clothes were finally ready. She hadn't eaten all day, and had been going through lollipops by the case, to keep going. And then one of the light bars went out again, and she climbed up on the runway herself to take a better look at it from below.

"Watch out it doesn't hit you," David said, only half-joking, as it literally began to fall from the ceiling, and Timmie took a step backward to avoid it. She managed to duck, but at the same time she fell backward over one of the remaining speed bumps on the runway, and fell flat on her back on the floor as everyone gasped and then rushed to her. Only David and Jade knew she was pregnant, but she had taken a hell of a fall, enough to frighten everyone around her. He wasn't sure if she'd hit her head, but she looked dazed and gray when he got to her.

David knelt down next to her and looked into her eyes. She was lying flat on her back and hadn't moved yet. She was winded. "Hey . . . are you okay? . . . Talk to me . . ." She looked up at him and seemed a little out of it for a minute as everyone stared at her and David left her with Jade.

"No doctor," she whispered to her assistant. "Don't let them call a doctor." Jade nodded, but she had a feeling she knew what David was going to do, and she couldn't leave Timmie to stop him. Timmie looked frighteningly pale, and when she tried to sit up, she was dizzy and let out a shout of pain when she tried to stand up. Her ankle was swelling to the size of a balloon as she grimaced and leaned against Jade. "I think I twisted it," she said, and collapsed into a chair, while one of the light techs went to get her some ice, and an assistant manager showed up to check on her. Someone had called him, and he offered to call the hotel doctor. Timmie emphatically declined. She insisted she was fine, but didn't look it.

"Maybe you broke it," David said, looking worried, when he returned. He didn't dare ask her about the baby, and he had seen her rub her stomach. "I think you should go to the hospital," he said, as Jade ran to tell the models there had been a delay and they would start the rehearsal in a few minutes. The assistant manager went to report to the general manager then. He knew just how important Timmie was and it was obvious that she was hurt.

"I'm fine," Timmie said, and tried to stand up again. "Let's get started," she said, looking like the ghost of Christmas past.

"You're crazy," David said, as she struggled to organize the rehearsal, looking like she might faint. Twenty minutes later, Timmie turned and much to her horror, she saw Jean-Charles standing a few feet away, observing her. Her worst nightmare had just happened. He was there. She had no idea who had called him, but someone had. She looked at David, and he turned away to say something to Jade, and avoided Timmie's gaze. Jean-Charles didn't look happy either. As soon as she saw him, Timmie looked panicked. And for a minute she looked as though she really might faint. Jean-Charles made her sit down and put her head between her legs, and when she sat up again, she looked at him with a tortured expression.

"I don't need a doctor," she said firmly, "but thank you for coming. I'm fine. Just a little winded." He had already looked down and seen the ankle. And was taking her pulse while he listened.

"It looks broken," he said, and then bent to look at the ankle, while Timmie looked frantically at David. But he would not help her escape him. This was fate doing its job, in his opinion. With a little help from him. "You need to go to the hospital," Jean-Charles said quietly. This was the first time they had seen each other since April, and it was visibly painful for both of them.

"I don't need a hospital. We're about to start rehearsal."

"I think we've had this argument before." Jean-Charles looked as miserable as she did, when David interrupted.

"I'll deal with the rehearsal. It's just a run-through, for chrissake. You get that ankle looked at." He helped Jean-Charles get her to her feet before she could object, and she pulled her draped top around her and fluffed it. She looked chic but deathly pale, and she couldn't take a single step on the ankle. They produced a wheelchair from somewhere while she argued with both of them to no avail. And the manager looked relieved to see a doctor on the scene.

"I'll drive you if you like," Jean-Charles said drily. He had been at his office when David called him and he had come immediately.

"I can take a cab," she said, avoiding looking at him. Her heart was pounding just knowing he was there. She didn't want to see him, or be in a car with him. She didn't want to be anywhere near him. Just feeling his presence made her heart ache. She knew she would be in love with him until the day she died. She didn't want to see him again. She had already resigned herself to losing him. That had been hard enough. Seeing him was worse. She would have been angry at David for calling him if she weren't in so much pain. David's guilt for making the call was all over his face. But he knew he had done the right thing. Someone had to step in, for both their sakes and the baby's. So he had.

"You shouldn't be alone," Jean-Charles said practically. "I don't mind. I have to see a patient at the hospital anyway." She said nothing, and one of the light techs rolled her through the lobby and out the front door as Jean-Charles followed.

The doorman brought his car around, and Jean-Charles helped her get in. She was obviously in a lot of pain and nearly cried while he did it. She was trying to be brave.

"Sorry," he apologized, and they said nothing to each other on the drive to the hospital in Neuilly. It brought back old memories for her, as she avoided looking at him and stared out the window. The ankle was killing her, but she said nothing. And she was relieved to feel the baby kick her. At least it was still alive. And then finally Jean-Charles said something to her. "I know this is awkward for both of us. I'm sorry you got hurt." He looked as handsome as ever, and she tried valiantly not to notice. She just wanted the ride to end.

"I told them not to call a doctor," she said firmly.

"You would," he smiled, "even with an ankle like that." He was happy to see her again, although he knew it was painful for them both. "I think you broke it. What happened?"

"I fell backward off the stage onto my ass, while trying to avoid being hit on the head by a light bar. It's been a bad day." And worse now, after seeing him.

"Occupational hazards," he said as they drove through Paris. He thought her face looked fuller, and it suited her. In spite of the accident, she looked very pretty. "You're in a dangerous business," he said to distract her, and she didn't comment. And at last, they got to the American Hospital in Neuilly. He had someone come out with a wheelchair for her, and then took her to X-ray himself. "I called an orthopedic surgeon before I came to the hotel, just in case. He's on call, and he'll come down to see you after they take the X-rays." She remembered perfectly how he had held her hand in surgery a year before. And if things had been different, she would have asked him to do it again, or he would have offered. As things were, he didn't. And she didn't want him to stay.

The X-ray technician wheeled her inside, where the radiologist on duty was waiting. She turned back to look at Jean-Charles, and saw that he was watching her. Their eyes met, and then Timmie looked away. His gaze had been agonizing on hers. It was hard to say which of them looked more wounded.

"I'll come back to check on you in a little while," he said, and she nodded. She knew there was no point telling him not to. He would anyway, whatever she said. Jean-Charles disappeared, and the radiologist asked her how it had happened. She told him, and then he wheeled her into the X-ray room, and put her on a table to take some pictures. She knew she had no choice but to tell him.

"I'm pregnant," she said softly, as though Jean-Charles were standing just outside the room, which she knew he wasn't. He had gone off to see his other patient. He could have taken her to the Pitié Salpetrière too, but he thought this would be gentler for her.

"You are?" The radiologist looked surprised by what she'd said, and she pulled back the draped jacket then and showed him. He was impressed. She had concealed it very efficiently, but he could see that she was at least six months pregnant, perhaps more.

"Please don't tell anyone," she said as she lay down. "It's a secret."

"Are you a movie star?" he asked, looking impressed, and she shook her head and smiled. He put a heavy lead blanket over her then to protect her. The ankle was excruciating, but he was nice. Jean-Charles had told him only that she was a good friend. The radiologist would have been stunned to know she was carrying Jean-Charles's baby. So would Jean-Charles.

The X-rays only took a few minutes, and then the orthopedist came to look at her. He checked the X-rays carefully. Jean-Charles was right. It was broken. He said she would need a hard cast, and by the time Jean-Charles came back an hour later, she was on crutches, with her ankle in a cast, and she was even paler than before. She was feeling sick but didn't want to admit it to him. He could see how shaky she was, and trying to hide it from him.

"You were right," she said politely. She could tell that he had lined up good people for her, and told them to take special care with her. They had all been exceptionally friendly, attentive, and efficient. She could sense his hand in the arrangements he'd made for her.

"I'll take you back to the hotel," he said, thanking both the orthopedist and the radiologist, whom she could tell he knew well from the way he talked to them and thanked them.

"You don't need to take me back," Timmie said, and then noticed she hadn't brought her bag with her. She had forgotten it at the rehearsal at the hotel. "Well, maybe you do." She looked embarrassed. "I don't have any money with me for a cab." The doorman would have paid the fare for her, but it seemed easier just going back to the Plaza Athénée now with him. She was feeling dizzy from the pain, and the shock of seeing him. "Do you mind?"

"Not at all," he said formally, glancing over at her. Something about her looked different, but he wasn't sure what. It wasn't her hair, maybe it was her face. It was not only fuller, it looked softer to him somehow. She didn't seem as sexy, but she was even more beautiful than he had remembered. He helped her gently into his car, and they drove off, toward the hotel.

"I'm sorry this happened to you, Timmie," he said on the way back. "It really is bad luck." He knew it must be hurting a lot, but she didn't complain. They had offered her pills for the pain, but she wouldn't take them because of the baby. She insisted she'd be fine, and put the bottle of pain medication in her pocket, without taking any. Jean-Charles thought she was foolish and very brave.

"It's all right." She shrugged. "It could have been worse." She could have hurt the baby, and was glad she hadn't. It had been kicking like crazy for the past half-hour, and she was relieved. All she wanted to do now was go to bed. Rehearsal would be over anyway. She hoped it had gone well, but really didn't care anymore. All she could think of was Jean-Charles, as he drove her back to the hotel. She thought she'd never see him again. And then he startled her, as he glanced over at her when they were stopped at a light. She was still looking very pale, and he didn't mention it to her, but he was worried about her.

"I'm sorry about everything that happened between us. You were very patient, and you were right. It was inhuman to ask you to go through all that with me. I'm sure you waited longer than most women would. I never expected all those things to come up."

"It's all right," she said softly. "It wasn't your fault. Shit happens, as they say." He smiled in answer. He still loved her, and knew he always would. She noticed that he wasn't wearing his wedding band, he saw her glance at his hand and met her eyes.

"It was time. I finally moved out last weekend. I wanted to do it before, but I just couldn't. I figured my kids will survive. My wife is doing better. I did my job. I had to get out." Timmie sat staring at him as he said it.

"You moved out?" He nodded. "How did they take it?" She was stunned.

"Everyone's angry right now. It turns out no one thanks you for what you did. They just remember what you didn't do. The children will be all right." He seemed very calm, and very quiet, and when he looked at her again, his eyes were sad. "I'm sorry I got so angry about your seeing someone else. It was a terrible blow. But you were right. Why would you wait around forever for me?" She felt like she had missed the train, and only by minutes. He had moved out. He had taken off his ring. He had finally moved on. She was having his baby.

And she had told him she was seeing someone else. "You look differ-ent," he said, to change the subject. She was staring at him, and had no idea what to say.

"I gained some weight," she said vaguely, as they drove through the Place de la Concorde. Her ankle was throbbing, and she was feeling sick.

"It suits you," he said, as they headed toward the hotel. "How long will you be in Paris?"

"I'm leaving day after tomorrow," she said, and then smiled, re-membering when he invited her for a drink in February. He had asked her the same question at her dinner party, and she had answered the same thing. And the next day, they had fallen madly in love. Love at first sight. "I think I've already seen this film," she said, suddenly laughing, as he turned to smile at her. He had been thinking the same thing. The words had echoed in his head as well.

"Maybe we should go to the Eiffel Tower," he said then, "and pre-tend it's the first of September . . . but then again, I suppose not. The new man in your life might not be too pleased." She sat staring out the window for a long minute and then turned to look at him. It was too late to play games with him. She never had until the end, and had regretted it ever since.

"There is no new man in my life, Jean-Charles. There never was. Only you." It had the ring of truth.

He looked puzzled. "Then why did you say it? Just to hurt me?" It wasn't like her to be cruel, but she had been in the end. Perhaps she thought he deserved it, but he didn't. He had been stupid, but never cruel with her.

"I had more complicated reasons. It's a little hard to explain. I wanted you to think I'd been unfaithful to you," she said with a sigh. She felt like a lunatic trying to explain it to him now.

"Why would you want me to think that you were unfaithful to

me?" he asked with a stupefied look as they stopped at a light. She was not making sense. They had loved each other, and been faithful to each other. Why try to turn it into something else in the end?

"Because if you weren't coming back to me, and staying with your wife, as I thought you were, I didn't want you to know that the baby was yours."

Jean-Charles stared at her in amazement. He looked shocked by what she had just said. "What baby?" He had no idea what she was talking about, and with a graceful hand she pulled back her jacket, and he saw what was there.

"Our baby," she said softly. "The one I didn't tell you about because I didn't want to put pressure on you. I only wanted you to come back if you loved me, not because you thought you had to come back, or felt sorry for me." As she said it, tears slid slowly down her cheeks.

"You're insane... oh my God... you've been pregnant for all this time and you never told me?... oh my God... Timmie..." He reached out his hand, touched her belly, and felt their baby kick, as he began to cry too. "How could you do something so crazy as not tell... I love you... I wouldn't have felt sorry for you... what a brave, crazy girl you are," he said, as he took her in his arms and held her, and then he kissed her, as horns blared, drivers screamed, and traffic eddied around them. He looked down at her with more love than she'd ever dreamed. "I love you. How pregnant are you?"

"Six and a half months."

"I can't believe you kept it from me," he said in disbelief as he moved forward in the traffic again, much to everyone's relief.

"I was going to, and then your wife got cancer right after I found out. It didn't seem right for me to pull on you too. And then I was going to tell you in September, at the Eiffel Tower... but you canceled and got stuck in Italy for a month with Julianne... and then..."

"Timmie, please . . . I'm sorry . . . I had no idea . . . I wanted to do the right thing, and the one I didn't do the right thing for was you. Can you forgive me?"

"I don't need to," she said simply. "I love you. It was stupid of me not to tell you. I didn't want you out of obligation or duty or by manipulating you. You're always doing the right thing for everyone. I only wanted you if you loved me, not because you thought it was the right thing to do."

"I do love you," he said softly as they drove into the Avenue Montaigne. "I love you. Now what do we do? When is the baby due?" He could hardly think. It was a lot to absorb all at once. She loved him. She always had. She hadn't cheated on him. There was no one else. There never had been. She had been faithful to him all along. She was having their baby. And she still loved him. She hadn't stopped loving him, just as he had never stopped loving her. He had been devastated ever since she had ended it with him. And then he thought of something else. "Are you sure the baby is all right after your fall? Maybe we should go back to the hospital and have it checked." He looked suddenly very concerned.

"It's due in January, and it's fine. It's been kicking like crazy for the last half-hour."

"I want you to lie down as soon as we get back to the hotel," he said sternly.

"Yes, doctor." She smiled.

"You're making fun of me, Madame O'Neill," he said with a smile. He had missed her humor and face and her arms and her kisses, her voice, and most of all her love.

"Yes, doctor, I am," she said, smiling broadly, as they drove up to the Plaza Athénée. "Would you like to come upstairs for a glass of champagne or something?" He looked at her and smiled.

"And after that, Timmie? What do we do now?"

"What would you suggest? I don't know if I could run my office from here, but I could try." She wasn't going to ask him to give up his practice and move to California, since he couldn't practice medicine there. If anyone was going to move, it would have to be her.

"And then?" He looked at her with a broad smile.

"What are you asking?" she said, looking shy. Their dreams had suddenly been returned to them. She thought she had lost him forever. And instead, she was looking at him with love in her eyes. He had come back to her because of her broken ankle and David's call to him. She was grateful now for that.

Jean-Charles leaned over and kissed her then. It was the kiss she had remembered and longed for, for all those long, lonely, agonizing months when he was gone. "I'm asking you to marry me," he said softly. He had never asked her that before.

"Because you feel sorry for me?" she whispered. "Or because of the baby?" Her face was inches from his as she asked and looked at him intently.

"No, because I love you, silly girl. I always did. I'm sorry it took such a long time."

"Then I accept," and this time she kissed him. After she did, she sat back against the seat and looked at him with a huge, happy smile. "I guess that means I won't be going back to the orphanage again." The orphanage was gone forever. She knew that now.

"That's right," he said, as he got out and came around to her side of the car. "You're never going back there again. You're coming home with me, Timmie. Forever," he said, as he picked her gently up in his arms and carried her into the lobby of the Plaza Athénée, where it all began.

Danielle Steel is one of the world's most popular and highly acclaimed authors, with more than eighty international bestselling novels in print and over 600 million copies sold. She is also the author of *His Bright Light*, the story of her son Nick Traina's life and death, and the memoir *A Gift of Hope*. She lives in California and Paris.

To discover more about Danielle Steel and her books visit her website at www.daniellesteel.com

And don't forget to join her on Facebook at www.facebook.com/DanielleSteelOfficial